The
Iron
Princess

The Iron Princess

BARBARA HAMBLY

OPEN ROAD

INTEGRATED MEDIA

NEW YORK

Copyright © 2023 by Barbara Hambly

ISBN: 978-1-5040-7902-0

Published in 2023 by Open Road Integrated Media, Inc.
180 Maiden Lane
New York, NY 10038
www.openroadmedia.com

For Mark W.

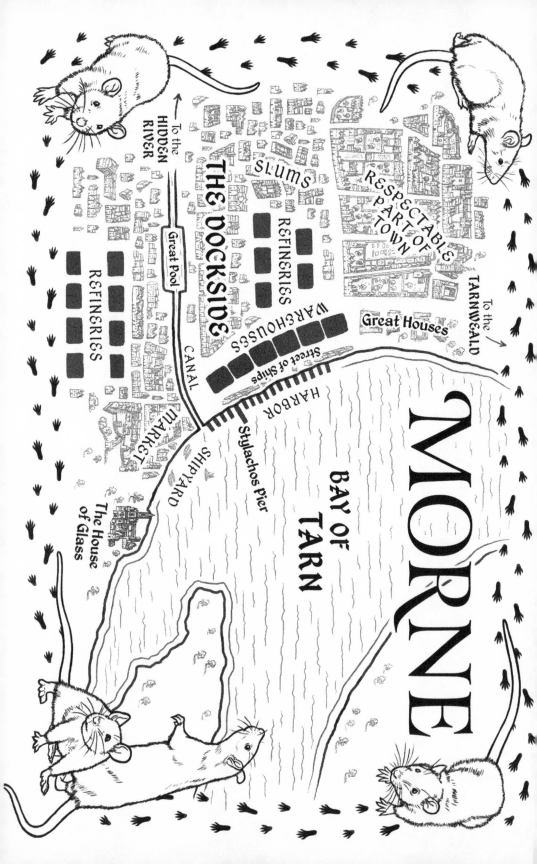

To the
HIDDEN
RIVER

THE DOCKSIDE

SLUMS

RESPECTABLE
PART OF
TOWN

To the
TARNWEALD

Great Pool

REFINERIES

REFINERIES

WAREHOUSES

Great Houses

Street of Ships

CANAL

MARKET

HARBOR

SHIPYARD

Stylachos Pier

The House
of Glass

BAY OF
TARN

MORNE

The
Iron
Princess

One

They said in the villages that what the travelers heard, thin and distant from the high bare crags of the Desolate Mountains at certain times of the day, were the screams of a god.

He had been chained to the rocks by the other gods and left, the storytellers said, for the eagles and vultures to tear out his heart and entrails: punishment for some outrage or horror—slaughter, disobedience, impiety, rebellion. Each night his body healed, that the birds of the air might rend him anew, forever. Now and then scoffers would contend that the sounds they heard were only the wind. Now and then a shepherd, braver than the others, would endeavor to climb those harsh ridges of lava and basalt, the dry gorges that flooded unexpectedly in the hammering rains of winter, and most of those didn't return. It was a place haunted by mountain-lions and wolves, as well as the deadly raptor-fowl of the upper peaks.

Those who did return would not speak of what they'd found.

Clea Stylachos whispered, "God's braies!" as the first of the eagles swept down on them—if an eagle it was, she'd never seen one that size—its talons were wider than the hands of the biggest man she'd ever seen. But as she cursed, she was already bringing up her bow. The bow was written with runes of silvery adamine, the arrowhead wrought of blacksteel, which held and magnified spells of power and ruin. It should have stopped a lion. But though the arrow went into the bird's breast halfway up to the feather, the eagle still drove at them like the bolt from a catapult. Clea barely had time to shove the bow into the hands of the shepherd who had guided her thus far and yank her sword free, cutting at the eagle (*Die, you damn hell-chicken, what the hell's wrong with you?*) as it smashed at her with wings strong enough to knock her and her companion off the rock ledge.

Hamo the shepherd struck at the eagle with his crook. Splattering blood and screaming like a marsh-wight, the bird dove on them twice more before it fell hundreds of feet down the cliff to their left, still screaming.

"Sons of Death." Clea wiped the blood off her blade, breathless with the shock of the attack, and checked the rest of her arrows. The eagle's wing-blows had pulled her red hair loose from the warrior's topknot she'd had it tied in; she pulled free one of the ties that held her doublet-sleeve together, used it to wind the trailing ends back. "I guess that part of the legend's true, anyway."

Hamo, panting, raised his eyes from staring down the cliff. The trail was barely a foot wide here, a sort of crack in the gray-black stone. Clouds of sand and dust still drifted down into space. There was a trace of accusation in his blue gaze. "It's *all* true, my lady."

Clea only shook her head. It would be useful if it were, of course, considering what was at stake. . . .

But part of her hoped that it was not.

Ithrazel had long since lost count of how many days—years—he'd been stretched upon the rock in his chains, each day's agony as fresh and singular as the first had been: *If the nerves and flesh re-grow in the night, of course they're tender as a baby's when the birds come back in the morning . . .*

He wondered if these were the same birds after all these years. Immortal, as he himself now seemed to be.

There was always an hour, just as the sun came up, when he'd hope that somehow—the gods knew for what reason!—the birds wouldn't come. That they'd died of old age, or been trapped by some monstrous cat—only knowing the lords of the Mages' Council, if the birds had fallen victim to a monster-cat, one could be sure that animal would be on its way up to the crag in its turn . . .

And always—*Why do I never learn? CAN I never learn?* there'd be the sickening moment when first he'd hear their hoarse screams in the distance, and see the circling specks of them against the brightening sky. When the shadows of their wings would pass across him, and he'd know the horror was going to start all over again.

Considering how long he'd been up there, each day still seemed endless. Each freezing night an event separate to itself.

And the dreams that came in the small hours were worse than waking.

At first he'd thought that this place, these mountains, these forests where he heard the howl of distant wolves, was the Pit, the abyss of demons and devils where the souls of evildoers were tortured forever when they died. That this was death.

This hadn't surprised him. He knew his own deserving.

But it seemed there was a village nearby, maybe more than one, and its dwellers didn't seem to be either evil or in torment. . . .

There had been, altogether, more than a dozen shepherds. He'd used to keep track of their names. They all seemed to be called Coulm or Hamo or Davo—*Don't they name boys anything else in those villages?*—and merely their presence, the sound of their voices, was a comfort. Some would try to bring him water, if they could. Others just stared, shocked and aghast that the stories of the shackled god were in fact true: stared, and ran away. The youngest—a Hamo or a Davo, years ago now—Ithrazel guessed had been barely seven. He'd run away the first time, but had come back, weeks later, with water. One day he'd stopped coming. Ithrazel guessed he'd fallen from a crag, or been killed by the birds himself—the old man could see a long distance from his rock, and had seen where the birds gathered among the gorges for several days in succession, as they did when a goat missed its footing and fell. And maybe it only was a goat, and little Davo (or Hamo) had merely grown bored with the long scramble up the mountain just to drive the birds away from an old man who would never be free of his chains.

Another had made the climb—Coulm, Ithrazel recalled his name was, many years before poor little Hamo (or Davo)—once every few days, for two or three years, and then at intervals after that, growing from shock-haired shepherd lad to a curly-haired young man. The last time he'd come, his hair and beard had been starting to thread with gray. Then he'd stopped coming as well. Ithrazel had no idea why.

It had been years since anyone had come. Even when snowstorms had scoured the rock, the birds would come, seemingly impervious to the bitter cold. Three times since he'd been here, he'd seen plumes of smoke rising into the sky when the village was burned—why or by whom he had no idea. He knew someone was scrambling up the trail now, by the shrieking of the birds and the way they gathered overhead, plunging on the intruder with hoarse cries.

It was late in the day. Under the grilling glare of the sun, Ithrazel had reached the point of death, his whole body a flame of agony, too exhausted even to groan and another two hours of daylight yet to go. He heard a young man's voice curse, a flurry of avian shrieks. One of his eyes had been gouged out—he knew that it, too, would grow back in the night—but with the other, burning with blood and dust, he saw the young man who scrambled and slid down the side of the crag in a shower of gravel, to the rocks next to him.

"Here he is!"

Clea whispered again, "Sons of Death . . ."

It was true. The stories were true.

Blood covered the rock, the body of the man stretched upon it in his chains. He was dead—no man could live, that far gone. Torn and scattered entrails glistened in the sinking light: lungs, liver . . . huge gouts marked where blood had fountained, when his heart had been torn from his ribs. She saw he'd been a man of no great stature: fair, to judge by the sun-grilled red of his skin. Though nondescript, his thin features were Telmayrian, like her own. The stubble on his jaw and scalp was a sandy brownish gray.

Ithrazel the Brown.

Ithrazel the Cursed, who had destroyed the city of Dey Allias and all within it out of hatred for his own people.

She had risked everything, and had arrived too late.

Another vulture—larger even than the eagles, the span of its wings must have been ten feet—dove from the flock that circled in the sky, and Clea, remembering the journey here, straightened up in anger and loosed an arrow at it. When it veered toward her grunting and hissing, she drew her sword, blacksteel like her arrowheads, the magic in it gleaming red. The bird snatched at her with beak and claws and she hacked at the naked gray neck, cutting it half-through. It fell on the crag, bleeding, and tried to crawl toward her, still snapping with its straggly beak. Hamo stepped gingerly forward and shoved it down the rock and over the edge with his crook.

It would have taken my hand off, if I'd tried to get my arrow back. She had barely a dozen left.

Scores of raptors still circled overhead. The rock-face was nearly black with old blood.

Clea knelt to one knee, looked across at the chained body, fascinated and sickened. She'd seen men—women, too, in her days with the Thieves' Guild—eviscerated in the public markets, traitors flayed and quartered. Seen the men who had been accused of being her mother's lovers. This was the worst she'd seen.

All this way . . . up the gorges, and the goat-trails, creeping across vertical rock-faces like bugs, with the birds circling over us . . . Only to find him dead . . .

Ithrazel turned his head, regarded her with his remaining, blood-gummed eye. "By the gods, a girl," he said.

In spite of herself Clea startled back. "You live—"

"You think the Mages' Council would let me die this easily?"

"Rope," she said, and held out her hand, and Hamo unslung the coil of strong light rope that she'd brought all the way from Morne for the purpose. The shadows of the birds fell across them. "Take the bow," she commanded. "Keep them off me if they attack again."

"They will," Ithrazel whispered. "You don't happen to know if they're the same birds after all these years, or descendants . . . How long has it been?"

"Seventy-five years." She edged out to him, leaning into the rock. The crag was a giant slab of pale-gray stone, sloping down to the drop-off into a chasm below. Hamo the shepherd braced his feet behind her, the heavy compound bow in hand, blue eyes narrowed to watch which of the birds would attack first.

"Don't waste your time, girl," the wizard muttered through cracked lips. "The chains are pure blacksteel. There's enough spells in them to break any chisel forged."

"Yeah, well, my pick-locks are pure blacksteel, too." She produced them from the bosom of her doublet, the final legacy of her master Rat-Bone, that genius in the arts of larceny and sneaky death. Diamond-hard, obsidian-black, they were so full of cold wicked magic that even Clea could almost feel the spells through her fingers—and she was certain there were rats in the city prisons more mageborn than herself.

"Can you drink?" she added, with a glance at the ripped horror of Ithrazel's belly. "Or will that make matters worse?"

"Doesn't matter."

She hooked her knee into a loop of the rope, untoggled a gourd bottle from her belt.

The agony of being carried down the mountain turned out to be a thousand times worse than the depredations of the birds.

The birds followed them like a black cyclone, plunging in, tearing, screaming in their rage. Hamo carried him, slung over his shoulders like a dead deer, and Ithrazel, with what consciousness he had left, tried to turn his mind aside from the nightmare vision of what would happen if the young man lost his footing on any one of a score of steep trails, or on one of the deadfall pines that bridged dry gorges hundreds of feet deep. He'd lie at the bottom, every bone in his body broken, prey to the god-cursed fowl and the mountain wolves besides, healing every night but never enough to flee before they returned in the day . . .

He didn't know if he fainted. Later he couldn't remember doing so.

The girl—Hamo called her "my lady"—conserved her arrows like a soldier and struck at the birds, when she could, with the sword she wore on her back, or with Hamo's crook, handling them like a professional. The sword was a professional's weapon, and for all her skinny build she was strong and very quick. Many times they barely had enough of a rock-ledge to put their feet on—in one place Clea bound Ithrazel's wrists together, so that he hung around Hamo's neck as they crossed a rock-face on a series of hand-holds and crevices, the eagles circling and plunging. In a gorge at the base of the mountain they made camp at twilight. With darkness, the birds left. They always did.

He woke in the bitter black cold before dawn. In its way, the pain of the flesh growing back was almost as bad as having it torn away.

They'd put a sheepskin blanket over him and built a fire against the rocks that sheltered them. The small wolves of the mountains—colyutes, one of the shepherd-boys had called them; in all his years on the mountain Ithrazel had never seen one—yikked and cried in the darkness. A stream babbled somewhere close by.

Wrapped in another blanket, Hamo slept on the other side of the fire. Ithrazel recognized him now, though it had been—twelve years? fifteen?— since he'd seen him last. He had grown from a big strong lad into a young man, thick bronzed muscles showing through the hand-me-down home-spun he wore. He'd climbed, all that frightful distance, up the mountain, and risked attack by the birds, to bring water to the chained and half-eviscerated man stretched on the blood-slicked rock, and that was what the wizard chiefly remembered.

His kindness.

Not his conversation, that's certain. Ithrazel guessed that those boys who got stuck with herding the sheep weren't the sharpest knives in the village box.

But the young man had remembered the way, and had been willing to lead this sharp-featured Telmayrian warrior girl to him.

She sat by the fire, keeping watch. He judged her well-worn green leather boots at three silver pieces, her doublet at twice that. He saw now that she had tawny hazel eyes, a few shades more golden than his own, and the red hair of one of the northeastern kinships of the Twilight Lands. *Ashupik or*

Setuket, probably . . . Her height and her aquiline nose shouted the blood of the conquerors.

When she looked across at him, she could tell by her flinch that the eye the vultures had torn out yesterday had grown back.

She fetched him water, ice-cold from the spring and tasting of iron. He was surprised to find himself hungry.

"The stories are true," she said softly, as she knelt at his side. "You're Ithrazel."

"You'd feel damn silly if you went through all that to rescue the wrong man, now, wouldn't you? As if there's anyone else stuck up on a mountain-side being eviscerated by birds. Or has that become common these days? Where are we?"

"You don't know?"

"I've been hanging in chains on the side of a rock for—what'd you say it's been, seventy-five years? I certainly didn't have time to climb down and buy a map." He reached—gently, and shuddering in spite of himself— under the blanket, touched the flesh of his belly, his chest and loins. It was whole again, though painful as the worst of burns. He wondered if that would go away. That their spells could still do this to him, to his body— that *they* could have done this, the mages of the Council—made him feel queer inside, and sick.

What could they not do?

"I'm Ithrazel," he said. "And you are?"

"Clea Stylachos."

His eyes narrowed. "Old Tethys Stylachos's . . . what would you be, his grand-daughter? Great-granddaughter?"

She frowned as if in thought, like someone casting her mind back, then shrugged. "I think I had a great-grandfather of that name. He was a mer-chant, wasn't he?"

"And your father wasn't? Isn't?"

She shook her head. Her features were delicate in the firelight, but there was a hard wariness in the hazel eyes, and premature lines in their corners. He guessed her age at eighteen or nineteen. An old eighteen.

"What is he, then?"

Her mouth tightened, and she looked aside. "A man of little worth."

House Stylachos, fallen. Ithrazel remembered those professional-looking pick-locks. *Well, they always were thieves* . . . All the merchant houses of Telmayre were.

Thieves, rapists, murderers, and slave-masters.

He would have bet money against it. The Stylachos had been among the strongest, like kings on the Bright Isle of Telmayre, for all that the ancient nobles looked down on them. Like High Kings where Telmayre had set up ports in the Western Lands—the Twilight Lands—to dig adamis from the deep gray sands of the river-mouths. House Stylachos had controlled the Emperors of Light, the lords of the Bright Isle, whose rule supposedly came from the gods and came in fact from the weapons of adamine forged and refined from the glittering stuff . . .

His thoughts stumbled. *Wait, there was something about adamine . . . something important . . .*

Something that I knew. Or thought I knew.

Wasn't there?

He couldn't recall, and that gap in his memory appalled him.

What don't I remember? And why don't I remember it?

The Mages' Council also had been very solicitous to do the bidding of the House Stylachos, that he *did* remember. A war between the Stylachos and another of the merchant houses? The Kinnesh, or the Othume . . . Regard for the emperor made them mind their manners on the Bright Isle itself, Ithrazel recalled from the days of his youth in the royal city of Esselmyriel. But once away from his rule, in the Twilight Lands of the west, the rivalry between them had been brutal.

And who knew what had transpired since the Marble City of Dey Allias had been devoured by fire and demons from beneath the ground.

Had the emperor come to blame the House Stylachos for that horror? For the tens of thousands whose dying screams still tore his dreams to bloodied ribbons?

He wouldn't put it past the little bastard.

Clea still watched him, arms wrapped around her drawn-up knees. "The stories say you heal every night."

"If I didn't, there'd be precious little left of me by this time but bones and bird-droppings. I've never figured out whether they put spells on me to do that—"

He frowned as another thought winked past his consciousness, vanished again: *Something I dreamed?*

No . . .

"—or whether . . . This is another world, isn't it? Another cosmos?" He moved his shoulders a little to get a better look at her—it hurt just as badly as he'd been afraid it was going to—and pulled the sheepskin tighter around his neck. "I didn't dream that part? But you're from Telmayre." The boots anyway were unmistakable.

"This is another world, yes," said Clea. "And yes, my father was from Telmayre. I was born in Morne." She obviously interpreted his puzzled frown at the mention of that Darklander fishing village, because she explained, "It's the principle port of the Bright Lords' holdings in the West now."

She didn't say "*since Dey Allias was destroyed*," and she didn't need to.

Of course. Smash one of their fortress-cities and they'll only put up a new one. They're never going to loosen their grip on the amount of adamis they can dredge out of the river-sands. And they're certainly not going to dig it out themselves.

"My friend Graywillow—she's one of the White Sisterhood—opened a Corridor of Mirrors through from our world. She's waiting there to lead us back."

"Have a nice walk. As I was saying, I have no idea whether this healing that takes place every night . . ." In the waning glimmer of the firelight he drew the blanket down to uncover his chest. Even the scars were fading. ". . . is some effect of this world. Were I to follow you back to the Twilight Lands, or Telmayre, or anywhere on our own earth, I might actually shrivel into a little pile of bones and bird-droppings—"

"We need you."

"Do you, now?" Ithrazel pulled the blanket back over himself, and turned, rather gingerly, onto his side, with his back to the red-haired girl in the firelight. "Pigs eat your soul. Let me alone."

Two

By the glow of the sinking fire, Clea watched the wizard as he slept. Remembered what she had heard, of what he had done.

Since first he'd come to the Twilight Lands of the West—trained in the arts of the Brown Mages of Telmayre—he had hated the merchant lords of the Marble City of Dey Allias, they said: hated the city itself. The mages had come first from the Bright Island, and had been welcomed by the nations that dwelt in the coastal fogs and the endless forests of the Mire: the Ashupik, the Lhogri, the Placne, the Setuket, the hundreds of lesser kinships allied with them. The native shamans had welcomed their wisdom, and the local Darklander clan lords had been glad of the trade that came after them. The mages had taught the Darklander farmers more efficient ways of bringing food from the land, and the Darklander healers stronger and better magics. Those who mistrusted and rejected the tall strangers from over the sea were defeated by the weapons of the newcomers, forged of adamine, the blacksteel that held stronger spells of destruction, of strength, of victory than any Darklander mage could lay on ordinary iron or steel.

Long before Ithrazel came from Telmayre, men of his islands had discovered adamis in the river-sands. The Emperor of Light in Esselmyriel had given the merchant houses "concessions" in the Twilight Lands to dredge adamis, first from the river-sands, then years later, from the endless miles of flooded canyons that made up the Mire, inland beyond the western hills. The streets of the Marble City had blazed with the fruits of the wealth being drawn from the land, mostly by Darklander labor: shops crammed with silk, with silver, with cunning works in leather and glass. Wharves jostling with ships, warehouses stuffed with wheat and hides from the farms that stretched up and down the coast—not that any Telmayrian ever turned soil with his own hands.

Warehouses stuffed with adamine.

And the mages, whose coming had begun it all, all had Houses there: the Brown Mages in a compound beyond the North Harbor, the Black Mages in a painted basilica near the river-mouth keeping their hands carefully clean of the affairs of either the Telmayrians or the Darklander clans; the Red Mages among the palaces of the rich. By the South Harbor had stood the House of Glass, beautiful and amazing and shimmering like a jewel, where the New Order, the Crystal Mages, had established themselves only a dozen years before the destruction of the city, startling the ancient orders with the strength of their spells, the rapidity and depth of their learning.

Even in the deeps of night, the stories said, Dey Allias had glimmered like a lake of jewels, a bed of embers, illuminated windows like twenty thousand topazes in the darkness. Torches burned before the temples of the gods, brighter than rubies and citrines.

It had been night when Ithrazel had destroyed the city.

Archmage of the Brown Order, he had called the domination of the Lords of Telmayre over the Darklanders slavery and denounced Dey Allias as a cesspit of oppression, of power misused and justice twisted. Even the gods, he had cried, must hate the stink of the place.

He took a small group of renegade mages out of the city only days before sickness broke out there, a plague that the other Orders—and both Sisterhoods—struggled in vain to cure. And on a midsummer night, seventy-five years ago, he and his followers had returned to the Hill of Oleanders outside the city and formed a vast sigil that had glowed—said the hill-shepherds who had seen it—in a misty light. Their small forms, hard and dark, had moved through that light, raising their hands, calling down their curse . . .

He woke screaming "NO!!!" and the pain that went through him, like hot knives as his muscles convulsed, was a thousand times worse than the claws of the birds. He was weeping as hard, slim hands gripped his arms, and fought to turn away from Clea's shoulder—

"What is it?"

He thrust her aside, horror wrenching him until he thought he must be physically crushed by it, physically twisted to pieces.

Hearing them scream, every one of them, as the city went up in flames.

The air was gray now. The hollow in the rocks smelled of campfire smoke. Clea backed away from him, and for a time he could only huddle where he lay, his head buried in his arms, weeping, and waiting for the grip of the dream to slacken.

It left him shaking, like a physical purge.

In time he thought, *the birds will be coming soon . . .*

He heard Clea's boots scrunch in the sand, the creak of boot-leather and the scent of her doublet as she squatted beside him again. "Can I help?" she asked.

"You can go to hell."

He heard her drop something—cloth—on the ground beside him. "Can you eat?" she asked, in another tone, and walked away, back to the fire. "We have to get going, if we're going to reach the Corridor of Mirrors back to the real world."

Ithrazel sat up and flexed his hands. It had been a long time since he'd seen them really: square, strong, with short, powerful fingers. His beard and his fine-textured hair were barely stubble. *Did they re-make themselves— like my fingernails?—every night when I healed?* The pain of healing was almost gone.

He pulled on the coarse shirt she'd left beside him, the peasant breeches and boots. "*You're* going to reach the Corridor of Mirrors," he corrected her. "I'll be staying here, thank you."

Hamo the shepherd, sitting on the other side of the fire, glanced nervously from Clea to Ithrazel. "The birds . . ." There was something in his doglike gaze that made the old mage want to go over and slap Clea. *The damn girl's put a love-spell on him, to make sure he'll do as she bids him . . . Or had her White Sister friend do it.*

"I'm sorry." Clea walked over to Ithrazel—now that he was on his feet again, he saw that slight as she was, she was tall, his own moderate height. She took his wrist, where the shackle of his chain was still locked around it, touched the sigils that traced the incorruptible blacksteel. "We need you and you have to come. I'm guessing the chains they put on you keep you from doing magic."

He jerked his hand from her. "Or it's just this world. Or the spells they laid on me—"

"Can you do magic now?"

He couldn't. He knew it in his bone-marrow.

Hamo startled, looked skyward as a shadow passed over them.

Damn rotten filthy hell-chickens . . .

"Let's go."

Typical arrogant Telmayrian bitch . . .

Leaving the blankets where they were, Clea scooped up the water-bottles and the remains of a satchel of bread and cheese and handed them to Hamo. Slipped her blacksteel sword from its sheath with a deadly metallic whisper, and led the way down the gorge.

I may be Telmayrian myself but I NEVER behaved like that. Well, not after I'd been in the Twilight Lands for a couple of weeks . . . or a season . . .

She didn't even look back to see if he were following.

Serve her right if I just dodged into the brush . . .

Only of course the presence of thirty or so swooping, screaming, flesh-tearing eagles and vultures would probably give me away.

Hamo glanced back repeatedly to see if he was following. Ithrazel couldn't make up his mind whether that was better or worse than Clea's blithe assumption that he'd obey her, but it felt good beyond anything he'd ever imagined was possible to be walking again, birds or no birds.

"Do you need a stick?" she called back over her shoulder as they reached the end of the gorge, where it dropped off into another sickening scarp of bare rock.

"No, I don't need a stick! I'm not in my dotage!"

She stood aside, sword in hand, to let Hamo and Ithrazel precede her down the hair-raising goat-trail that led down, gauging the circling eagles. But she spared the wizard a grin. "By my reckoning you're a hundred and forty," she said. "Just thought I'd ask."

"Minx."

It was probably, Ithrazel calculated, another three miles to the shoulder of the mountain where Clea's friend Graywillow waited for them. Three miles that they could never have done in bird-free darkness, or, he estimated, had Hamo been burdened with an injured man's weight. Only the last half-mile or so was meadow, roughly slanting and knee-deep in dry mountain grass, and by the time they reached it Ithrazel was trembling with exhaustion. The smoke of the village rose beyond the trees. Goats and sheep scattered, and a boy of eight or nine stared at them in shock from a little hillock at the far end. Ithrazel felt a curious pang of regret that he'd never see the village itself, the place from which his young friends had come all down the long years.

Were they a part of this world, like the birds? Was there anything else here, any cities, any trade, anything beyond scrabbling for the existence that the boys had from time to time described to him? Raiding the next village for stolen sheep, being raided over blood-feuds and women?

The birds fell upon them like a deadly plague, shrieking, gouging with their beaks, buffeting with their wings. At the top of the meadow, the girl cut them both branches from the stoutest plants she could find—drought-twisted acacia more like brooms than staves. The House of Stylachos, Ithra-zel guessed, once the greatest among the merchants, were probably assassins these days. *Not that they haven't always been that . . .*

Blood ran from his torn shoulder and back where he wasn't quick enough to fend off the eagles. He wondered if those cuts would heal come night. It was good to be able to hit back, wonderful to see Clea get in a good blow now and then and send another one of those filthy brutes screaming and bleeding to the ground.

More of them came down as the three fugitives crossed the open grass-land, thick in the sky as monstrous blackflies. At the bottom of the meadow was a hillock, where a clump of bedraggled fig trees marked a spring. In their shade Ithrazel saw another girl get to her feet. Patchy sunlight glinted blindingly on glass, a halo of fire around her, and like the wash of heat from a kiln-door he felt it, the glittering whisper of magic in the air.

The girl stretched out her hands . . .

"Damn it you fool, DON'T!" Ithrazel halted in his tracks, shouted at the top of his lungs.

Her concentration broken, the girl stepped back and the spell—prob-ably to drive the birds away—dissolved: *The gods only know what it would have actually done!* He yelled, "We're in a different world, you idiot!" and turned to smash his raggedy branch of acacia at the eagle that slashed and dove at him, eight feet of wings thrashing at his head and face.

Clea called out, "Torches!" and the girl in the grove scrambled to gather and light sticks of firewood, while the fugitives raced the final hundred feet. Ithrazel stumbled. Hamo caught him under the arms and half dragged him to a little clearing among the fig trees, where three mirrors had been set up and a Gate-Sigil had been drawn on the ground. Clea grabbed a burning brand from the girl—Graywillow, Clea had called her, a few years older than Clea, clothed in the white robes of the Goddess Nyellin's order, dark brown hair braided down past her hips—and strode out among the birds, trailing smoke and flame.

The shepherd Hamo dumped Ithrazel to the ground beside the girl, caught up another torch, and sprang to Clea's side.

The birds retreated, screaming. Ithrazel pressed his hand to his side, muscles long unused cramping horribly, and wondered if it were possible to vomit when one hadn't eaten anything in seventy-five years . . .

"Here." Graywillow knelt beside him, offered him a water-bottle. Only when he'd drunk did she draw back a little, as if only just realizing who this ragged little man in his bloodied clothing was or had to be. Staring in shock. In horror.

The dreams were true, then . . .

Not that he had ever doubted. But there had been mornings on his rock when he'd hoped.

Gruffly, he snarled, "It's me, all right. Don't gawp at me as if I were a monster—"

With hasty obedience she turned her eyes aside. Dark eyes, like a Telmayrian, though she had the cheekbones of a Loghri.

"What the hell's all this?" He jerked a hand at the mirrors, the sigil.

"The Gate," she whispered. "The Corridor of Mirrors . . . I have to help them." She looked swiftly back at Clea and Hamo.

"Don't be an imbecile. This is a different world. You have no idea what you're sourcing your magic from. None of the gods you know have power here. Your bird-spell could open a chasm that could swallow us all, or could summon every mouse for a hundred miles around, or smite us all with leprosy—"

"But if we're in another world—" The velvet-brown eyes were wide with panic. "What's happening in our own shouldn't be happening here. With magic," she explained, seeing his eyes, in their turn, go blank with puzzlement and shock. "With magic changing—"

"Magic *WHAT*?"

Clea sprang up the hillock as the birds drew back, her forehead bleeding from a claw-gash. "Take the spell off him," she said, with a fast glance behind her at Hamo, who was faithfully guarding her back. "Now, quickly— Lord Ithrazel's right, we can't use magic against the birds, we're lucky the spell you put on Hamo worked. We have to flee. I'm sorry—I wanted to say goodbye to him—"

"You can't." The young Sister got quickly to her feet.

Clea stared at her, appalled. "Can't what?"

"I thought you knew." The girl's gentle eyes filled now with tears. "You can't undo a love spell, Clea. You can't take it off like a blindfold. It has to wear off, like love does . . ."

"Or doesn't," said Ithrazel grimly. "As the case may be."

The girls looked at each other, then back at him: *Gods, if you tallied their years together in a pile, they still wouldn't equal my daughter's age when last I saw her . . .*

"Leave the poor bastard here, then," he advised sarcastically. "You're never going to have to see him again. The birds should go away once I'm gone."

The last of the flock had risen higher in the air, circling, screaming defiance down at the young man with his torch. Hamo came running back to the others, handsome face earnest. "That's done them," he panted. "Lady Graywillow can open the road, we can be gone—"

"I can't take you," said Clea, and Ithrazel observed—with a combination of wrenching pity and bitter satisfaction that this bossy tomboy was being forced to admit a miscalculation (*And what the hell did she THINK was going to happen?*)—the expression of shock, of heart-broken grief, that swept Hamo's face.

"Hamo—" Clea stepped toward him, reached for his hand, which he pulled from her, as if her very touch would lacerate him as the birds could not.

"I'm sorry. I can't take you away from your family, from your village—"

The young man whispered, "My lady—"

And don't you dare, don't you DARE tell him he loves you because you got your White-Sister friend to slap him with a spell because you needed his services.

Don't take from him even what he has . . .

Ithrazel got to his feet, caught Clea's arm when she looked as if she were about to do exactly that: stammer explanations, beg absolution, say she hadn't meant any harm. He held out his hand to the young man, said gruffly, "The lady is right, Hamo. Your family needs you. Your people need you. Thank you—eternally—for what you've done. Not just for helping her to get me down from there . . . Thank you for coming up to the crag in the first place, all those years ago. For giving me water. For letting me know I wasn't alone."

The young man's blue eyes flooded with tears. Went from Ithrazel's face to Clea's, begging.

Ithrazel said, "We must go, before the birds come back. They'll disperse once I'm gone—"

Gods of mercy, PLEASE make that true. Don't let it be that our flight's going to leave him in the lurch. . . .

But of course there was no way of knowing, once they passed beyond the sigil and into the Corridor of Mirrors, whatever the hell THAT was . . .

Hamo only shook his head. He looked stunned, as if this were the last thing on the earth that he expected, to be deserted by the woman he had taken for the queen of his heart and life. Ithrazel caught him in a swift, rough embrace, like a son . . .

Seventy-five years. That means all my children are dead.

Not only my son . . .

He wrenched his mind from that new abyss, made himself say, "Thank you. Forever. Thank you, my boy."

Turning, he caught Clea by the arm, shoved her in the direction of the sigil, beside which Graywillow stood in an agony of compassion and uncertainty. "Open it," he commanded. "Let's don't draw this out . . ."

She turned obediently to the sigil, raised her hands. The hot tingle of magic filled the air, mixing with Hamo's whispered protest, "My lady—" and the harsh screams of the birds.

And let's hope the spell to open the gate and get us back to our own world works properly in this one. . . .

Three

Graywillow called a whisper of witch-light, like a corpse-candle, to float before them as they walked. Beyond the narrow road of stones lay nothing: pitch-black darkness like a foggy night. Now and then something that could have been a mirror flashed ahead of them, with a cold, steady light. Between those bluish gleams, the road was dark indeed.

For a time Clea could hear the birds shrieking in the distance behind them. Then that faded. She wondered, sick with guilt, if the young man Hamo had gotten away.

The brutal experiences of her childhood had taught her—*You don't make excuses. Nobody cares why you did what you did.*

But her heart cried now: *I had to. We didn't have time, I HAD to have a guide, and I had to have one who wouldn't take fright and desert me on the way up the mountain.*

Who would do whatever I said.

She'd never had the slightest interest in love-spells, and had never asked how they worked. In her crowded life she'd simply not had the time to think of them. In the Dockside and the Tunnels, she'd known a lot of grannies who dealt in love-spells and had seen a lot of the girls put them on men, or seen the pimps put them on their girls. Generally they didn't last long.

After the age of six she hadn't trusted love anyway. Her father had said he loved her.

Hamo will get over it.

She remembered what it was like, to lose love—real love, not love-spell love like The King (as the chief pimp of the Dockside called himself) put on his girls. She'd loved her father.

As Rat-Bone the Assassin had always said, *you do what you have to do*. . . .

Beside her, Graywillow stopped and turned. Looking back, Clea saw that Ithrazel the Wizard had halted in his tracks and seated himself cross-legged on the flat stones of the road. "Now," he said. "Suppose you tell me what this is about, young lady. And don't lie to me."

Clea and Graywillow traded a glance.

"Or shall I guess? Let's see—you need my help." Irony glinted in those hazel green eyes. "One of the orders of wizards has managed to get the Emperor's favor—or maybe it's the favor of the merchant house that holds the biggest adamis concession these days. Doesn't matter. They've driven out all the other orders and are now doing Bad Things. Did the so-called New Mages ever come to anything, by the way? I always felt there was something . . . *fraudulent* . . . about their magic . . ."

He hesitated, as if trying to remember something about the New Order of Mages . . .

Something he'd forgotten . . .

"Powerful spells," he went on, with a slight shake of his head. "But slick little courtiers, the lot of them. In any case, you reason that since wicked old Ithrazel had sufficient power to wipe out a city of fifty thousand innocent people just by standing on a hill and lifting his hands, he'll be the very person to help your cause—whatever it is. And he'll be glad to do it out of gratitude to you for breaking him out of seventy-five years of unspeakable torture . . . Is it something like that, my dear?"

"Not really." Clea perched on one of the larger stones that bordered the roadway and unwrapped her satchel. The thread of magelight, like a tuft of raveled wool, settled between them, close to the ground. A tiny bubble of light against darkness like death.

She handed bread, cheese, and a gourd bottle of water to the wizard, and portions of the same to Graywillow, who seated herself—with a worried look around them at the blackness—on the short, dew-silvered grass that grew between the roadbed and the bordering stones.

The wizard's hand brushed at the dew, raised the droplets of it wonderingly.

"We do need your help," said Clea, "yes. And yes, the Crystal Mages— that's what they call themselves now—are still around. They haven't attacked or interfered with the other orders at all, except that they're the only order whose powers haven't been affected—"

"Affected by what?" Ithrazel shot a glance at Graywillow from under those long, tufted brows. "You spoke of magic *changing*—"

The novice nodded. "But that's what we don't know," she said, and looked up at Clea. *How much does he need to know?*

Clea sat silent for some moments, gathering her thoughts. *How much DO I tell him?* "For . . . I don't know, twenty years? Thirty?"

Graywillow shook her head to Clea's inquiring glance.

"Maybe longer"—Clea gestured time aside—"the spells of the Black Mages, and the Brown, and the Red have been . . . *unreliable*. At first—I'm told—it was something that happened very rarely, at intervals of years, so we don't even really know when this started. But either a spell would fail to work entirely, or more often, something else would happen, the way you feared it would if Graywillow tried to cast a spell against the birds in the meadow. Spells to ward a house, or a barn, against mice would cause the roof to catch fire. Or the spell wouldn't work on the mice, and that night the roof would catch fire—or a week later the horses would all go lame. Spells of good fortune on cargoes of salt fish or potash would result in the boats that carried them being unable to navigate, even the simplest instruments failing. It took a long time before anyone could see a pattern. Could see that this was something beyond a single, simple oddity. Well, in the past eight or ten years, it's become worse. Much, much worse."

Ithrazel shivered, as if a night-wind had brought him the heat of flames, the sound of screaming. He started to speak, stopped—as if he had for a moment lost his train of thought—then asked, "And the New—the *Crystal*—Mages do not seem to suffer from this . . . *malaise*?"

"So far as we can tell, no."

"I should imagine they've become very powerful as a result."

He was watching her face as he spoke, and habit made Clea close her mind on the pain—the rage—that his words brought, as if they meant nothing.

But for a moment she wasn't able to speak. So Graywillow put in, "The Lady Anamara—the Goddess's Hand—says that the magic of the Crystal Order feels . . . *sharper*, is the word she uses. Lighter but sharper. The difference between wielding a weighted wooden training-sword, and one of steel."

"Yes," agreed the wizard softly. "Yes, it felt that way to me, too. And . . . slick."

"And much more powerful. The magic that the gods channel through the Sisterhoods doesn't seem to have been affected," the novice went on. "But it never was as strong as the Orders of the Mages. And according to the Lady Anamara, and the older Sisters in the shrine, the gods work their magic much less than they used to. I've never heard the Great Goddess Nyellin speak—none of the girls of my year have. Nor those for five or six years before me. It's as if the gods themselves have gone away." She gazed down unhappily at the interlocking pattern of black and gray that bordered her sleeves.

"So where do I fit in?" Ithrazel folded his hands around the sharp bones of one kneecap. "I'm flattered, naturally, and eternally grateful, but murdering an entire city of Telmayrians and their servants scarcely qualifies me to analyze the nature of magic. Is this effect—this *malaise*—in force both in Telmayre and in the Western Lands?"

Clea nodded. "So I've heard."

"And have the New Mages expressed the slightest interest in repairing the problem, since they're not affected? And how do you know they're not affected? In my day they were as shy with their secrets as springtime brides. *Not affected*, I should say, except insofar as this change—whatever has caused it—has of course given them vastly more power? Who are you working for, by the way, my dear? Other than 'all of humankind,' naturally . . ."

"Specifically"—Clea fought down the impulse to box the old man on the ear—"you could say I'm working for the people of the enslaved villages of the Mire. And probably—I'm guessing, in a very short time—the people of the City of Morne. Because that's who's going to die if the thing that's risen out of the Mire isn't stopped."

That jolted him.

"*Thing*?"

"The villagers called it a *zai*," said Clea grimly. "After the water-monster of Darklander legend," she added, cutting off his observation—she was willing to bet—that if the fishy predators of Darklander legend had ever existed, none had been seen for thousands of years. "It doesn't look a thing like the legends. Doesn't look like anything *anyone* has ever seen—and by the few accounts I've heard of it, it's almost impossible *to* see. It destroyed a village called Turtlemere four days ago. The survivors tell me that there was another village wiped out six months before that, but my father had it hushed up. The survivors of that attack were transferred to another village . . . supposedly. I haven't been able to locate word of them."

"Turtlemere's in the Mire," protested Ithrazel. "It's the main village of the Ghoras tribe, I hid there for days . . . It's fifty miles from the coast, on the other side of the hills in the Nightshade Maze canyons—"

"That's where they're getting adamis from these days," said Clea. "They worked the river-sands bare decades ago. The clay at the bottom of the canyons in the Mire is shot through with adamis, veins of what they call 'diamond-clay.' Like a crystalline powder. Not all of them have these veins, not even most of them. But the merchant houses all have concessions to the ones that do. They're dredging it out by the ton, and processing it to adamine, and then to blacksteel and white-steel, in Morne. All the villages for a hundred miles into the Mire have been . . . *protected*, is the word the merchant houses use. *Enslaved*, is what they really mean."

The rage in Ithrazel's eyes turned suddenly deadly, a hatred that had crushed a city. But he only asked, "And who is your father, Missy, to be able to 'hush up' the obliteration of a village? Not 'someone of little worth,' I take it?"

"That depends," returned Clea dryly, "on one's definition of 'worth.'"

"Let's start with money and power," suggested the wizard. "Later we can move on to how he treats his daughters."

"I don't need your pity—"

"The gods assist the man who pities you, my dear. It sounds to me as if the House Stylachos remains a power among the merchants, after all—the 'protector' of villages whose inhabitants now spend their lives dredging clay off the bottoms of submerged canyons in the Nightshade Maze."

After long stillness—it was eerie, how still the iron-dark mists around them were—Clea drew a deep breath, putting aside the memories of her mother's trial for witchcraft, of her own years in the prison, and what came after. "My father is head of the Darklands Council," she said, keeping her voice level as frozen water. "The most powerful member of House Stylachos in the Western Lands. He holds the concession on half a million acres of the Mire—six canyon systems, the richest, as far as anyone knows. With what he sub-leases from the Crystal Mages, and the concession that's held by our cousins in the other main branch of our House, it's nine hundred thousand acres—plus a reversion on expansion inland—though actually Tykellin Stylachos is more a danger to us than a help. . . ."

She shook her head, pushing away the politics of the House. "But that isn't the issue. This thing—this zai—came out of the Mire. It was in one of the caves in the side of a canyon. The men took me there—"

"In seventy-five years," broke in the wizard curiously, "has anyone ever managed to cross the Mire? Or even determined how big it actually is?"

Again Clea shook her head. "It just goes on. The emperor has offered rewards, and expeditions have set forth, either in boats down in the canyons themselves, or up top, through the forest. Some have come back without reaching the far side of it. Others haven't returned at all. And the water down at the bottom of the canyons—in some gorges it's six or seven feet deep, in others it's a hundred or more. In a lot of the caves that cut in under the banks, they have no idea how deep it is."

"So these things could be as common as sticklebacks, further in."

"I don't think so," she said. "I have friends in the villages, and in the Old Town in Morne. None of them had ever heard of this—this thing. This devouring darkness. This creature—if it *is* one creature in the darkness that it holds around it, or many—that tears down houses and stone walls. That strips flesh off the bones of men and beasts. The men took me to the cave where it rose up—"

"And your father let you go? How old are you anyway, girl?"

"That's none of your business," she flared. "Old enough. And my father didn't know. Well, word reached him from the overseers of the village, but the dredgers came to me first, because he'd had the survivors of that first attack silenced, so the emperor wouldn't get word of it and give our concessions to another House. We got out of town and on the road while Ganzareb—Father's Master of Swords—was still collecting his men."

Graywillow had sent her a dream—a stout tradesman who'd walked into one of her troubled nightmares about her mother's trial and told her, *You have to wake up*—and she'd slipped away from the attic where she'd been sleeping to meet the novice Sister and the dredgers in the stables, without the ladies-in-waiting her father had assigned her ever being the wiser. These days she had a fair suite of rooms in Griffin House—one of several mansions that comprised the Stylachos compound—but she never slept in her elegant bedroom.

Her father was currently on his fourth wife. The gods only knew when he—or one of his new wife's family, which included the Master of Swords—would consider Clea threat enough to have her either arrested, kidnapped, or killed in her bed. Better safe than sorry.

"The thing is," Clea went on, "among the men my father sent was Himelkart, the chief disciple—the chief student—of Heshek the Fair. Heshek's the Archmage of the Crystal Mages here in the West and the head of the Mages' Council. My father favors the Crystal Order—naturally. The Crystal Order owns concessions on close to thirty canyon systems and leases them to all the merchant houses. And, these days they seem to be the only ones with reliable power. My brother Pendireth is mageborn. He's already being trained to enter the order. They're having the law changed," she added, seeing the old man's craggy eyebrows dive down. "And the Crystal Mages are perfectly happy to have merchants and lords educated in their secrets."

"Oh, they are, are they? And does the fact that this brother of yours is a member of House Stylachos have something to do with that?"

"Something." She kept her voice flat and cool. "My father put aside his first wife—my sister Shumiel's mother and the daughter of the lord of the House Shiamat—in order to marry my mother, who was mageborn. Then when I was born a girl—and about as mageborn as an old shoe—he had her tried by the Mages' Council and killed for misuse of magic, so that he could marry another mageborn girl, Pendri's mother. So you see I wasn't terribly surprised to see Himelkart—Heshek's favorite pupil—turn up in the cave where this thing—this zai—had appeared. I just wasn't prepared," she went on, "to see Himelkart command it."

"*Command* it?"

"Turn it away from himself. He let it devour the two guards with him," she added drily. "He didn't speak to it, exactly, but it . . . it hung above the water before him, gleaming in its darkness. He was holding to the big canoe that the thing had overturned, and he didn't seem afraid. The light wasn't good," she admitted. "And I was hiding, holding to rocks just beyond the mouth of the next cave—there was a series of grottoes, opening out of one another. I'd sunk my own canoe when I heard Himelkart and his guards enter the outer one—I knew it was him from his accent—and had swum for the wall. . . ."

"You'd risk being eaten by this thing rather than have this Crystal Mage know you were there?" His narrowed eyes glinted in the witchlight. "What could they have done, to the daughter of the president of the Darklands Council?"

"Well," said Clea slowly, "that's something I don't know. I knew Himelkart was trying to keep the news of this thing's attack on the village a secret. I don't think my father would sacrifice my sister Shumiel rather than lose the lease-hold on the two canyon system concessions he holds from the Crystal Mages—but then, Shumiel's a true princess. The Golden Princess, they call her in Morne. Her mother's family would ask questions if anything happened to her. Me—" She shrugged, trying to keep her bitterness from her voice. "I've been declared a bastard and legitimized twice. And my father knows I have . . . *friends* . . . among the Twilight Kindred, both in the villages and among the workers in Morne."

Ithrazel raised his brows. "Doesn't trust you, does he? Especially not if you were out poking around in the Darklander slave-villages?"

"I didn't want to take the risk." Clea dismissed his words with a wave. "So I hid, and I didn't see very clearly. But I saw enough."

Enough to give me nightmares for the rest of my life . . .

Don't be silly, the strong don't have nightmares.

She closed her eyes, remembering for a moment the freezing cold of the water—hundreds of feet deep by the dredgers' estimates—and the soft surge of a bow-wave going by under her feet as *something*, the gods only knew what, passed beneath her.

Remembering that thin, agile mage—barely her own age and without a whisker on his angular chin—stretching his slim hands out over the water, his eyes half-shut, his dark, thick hair bound up into a topknot decorated with gold. He'd turned his head, as if smelling for something, and all around his canoe the obsidian-dark water began to release not smoke, but darkness itself.

And the two guards with him, in the scarlet tunics of her father's household, clung together, staring, hoping this smooth boy-mage would save them.

"But if Himelkart commands this thing"—she pushed aside the recollection of what had happened next—"I can't know that my father isn't aware of it. I can't know that Heshek didn't somehow create it, either deliberately or by some kind of accident. Heshek hasn't been seen by anyone outside the House of Glass—their compound—in about five years. And I can't know that the Brown Mages, or the Black, or the Red, aren't somehow involved as well. They'll do pretty much anything to please my father these days, or Heshek. Or Himelkart, since he's the one they have to deal with most of the time. To deal with this thing, I needed to find someone who I *knew* wouldn't be working for my father, or Heshek, or anyone."

She studied the old man's features, outlined in the glow of Graywillow's witch-light.

"When people talk about what you did, they always said you were killed for it. I only heard recently the rumor among the Darklander beggars in the Morne Dockside what the Council really did to you. And how to get to where they'd put you. Then Graywillow and I had to track down—well— somebody who knew about the Corridor of Mirrors."

His shaggy eyebrows quirked up. "My dear girl, I'm hardly going to turn monster-slayer at my time of life. Particularly not, as you say, if some or all of the Council might be in on it. It was very nice of you not to demand my oath to aid you before you freed me—though I can assure you I would have lied—"

"You'll have to help," said Clea. "You said yourself, those shackles you still have on your wrists are pure blacksteel. They soak up spells like dry moss. While you slept Graywillow added a spell to them, which will let any mage find you with a scrying crystal, as if you weren't mageborn at all. Your life won't be worth two coppers the minute we come out of this Corridor into the real world again."

Ithrazel opened his mouth to snap a furious reply, then seemed to remember the way the birds had been drawn to him, not only on the crag, but the following day.

"I'll have Graywillow temporarily negate the spell when we come out, but if you run off, or disappear—"

"If I was your father, I'd take a strap to you."

Clea grinned. "If you were my father—" Her jest faded, though she could speak of Minos Stylachos quite naturally to his steward, to his guards, to her brother and sister and ladies in waiting. "If you were my father, I'd have left you for the eagles," she said quietly. "Forever." She got to her feet. "Now let's go. Khymin—the Black Mage who told us about the Corridor of Mirrors—said that time doesn't elapse once you enter the Corridor. But since he's never used it himself, he couldn't attest to this from his own experience. And we have no time to waste. This creature, this zai—"

She turned her head sharply, and when Graywillow opened her lips to ask what was wrong, she made a slashing gesture with her hand: *Shut up!*

In the silence, Ithrazel listened, too.

Thin and infinitely far off, Hamo's voice, crying, "My lady!"

Hoarse with terror, like a man lost in the darkness that lies between one universe and the next.

Four

Clea used a phrase that would have made a storm-trooper of the Imperial Marines blush.

"The idiot followed us!"

"Of course he did," retorted Ithrazel. "What did you think he was going to do? You're the love of his life."

The younger princess of the House Stylachos cursed again, and Ithrazel made a mental note to ask her where she'd picked up her vocabulary. To Graywillow she said, "Can you make that light stronger? *Hamo!*" she added, stepping to the very edge of the Road, standing on the uneven stones that bordered it (*Who set them there? Who paved this road?*) "*Hamo, we're here!*"

And in the blackness beyond, a sound, like something huge and soft passing unseen. A growling whisper. A smell that raised the hair on Ithrazel's neck.

Then silence again.

Damn it. Damn it, damn it . . .

Graywillow shook her head. Her velvet-brown eyes were stretched with fear and shock.

"Can you attach it to me, then?" Clea drew her sword, and Graywillow caught her by the arm.

"Don't leave the road! Khymin said—"

"I'm not going to leave that poor oaf here alone. Listen, he's still alive out there—"

"Or something that sounds like him is," pointed out Ithrazel.

"You—" Clea rounded on him, jabbed at his nose with one long finger. "Keep your god-damned mouth *shut*. Can you attach that light to me?"

The White Sister shook her head again. "I can't—"

Ithrazel got to his feet, held out his hand. "Give it to me, then."

"You can't touch magic—"

"Well, these bloody shackles are soaked with it," he retorted. "Attach it to the shackle and don't be a fool. D'you have a spare weapon of any kind?" He turned back to Clea. He thought she was the kind of girl who would and yes, she produced a dagger as long as her forearm from her boot. For a moment she hesitated, their eyes meeting, and he could see the calculation in hers. He was a mage, with a mage's perceptions even if the spells on the metal prevented him from magic itself. Though they were of a height, and he was slightly built for a man, he still outweighed her. By the way she gauged him, he could tell that she knew what her own limitations would be against a man's heavier muscle. Armed, he would have an advantage.

She passed him the knife. Ithrazel held out his arm toward Graywillow and the smidge of witch-light floated upward, calved itself into two. One of them drifted out in front of him. "Stay back," he ordered, stepping to the border of stones, and Clea obeyed him, a fact that he found interesting. "Graywillow, what else did you find out about this Corridor when you were learning the spells to open it? Anything I should know?"

"Only that Khymin said we mustn't step off the road. He said that things—creatures—moved through the darkness. He didn't know what they were, or where they came from."

Ithrazel grunted. "Useful." He could feel the creatures out there, sense them, though the darkness was nearly as impenetrable to his mageborn senses as it was to Clea's ordinary ones. He called out, "HAMO!" in his cracked voice, and far off, heard a despairing wail that could have been, *Help me!*

"Hamo, can you follow my voice?" After seventy-five years of screaming in agony, he was a little surprised that he still had any voice left at all. Like his flesh and entrails, that, too, must have re-made itself in the night. "Can you see light?"

"I can't see you, my lord!"

Damn, what if there's something out there that calls to us in the voices we want to hear? He'd encountered such things while journeying deep in the Mire, and in the coastal hills behind Dey Allias. *Green children*, the Dark-landers had called such things, though no legend preserved the origin of the term.

"You still got that rope?" He tossed the words over his shoulder. "Good—"

"There's only about fifty feet of it."

"It's all I need for the moment. Stay where you are." He knotted the line around his waist, stepped between the border-stones and into the darkness, the knife ready in his hand. The clammy air was cold and left him short of breath, as if he were trying to inhale water. Whatever was underfoot gave queerly, and seemed to be jaggedly uneven: *Just what we need, unseen chasms . . .*

Movement nearby in the darkness. A stirring, gliding past him like a shark.

He walked to the limit of the rope, turned to look back.

The road was visible. The girls visible, Clea standing on the rock border, sword in hand, terribly thin and tiny against the wan glow from the mirror-light that defined the path. "Can you see me?" he called out, and Clea called back, "I can see the witch-light."

"Good. Come out here, keeping hold of the rope. HAMO!" he shouted again into the darkness.

Movement again, to their right, coming at them this time. He shouted, "Clea! Close up!" and she broke into a run toward him. "Something coming from the right—"

She reached him at the same time it did, whatever it was. The faint witch-light glistened on an agglutination of wet shapes, and when Clea slashed at it with her sword, there was a thick slurp of parting tissue and a blast of horrific stench. Something that looked like a thick paddle, or a sheet of leather, curled out of the dark and Ithrazel cut it before it could get around him. Clea put her back to his and slashed again, the well-trained strokes of one who has been professionally taught and has practiced daily. Droplets of flying fluid burned Ithrazel's cheek and hands, stinging even when he wiped the stuff off. He heard Clea swear. The thing made a noise at them, like the deep-voiced pale cats of Telmayre, and retreated. He could still smell it.

"My lord!" Hamo's voice sounded closer, frantic with terror. "My lady—"

"Here!" yelled Clea.

"I see light—Oh, gods, there's something—"

As one, Ithrazel and Clea strode into the darkness, slipping and off balance on the uneven surface underfoot. Once Clea glanced back and said, "I can't see the road."

"I can." Or at least there was some thread of silvery pallor in the abyss behind them. *That BETTER be the road . . .*

"My lady! My lady!" cried Hamo's voice, and Ithrazel could see movement again ahead of them, dark forms swirling and circling in the blackness.

Clea grabbed Ithrazel's belt from behind, called out, "We're coming, Hamo!" and Hamo screamed.

The witch-light glistened on the huge, floating shapes. Out of the darkness around them other forms materialized, human or almost so. Clea yelped, cursed, and let go of his belt—he could feel her movement as she slashed with her sword. Whoever—whatever—they were, they were armed only with what felt like sharp stones and sticks, and their eyes flashed like the eyes of beasts. Ithrazel smelled blood behind him, and again when he slashed at the grabbing hands. The things opened huge mouths like dogs' and bleated at them, then scattered as the larger shadows drew nearer, glistening darkness within darkness. The movement within the blackness showed him Hamo, on his knees with blood on his face, his shepherd's stick in one hand and his dagger in the other, and Ithrazel strode to him, the shred of witch-light trailing behind him like ghostly comet-hair.

"Can you run?"

The young man nodded, beyond words; Ithrazel jerked him to his feet.

"My lady?" sobbed Hamo, and the wizard firmly crushed a desire to go back and shake Clea until her teeth rattled, for doing this to a poor well-meaning bumpkin who was only out minding his sheep. . . .

At least she came and got him.

"Can you see the road?" She strode to his side, sword-blade smoking with fluid that stank. She reached out and caught Hamo by the hand—*Thank you, good man, thank the gods you're alive,* all in one hard grip, one sharp dazzling smile. And Hamo, Ithrazel was interested to note, had the sense not to tie up her sword-arm by flinging his arms around her, something he clearly wanted to do.

The cold around them was deepening, the black shapes closing in. "Put this through your belts." Ithrazel shoved the rope into their hands. Even Clea's fingers fumbled with it, her breath a fume in the witch-light. Hamo shivered in his ragged breeches, his shirt and jacket half torn off him and gaping with holes. Ithrazel realized that where he'd wiped his hands on his own clothing, the dripped ichor of the creatures they'd slashed had eaten through the cloth. A dozen yards back toward the glowing line of the road they came on the corpses of six or seven of the human-like things that had attacked them—six or seven was only an estimate, counting pieces. A lot of flesh remained on them. A lot didn't.

"What are those, Lady Clea?" panted Hamo, glancing over his shoulder as they strode. "Where is this? Is this the world far away that you spoke of?"

"Nothing you need to worry about right now." Clea had put herself in the rear of the line, and Ithrazel guessed that being joined by the rope gave her a better chance of watching behind them for another assault. He himself wasn't going to look back to see.

There was one more quick attack before they reached the road, but Hamo and Clea closed up behind Ithrazel immediately, and the three of them together cut at those bulbous, glimmering shapes that loomed out of the darkness. What this place was that lay between worlds—what other worlds might be reached through it, on other roads, by other spells—was a question that Ithrazel dared not think of at the moment, but which he knew would consume him later. *What Black Mage—this Khymin of hers?—would part with secrets like this?*

The line of stones appeared before them, the reflected gleam of the mirrors. Ghostly phosphorescence outlined the White Sister where she stood peering into the darkness. Slim and beautiful, dark hair and creamy brunette complexion a foil for Clea's auburn brilliance. She dressed like a novice and spoke like one, too, and the power of women's magic had always been less forceful than—and hugely different from—that of men. *No wonder Clea's father hadn't any use for a girl, even if she had been mageborn....*

They sprang over the barrier of stones. Graywillow—no warrior—caught first Hamo, then Clea, in a welcoming embrace, even as they swung around, weapons ready for an attack on the road itself.

None came. Ithrazel had guessed already that whatever spells had made this road also guarded it.

Watching the three young people, remembering what the girls had said of their world, of the House Stylachos . . . *Good gods, a mageborn merchant-king! He'll tear the world to pieces, unless he's decently taught....*

He saw in his heart the marble palaces of Dey Allias, the miles of trenches and furnaces that had turned the river-mouth beds of adamis into a gray wilderness of cinders. Saw the swarms of enslaved Darklanders digging, and the hatred he'd felt toward his countrymen, toward the arrogant, self-satisfied greed of the Lords of the Bright Isle, rose like bile in his throat.

And they've started to work the Mire—how could you even DO that?

The thought of the labor entailed—of where, and how, they'd secure that labor—prickled the hair on his head.

They worked the river-sands out decades ago. And how many men lay dead, their bodies simply dumped into the crumbling trenches when they collapsed with exhaustion and malnutrition? How many women and children killed in the hostage villages whose existence kept the men at their labor? From his own day he remembered the piles of children's severed hands heaped on the edge of the villages in the twilight. Strings of small ears threaded like dried apple-slices. The sound of fathers weeping.

To what world am I going? A shudder went through him, and the pain of the eagles' beaks and claws, the vultures' tearing talons, woke in his flesh like an echo of dread.

Magic changed and the gods in retreat.

Magic changed . . .

Again his mind groped at the flicker of a memory, the winding-sheet of a ghost whose name he had forgotten.

And what the HELL is it rising out of the Mire? At whose summons, and why?

This Heshek of the New Mages? For what earthly purpose?

"You idiot—" The relieved laughter in Graywillow's voice turned the words into kindness, the tone one would use to a beloved brother. "You shouldn't have come after us! You could have been killed!"

"Lady Gray, I'm sorry—" Hamo hugged her like a brother indeed, already forgetting—Ithrazel could see it in his smile—the worst of the terror, the cold, the horror of being lost in the darkness alone. Forgetting them in his relief, and he laughed when Clea gave him a sisterly shove . . .

Ithrazel looked back along the road, in the direction in which they'd come. No glimmer of the mirrors that burned on the road ahead. Black mists drifted over the stones, and anomalous shapes stirred in the mists. *If we walked back, would the road still be there?*

Is there ever a road back from anywhere, to anywhere?

Anaya gone. He closed his eyes briefly, at the recollection of his wife's name. *My children gone. My grandchild.* Whatever lay ahead, he already knew that that was going to be the worst of it.

The others joined him. *Children, really,* he thought as they gathered around him: warm arms, warm hands.

Puppies. Idiots . . .

For a time they, too, gazed at the road that might or might not lead back to wherever it was, where a village had huddled at the foot of a mountain crag. Where in the hot bright mornings the sounds that drifted down from the rocks sounded like a man screaming in agony. Where shepherd boys tended their sheep and fell in love with village girls who weren't beautiful iron princesses and wouldn't break their hearts.

Clea said, "Let's go."

* * *

They came out of the Corridor of Mirrors a few hours before sunset, at the top of the low hill called the Star-Back: the memory of the place hit Ithrazel as if he'd been rammed with the end of a barge-pole over the heart. The pillars around the open Circle at the top had been thrown down. He remembered seeing them as he'd been carried away in his tangled stupor of shock and spells and chains.

Brownwaith—the little colony of his students—had lain about a hundred yards from the hill's foot. He saw it with a kind of shaken numbness, memory re-forming the few remaining fragments of a dream. The building where he'd taught—like a small stone barn—was utterly gone. Trees grew where it had been. Some of the houses of the other Brown Mages were dimly recognizable: a wall, or a broken chimney.

He remembered the names of his students who'd lived there. . . .

Vetch, a Ghoras from Turtlemere. Goerk, from Yellenth in Telmayre. Another Telmayrian, Dacro, who was frantically in love with a minor nobleman's daughter back on the Isle of Caith. He saw their faces, as if they'd parted yesterday.

In front of his own house—as Archmage, his had been the largest in the little colony—the ashes of a campfire still smoked faintly, and a couple of horses grazed on leads. The house itself was nothing more than three broken walls and some bracken, where a shepherd or a hunter had put up a shelter. He whispered, "Dear gods—"

He hadn't even considered that they'd come out in the same place where the Council had taken him in.

The place where the Imperial Marines—where Machodan Indigo of the New Order—had run him to earth.

He remembered, as if recalling a dream, that he hadn't struggled. What had become of his students, he wondered. And those other Brown Mages of his Order who had remained faithful to their vows to keep their hands out of human affairs. They would all be dead now . . .

But dead how? At whose hands?

The hills to the south, almost bare in his day, were thickly wooded now.

Beyond them would lie Dey Allias, the Marble City, beside the gutted estuary of the Dey.

Clea said, "Sons of Death!" and walked from the wide sigil that had been written on the Circle's paving-stones—carefully, through the "gate" that broke its lines—to the nearest of the five firepots that had been set to mark the sigil's points. The pot still smoked gently. "I think this is really the same day!"

"It is," affirmed Graywillow at once, and guided Hamo out through the "gate," Ithrazel following behind. There was nothing that said you couldn't remain within the Sigil's wide ring for as long as you liked, and no real reason why you couldn't walk over the spell-lines once the spell was concluded, as this one was. But among wizards it was said that those things brought bad luck.

Or if magic has changed, reflected Ithrazel wryly, *the gods know WHAT they'd bring now.*

Graywillow briefly knelt, and drew the lines, first to close the sigil—nothing showed in its center to mark where the entrance to the Corridor of Mirrors had lain—and then to dismiss the energies that had formed it. Hamo started to go to one of the burnt-out firepots, but Clea said, "Best let Graywillow do that." The young man nodded, flustered, staring around him at this unfamiliar world. Geese flew, honking, toward the south. The chill of autumn lay like smoke in the air.

My own world. Home.

I knew I'd be home, he thought, dazed. *But not my ACTUAL home. . . .* The home where he'd lived for so many years with his family and his friends.

His eye traced the path that Anaya had walked, from their doorstep up Star-Back Hill to the paved Circle where the Brown Mages had worked their spells. Early dawn, the first morning she'd come to this place. The first morning she'd woken in his arms. The memory was brutal.

"There should be tack in that ruin there," said Clea, pointing for Hamo. (*MY house! That was MY house . . . How DARE you call it 'that ruin'?*) "Have you ever tacked up a riding-horse? Excellent! Bring the saddlebags up here first, if you would. Graywillow, do you need help with the mirrors and things?" The White Sister had made the circuit of the outside of the sigil, dismissing the energies from each firepot, each water bowl, each cardinal point, dusting away the salt and silver and—Ithrazel was interested to note—squiggles of raw adamis, like faintly glittering powder of diamonds.

Spells fade from silver and salt. Adamis—and especially its refined derivative, adamine—held magic longer. *I'll have to learn if newer spells have been devised to disperse its power.*

I'll have to learn a lot of things.

Five mirrors had been set up around the outside of the sigil. Their frames were blacksteel, set with crystals of sulfur, silver, and salt.

Is this Corridor a spell that can only be worked with adamine? He remembered that the New Mages founded their power in the stuff. Rumor had whispered the Black Mages had some knowledge of such a thing. A terrible sense of being out of touch seized him, of being old, like chill wind on naked flesh. The sense, even more disconcerting, of things unrecalled, things that were vital that he should remember . . .

A blink of rage, panic, terror, that disappeared in the next instant, like a shadow in the corner of his eye.

What?

Is it also part of the sorcery of the New Mages, which they keep so secret? To make people forget?

Hamo came running back with the saddlebags, large enough to contain the mirrors, the pots, the paraphernalia of the spell.

Clea thanked the shepherd with a handclasp on his arm, and another smile that dissolved the young man's worried expression, banished the shock and the fear he'd felt in coming out of that dark road into this place. The smile that said, *You're one of my men. I take care of my own.* The smile that said, *Don't worry. You didn't make a mistake, to follow me.*

No wonder her daddy worries about her "friends" among the Darklanders, among the enslaved, among the dispossessed. In his own day, three-quarters of a century ago, the rage of the Twilight Kindred against those who'd taken their land and their menfolk had been a smoldering brushfire, held in check only by better weapons and stronger magic. *I'll bet Stylachos's own troops adore this girl, who speaks their language and handles her weapons like a champion.*

Down the hill from the ruin of the little settlement, horses broke from the trees. A dozen riders, black mail glittering against scarlet tabards, black helmets crested with crimson and gold. A dozen sword blades flashed in the westering light, and Clea said, "Pox rot it! It's my father's men."

Five

There's a hut down that side of the hill." Ithrazel jerked his head at the slope hidden from the riders. "Or there was, anyway—"

"It's gone."

Of course she did a reconnaissance. . . .

"The cellar's still there but they'll search it—"

"Did you find the sub-cellar? Triangular paving-stone in the northeast corner, there's a slit you should be able to get an arrow down. Turn it so the barbs catch and pull straight up—"

Clea dropped flat and pulled the startled Graywillow down behind one of the fallen standing-stones—Ithrazel had not entertained the slightest doubt that the girl had the wits not to silhouette herself against the afternoon sky. He didn't even look back to see them depart, but grasped Hamo by the elbow and led the way down the hill toward the advancing troops, praying they hadn't seen the girls.

One good thing about having been dead for seventy-five years, at least nobody will recognize me.

He shoved the shackles up as tight as he could on his forearms and shook down his too-big sleeves to cover them. *All I'll need is for one of the New Order to be riding with those soldiers. . . .*

Machodan Indigo, Archmage of the Order's House here in the western land, could practically smell blacksteel, Ithrazel recalled. Even after all these years, the recollection of that smooth, boyish face, the Sea Islands drawl of his speech, made the old man's nape prickle. The sense of dealing with something that was not as it seemed . . .

And a sense there was something worse, something he couldn't remember.

"Keep your mouth shut," he whispered to the young shepherd at his side. "You're my grandson and we haven't seen the girls."

"What will they do?" Hamo's eyes filled with trepidation as the warriors clattered up the hill.

Ithrazel didn't answer. You never *did* know what the merchant houses— he recognized the black griffin of House Stylachos on their tabards—would think was a good idea.

The captain was Telmayrian, the aquiline features of the Lords of the Bright Island craggy on a face that was wider at the jaw than the forehead, and wider at the neck than the jaw. The small red jewel of the ancestral Telmayrian nobility winked on his brow. A couple of the troopers wore these as well—younger sons of younger sons, the wizard guessed. He recalled how they'd swagger through the streets of Dey Allias: young men who came to the Twilight Lands to hire out their swords but who despised the merchant houses they worked for. Others among these guardsmen bore the features of various Darklander kindreds: the thin Loghri build, the freckled fairness of the northern Ashupik. . . .

"Where did they go?" The captain snapped as if to servants, and didn't bother to dismount.

Ithrazel made his whole face brighten, as if with revelation. "You saw them too, then, my lord?" He looked back up the hill, toward the circle of fallen pillars at its summit. It was six hundred feet to the edge of the trees, there was no way the men could have been sure of what they saw among the pillars. "A girl and a young lad, it looked like—"

The riders spurred on past them, almost riding them down. Ithrazel— with Hamo firmly in tow—hastened up behind, hobbling like the tired old man he thoroughly felt like.

"Search those huts down there." The captain swung down from the saddle, scuffed with his boot at the half-effaced markings of the sigil. As the men rode down to the ruins of the old settlement, Ithrazel tagged at the captain's heels, making sure he was always under the man's feet when he turned around.

The captain shoved him roughly aside, and Hamo, gods bless the boy, caught him by the arm and urged, "Grandpa, come away—"

Ithrazel shook him off, and bumbled into the captain's way again. "They came right out of the air, I tell you . . ."

The man turned, caught him by the shoulder of his dirty homespun jacket. "What did you see, old man?"

Ithrazel widened his eyes. "A girl and a lad!" he cried breathlessly. "They just—just stepped out of thin air! They looked around them . . . My grandson and I were just down the hill there, in that hut—" He pointed toward the ruin of what had been his own house, where the horses had been tied. *How much does this neckless lout know about the Corridor of Mirrors? Not a lot, I'll bet* . . . "We're on our way to Morne, you see, sir. My granddaughter—not Hamo's sister, but the daughter of my son Bellu—is going to have her first child, and her not yet eighteen years old, and her mother only this year dead of the lung-dropsy—"

The captain slapped him impatiently across the face. "Devils eat your granddaughter. What did you see?"

Ithrazel cringed, convincingly, he hoped. After seventy-five years of having his entrails torn out by eagles, the slap was surprisingly irritating. "They were . . . I swear they weren't anywhere here when we got here! We found the horses down there near that house, you see, sir. One of them had got loose and strayed, that nice-looking bay, like my old master used to ride, except my old master's had white socks. Miss Daisy, her name was, and my master'd trained her to come when he called. I thought they might have been stolen," he went on as the captain shook him. "Or left by someone . . . so we were watching the trees all around, for them to come back. Whoever owned the horses, I mean. We were hoping for a reward of some kind, you see, sir. Neither of us had eaten all day, and we've come so far . . . Then all of a sudden, there was a sort of flickering, like light and movement, here on the top of the hill. And it's like they just stepped out of the air! Like fairies, but if they were fairies, they couldn't have left horses here, now, could they? Hamo and I ran up the hill toward them, but they just . . . just stepped back, and there was another sort of flicker of light, and they were gone!"

He scampered, to plant himself in front of the captain as the man crossed back and forth through the ring of scratched-out sigils.

A soldier came up the hill, blacksteel mail glittering in the fading afternoon. "They were here all right, Lord Ganzareb. Both horses are from the Lady Clea's stable. Blooded racers, both of them—"

"Bitch," said Lord Ganzareb. "Take them, and the rest of the gear—"

"We did find them, sir," pestered Ithrazel. "Wandering stray, they were. And we've stayed here all this time watching over them—"

Ganzareb shoved him aside, with the casual brutality of a man kicking a dog. Hamo caught him as he staggered, and glanced pleadingly toward the edge of the woods. Ithrazel tightened his hand on the young man's wrist. *Stay* . . . "Anything?" Ganzareb asked as two of the troopers clattered up to him, and the men shook their heads.

Good, the girl found the trapdoor into the old drain . . .

"It's witch-work, sir." One of the Telmayrians kicked at the traces on the ground, and used the Telmayrian word for the street-corner fortune-tellers and granny-wives of the city slums. In his own time, Ithrazel had heard it applied both to the shamans of the Twilight Kindred, and to the two orders of priestesses who sourced their power from the gods of the land. "The Iron Princess is supposed to be damn thick with the Sisterhoods. Could they still be here and—you know"—the young man looked around him fearfully—"invisible?"

"'Fraid they'll kiss you when you're not looking, Ranko?"

The other men laughed, but the oldest of the troopers, with the long, hooked nose of the Placne tribe, said, "There's no such thing as invisible, Lord Ranko. Not even the Crystal Order can do that. They just make you think you're seeing something else. My guess is, since it looks like they came here to practice some kind of magic, they'll have gone west to the Sisters in the marshes by Serpent Lake. It'd help if we knew"—he glanced at Lord Ganzareb suggestively—"what the princess is supposed to be doing and why her dad wants her back so smart . . ."

"And would you like him to tell you also, Sarpellis, what he plans to have for breakfast tomorrow morning? Or if he's a mind to bull his wife tonight? You think any of that might be your business?" Ganzareb planted himself challengingly in front of the Placne.

"No, my lord." The trooper Sarpellis pressed his knuckles to his brow and retreated.

"Mount up." Ganzareb slashed his hand at his men. "I'll wager you're right, and the bitch will be on her way to the Serpent Lake. She has to get across the Marble Bridge, so we'll wait for her there . . ."

"Fetch him his horse," whispered Ithrazel, shoving Hamo in the direction of the big gelding that stood ground-reined where the captain had left it. "And look humble."

The young man scurried to obey, and Ganzareb took the rein and swung into the saddle with barely a glance at him, like a man taking only his due.

The troopers cantered off down the hill, too intent on their own mission to ask themselves, presumably, why the two wanderers they'd encountered on the scene of Clea's "magic" had only a small satchel of bread and cheese between them, and a gourd of water.

Ithrazel watched them out of sight, then led the way down toward the bank of Sweet Creek, where the drainage tunnel from the old settlement bathhouse ended.

"Wish I knew if my father had heard anything specific about my plans," said Clea when the wizard relayed the details of his encounter with her father's Master of Swords. "Or if he's just worried about the Darklander Kindreds rising in rebellion. They're ripe for it, and they'd follow a single leader, but their shamans are no match for the Crystal Mages. I keep trying to tell them that. . . ."

She stopped herself, under Ithrazel's sharp sidelong glance.

"And what makes Daddy think you'd be that leader? In my day you could barely get a Setuket to drink water that a Loghri drew for him, or a Ghoras to let an Ashupik walk across the Gray Hills without getting an arrow in his back. I daresay," the old man added, "that seventy-five years of closer acquaintance have changed that."

"They have." She was silent then, observing that the wizard seemed to know this path well, even in the gathering dusk. Ahead of them, above the Gray Hills, the fingernail-clipping of the new moon followed the sun to its rest; the world breathed of sage, and of the wet stones of the creek.

In time she went on, "My grandfather—my mother's father—was a shaman and a scholar, one of the guardians of the books among the Ashupik. Greenshield was his name among the Kindred. He was called Elannin when he came to Morne to be a healer among the Ashupik there."

"And do the merchant houses still hire the Ashupik as their clerks and their bookkeepers?" He sounded genuinely curious, and for the first time no longer wary. She remembered that he had destroyed Dey Allias from his own hatred of what was being done to the tribes.

"Mostly," she said, "yes. Grandfather worked in Morne to unite the schools of the Kindred in the city, even after the emperor suppressed them. Brought the elders and chiefs of the different Kindreds together, first in Morne, then in the other towns like Aktas in the north, and Chrisankus— that's the House Othume headquarters south of here. Then out among the Kindreds in the Mire.

"I didn't know him well," she added. "I was only six when my mother was arrested, and Father had most of her family killed, including Grandfather. They were supposed to have helped her bewitch Father into getting rid of his first wife. Shumiel's mother—she was an heiress of the House of Shiamat. I think it was because of the Shiamats that I was put in prison rather than just sent to some distant manor-house." She shrugged. "But it could have been because I was Elannin Greenshield's granddaughter. Even after I was re-legitimized the first time, Father's never known whether to play me as a card to keep the Ashupik on his side, or to get rid of me as a possible troublemaker."

"Given that he murdered your mother," commented the wizard, "I can appreciate his concerns about your loyalty."

Clea concentrated briefly on the mental image of the Greenflood River where it rose in the Gray Hills and tumbled over rocks on its way down to Morne, as she had trained herself to do when the subject of her mother, or her father, arose. *It all happened a long time ago to someone else and it gave you some very valuable information about Minos Stylachos. That's all it was.*

If you feel anything inside, your hands will shake. The strong don't shake.

"The Ashupik are a strong Kindred," she said, after barely a pause. "They still have actual cities, out in the Mire, and trade with the merchant houses. The Kindred in Morne . . ."

She stopped herself, reflecting that now wasn't the time to admit that she even knew about the Councils of the Kindred among the Darklander servants and artisans and slaves of Morne. Instead she said, "Father spent a lot of time and money—once my brother Pendri's mother died and he could do it without offending the House Shiamat—trying to get me and everyone else to forget that he married Elannin Greenshield's daughter, and turn me into a usable princess for the House."

Ithrazel said, "Hah!"

Needless to say, after Ithrazel's account of his meeting with Ganzareb, Clea steered well clear of the Marble Bridge that crossed the River Dey on the road back toward Morne. There was a fording-place that the Ghoras used, where the waters tumbled between the Dark Hills and the Gray. Pressing on hard, they reached it before twilight grew thick, through what had been the fertile hinterland of Dey Allias. Woodland now covered the abandoned fields, silent save for the passing of deer and rabbits in the darkness, and the occasional scream of a lynx. Even now, the younger sons of Telmayrian merchant nobility would occasionally put together schemes to go in and start working the old adamis beds of the Dey estuary, fat with diamond-sand. One could still see the long coves scooped into what had been the bluffs along the city's harbor, the huge rectangular sump-ponds, where the sand had been gouged up and the slag-waste dumped back, now only mile after straggly mile of salt-bush and water-weeds.

Clea was familiar with those keen-eyed young gentlemen, elegant in the artificial austerity that was fashionable in the cities of the Bright Islands these days. (*And who the hell EVER told them those flower-shaped hats looked good on ANYONE. . . ?*) They'd display beautifully bound volumes of notes to her father in the hopes of getting House Stylachos's backing and House Stylachos's credit, and drop subtle hints that if House Stylachos wasn't interested, perhaps the Othume might be, down in Crisankus . . .

And Minos Stylachos would stroke the oiled, golden curls of his beard and agree that yes, it certainly looked like an interesting plan, and there was certainly a great deal of diamond-sand there for the digging. He did not say (for it did not, after all, pay to offend even the younger sons of minor nobility by laughing in their faces) that they could go peddle their scheme to the Othume or the Kinnesh or the Vrykos or to his abominable cousin Tykellin, and the answer would be the same. The output of the diamond-sands of the Dey estuary had been shrinking for two years before the catastrophe that destroyed the Marble City. These days, dredging operations in the flooded canyons of the Mire were firmly in place and turning out barges loaded with adamis. Whatever profits might be generated in Dey Allias, after new equipment was brought in and set up, would be undercut by dredgers who dragged their feet or refused to enter the pits, who broke machinery, or died by the score in the diggings. Men who fled—as if from the demons of Hell—at every opportunity no matter what threats were made . . .

Because of this man.

Clea glanced behind her, at the small, sturdy figure in his homespun rags and grimy sheepskins.

Ithrazel the Brown.

Ithrazel the Cursed.

He moved stiffly, blood from the cuts he'd taken in the final fight with the birds crusting the back of his too-large, homespun shirt. There was an acid-burn on the side of his face. *Will those disappear tonight?* He was slowing down—they all were, even Hamo—and Clea was already calculating how much strength each of her party had, against the slender supplies of food and the oncoming cold of autumn night. The loss of her horses angered her, for she knew Ganzareb treated beasts no better than he treated the men of the Twilight kin. But she guessed she could get them back eventually—Ganzareb never could resist money. Between the addition of Hamo to the party, and the need to circle through the hills to avoid pursuit, she knew they would have been slowed down in any case.

* * *

For hours after fording the Dey she listened behind her, aware that Graywillow's novice scrying-spells might have been no match for whatever amulets of concealment an ambush party might have gotten from Himelkart. And though she heard nothing, sensed no threat, she guessed that her father—or the Crystal Mages—might have other searchers than Ganzareb out in these hills.

There was a landing called the Dogpond, three days to the west, where an elbow of the Mire curved into the hills. From there they could get boats, and return—carefully and circuitously—to what was left of the village of Turtlemere.

To see what there was to be seen.

She glanced back at Ithrazel again. The old man stumbled, but caught himself and moved stoically on. Wizards were tough—tougher than assassins, some of them—but he was coming to the end of his strength, and Graywillow was being helped at nearly every step by the sturdy Hamo. Definitely time to stop, at least for an hour's rest. None of them were more than a shadow in the dusk now, but she saw the old man's face in her mind: nondescript, gouged with lines of pain and watchfulness, hazel-green eyes cautious under tufted sandy brows . . .

Will he run when he gets a chance?

Not if Graywillow can call the Mages' Council down on his back.

Will he think it's a good idea to trade us to Father to see what he can get?

He can't think he won't be double-crossed.

The thoughts clicked through her mind like the flicked beads of an abacus, while her eyes and ears scanned the landscape, systematically searching for anomalies in the familiar patterns of early night.

And he doesn't know the politics. Everything has changed, since last he breathed this air and looked up at these stars—disconcertingly, there had been no stars in that strange enclave world where Hamo had tended his sheep. *Right now he doesn't know who to sell me to or who might consider his death a more profitable prize than mine.*

Movement to her right—the deadly wraith of a hunting owl. The red Blood-Star hung low over the rise of ground behind and to the east that hid Dey Allias's corpse.

And I've got to keep him on my side—keep him looking to me for protection—until I can figure out what the hell Heshek Paramos is up to and how to combat the thing that, even if he didn't create it, he seems to be trying to turn into his servant.

Six

Darklander scouts met them their second night in the hills.

After a brief rest to eat, Clea had led them—slowly, for Graywillow was almost spent—until nearly dawn. First light found them still in the Gray Hills, the valley farms that had once provided grain and cattle to the lords of Dey Allias. They had gone to ground in the ruin of a stone cottage whose overgrown orchards Clea and Hamo scavenged while their companions slept. *The spell will wear off,* Clea told herself, watching the young man sling-stone a squirrel from the trunk of a tree with silent swiftness that would have done any assassin of her acquaintance proud. *It will wear off, and he'll ask to go back—and by the gods I'll find a way back for him, blacksteel mirrors, adamine firepots, and all!* Knee-deep in chilly water by an old fishing-weir, she watched him gather up the squirrel. *All the girls in his village will thank me . . .*

He was, she had to admit, a comely young man, tall and broad-shouldered, with his thick black curls and honest, open blue eyes. *Dumb as a paving-stone, of course . . .*

"Thank you." She gave him a rueful grin when he came up to her. "You're good with that—but you were an idiot to follow us! You could have been killed!"

He pressed the limp little corpse into her hands, his own fingers big and rough over hers. The whole of his heart was in his eyes as he said, "You know I couldn't do otherwise, Lady."

Dear gods, I'll bet he's a virgin.

At least a virgin in respect of being in love.

Clea's own virginity hadn't survived her years in the underground slums of Morne after her escape from prison, but it wasn't something she thought of, much. She hadn't dared tell Rat Bone. Female assassins were not encouraged to put themselves in danger of pregnancy. But she'd bided her time, until she'd been able to trap, geld, flay, and eviscerate her rapist without possibility of detection or reprisal. The man, a well-known pimp, had been her first independent kill. She'd never been able to count him in her official Guild tally, but it had been good practice.

Now she looked aside from Hamo's ardent gaze and said, "Well, thank you. You shouldn't have done it but I'm glad you did. You've been tremendous help." She met his eyes again and added, "This is a pretty poor introduction you're getting to my world. The rest of it isn't like this."

"When I was a little boy," said the shepherd, with the first un-self-conscious grin she'd seen from him, "I used to dream of seeing something beyond our village, our valley. I didn't even know what it would be like, you know. So I guess I'm getting my wish."

"My nurse always said, 'Be careful what you wish for, because you might get it.'"

He laughed at that. "My granny said that, too. And then she'd tell me these horrible stories, about little boys who wished for things that turned out to be just awful—"

"My nurse, too! By the gods, I think they were sisters!" Her nurse, Clea was almost certain, had been one of those who'd gone to the Mages' Council with tales of her mother's adulteries and rites of forbidden magic. But that, she understood, was beside the point. Her words made Hamo laugh, and put him at his ease with her. The actual truth was nobody's business.

With the squirrel and the few fish she caught, and a dozen early apples, they had moved on the following afternoon, and toward sunset Clea became aware that they were being dogged. *Probably Ghoras*, she calculated, the second time she caught the fleeting impression of movement in the woods to her left. Villages of the Ghoras tribe had held this whole stretch of coastline, from Dey Allias north to the Bay of Tarn, before the coming of the ships from the Bright Islands. She cut a sapling, and tied her neck-scarf to the end of it in the fashion accepted throughout the Twilight Lands: *Do we have permission to pass?*

A brown owl hooted, several hours before such a bird would have been waking.

Clea stopped, and the hunters melted out of the trees.

They knew her, and she recognized their leader, a woman named Star, graying fair hair cropped short as some of the tribal women did to indicate mourning. She was one of the many hunters who moved back and forth between the villages of the Kindred and the Darklander communities that made up well over half of the underworld slums of Morne. Star herself, Clea knew, was an escaped slave: her hands were knotted with arthritis and she was missing three fingernails, from work at the washing-baffles where they cleaned adamis-bearing diamond-clay. "The men of Turtlemere said you would be returning to the Mire," she said.

"This thing, the zai," asked Clea. "Has it struck again?"

The woman shook her head. "In the towns they're saying now that Turtlemere was destroyed in an uprising. That the village men attacked the guards and tried to break the dredgers, and the guards killed them. Their families were taken out of the hostage village and sold as slaves."

"What about the rest of the people in Turtlemere?"

"Moved to other villages, they say."

If it was a choice of believing that, or accepting a rumor about a giant murderous shape of darkness that came out of nowhere and killed at random, she knew which story she'd pick.

"What other villages?"

"No one knows. No one who has asked in any village has heard of people from Turtlemere being brought in."

Clea whispered. "Pox rot them—"

"But it was a zai?" asked the woman softly. "A—a spirit from out of the Mire, and not a rebellion against the Outlanders?" Her colorless eyebrows pulled down over the low bridge of her nose. "This is not just one of their lies, to keep us from knowing that there are some who have the courage to rise against these Clay-Grubbers, these Easterling murderers and thieves. . . ?"

And one of the young men with her—Kingfisher, Clea remembered him from a secret gathering in the Tunnels below Morne—murmured, "We thought it might have been you."

The huntress's green eyes slid sidelong to take in the shape of Ithrazel's features and the color of his sandy hair, and her lips compressed with hate. "This one you travel with—"

"Is my servant," said Clea. "It is a zai that destroyed the village. I saw it. I saw what was left. And, if the men of Turtlemere really did plan a revolt, I think they'd be smarter than to attack the garrison in a locked village at night, with nothing but dredging-tools." She added, her eyes meeting Kingfisher's, "*I* would be."

The other hunters looked one another doubtfully; Kingfisher's eyes remained on hers. "If someone had led them against the Clay-Grubbers, they would not have fought alone."

Clea held up her hand. "Don't talk about hunting rabbits," she said, "when you've got a wolf coming in through your window. What's happening in Turtlemere now?"

"It's surrounded by your father's men," said Star. "There are soldiers at the dredging-stations in the Nightshade Maze, too, keeping the men there at work but also keeping anyone from getting near the village. In the woods you can smell the burned houses, and the corpses of the unburied dead."

Three of the men made the sign against evil. Clea didn't blame them. There were magics that could be sourced from the energy released at death, and bodies that had not been properly given back to the earth—and souls to the gods—would go on releasing those energies for a long time, to say nothing of the stink of their rotting remains. She saw Graywillow shiver. Ithrazel folded his arms, listened without change of expression.

"Are they in the village itself? Either wizards, or soldiers?"

"That I don't know, Lady. I doubt you could get soldiers to stay in the place. There are mages with the soldiers . . ." Her mouth pursed again, with contempt this time. "*Mages*, they call them. Smooth-faced boys who should be at their nursie's tit. Yes, they have power, and the god who gave it to them should take shame on himself, if they're truly as young as they seem. They have power, but not the understanding of men. Neambis, of the Gray Sisters of Farrawen, has said to me that these Crystal Mages—these unbaked biscuits!—have found spells that will lengthen a man's life: is that why they all seem like children? Are they in fact men of forty and fifty, who only look like youths?"

Ithrazel's tufted eyebrows shot up, and Clea tried to remember when the New Mages had started contriving spells that would extend a man's days. The Crystal Mages were superb healers, and there'd been talk for years that those of the order who returned to the Bright Island were able, in addition to curing some of the worst diseases of human and beast, to simply add years to a life that would have quietly snuffed out. This, some said—mostly mages of the other Orders that hadn't discovered these spells themselves—was what earned the Crystal Order the favor of the emperor and the Great Lords of the Bright Island. And it was true, Clea knew, that the emperor, who'd been an old man already when Clea was a child, still sat on the Throne of Light.

But she'd seen the wizard Himelkart first as a child, when she'd been a child herself, not quite ten years old, picking pockets in the crowd as that thin, raven-haired boy rode by among the handsome young wizards, in the entourage that escorted her infant brother to the temples of the gods.

Remembered the blast of resentment she'd felt, that this favored mageling with his whole clothes and his clean hair was a lad no older than she.

"As far as I know," said Clea slowly, "those youths are youths indeed. They really do come to power that young. But I'm not a wizard, Star. I don't know the truth of what I hear. Are the wizards camped with the soldiers, or do they come and go from town?"

"They come and go. *He* comes and goes—the Archmage's pretty-boy. He's been out among the soldiers, asking questions, they say. He had two others with him yesterday." She shook her head. "What will you do, Princess?"

"First," said Clea, "find out what we're talking about, if I can. Will you help me, Star? Can you get us a canoe, and guides to take us as close to Turtlemere as we can get? Food, too, if you would," she added. Those fragments of squirrel and fish had been a *long* time ago. "We had to flee my father's men, and lost our supplies—"

With Star and the Ghoras warriors around them, they moved forward as darkness deepened. The air grew moist on Clea's skin, and as the ground sloped down beneath their feet, from out of the formless lands below rose the vast, sour pong of the Mire: the smell of water and decay; the smell of endless miles of trees. Now and then the whiff of wood smoke touched the air, where villages of the Twilight People, the Darklanders, nested in their rings of fields and gardens. There were few hereabouts, Clea knew. Completely aside from the slave-hunters in quest for workers in the diggings, even after seventy-five years nobody wanted to dwell too close to the ruins of Dey Allias.

Clea glanced up the line of the marchers at Ithrazel again. The old man strode stolidly, glancing to the right and left as if he could see, through the blackness, the tangled hells of laurel and cane that had swallowed up what had once been farmland.

He must have known this land well. He'd remembered exactly the layout of the little sanctuary of Brownwaith, and how to open the sub-crypt—which had eluded her earlier investigation of the ruins—that had contained the old drain that led down to Sweet Creek. *Better than I know it, even now.* Back at the deserted farm in the hills where they'd slept the daylight hours, she'd considered asking Graywillow to guard him for as long as it took Hamo and herself to get food, but a second look at her friend's discolored eyelids and haggard face had closed her lips on the words.

Far off she could hear wolves howl, the big hill breed that ranged all of this land. But the deer were fat this time of year—she'd seen plenty of droppings before the light failed—and she guessed that the wolves would avoid the scent of humankind.

The old man's no danger to me yet . . .

But it was only among the Sons of Telmayre, she was well aware, that he was called Cursed. Only among the wizards whose teaching he had betrayed.

To dredgers like Star's brother, who had wives and children in the hostage villages—to Rediron and Pikefish, who'd slipped over the stable wall five nights ago to tell her that a creature had come out of the Deep Mire and destroyed Turtlemere village, who had known men in Sandmire village that had been obliterated last year in exactly similar circumstances—to all those who had good reason to hate the shining Easterlings from out of the sunrise, Ithrazel was the Destroyer, whose demons had swallowed Dey Allias whole.

An inconspicuous little man, reflected Clea, *until you met his eyes.*

A weapon in my hand . . .

Or in the hands of this land's angry gods.

"How do you fare, sir?" Hamo picked his way across the half-buried ruin of a stable where the little band had gone to ground with the approach of day. The Dogpond, first of the canyons of the Mire—steep-walled and flooded fifty feet deep with dark waters that moved very gently toward the far-off Marsh of Serpents—still lay ten miles off, but Ithrazel could smell the Mire. Thick growths of fern and bog-laurel all around them now spoke amply of the wet fogs that would rise from those endless meres.

The new moon had set. Dim color stained the east. There could be no fire in this place, and the hunter's pemmican the young man handed him was cold and slightly mealy, but Ithrazel was too hungry and too weary to care. When he'd lain down yesterday, at the empty farmhouse, he'd fallen asleep instantly from sheer exhaustion, though he'd have gone back to his crag and his eagles rather than let himself be outwalked by a couple of girls. Now he looked up into the young man's face and said, "Thank you."

He scooped the pemmican from its sheep-gut tube—fat, meat, and dried berries mixed, with a texture like very soft sausage or very firm porridge—divided it between two enormous sycamore leaves and handed one back to Hamo. He was aware of the young man's discreet glance at the burn on his face, and chuckled grimly. "Better today. I must really be alive—" Gingerly he touched the blistered flesh. "I suppose it should be a comfort, but it's not. I still have claw-gashes on my back—"

"The lady Graywillow should see to those." Hamo ducked his head, a little shyly at having his curiosity detected.

Ithrazel growled. "The gods only know what this"—he gestured with the blacksteel shackle—"will do to a healing-spell, but I'll ask her." He shook his head, and returned his attention to the pemmican. "All those years of dreaming about being able to run away, and I never once thought about how far or how fast I'd be able to run if I got the chance. It's hard to believe I'll ever stop being hungry, though."

The young man laughed, and scooped up the soft mixture with two fingers. *They must have something similar in his home village,* reflected Ithrazel, watching him as he did the same. This made sense, if you needed something to keep you going for long distances.

"These people—the Ghoras—" The shepherd signed toward the guards, nearly unseen in the thickets around the broken walls. "Star and her kinsmen—they tell me the Bright People, the Easterlings, will hunt us now, if they get wind of us. That they'll be hunting the Lady Clea."

Pity on the poor bastards if they catch her. "I doubt they'll succeed," Ithrazel said. "The Twilight Kindred are masters of the woodlands. Once we enter the Mire, we should be able to move quicker."

"They say these Easterlings—these Bright Warriors who enslave them, and make them work digging magic mud out of the bottoms of the canyons—kill and maim their children, if they don't work." The young man's heavy brows crumpled deep over his nose. "They tell me they have powerful wizards, more powerful even than the gods of this land. They cast spells to hold the workers prisoner, and to force them to do as they're told. They dig this stuff—this *adamis*"—he mispronounced the unfamiliar word—"out of the mud, housefuls of it, and send it to the cities of the . . . the *sea*—" Again his tongue fumbled on the name of a thing that he had never seen, never imagined. "And they use it to make their magic even stronger."

After troubled silence, the young man went on, "They say that *you* are one of these Easterlings. These Bright Masters."

And, when Ithrazel did not reply: "I thought you were a god."

Ithrazel made a single harsh sniff of laughter. "I wish I were."

"Do you?" Hamo finished his meal, licked the leaf, then rubbed it, greasy side down, in the thin dirt of the floor, to obliterate any trace that men had camped in that place. "Do gods like being gods? Does it make them happy?"

"If I were a god, I could tell you."

The young man looked crestfallen, and disconcerted. Ithrazel remembered him as a sturdy young boy, balanced precariously on the rocks beside his mountain crag, staring at him in horror and shock and pity. He had asked then, Ithrazel recalled, *Are you a god?*

He didn't remember what he'd replied.

Hamo had been ready to creep out across the rock-face to give him a drink from his own water bottle, Ithrazel remembered, even though the birds circled screaming overhead. Ithrazel had called out to him to wait until twilight came, when the birds would depart.

"Why do you ask?" he said now.

By the way Hamo ducked his head and glanced aside, he knew.

"I thought . . ." The young man hesitated. "They tell me—Star, and the hunters—that the Lady Clea's mother was an enchantress of . . . of one of their great tribes. That her father is a great lord of the Bright Island. I thought maybe a god would know how I can win her. Win her love, I mean. I would give my life for her . . ."

Don't be an idiot, boy. In a year you won't want her. Less than that, if you're lucky.

Ithrazel took a deep breath. "Don't hurt yourself," he said gently. "Don't give your life for her."

"Why not?" The azure eyes stared desperately into his. "She means more to me than my own life! I've never felt like this before. If I cannot be with her always, I feel that I *will* die!" He glanced over his shoulder a moment later, though he had spoken in a whisper, but Clea was at the top of the rough slope that led up out of the ruin, talking to Star about canoes.

"You won't die." The kindest thing he could say, Ithrazel reflected, would be to put this ardent boy out of hope. Instead he remembered the first time he'd seen Anaya, sixteen years old and betrothed to the son of her father's business partner—he ran one of the biggest silk factories in Yellenyth, in the cool uplands above the Fire Lakes. . . .

It had felt like the world coming to an end.

Or a new universe beginning.

He'd gone straight to his teacher and asked about a love-potion, and nearly had his ears ripped off by the old man's blistering lecture.

Hamo asked again, "How can I win her?"

Not, *You're a god, I brought you water, make her love me . . .*

And he was a good seven years younger, Ithrazel guessed, than he himself had been when old Brancas had verbally flayed him about love that is won, and love that is bought.

"Do your people believe," he said slowly, "that love is a gift of the gods?"

"All things," returned Hamo, "are gifts of the Good God."

"It is generally held to be unwise," continued the wizard, "to snatch what you want out of their hands."

Like the destruction of a city of murderers and tyrants . . .

Hamo laughed: soft, bitter laughter. "That's funny," he said, to Ithrazel's lifted brows. "That's exactly what my granny said to me. And she—Lady Clea—said her nurse said it to her. She says they must have been sisters. *Be careful what you wish for . . .*"

Ithrazel laid his hand—soft and unworked as a woman's, though the blacksteel shackles were beginning to leave a ring of sores on the bones of his wrist—on the boy's huge brown one. "It's hard to hear it," he said. "Be the man you would wish a woman you care for to have in her life. A man who is brave without bravado. Who is kind without hope or expectation of either praise or reward. A man who cares not only for her happiness, but for the happiness of those around her. A man who walks at peace with who he is, and who *she* is. A man who trusts her enough to leave her—and himself—in the hands of the gods."

And incidentally, one who doesn't call up demons and fire to kill fifty thousand people . . .

"I want her," Hamo whispered. "More than life."

"I know." Ithrazel took the boy in his arms, held him like the son he had lost, the son he knew had never grown to manhood . . .

The son he knew had been in Dey Allias the night it was destroyed.

With Anaya.

As he had known at the time.

Seven

Lady—"

Clea was already awake as a man's hand touched her shoulder. Her own knife was in her grip and her breath short with shock, as if every hair on her head stood up . . .

WHAT IS THAT SMELL???

She was shaking.

The Ghoras hunter—Second Rabbit, his name was—had had the wits at least to shake her from arm's distance away and behind her head, probably the only reason she hadn't stabbed him. He still backed up fast.

But it wasn't waking that blazed along every nerve like pitch-pine.

Fog covered the ruined farm, threw back reflections of their tiny fire. Fog rank with the smell of the Mire, the wet scents of fern and forest, and something else . . .

"What *is* that?"

"We don't know." Second Rabbit drew close and spoke in a whisper. The other hunters—and Hamo—made a tight ring with the fire at the center, facing outward with bows, spears, knives. Ithrazel sat up, blanket half drawn around himself, looking around, and she saw fear in his eyes.

"What is it?" She turned to him.

For a moment their gazes met. He said, "I don't know," and the lie moved across his face like the shadow of a serpent.

The smell was everywhere, thin and penetrant, like burning metal. But something in it told her it was the smell of a living thing. She remembered the darkness beyond the Corridor of Mirrors, the horrible sense of unseen things gyring there.

She had just time to say "Pox rot it" and catch up her sword when something rolled or swam or flew out of the fog, the bulk of a man but of no man's shape—of the shape of nothing she'd ever seen or imagined, shapeless as a monstrosity dredged out of the deeps of the sea. It had eyes because they gleamed in the light, instants before it materialized from the darkness. Kingfisher struck at it with his spear, and with a retching bellow the thing wrapped its tentacles around the spear and around the man's legs. A second monster, like the first, flashed out of the fog and fastened itself on Kingfisher's back, and Second Rabbit and his brother Boar sprang to spear it, tear it free, while the young hunter screamed in shock and agony. Blood spouted out between the writhing tentacles, the blue, squamous flesh.

Graywillow raised her hand and Ithrazel grabbed her wrist, as he had done before. This time she pushed him off with surprising strength, made the sign of Summoning, calling fire, a flash of bitter pain, onto the attacking creatures. The flame ran slithering off them like water, and if they felt pain, they made no sign of it. Two more of them appeared from the darkness, Star and her hunters slashing at them with knives and shortswords. Clea bent, caught up a brand from the fire and strode toward the struggling mass, Ithrazel behind her with another burning stick likewise in his hand.

There were tiny eyestalks at the base of the greater tentacles—Clea had seen them swivel toward the attackers—and she rammed the fire into them, the wet flesh hissing. The creatures writhed but did not release their hold on their prey. Rather, they backed away into the fog and the darkness, fast as wolves running, Kingfisher still bucking and screaming among the blue, wriggling tentacles. Clea could see the flesh of his face, arms and breast dissolving already, like sugar, dribbling in lumps on the ground. Clea slashed again with her torch but the creatures were shockingly fast, rolling and tumbling away from the flame among the bracken. She grabbed for a tentacle, felt the horrible flesh surge and give under her fingers before it slid away.

What if there are more of them in the forest?

She plunged after the things anyway, Star and the others behind her, trying to follow the sound of Kingfisher's screams. "What are they?" Star gasped. "What are they?"

Not even legend, thought Clea, *spoke of them . . .*

As no legend had spoken of the thing that had destroyed Turtlemere Village, that had been given the borrowed name of zai.

The smell was beginning to dissipate. Only wet echoes of it drifted in the fog.

They hunted the darkening mists of the woods for as long as the screaming continued. Twice they found pieces of its victim, but there was no trail—not even for the experienced hunters of the Ghoras—in the brown ferns, the dying autumn leaves underfoot. As the smell dispersed, the fog did also. "Can they summon fog?" whispered Star, and behind her, Second Rabbit cried out and whirled, but it was only an enormous tree spider, its outspread legs the width of his hand, which had dropped onto his arm.

"Are they demons?" asked Boar, glancing nervously around him. "They're like no demons I've ere heard tell of. Lady—?" He looked at Graywillow, who shook her head, then swatted at a centipede—curiously aggressive—that came crawling toward him through the leaf-mast of the ground.

"I don't . . . think so . . ." She looked uncertainly toward Clea in the shadowy torch-glow.

"'Twas demons that destroyed Dey Allias," said Star. "And we're not so very far from its ruins yet. Yet I've never heard of them—or things such as these—lingering still."

Clea said softly, "No. Nor have I." Her glance returned to Ithrazel, and saw his eyes as he listened to the darkness that pressed around them. *Haunted,* she thought, *not by fear of the unknown, but by the horror of recognition.*

Later in the night, as they made their way toward the deep gorge of the Dogpond, they smelled an echo of the Night Gluttons (as the Ghoras named them) and following it, found most of Kingfisher's skeleton, wedged high in the fork of a cottonwood tree.

Clea whispered, "Is it a trap?"

From the thickets of swamp-laurel where they hid, she scanned the broken houses, the charred roofs of Turtlemere in the chilly forenoon light. From the Dogpond they had paddled nearly fifty miles through the cold dead of the moonless dark. With dawn they'd hidden the canoes and climbed the canyon wall, to approach the village through the woods. Concealed at the far edge of what had been the town's cornfields—when Turtlemere had been an actual town and not a dredger slave-village—it was still possible to view the place with a mariner's seeing-glass that magnified fivefold, a purchase from the best instrument-maker in Morne. At a gap in the wall Clea picked out the black helmet of one of her father's troopers. A little farther off, near what had been the village hall, she glimpsed another.

"Or illusion?" She took the brass tube from her eye, looked beside her at Graywillow, then across at Ithrazel, who lay on the girl's other side in the near-impenetrable tangles of leaves and choke-vine. "Am I deceived, or are there no mages there?"

Ithrazel shook his head.

The smell of burning lingered over the village, as it had six days ago. *Only six.*

The men who'd come to find Graywillow seven nights ago, at the goddess Nyellin's shrine in Morne, had done so a few hours after dark fell, with the horrified tale of the creature that had risen from the waters of the Nightshade Maze and destroyed a dredging-crew carrying adamis down to the barges. The men of her father's garrison at the village had sent word to her father, they'd told her. The surviving dredgers were terrified they would be sent away, as the folk of Sandmire had been (or so the rumor went) six months before. Graywillow had brought the messengers to a quiet courtyard of the stables and had summoned Clea, shortly after midnight. Knowing it would take her father a good five hours to arrange troops, send word to the Crystal Mages at the House of Glass, get horses saddled, and come up with a plausible story as to why he was doing all this, Clea had set forth at once. The houses in Turtlemere had been still burning when they'd arrived there, shortly before noon.

About a hundred yards from the gate of the village, they'd found the body of a man, the flesh of head, shoulders, and one arm either torn free of the bones or melted off, reeking brown gobbets soaking into the dank mold underfoot, as Kingfisher's flesh had done yesterday evening. Pikefish, one of the dredgers who'd ridden with them, had known him.

But by then they'd smelled the smell of burning for a mile or more, and heard the wailing.

In a way, Clea had been glad of the wailing. Since that first whiff of smoke, she'd been afraid all that would meet them would be silence.

Two women had run out the half-opened gate, grabbed at Clea's stirrup-leather: "Get us out of here! Help us, oh, Lord—" People often mistook Clea for a boy when she had her hair up under a cap. Laundresses, Clea guessed—the polite word for the prostitutes that the merchant lords would have sent to the villages, for the use of the miners and the garrison—but Pikefish had slid from the saddle and comforted them. "It took Jade!" one of them sobbed. "It took Jade!"

"Jade is her boy," Pikefish had said.

That was when they—and other survivors—told her that the zai had struck the village.

*   *   *

She moved in cautiously now, circling the palisade around the village and watching the forest on all sides for outlying troopers. The palings were wood, built to keep the dredgers in rather than any foe out. In four places they'd been torn to kindling, and at the rear of the village had been burned.

Just outside the ruined western gate lay a small temple, marked by the double serpent carving of Kochmal, lord of all that lay beneath the ground. A remnant, Clea guessed, of the original Ghoras town; by the smell of it, now used as the dumping-ground for the dead.

"What is here?" breathed Hamo, silent as a shadow among the ferns at her side. "It's like the House of the Ancestors in my village."

Brush and tinder piled along its walls. Presumably the whole thing would be burned.

Possibly, reflected Clea, *the entire village as well.*

A single guard stood just inside the west gate, keeping a wary eye on the little building. The roof was black with crows, ravens, and kites. The razor-backed wild hogs of the forest trotted in and out of its open door.

"I'm not sure Ganzareb and his men will have made it back to Morne yet," murmured Clea doubtfully, as Star and Graywillow melted from the green shade to crouch at her side. "So my father—and Heshek—may not know I went to Brownwaith. But if they're trying to keep the attack here a secret, they've got to have mages here."

"I haven't felt any warning-wards so far," Graywillow whispered.

"You can be sure they'll be closer in. I wonder if they're just on the gates, or on the palisade as well?"

That first day, Clea had tried to get a description of the creature from the survivors. It had struck in darkness, shortly before dawn, and most of those she spoke to then were still incoherent with shock. She'd gone to see the bodies, to get some idea of what they might be up against, but had not dared linger in her examination. Though she was careful to buy the fastest horses in the country, and keep them in training, she knew her father and his men wouldn't be more than a few hours behind. The second-in-command of the village garrison had told her that at news of the initial attack on the dredging-party, the commander had locked the gates, sent word to Lord Minos Stylachos, and waited.

The commander hadn't survived the attack on the village itself. Clea wondered now what had become of the second.

* * *

A hunter emerged from a laurel thicket deeper in the woods behind them, signaled to Star. The whole small party withdrew from the edge of the ruined fields, followed the woman into the deeper woods. A wooden bridge near the village crossed a small canyon close by: seventy feet in depth and less than half that across. A small guard shack beside the bridgehead had been smashed, the bridge itself bitten through and burned. In the green water far below a body floated in an uneasy cloud of feasting gar-fish.

"There were two mages here." The hunter's whisper was like the susurration of a small bird's wings. "Boy mages, beardless as girls. This morning the boy mages rode away with half the guards." When the hunter turned her head, Clea saw that her left ear had been sliced off, years ago—a favorite warning from the overseers of the hostage villages, to keep the workers in line. "Later I heard the guards say the mages had had word through their scrying-stones that the Lord Stylachos's son was taken ill, and they had to go help."

"Pendireth?" Clea glanced quickly at Graywillow.

"So they say," the hunter affirmed. "He's been taken to the House of Glass, they said, to be cared for—"

"He'll be all right." Graywillow laid a quick, comforting hand on Clea's arm. "The last thing they'll want is for harm to befall him."

"We have to go there." Clea turned to Ithrazel, her stomach chilly with dread. "Now, today—tonight. You know the Crystal Mages. What can they do—what *might* they do—to a boy of eight, in their House of Glass? Can they . . . deceive him? Weave his dreams with lies? Work spells on him, to make his heart their slave?"

Graywillow gasped in shock at the idea, but the old man only looked amused.

"You have no great trust in mages, do you, girl?"

"Do you?"

Something changed in his eyes. "Not by the weight of a poppy-seed." His voice was barely a whisper. "Myself included."

Nevertheless—though Clea's heart screamed at her and her mind flung up a thousand images of what the child-faced Crystal Mages might be "curing" her brother of in addition to his disease (*And I'll bet they GAVE him the disease, too, to get him into their house . . .*)—she knew that the chance to see what was to be seen in Turtlemere without fear of meeting the members of the Crystal Order was not to be passed up. Six nights ago she had barely looked about her at the village itself, knowing her father's troops were only hours behind her. At that time she had counted the obvious dead, noted the damage, estimated the size of the creature from the size of the holes ripped in walls, roofs, barns. Seen how the burning roofs had been stove in from above: *It flies, then, like dragons are supposed to. . . .*

She had noted how the store-sheds had been reduced to heaps of charred beams and cinders. The diamond-clay—so painfully dredged and dried and borne to the village—was mixed, glittering darkly, far and wide into the ashes and dirt, or melted in puddles on the rucked and churned-up ground.

In the open square where the miners would be assembled for their shifts, two mules, a dog, and two men had lain dead. One of the men had been bitten in two, only head and shoulders and part of one leg remaining. Graywillow had turned her face so violently from the sight that she'd staggered: "Don't you *dare* faint," said Clea.

"Forty feet, I swear it, my lord, wing-tip to wing-tip—" one guard had babbled in his terror.

"'Twas invisible," had said another man. "Just shadow, darkness . . . looking at it 'twas like being blind—"

"I saw it!" insisted the first, and there were confused shouts of agreement and dissent.

"'Twas pitch-dark—"

"It came on us whilst we slept . . ."

"Every dog in the village barking—"

Women had dragged bodies—or pieces of bodies—toward the longhouse that served as barracks for the guards. Beyond it, the pen where the pigs were kept for slaughter had been broken down, and dead animals—and fragments of animals—lay everywhere.

"Flew away off over the Mire west—"

"Just disappeared, like smoke—"

Hands mutely pointed north . . . and south. And west.

A dredger had stumbled past them, carrying a man's head between his hands and weeping.

All this Clea had seen through the cold bright inner flame that seemed to slow time down and sharpen her senses, which came on her in a fight—or when, in those queer warped days of her later childhood, she'd be sent out on a robbery or a kill.

Now she, Graywillow, Hamo, and Ithrazel moved like cats among the charred houses, surrounded by the faint veil of Graywillow's spells. Those guards who had been left in the ruin seemed to be clustering together by the gate. The smoke of their fire lay thin in the chilly air. Upon this second viewing, her assassin's training noted every detail that could tell her anything further about the attack; that might mark it as different from the depredations of a beast. That might sound a warning-bell of some kind in her mind, or in the minds of a young shepherd who'd hunted all his life and of two wizards with radically different power and experience.

With that same training, she forced back into her heart the icy urgency that whispered her brother's name. *We have to get him out of there . . . or at least make sure what they're doing to him . . .*

She made her heart smooth as silver, concentrating as she'd learned to do as a child, when she'd be whipped if she missed anything while casing out a house.

She saw little now that she hadn't seen six days before, or guessed later from her nightmare glimpse of the creature itself in the grotto. Something— a limb? a tail?—could be wielded as a club, leaving long and characteristically shaped holes pounded in walls and roofs. Its claw-marks were spaced apart to the length of her finger; it had a bite-radius the length of her lower arm. To judge by the marks where something had rolled in the glittering dust before the smashed adamis sheds, she'd guessed the body at twenty feet, with who knew how long a tail. The charring looked sometimes like open fire, sometimes more like the splattering of burning liquid, naphtha, or phosphor.

The only effort that seemed to have been made toward repair, she noted, was that the ashes of the ruined adamis sheds had been carefully scraped up sometime in the last week. Presumably to be sifted, to recover the dust . . . *Trust my father for that.*

Or had it been because the sole mark of the creature's body had been there?

Nowhere a track, as if its feet—*Does it have feet?*—never touched ground.

"What did it want?" she breathed, crouched behind the wall of a barn in which the dead animals had been stacked, now a seething nightmare of flies. "These corpses weren't eaten. This looks like killing for killing's sake, like a wolverine in a hen-coop."

"If it had been hunting"—Hamo gestured toward the gaping holes in the steep, crudely-thatched roofs—"would it not have gone for the animals in pens, rather than men and women hiding in their houses?"

"And if it were only hunting," Clea agreed, "the village hunters would have found its traces weeks before."

"Might it have been a curse?" asked the shepherd hesitantly. "A—a visitation, to punish the men and women of the village for some impiety or trespass?"

Clea glanced sidelong at Ithrazel, though it was to Hamo she replied. "You mean, did it slaughter on its own, or was it sent? And if it were sent . . . Why?"

"I should imagine"—the mage's eyes were like stone—"that everyone asks such a question in the circumstances."

They withdrew as quietly as they'd come, slipping through a gap where the palisade had been beaten to kindling, the wood scorched and stained. The guard at the western gate didn't even turn his head as they crossed the weeds and scrub of the abandoned fields.

"Will you seek this zai?" asked Star softly, when they rejoined the hunters in the thick of the laurel and wild grape that tangled the edge of the deeper woods. "Lynx Child"—she nodded to the young hunter who had brought word of Pendireth's illness and the Crystal Mages' departure—"says our kin in the deeper Mire have seen nothing of it, but such a thing as killed Kingfisher attacked a hunter of the Reed Clan two nights before the new moon. A day's paddling will take us to the Place of a Thousand Frogs, where my people are camped. With a bigger canoe and more paddlers, the Lake of Serpents lies but a day beyond that, where we can take counsel of the Lady of Serpents."

"Thank you," said Clea. "Ten thousand times thank you, for that and for all you have done, sister." She tapped her chest in thanks, gripped the green-eyed hunter's shoulder. "But first, and before all else, I need to go to Morne. I need to," she added, seeing the hunters look at one another. Reading in their eyes the danger, from the soldiers of the merchant houses, and the slave-takers who haunted the city's dockside slums and the landing-places along the Denzerai, the canal that cut from the Mire into the Gray Hills.

"They have my brother in their House of Glass. They claim he's deathly sick, that only they can cure him. I need to know if that's true, and to get him out of there if it's not."

"Will they make him like them?" asked the hunter Second Rabbit, whose sun-bronzed face bore the marks of old scars, wildcat or wolverine.

"I don't know what they'll do," said Clea. "Or what they *can* do." She glanced beside her at Ithrazel, who was listening with a look of calculation in his eyes, as if adding pieces of information together in his head. "But he is born with a mage's powers, and is the sole heir of the House Stylachos. I don't want to see him become a weapon in anyone's hand."

Again the hunters looked at one another, and Graywillow asked, "Could you get us into Morne if there was a fog?"

Clea shot her a glance. The magic of the Sisters—White or Gray—was subtle, and though as far as anyone knew it had not been affected by the twisting of magic, she knew her friend was young in her craft. She might weave spells around herself and her companions to fool the eyes of casual watchers, but they wouldn't escape the scrutiny of those searching specifically for a dark-haired Loghri sister and a red-haired warrior girl.

But Graywillow lifted her chin and returned her look, then turned her head to meet the querying lift of Ithrazel's brow.

"Redhawk and his rowers are down at the old town landing." Star nodded toward the place farther along the canyon, where, presumably, the hunter Lynx Child had come up to search for them. "You can reach the gates of the Hidden River just before sunset—where the tunnel runs under the hills," she added, seeing the incomprehension in Hamo's eyes. "The tunnel his people"—she jerked her head scornfully at Ithrazel—"hewed from the rock through the very bones of the earth. Twenty-two miles in darkness, where five thousand of *my* people died, that the merchant houses might have their diamond-clay and their wood and their gangs of slaves a few days quicker."

The canoe that waited for them, hidden in the foliage that everywhere draped the canyon walls down to the waterline, was longer than Star's small hunting-vessels that had brought them here from the Dogpond, and crewed by a dozen Ghoras. Star and Second Rabbit fetched the long, light ladder of braided deer hide that Lynx Child had hidden in the roots of a hollowed oak; Clea descended last, noting with approval that Hamo, for all his slightly bumpkin air, was clearly familiar with something similar in his own world.

Good, she reflected. *One less thing to worry about.*

Ithrazel moved down the knotted rungs like a spider: *Of course, if he hated the Telmayrians, he must have spent time among the Kindred in the Mire.*

"Remember," said Star softly as Clea started down. "If there's trouble, Redhawk and his rowers will have to flee and leave you."

"I understand." She gripped the thin lines, hooked a foot into the fragile sling of the next rung, then stopped and looked up again. "We should be back here tomorrow, and then we will go on to the Lake of Serpents, and the Reedmire beyond it. Those things have to be coming from somewhere. Will you do this for me, Star? Will you send out word, among the hunters, among the Kindred? Anything, any word, of the zai, or these Night-Gluttons, or of any strange creatures . . . Anything will help us."

The hunter tapped her chest in assent.

When Clea reached the bottom, and Star untied and dropped the ladder down after them, she found Graywillow already seated in the waist of the canoe, the tiny ivory drinking-cup she carried in her belt filled with water dipped from the still channel around them. As the rowers pushed silently away from the cliff, the dark-haired Sister blew gently across the top of the cup, whispered, "Neambis . . ."

Clea recognized the name of the Mother of the Gray Sisters who tended the shrine of the goddess Farrawen, out on the marshy Lake of Serpents. As a White Sister, Graywillow should by rights have called on her own Lady Anamara—but Clea guessed that the tall and queenly Telmayrian Mother would almost certainly have taken a dim view of her novice's behavior.

"Mist on the land." Graywillow mumbled the words in the Loghri tongue, gazing into the cup, and Ithrazel, just behind her, bent his head also to watch the water, his eyes half shut. "Trust me, believe me—this is for a great good. I swear by the white hands of Nyellin, by the beautiful heart of Farrawen, by the songs of morning light. There is no ill in this that I ask."

Stillness for a time, broken only by the lap of the water against the bow, the silvery drip of the paddles as they rose and fell together, like the feathers of a single beating wing.

Mist curled, very gently, over the face of the water. Far overhead, a fragment of cloud veiled the autumn morning.

If all went well, reflected Clea, picking up her paddle, *it would be a foggy, foggy night in Morne.*

Eight

I take it," murmured Ithrazel as the long canoe slid through the drowned canyons, "you have some idea of where the boy's going to be within the House of Glass? As I recall, the house of the Crystal Order in Dey Allias was rather large. . . ."

"I don't know it now," retorted Clea grimly. "But I know who will."

"Of course you do." The old man smiled, as if pleased to have guessed her answer before she spoke.

The fog didn't grow thick until the canoe was almost at the stone-founded gates that defended the entrance of the Hidden River. But through the morning, and as noon passed over into afternoon, whenever they passed the barges, heavily laden with wood or adamis, or with sacks of grain, or apples for the city's insatiable markets, the barge-crews barely glanced at the slim, dark craft being paddled by them with such purposeful speed. Then—with the slightly glazed expressions of boredom or daydream—they glanced away. Graywillow on her narrow bench sat with eyes three-quarters shut, her mind whispering to the minds—the spirits—of the Gray Sisters far off in the Serpent Lake marshes, though sometimes she reached out a little with one hand and moved it over the mists that rose above the water.

Ithrazel, too, seemed half in a doze.

Isolated in the silence, Clea shivered. She'd heard it explained to her a dozen times—differently with every different expositor—how and why the magic of the older orders of wizards had become unstable and unreliable. Most of them seemed to agree that the lower-level spells, like Insignificance—Disvisibility, as it was sometimes called—were seldom affected. As a former assassin and part-time Thief's Brat, Clea's wariness of such spells was deeply ingrained. Penalties for using magic for such purposes were frightful, so those who could use them were generally on the side of the householders—potential marks—and Emperor's Law. Rat Bone himself regarded such cantrips as cheating anyway: "Seventy-three I've killed, without once having to hide under a fake shadow. And what'll you do if something goes wrong, eh, girl? If your wizard stubs his toe and loses his concentration, or you run into a counter-spell. *Pff!* There you are in your enemy's house with your backside hanging out."

Having her backside unexpectedly hanging out while in the House of Glass was *not* the way Clea wanted to end the evening.

Not with her father's men hunting her. Not with that smooth-faced pimp Heshek just as happy if she'd disappear with no questions asked about what she'd seen.

Redhawk's men paddled like machines, dripping blades rising and falling smoothly, with barely a sound. For most of the autumn and winter, the canyons of the Mire were fogged, so today's damp brume wasn't in any way unusual. She'd counted the dredging-stations as they'd passed them in the opal whiteness: on their long platforms of planks where the water met the cliffsides, the dredgers with their brown naked bodies had seemed barely more human than ants. Beside her, she saw Ithrazel turn his head to watch them, and recalled that this man had destroyed Dey Allias out of hatred for what the Telmayrians had done to the Kindred.

His eye caught hers; he said, "They seem to hold you in esteem, Princess."

"They know me," returned Clea shortly. "I lived among them in the city: the Kindred who clean the stables and dig the ditches and carry wood and sell vegetables. From the time I escaped my father's prison when I was eight, I hid among them, the Kindred who hide in the drainage tunnels, and scrounge for a living, if they've escaped from the dredger barracks. By the time old Lord Shiamat died—the father of my father's first wife—and Father figured it was safe enough to use me as a pawn, I'd spent time among the Kindred, and they knew me as Elannin Greenshield's blood."

The Cursed Wizard looked as if he might have said something to that, but only sniffed, and settled back within himself, watching the thin murk that stirred above the water. In her mind Clea heard old Khymin, the Black Mage whom the thieves in the Tunnels had hidden for years: "Used to go out among the Kindred, he did." The frail voice was barely a whisper among the ruined archways that Clea's great-grandfather had had built, in the days when adamis had first been dredged from the Tarn Estuary's sands. "Read their scrolls. Learned the shamans' spells. Spoke with the demons the shamans could call up from water and night. It turned his wits . . . Some say, one of their demons entered into him, drove out the man he'd been born."

Did he think that by destroying our city, he'd drive us from these shores for good?

She studied the lined face, the scrubby brownish-gray beard that had begun to sprout in the days since they'd left the Hell of the Birds.

Did he think the traders of Telmayre were just going to walk away from a land where adamis lay in the ground for the taking?

Does he still think he can frighten us away?

Or destroy us?

Destroy THEM, she reflected. *Am I "us," or "them"?*

Pendri at least was "us." Her heart clenched at the thought of her brother, golden and sunny and chubby, though as he'd grown he'd thinned, it seemed, before her eyes. By the time she'd been taken back into her father's good graces, two years ago, the child's powers had begun to manifest themselves and he'd been clamped into a routine of tutors, mentors, classes. First to teach him the difficult arts of reading—which he'd taken to, as she herself had at the age of four, like a fish to water, the gods be thanked—and then to use those skills in the long and painstaking process of learning names, spells, sigils, principles, theories. Pendri's mother, a novice White Sister whose powers had only begun to blossom, had been seventeen when Minos Styla-chos had chosen her for his third bride. Thieves' Market rumor ran that he'd asked the Mothers of all the Shrines in the city for the names of the girls who had the greatest natural power, and had made his choice from among them.

He wasn't about to wed a mageborn woman with whom he'd actually fallen in love.

Not again.

Clea had been eight years old, still in prison when her father had married Melzael Lissona. She'd stolen food from the other prisoners—or the guards—to keep from starving, or to bait traps for the rats that for long periods were her only sustenance. After her mother had been executed, Clea had more or less been forgotten. When she found a way to slip out of the cell where she was confined, she didn't think the guards had looked for her very hard. They certainly hadn't told their commander—or her father—that they had no idea where she was. It had taken her, she'd later estimated, almost another year to get out of the dungeon itself: they were that careful, at least. And then it was only because Rat Bone had taken her with him when he'd escaped. In any case she'd completely missed her father's wedding, though six months after her escape she'd stood in the crowds watching her new little brother carried in procession from Shrine to Shrine for the blessing of the gods. She'd been almost ten by then.

Huge crowds, and people so busy cheering they'd completely forgotten to watch their purses. Rat Bone had embraced her in ecstasy when he saw her takings that day.

Melzael Lissona had already looked ill, Clea recalled, carrying her precious gold-wrapped infant through the streets to show him to the gods. To Nyellin the Lady of the Moon, and Tianis the Lord of the Dead. To Father Ominda and Mother Nie and Gingul the Lady of Mice. The tribes had other gods, and worshipped other things. Clea distrusted them all.

Haggard and thin in her refulgent golden gown, her father's third wife had reminded Clea of a starving child herself. She'd died two weeks later, leaving that sunny little mageborn soul alone among those who expected to use him at the earliest possible moment.

Pendireth.

Pendri.

Whom she'd wanted so badly to hate, but could not.

The fog was thick, and the sun just down as the canoe shot through the growing traffic of what was called the Denzerai: the artificially widened canyon that had been dug out toward the Gray Hills. Before the Hidden River tunnel had been excavated, cargoes of adamis had had to be unloaded there, carried by mule-back (or on the backs of Darklander slaves) twenty miles up over the hills and down to the coastlands where Morne lay beside its harbor. At the eastern end of the Denzerai—crowded with barges and the canoes of farmers—stone gates guarded the black mouth of the tunnel itself, twenty feet high and flanked with guards in the colors of the various Houses that held concessions on the Mire. These were mostly the men of House Stylachos, in the familiar red and black: the Vrykos had their own port, at Aktas in the north, and the Othume at Crisankus south of Dey Allias. But neither of those dreary towns had a harbor like that of the estuary of Tarn, nor the volume of trade from the East. Even the lords of the Vrykos preferred to make their headquarters in Morne.

Clea ducked her head, knowing that these were the men who'd be watching for her.

Torches and lanterns burned every two hundred feet in the tunnel for the whole of its twenty-mile length. The slick black walls were cut from bedrock; without adamine tools and the spells of the Crystal Mages it could never have been done. In three places, short stretches of the channel passed through valleys in the hills, a hundred or two hundred feet of open sky before passing into darkness again. Moss crusted the edge where the water touched stone. With the fog that rose from the water, the lamps along the tunnel walls were little more than smears of yellow in the dark, and the bobbing lanterns of the wood-boats and adamis-barges like the eyes of sea-monsters. Sometimes the canoe passed so close between them, Clea could have put out her hand and touched the wet wood of their sides.

Yet no one gave them a glance.

Cheapjack tricks. She could almost hear Rat Bone sniff, and smiled in spite of her dread for her brother's sake.

"We should be back by the eighth hour of the night," she whispered as the vessel glided at last to wharfside in the crowded waters of the Great Pool at the Hidden River's end—yet another great feat of engineering, melding the skill of the Bright Islands with the magic of the Crystal Mages. "Hamo, you stay here." She held up her hand to still his protest. "That's an order, soldier. Will the fog hold?" It was thick now as porridge, the shapes of the barges docking all around them little more than jostling blocks of darkness, like giant cattle settling down for the night. Red and green lights, unnaturally bright, burned at the ends of the wharves, and the whistles and calls of the pilots and wharf-gangs pierced the murky gloom.

Graywillow nodded almost absently, deep within the trance of her concentration. Eastward, along both sides of the smaller canal that led from the Pool to the sea-wharves two miles away, the Dockside stretched: warehouses, counting-houses, brothels, taverns. The mansions that the rich had built when the city first was founded, abandoned now in favor of more salubrious quarters elsewhere and rented out by the square foot to dockworkers, whores, and the poor.

Hamo, for all his evident determination to follow her to the gates of the Pit, looked stunned. *I am NOT taking him ashore in this place. . . .*

Ithrazel, wrapped in a hunter's coat of grubby wolf-skin, gazed around him, and in the torchlight the shock and disgust and pain in his eyes was terrible to see.

As they moved through the crowds of laborers on the docks, the wagonloads of adamis, the stench of burning and sewage and poverty, he whispered, "What *is* this place?"

With a kind of irony in her voice, Clea replied, "This is Morne."

He'd been angry in Turtlemere.

He had known the place as a free fishing-village, safely ensconced in the north and away from the glittering river-sands where adamis had been dredged. Had known the longhouses there, the garden plots that ringed the houses, the myriad of little shrines in the nearby woods and the drying racks where fish and venison were preserved for the winter. His memories were memories of friends, of welcome, of women healed and children who'd asked if he could really turn people into frogs. At Turtlemere today, his eye had taken in the marks of wholesale slavery that characterized the place now: stone barracks instead of family longhouses, huge communal pens for swine and sheep, storehouses for cheap dried food brought in, instead of the gardens that the families raised.

There were no families anymore in Turtlemere.

Only barracks of slaves.

And Clea—he could see by the way her attention had gone to broken rafters, smashed walls, to the scraped-out vacancy where the store-sheds had been and to the marks of charring and ruin rather than to the shape of the village itself—she was so used to such places that she didn't even see the obscenity of it. He'd struggled not to seize her by the arms and shout.

The line of whipping-posts along one side of the square. The assembly ground where workers were marched each day to begin their work. The spikes on the top of the wall, pointed to keep the villagers in rather than wolves or tree-lions out.

That was Turtlemere now.

Morne was worse.

Infinitely worse.

Fog cloaked this swathe along the canal that joined the Pool and the wharves, shut out moonlight or starlight. He wasn't sure he could have followed her, kept his mind on the soft little ripples of There's-Nobody-Here, had it been otherwise. The place stank ten times worse than Dey Allias had: cheap cooking, choking wood-smoke, the throat-ripping reek of diamond-clay being roasted in the kilns. The stink of thousands upon thousands of the poor, crowded together in sheds and shanties and crumbling apartment blocks. Cows and pigs and chickens crammed in unspeakable conditions, lowing and crying. Human voices shouted, quarreled, called out wares: "Old shoes! Old shoes!" "Milk here, fresh!" "Rags and bones, penny a pound . . ."

At this hour of the evening, rasping, discouraged, exhausted.

"Dreamsugar—buy you a lovely dream . . ."

"Hey, mister, my sister, she says she loves you . . ."

And the stink that hammered at his mind—hopelessness, directionless rage, the savage greed of desperation—was ten times more terrible still.

Two guards marched a double line of slaves past them along the water-front, men and women bent under loads of sacks, stumbling on feet that bled. Somewhere close wagonloads of wood were being unloaded into the furnace-mouths of a refinery, burning the adamis clay into the glittering dust of adamine to be pressed into blocks for export to Telmayre. As they moved east through the black gloom he heard the creak of rigging from the harbor, and the cries of a woman as she was passed around among a ship's crew. A whiff of frankincense snagged him: a tiny shrine, a Sister bent over a fire there. He recognized the shape of a single ruined arch: Rycellis, one of the forgotten gods of the fishing-village this had once been.

What have they done to this place?

He was trembling as Clea turned into what looked like the gateway of a merchant's town-palace—or what had been such a building, fifty years ago. The stonework was black with soot and plastered with filth, the court-yard beyond a squalid desolation of clotheslines, smoldering fires, middens, penned pigs. A woman skinning rats—a pile of dead ones on her right, a half-dozen stripped carcasses spitted over a low fire to her left—glanced up and wiped a dirty forelock from her brow with the back of a bloody wrist. "Hey, Princess," she called to Clea as she passed.

"Hey, Gerti," Clea returned. "Liver-Eater in?"

Gerti gestured with her skinning-knife toward what looked like the long-ago stable gate. Clea stepped around a swarming mound of feces and guts and led the way. In the doorway behind Gerti, a half-grown Dark-lander child performed fellatio on a drunk Telmayrian soldier.

I didn't know when I was well-off, reflected the wizard, nauseated, *there on my cliff with my eagles . . .*

What have they done to these people?

Liver-Eater was a square-faced, sturdily built man with dyed black sausage-curls, sitting over a brazier of coals in the mansion's old stable. A five-foot oak scythe-handle was propped at his side; before him on his knees balanced a bowl containing, rather than liver of any sort, oysters, which he slurped up with an expression of deep content. The stalls behind him held six narrow bunks apiece, built up in three tiers. Men slept in them under piles of dirty garments. Down at one end of the stable, to judge by the sound and the line of men, prostitutes received their clients. The other end was manifestly in use as an opium-den. Liver-Eater beamed as Clea and her companion entered. "Clea, my darling! It's been an age!" By his accent—and his alabaster fairness—he was of the Ashupik tribe. "And just in time to share a little supper with me, and a jug of the best—"

He reached down beside him and held up a bottle of extremely expensive Telmayrian wine.

"Now, don't argue, dearest heart—fetch yourself a glass or I shall pout. And your gentleman friend—?"

"Another time, Lord, with all respect." She inclined her head, and spit at his feet, in the fashion—Ithrazel recalled—of the thieves' guilds in Dey Allias in his own day. "With all respect, I have a favor to ask."

"Whatever you will, my darling. But I promise you, these oysters are the very sweetbreads of the gods."

"I'll spend the rest of the night weeping," Clea assured him, "at having missed them—and missed also the pleasure of your conversation, my lord. But we're in a hurry—"

"Well, with ten silver pennies out for anyone who'll turn you over to your father's guards, I expect you are."

Clea said a word that she'd obviously—Ithrazel reflected—learned on some previous visit to this quarter of the town.

"I need to talk to someone who knows the House of Glass," she went on, with barely a pause. "My brother's being held there—"

"Took him down there last night," agreed Liver-Eater. "Yellow sickness."

Clea flinched.

As well she might, thought Ithrazel. *If it's true, and not a ruse to get the boy into their power . . .*

The landlord—or whatever he was, in this dirty domain—half-glanced over his shoulder and called out, "Pig-Face—!"

A huge thug with iron muscles and suspicious (and heavily painted) eyes ambled out of the opium-den end of the stable, carrying a candle. "Yeah, boss?"

"Fetch the Quillet. You sure you wouldn't care for a glass of heaven while we wait, my Gloriana? No?"

"On a job," Clea excused herself. Ithrazel wondered how much a month this enterprising damsel contributed to Liver-Eater's coffers to elicit his tone of playful affection—not to mention to ensure that she wasn't assaulted on her way across the courtyard. The question of where she'd come by her blacksteel lock-picks, at least, was resolved. She asked politely after several mutual acquaintances with names like Stinking Groth, Big Blossom, and Black Khymin, and her brows quirked down with concern at the news that the last of these hadn't been seen around lately—

Hanged, belike, Ithrazel reflected drily.

"And does that have anything to do," inquired their host, "with those rumors I'm hearing from the Tunnels lately? Or do the things that old drunkard Ballygore claims he's been seeing down there just come out of a bad batch of rum?"

Clea frowned. "Things like what?"

The dark, kohl-rimmed eyes studied her face. "Things that aren't rats," Liver-Eater said softly. "Things that go straight over the rat-wards—even the wards those pasty-faced pimps from the House of Glass charge us two silver pieces a month to draw." He shrugged elaborately. "Maybe they ate old Khymin."

Further inquiry on that subject, however, was interrupted by the return of Pig-Face, leading a tall, thin young man in the ragged remains of a scholar's gown. Long mouse-colored hair fell in a braid down his back, and he had Loghri cheekbones like Graywillow's.

"This is the Quillet," Liver-Eater introduced him to Clea, and tapped the young man's shoulder lightly with his scythe-handle. "Quillet, this is—"

"The Iron Princess." Quillet spit respectfully in front of Clea's feet, then—for good measure—in front of Liver-Eater's as well. "How may I serve you, Lady?"

"The Quillet mucks out the latrines in the House of Glass," explained Liver-Eater. "You see the value of an education, at least to those of us with—um—*inappropriate* blood in our veins. Where would she find her brother in that place?"

The Quillet unhooked a pair of tablets from his belt and sketched something on them—standing too far from Liver-Eater's minuscule fire, Ithrazel observed with interest, for anyone who wasn't mageborn to see anything on them in the smoky gloom. When he showed what he'd drawn to Clea, she had to move him closer to the brazier. "That's Whispering Alley—the kitchen gate's there—go through the vegetable gardens and up the stairs back of the dairy . . ."

"Thank you." Clea handed the young man a coin. Ithrazel wondered if Liver-Eater was going to let him keep it.

"You're in luck tonight," said the Quillet softly. "They've got a council or something going. They'll all be in the front part of the House. The infirmary's in the rear, where it overlooks the sea. Those rooms across there are where the boys sleep, the ones who come there for full-time training."

"What's that?" She touched something on the sketch-map.

"Workshop."

"Those?"

"Classrooms, and the bath-house."

She nodded, satisfied that nothing could surprise them on the way in or out.

"And that?"

"I don't know." His voice lowered. "There's a stairway with a grille across it. They keep—prisoners, I think. Someone . . . I've never seen guards there, but sometimes I'll see one of the mages carry food up. And on hot nights, when the window-shutters are open, sometimes I'll hear one of them screaming."

Nine

Is it possible to counterfeit yellow sickness with magic?" Clea murmured as they made their way down Whispering Alley to the wicket gate. "So my father would let them bring him here—"

"A household healer would see right through it." The old man's voice had a slightly slurred quality to it, as if he were speaking in his sleep.

Concentrating, Clea knew. Listening, sniffing, stretching out his senses, for the slightest hint that Graywillow's spells of concealment might have been seen through or failed. Scanning the world around them, as the fog thickened and the city seemed to drift into a sightless abyss.

She waited. *Don't disturb him. Let him listen . . .*

It gave her time to stop shaking, to let the flush of rage and panic that filled her subside.

Damn them. Devils screw them senseless, and pigs eat their souls. . . .

The House of Glass lay close to the harbor, on a little rise of land thick with willow and poplar that not even the fuel-hungry refineries—or the desperate poor of the Dockside—dared touch. In the stillness, distant now from the noise of the waterfront, Clea could hear the sough of water around the little private harbor at the low hill's foot; the tiny, musical clinking of rigging-blocks. North along the long curve of the Tarn estuary, the fog hid the great harbor, the long line of the warehouses . . . and the compounds of her father and the other great merchant houses. Blurred spots of yellow light marked their walls and gates, and the dark bulk of the merchant craft at the quays.

At the sight of the witch-light that glimmered in the House's thousand windows, starlike among the luxuriant trees, hatred of all mages flooded her with the memory of her mother's trial. She saw again the mages of the Crystal Order gathered on the bench in their stylish doublets—*no old-fashioned robes for THEM . . .*—tamely assenting to her father's contention that Rethiel Elannis, as she had been called, had used love spells to make him divorce and abuse his first wife . . .

Heard Heshek the Fair—thin and fey with a kind of fascinating, jewel-eyed ugliness—agreeing, that for such illicit uses of her magic, she be condemned to death.

The mages of the older orders—the Brown, the Black, the Crimson, robed and solemn and looking very old by comparison—had gone along with them, as had the Great Mothers of the city's largest temple sisterhoods.

They cannot be trusted. Not any of them . . .

Prisoners, the Quillet had said.

Who would they be keeping prisoner?

"The healer Father employs these days is one of the Order," she whispered. "So is the brother of Pendri's tutor Berosale. He thinks the sun rises and sets on Himelkart." Like the judges at her mother's trial, she thought. Crystal Mages themselves, or Heshek's whores in the other orders.

She took a deep breath, put out her hand to the wet brick of the wall, and led the way toward the single smear of light that was the lamp above the kitchen gate. The smell of baking bread, of wet earth and compost, drifted on the fog. The latrines were down at this end of the complex of kitchen-courts. Without the summer scents of the flowers planted around them, jasmine and lilac and honeysuckle, despite the chill weather and careful cleaning, they still stank.

Why would they keep Pendri prisoner? she asked herself. *They have to stay on Father's good side. Why would they counterfeit something like yellow sickness to get him here, when Father's already given him to them, to tutor, to train. . . ?*

Something flickered in the corner of her eye. Not a rat. She knew, intimately, the way rats moved, and this was . . . different. Long, like a weasel. But she had the impression of a glister like wet, raw sheep-gut stuffed with blooded meat. And, just for an instant, a smell that jolted the blood in her veins.

Then it was gone.

She glanced beside her as she drew out her lock-picks. Ithrazel, too, had turned his head sharply. But he said nothing, and after a moment she returned to the task at hand, delicately inserting the tiny tools into the gate-lock by touch, as she'd been taught . . .

The flame in the gate-lamp, sunk to almost nothing, only outlined the tips of Ithrazel's sweat-spiked hair, the end of his nose, the coarse sprinkle of wolf hide where the collar of his coat caught the light.

You cannot trust any of them. Not old Khymin the Black, hiding in the Tunnels with his rotting books. And especially not the old man beside her.

The lodge by the gate was dark. She followed the wall around by touch, smelling the mulch of the vast kitchen gardens in the fog.

Father needs a mage—a mage who'll work for House Stylachos, not for the Archmage of some Order. He married Mother to get one, and Pendri's mother, and that poor girl Linvinnia he's got now . . . mageborn in her blood and stupid as a brick. Would it make sense for Heshek to hold Pendri here long enough for him to . . . to work some kind of spell on his mind? To force, or trick, his loyalty to the Crystal Order rather than to our House?

But he'll be able to do that in a few years anyway, when Pendri comes here for his training.

Unless Father's planning something . . .

The sickness has to be genuine, she reflected. *And if it's genuine, no wonder they're scared.* It was the sickly season, with the weather turning cold.

Faintly, less real than the half-heard lap of the sea beyond the walls, she heard wailing. Dim, muffled, almost below the edge of hearing. Like life being wrung out of flesh. A thought flickered through her mind, submerged at once by her greater fears for Pendri, and she put her hand on Ithrazel's arm.

"I've got to see it. See the place where they're keeping them. See who's there . . ."

"Don't be an idiot, girl." Still the slurred note in his voice, and Clea remembered what Rat Bone had said about breaking a wizard's concentration, even that of one who could do no more than listen for sounds that even she could not hear. *Leaving your backside hanging out in the middle of the House of Glass.*

"He's my brother—"

"Your brother's in the infirmary." He spoke as if from a great distance away, or three-quarters drowned in sleep: sing-song, dreaming.

And what will they do to him there?

She knew she was risking both their lives, but whispered, "Can they seize his mind? Bend his thoughts? Make him loyal to them, love them, hear what they want him to hear, cleave to them only?"

Rat Bone would have slapped her, for distracting her cover. . . . *Rat Bone would NEVER carry on this conversation . . .*

Ithrazel's half-shut eyes glinted a little in the reflected gleam of the kitchen's window. "Like you did to that poor sap Hamo? Probably."

Without another word Clea turned away, stepped into the fog-choked acre of the kitchen garden, gently tapping the side of her boot against the raised beds, counting turnings to guide herself as the map had shown.

The night tingled with magic. Ithrazel tasted it in his sinuses, in the back of his throat; it crawled along his skin like the forerunning itch of a rash. He'd always hated the aura of the New Mages' spells, which had a distinct flavor of its own, as visible and obvious to the mageborn as were the smoky warmth he sensed in the enclave of the Brown Mages, the velvety dark echoes thrown off by the Black or the strange misty whispers that surrounded the shrines of the goddesses. As obvious, and as completely invisible and intangible, to those without magic in their flesh.

And worse than that, a terrible vertigo seemed to nibble at the back of his brain, as if he were about to slide into one of his dreams again. Dreams of raising his hands and crying out words of power, dreams of seeing flames burst in a thousand places in Dey Allias . . .

The sensation that there was something he'd forgotten. Something he'd tried to forget, tried desperately, and that he stood in hideous peril of remembering.

NO . . .

Clea's hand touched his arm again. Strong and thin, a grip that wouldn't loosen on a sword in battle . . .

There was a wide door, just where the Quillet had marked it on his map.

A council, he'd said. *They'll all be at the front of the house* . . .

For how long?

And talking about what?

If the boy's really got the yellow sickness, he thought, *I hope to the gods the ward-spell that girl Graywillow lay on us can shield us from it*. In its early stages of fever and vomiting, the disease was horribly contagious.

A single lamp burned in the hall as they entered it, another at the top of the wide oak stair. The hall itself was reminiscent of his own half-forgotten childhood in Telmayre, with its carved paneling and rows of lamp-niches. He had to force those memories aside, focus his mind on the tiniest shreds of sound, of scent . . . concentrate on not feeling the burning along the edges of his shackles that had begun the moment they'd crossed the threshold of the Crystal Mages' gate. The sweet murk of incense. Healing herbs. The harsh sting of burnt adamis, the ghost of a woman's perfume.

Honeysuckle.

He followed Clea up the stair.

The Quillet had said it was the room at the right, at the end of the hallway. A night-lamp within outlined the bottom of the door in dim pinkish amber. A whisper of comfort, Ithrazel wondered, for a little boy far from his own bed? He himself remembered being able to see in the dark when he was tiny—or maybe it was only those few, earliest shreds of a toddler's imagination. Most mageborn children lost that talent when their powers went into abeyance at the age of three or four, only to have it blossom again when they reached puberty. This boy was, what? Eight, Clea had said? Nine?

Being schooled, trained, drilled to step into his powers when they returned, in the highly efficient way that marked everything the Mages of the New Order did.

Mages of the New Order came to their power earlier, he recalled. Sometimes as young as ten or eleven. *This boy may well have the beginnings of it now.* Gerodare, Machodan Indigo's favorite pupil (and more besides, it had been rumored) had come to the full powers of a mature wizard at fifteen.

With the scorched eyes of a man of ninety.

He had often wondered what that process was. How they accelerated those skills. Even more frequently he'd wondered what it did to them. They went into retirement—at least they had seventy-five years ago—at an age when Brown or Black or Red Mages were just coming into the fulness of their magic, at forty or fifty. At that age, sometimes younger, the New Mages returned to their Master House on Telmayre to study the deeper aspects of their discipline.

Deeper aspects to repair the holes left by that too-early flowering? He could only speculate.

The boy Pendireth looked younger even than eight, swathed in a too-large night-shirt of white linen. Propped on the pillows of a great carved bed, he resembled a little white finch in an eagle's cage. Under a cap of hair the same red-gold hue of Clea's, his face, like hers, was thin and delicate, without her strength. His eyes, when he looked up as the door was softly opened, were large and dark, and brightened with joy at the sight of her.

Clea looked swiftly around the room before stepping inside—*I'll bet she doesn't enter a latrine if she hasn't checked it for an ambush beforehand . . .*

Ithrazel put a hand on her sleeve.

Magic lay like a whisper of stardust on the air.

Adamine . . .

He looked at the parquet of the floor. The finest breath of dust lay there, thick in places and thin in others. Someone had laid out a vast design of interlocking sigils on the polished wood: adamine, silver, crystal, and salt. The adamine had left its invisible sparkle there, even when swept up and counter-spelled into neutrality.

Adamine was never entirely neutral.

He knelt and held his hands over the graceful patterns. No active spell, not the faintest trace of warding that would ring a bell in some other quarter of the house or cause a candle to brighten into flame or turn milk into blood.

He signed Clea to go on. The sigils were intense and powerful healing, resonant with the spells of the whole building. The Crystal Order had been famous, in his own day, for healing.

"Pendri!" She strode toward the bed.

"Clea!" He held out his hands to her. A candle burned beside him. He'd been practicing drawing sigils on a wax tablet, dropped now on the silk of the counterpane. His whole little face lit with joy.

"Are you all right?"

The child nodded, and those dark Telmayrean eyes went past her to Ithrazel, inquiring.

"This is my uncle Iohan."

Pendireth Stylachos held out a fragile hand, and smiled. "I'm honored, sir."

The moment Ithrazel's fingers touched those of the boy, the wizard could feel it, confirming what he'd already guessed from the sigils on the floor. "The sickness was here," he said quietly to Clea. "This was no sham."

"Oh no!" Pendri shook his head. "Two of Papa's stablemen came down sick, too, Gobby and Brue. Lord Heshek said he feared for my life. All last night, and today, they were here: Lord Heshek himself, and Lord Himelkart, and Lord Tsorkesh the Librarian, and the others."

"And they cured you in one day?" Clea's dark brows drew down. *As well they might,* reflected Ithrazel. The yellow sickness usually took a week to run its course, if the victim didn't die in the first day or two. Many of its victims died not of the disease itself, but of the effects of starvation or thirst.

The boy nodded, his eyes wide and grave. "I thought I was dying. Like . . . Like Mother. But they saved me—Lord Heshek never left my side.

He called the power of healing, spells like I've only read about! And . . . and now I know, Clea! *That's* what I want to do with my magic! It's like . . . It's like music, only better! To heal—to give somebody back their life . . ." His small fingers clung tightly to hers. "I know that's not really what Father wants of me, and I'll do everything I can to please him, of course . . . But the emperor will never really let me rule the House Stylachos if I'm a mage, you know. And while I'm studying with Lord Tsorkesh—he's the librarian here," he explained to Ithrazel, "I'll study this for *me*. How to heal. How to . . . to make the sickness dissolve like mist before the sun. How to breathe life back into the dying."

"There was incredible magic done here." Ithrazel knelt again, and held out his hand, palm-down, over the floor. He felt in his bone marrow the soft counterpoint of the chanting, could see the lines that had been drawn in the air with light.

"It would have to be," whispered Clea. "To clear away the yellow sickness—"

But with that power, something else. Something he knew he should remember and couldn't . . .

Honeysuckle perfume—soap—the whisper of silk in the shadows of the door and the quick delicate clatter of a lap-dog's toenails. Ithrazel wheeled around, still crouching, with a warning on his lips even as a voice asked, "And why should it not be so?"

Sons of Death—

But as he stood Clea put her hand on his arm—stopping him from diving for the window—and coolly returned the gaze of the woman who had slipped through the door. This newcomer wasn't dressed like a Sister, either of the Gray order or the White. Rather, she wore a pink gown stitched and trimmed with gold, clean and new. Wheat-blonde hair that contained no trace of Clea's auburn or Pendri's brighter amber, but eyes like Pendri's, dark hazel, large, and beautifully shaped. There was an echo of Clea's bone-structure in her exquisite face, but her features were more regular and far more beautiful. An exquisite little doll of a woman, like a rose in the darkness by the light of the single candle beside Pendri's bed.

"To save the life of our brother, Lord Heshek would call forth the greatest magics of the sun and the earth. Father would demand no less."

The sister, then, reflected Ithrazel, breathing deep to quiet the pounding of his heart. *What was her name?*

The daughter of that first wife, whom Minos Stylachos put aside.

Shumiel. *The Golden Princess*, Clea had called her.

And if she was twelve when her father put her mother aside for Clea's mother, that would make her thirty now . . . and because of the upheavals surrounding her girlhood, still unwed.

She stood looking at Clea, gold-flecked gaze expectant, and after a moment Clea dipped her knees in a slight genuflection and bobbed her head. "Shumiel."

Ten

S ister." Shumiel held out her hand, which Clea took but didn't kiss. To judge by the compression of her lips, Shumiel was clearly expecting this gesture of penitence. "Where have you been?" Her voice was high and silvery, curiously childlike. Her speech, the pure, trained accents of the noble houses of the Bright Islands. "Father sent out Ganzareb and his men three days ago, fearing some harm had come to you."

Fearing she'd run off to the tribes. Ithrazel recalled the arrogant Captain Ganzareb and his men riding up to Brownwaith on Clea's trail. They'd have returned to report by this time. *No wonder Daddy's got a reward out for her.*

He recalled, too, the way the hunter Kingfisher had spoken to her: *If someone had led them against the Clay-Grubbers, they would not have fought alone.*

Given the number of whipping-posts and slave-barracks in Turtlemere, small wonder they're looking around for someone to lead them in revolt.

No surprise this girl's father's nervous. I'd be.

"I had heard," returned Clea in a perfectly calm voice, "that people in Father's household have spread lies about me." She stooped, smiling, to let her sister's silky white lap-dog—who'd been eagerly pawing her boot-tops—lick her fingers. "I heard Father was seeking me to have me jailed. I can't risk coming forward again until I know for certain that isn't true. But I had to see Pendri. I heard he was ill . . ."

The determined sweetness of Shumiel's mask dissolved—clearly she, like her sister, adored their brother. For a moment she seemed unable to speak at the memory of how close they'd come to losing him.

"Why bring him here?" Clea scooped the little dog—a six-pound ball of overfed fluff—into her arms, and deposited it on Pendri's bed. "Couldn't they have worked their magic back at the Griffin House?"

The older woman shook her head, another abbreviated gesture. "The magic is stronger here, Lord Himelkart said."

Clea glanced at Ithrazel. *Is it?*

"He spoke truly," he returned. "There are deeper resonances in a place like this, where magic has been worked for years."

"Father couldn't endure the risk," said Shumiel. "And, he . . ." She looked sidelong at their brother.

"I have to get better quickly," provided Pendri in an eager voice, holding the dog tight as it licked his chin. "The magic is stronger here; they had to bring me. I mean, yes, Father would have had me brought here anyway, but . . . The Vrykos Family have a boy-wizard, Clea! A child-wizard. He's supposed to be stronger even than Lord Heshek or Lord Himelkart—"

"Can they prove that?" demanded Clea at once, and Ithrazel frowned sharply.

"What order is training him?"

Was that what bothered him, he wondered, about the magic he sensed here? An impression of power forced before its season? And now, were the other Orders doing it, too?

Shumiel glanced at him and raised her eyebrows, as if inquiring what "Uncle Iohan" knew about or had to do with the Orders of Wizardry.

Pendireth shook his head. "But Father asked for a meeting of the Mages' Council, to examine his claims. And when Tashthane Vrykos brings him into the city, I've asked Father to let me meet him! Vervaris is his name—somebody my age who can do real magic, great magic!"

Eagerness blazed in those expressive eyes. "I'm starting to have power—real power! But not like that! Not just studying and learning, but able to work great spells! Father keeps saying *Maybe* and *We'll see*, and Himelkart says he doesn't know, but I . . . I just want to talk to him! To learn what he's doing different! That's all. It shouldn't all be about whose House has the greatest power, should it?"

His brows—dark, like those of both of his sisters—puckered in consternation. "Father says it's what we have to think of first . . ."

"What *you* have to think of first," said Clea gently, "is getting well, Spellcaster. Will he?" She looked again at Ithrazel. "Get fully well? Not be left weak?"

The old man took Pendri's hand, half-shut his eyes. Feeling down through the skin, the blood, the soft muscle, the bright bone. Through the pain—and it was pain now—of the blacksteel shackles, he felt the boy's spirit, the strength in him . . . and magic, like a bright little flame. Pendri raised his eyes quickly to his, then looked down at the shackle, where the edge of it showed beneath his sleeve. Very slightly, Ithrazel shook his head.

Behind him he heard Shumiel ask, "And who is your friend, Sister?"—the last word pronounced as she would have said, "wench."

"An old man who was kind to me," returned Clea sweetly, "when I was a little girl in Father's prison. He's a healer."

"You don't trust Lord Heshek?"

"I didn't trust what I'd been told."

Shumiel made a sound like *hmff.* "You think everything is a plot."

"Many things are."

They'll be rolling on the floor pulling each other's hair in another minute . . .

"Did you come here to stay at your brother's side, Princess?" He turned to Shumiel, and bowed as he spoke in the accepted fashion.

She almost visibly preened at the deference. *How could she not, after her sister's lack of it?* "I came here to care for him, yes."

Ithrazel bowed again, even more deeply. He thought Clea was going to kick him. "I don't understand the sort of magic that was used to drive the yellow sickness away, of course; it is far beyond my small training." Ithrazel had never had any objections to laying it on with a trowel in a good cause, and he could see Shumiel's delicate shoulders relax. "Do you have remedies of your own, above and beyond what the good mages here recommend? Sometimes the spirit needs familiar things, good food and your sweet little friend there—what is his name?—as much as the body needs healing—"

"Snowball." Shumiel practically purred. "It's just what I always think! And when you've been sick, it helps to have one of your family at your side. My mother"—her words hesitated just for an instant on the name—"used to brew me a tisane of lavender and rose-leaves, with a little honey—"

"My aunt Chloellis used to make the same thing!" Ithrazel brought out the fabrication as if it were a treasured memory.

"Did she also make poultices of lemon-grass and oatmeal?"

"She did!" He responded to her eager delight as if to a light cue in a dance, despite his knowledge that a poultice of lemon-grass and oatmeal would be effective only for its warmth—and the fact that somebody cared enough to make it.

After another few minutes of listening raptly to her praise of Snow-ball's various perfections—the buggy-eyed little dust mop was currently chewing a hole in the pillowcase—he bowed deeply again, as if with very little encouragement he would kneel and kiss the hem of Shumiel's gown. "Lady, may I beg it of you—and of you, too, son"—he smiled at Pendri, who grinned back—"to keep it secret, that the Lady Clea and I even came here? In truth, where it comes to rivalries between the Great Houses, I would feel a good deal safer if all of this"—his gesture took in the chamber around them and the conversation of the past twenty minutes—"never took place."

Shumiel smiled warmly, utterly charmed. "Of course."

Pendri made the crisscross double-cross swear-I'll-never-tell signs that Ithrazel recalled from his own childhood, and would have spit on the floor to seal the vow if he hadn't been the son of the House Stylachos, in the House of the Mages.

"Thank you, my lady, my lord Pendireth. I take it the N—uh—Crystal Mages are in council about this Vrykos boy?"

"I think so." Shumiel gathered her pet into her arms again. "Lord Heshek himself came to speak to Father when he was here today—he *never* leaves his studies and meditations! But I think he's concerned that Father will take Pendri away from here, and put him to study with those teaching this Vrykos boy: Dalmin, I think the tutor's name is. A Red Mage, I believe. And Father says the Vrykos have sent word about their boy to the emperor, who's always been such a patron of the Crystal Order. During my two seasons in Esselmyriel"—she dropped the name of the emperor's city as casually as a handkerchief—"one saw a dozen or more at his court. Everyone says it's their spells of healing and long life to which His Majesty owes his good health—"

"And you still don't think," said Clea grimly, "that Pendri coming down sick like this was planned?"

Shumiel turned to Clea, sadness in her dark eyes. "Do not dismiss everything as a plot, Clyaris," she said gently. "Before all else, Father cares for Pendri, and would do so were our brother as powerless as you or I. I was in Pendri's chamber when Father came to him, when first he fell ill." She cuddled Snowball under her chin. "He wept." Her own eyes filled with sentimental tears.

"He probably wept," commented Clea softly as she and Ithrazel descended the stair, "at the thought that if Pendri dies he'll have to get a son off that greedy little hussy Linvinnia that he's married to now—who's exactly my age—and hope *he'll* be mageborn as well."

Ithrazel glanced sidelong at her.

Keeping her voice steady with an effort, she went on, "He wept at my mother's trial, when he talked about how much he'd loved Shumiel's mother before *my* mother bewitched him. Of course, Sylmane Shiamat was dead before he started accusing my mother—dead of pneumonia, from the place he'd locked her up in. Father's tears don't impress me. He sheds them easily."

From her belt she unhooked the tablet the Quillet had drawn for her, and held it under the lamp that burned beside the infirmary's outer door. "At the trial he said my mother had had her poisoned." The fog was thicker than ever. The world could have ended a foot from the door, and no one would have been able to tell. When she started to move off to the left, around the vast quadrangle of the buildings, Ithrazel whispered, "Where are you going? That's not the way to the gate—"

"I'm not going to the gate. I want to see where they keep those prisoners."

She was aware that with every minute she remained within the House of Glass, her danger increased. The more so now that Shumiel knew she was on the premises—and who knew what skillful questions Himelkart might put to Pendri, even, that would coax from him the information that Clea had been there with a "healer"?

She spared a moment to smile at the way Ithrazel had handled her sister, almost laughing, despite their situation, at how Shumiel had practically rolled over like old Snowball begging for sweetmeats. *I'll have to remember that, next time I'm with her. . . .*

But the news she'd given was disquieting. *A child as young as Pendri? WITHOUT the training of the Crystal Mages?*

Is that possible?

Then her mind returned to the matter at hand. To the screaming that wrenched the night.

Khymin . . .

Liver-Eater had said the old man hadn't been seen.

For all Rat Bone's contempt for mages, the little assassin had kept the secret of that withered old fugitive's presence in the Tunnels for years. Had taken him food and fuel to keep him warm, opium to help him sleep and booze to chase the devils out of his brain, and had let the other beggars in the Dockside know that whoever stole from him, or harmed him, or ratted him out to the City Guards, would be sorry for it. Khymin had been old when Clea had first encountered him, during her own period of hiding in the Tunnels at the age of nine. Wrinkled, white, and desiccated, he'd reminded her of a dried mushroom in the dark, huddled among the rotting scraps of his books, his crumbling parchment scrolls. But from him, Clea had heard stories of Ithrazel the Cursed—whom she'd thought had been simply a figure of Darklander legend. And once he'd whispered to her about what the Crystal Mages had done to the destroyer of Dey Allias: taken him down the Corridor of Mirrors, chained him to a rock in everlasting torment . . .

The kind of thing, Clea had thought even then, that wizards were liable to do.

Even after she'd been taken back into her father's house, she'd looked after the old man, for Rat Bone's sake. What he was doing down there in the dark, she'd never learned. He'd never even do magic, for fear that stories about him would get out.

Only now, with the rising of the zai—with the deepening sense that the Crystal Order controlled, or were trying to control, the thing—did it cross her mind to wonder if it was that smooth, fascinating, ugly Heshek and his Order, from whom old Khymin had fled.

Something rustled the myrtles to her right. Moved in the shadow, almost—but not quite—like a snake. Again that quick thread of fetor, nothing of this earth, and the blink of too many tiny eyes.

Then the sound of the screaming, muffled in the fog, raised the hair on her scalp.

She eased forward cautiously, left hand to the wall, the shuttered tin lantern she bore radiating heat upward against her hand. Seeing in her mind the neatly scratched map: *window, window, door. Window, window . . .*

The scream came down louder, almost directly above them. Harsh and terrible, beyond physical pain. Through her arm she felt the wizard's hand tremble, where it lay on her elbow. Across the wide garden, blurred spots of orange marked a window or two in the kitchen building. In this wing, all was blackness. Windows shuttered, or more likely the rooms were dark.

A second voice joined the first, frantically shouting words she didn't understand.

She felt the stone molding of a door. Quillet had said there was a grille over a stairway . . .

Ithrazel pulled her back. "Don't touch the grille. Don't go any closer to the door."

She breathed, "Spell?"

"Hundreds," he whispered. "Like iron barbs, in the air, on the ground—I feel them on every step of the stairway leading up to that place. Smell them . . . who the HELL do they have up there?"

Old Khymin . . .

Or someone else.

Another scream floated on the air, like the exhaled mist of blood when a man is chopped through the lungs in battle.

Ithrazel backed away, drawing her after him.

She didn't resist. She understood that here, there was nothing that could be done.

The screams followed them like the stench of burning flesh.

"Will Pendri really be all right?" Clea asked him as they moved through the Dockside again back toward the Great Pool. "The sickness leaves people weak, sometimes for years . . . sometimes for life." He would need his strength, she thought, if there was some kind of plot afoot from the Vrykos.

To get the emperor's favor? To take our lands from us? To render us powerless? She had seen what the great Houses did to those who were powerless.

I should want them to fall, for the sake of my people.

But one House falling wouldn't save us from the others.

"He should be all right." The old man's voice was curiously gentle, and she wondered if he, too, had had a son. And if so, what had happened to the boy. "His sickness was genuine—the healing, too. And both the least of his perils," added Ithrazel, "compared with the danger he's in from the people around him."

Clea couldn't argue with him there.

They walked on in silence. The fog was still thick. Here along the canal again, with the smeared gleam of bonfires burning in the mist-locked blackness of alleys and courtyards, Clea felt herself relax, and she shivered in her sheepskin jacket. For weeks after she'd gotten out of the prison she had emerged from the Tunnels only by night, for being out in daylight had filled her with terror. This was the world as she'd first remembered it, after that weird re-birth when she was little more than Pendri's age: whores from the Blossom Garden or the House of Drunken Thunder strolling the shadows in their threadbare finery, making eyes at the sailors; dream casters and cut-rate astrologers whining from the doorways, advertising blissful oblivion or fortune at the dice. Hollow-eyed old women, or children like little skeletons, gathering dog-turds in the gutters to sell to the leather-workers, glad not to be working in the slave-villages of the Mire. The blaze of cressets around the gate of the Courtyard of a Thousand Ecstatic Cries. The grease-salt wonderfulness of fried plums sizzling in a barrow.

Firelight gashing gaudy patches in the blackness.

Faces that came and went.

Her mind still heard the screams, and old Khymin's crumbled whisper of a voice.

After a long time, Clea asked him, "What made you decide to do it?"

"To do what?"

"Destroy the city," she said. "Burn Dey Allias. Half the people there were Darklanders . . . Was there some single thing that happened, some event that made you say, *This has to end, no matter what it costs?* Or was it just that you . . . couldn't endure seeing this anymore?"

He was silent for a long time, a shabby little man in a Ghoras hunter's borrowed wolf-skin coat. They passed a young woman selling scrap metal and broken lamps on a spread-out blanket at the head of a wharf, two children sleeping beside her under a sailor's blood-stained coat. The Monkey King passed them—she couldn't believe the old man was still operating, he must have been a hundred years old already when she'd first met him as a child—pushing a wheelbarrow that contained three suits of clothing, five pairs of shoes, a woman's dress and several thick coils of hair tied with string, plus two shovels and a pry-bar clotted with graveyard earth.

Still better than dredging . . .

At last Ithrazel said, "I don't remember."

Clea stopped in her tracks for a moment, only looking at him. It was not what she'd expected him to say.

"I don't remember," he said again as they walked on. "I remember doing it. I remember standing on the Hill of Oleanders, looking down at the lights of the city—it was late, it was like looking into a hearth where the embers are mostly burned out. I remember crying out the words, raising my hands . . . but I don't remember what was in my heart. What was in my mind. I know I'd planned it carefully, because four other mages helped me, raised power behind me on top of the hill. I remember searching them out, going deep into the Mire to find Khoyas White-Eyes, who was the most powerful of the Black Mages . . . Dershin Shalzaib, Eketas Elsynnin, Second Ox of the Ashupik . . ."

He shook his head. "I remember those things like yesterday. I see myself doing it—see myself every night in dreams. And I remember knowing that my wife was in the city that night, and our son. But in all those dreams, in all those memories, there is nothing in my heart. Not even darkness."

Eleven

They were on the move all the following day. When the canoe reached the little canyon below Turtlemere again it was well after daylight.

"A dozen of your father's men arrived last night," reported Star, when the Ghoras lowered their ladders from the canyon's edge and the hunters descended to the canoe. "Is your brother well?"

"My father's watching over him." Clea had already guessed, from the increased campfire smoke, that the defense force at the wrecked village had been re-enforced. "I'm guessing a couple of Crystal Mages will be on their way, so we need to get out of here. Can you keep up the fog for a few more hours, Willow?"

The older girl whispered, "I'll be fine." She was shivering, and Hamo had wrapped his sheepskin jacket around her shoulders. Behind her, Ithrazel seemed three-quarters asleep, huddled in his own scraggy furs. Clea wasn't fooled.

Noiseless as ghosts, a flight of pelicans swept past out of the thin mists that lay over the water. With the same dreamlike silence, three smaller canoes melted from the fog, Star's hunters and a half-score of Darklanders whom Clea hadn't seen before redistributing themselves to take the place of Redhawk and his weary rowers. "Your father has men camped in Sand Canyon," one of the newcomers informed Clea. "Another small camp in the Orchid Maze; both with those little baby-mages among them."

Clea cursed, almost absentmindedly, as she called to mind where those places lay in the watery wastelands that stretched to infinity beyond the narrow strip of Telmayrian settlement. "Thank you—Blackfeather, is it?"

The man smiled as he nodded, pleased that she'd recalled his name from a brief meeting years ago. A minor chief of the Gar Clan, Clea identified him.

"Both those places are in my father's concession near the Reedmire," she said after a moment. "But that area's never been worked, and it's miles from anybody else's concessions . . . I don't think there's ever been trouble out there with the Kindred, either."

Star shook her head.

"He's guarding something," Clea said after a time. "He has to be. There's no other reason to keep men out there."

"Guarding what?" asked Hamo, and Clea glanced back at the hunter Blackfeather.

"Any idea how long they've been out there?"

"Since the spring."

Sandmire Village was destroyed in the spring.

To Star, Clea said, "It sounds like it might be worth our while to go have a look."

At the same time that Clea's father had taken her back two years ago, she recalled, he had, rather startlingly, issued the statement that for the previous seven years, Clea had been brought up in virginal virtue in the House of the White Sisters of Kissare, on the small Lake of Kissare. She had been taken to visit this House—to make sure she knew the layout of the place, in case anyone asked—and had met the Sisters who were henceforth going to swear that she'd been raised among them. While there, she had sneaked out one night in the company of Rat Bone and two Ashupik grooms, to meet with the members of her mother's ancestral tribe. She'd been gone for two days. She had known the Kindred in Morne, in their slum communities and half-hidden retreats in the Tunnels; had learned their laws from the secret Kindred Councils, and their ways from the hunters who would come into the city. Their hopes, and their anger, from those who moved back and forth between the two worlds of the Mire and the Easterling dominion.

For two days, she had hunted birds from the reed boats used in the swamplands, slept in Darklander camps, listened to their legends. She'd mixed her blood in ceremonies with all the minor chieftains, spoken to the men who had known Elannin Greenshield, learned the depth of the taproot that connected the enslaved Kindred in the towns with those who hid like fugitive animals in what had been their own land. She had seen the wounds left on those who'd escaped the dredger-villages, the hostage-villages, whence the adamis came: the crusted masses of flogging-scars on the backs of the men, the stumps and empty eye-sockets of those women and children whose men had defied the forces of the Bright Lords.

She had come to understand the world and the ways of the Kindred. Had heard the voices of the so-called Green Children, who whispered and tweeted in the fog. Had spent an afternoon at the great shrine of Farrawen, the Goddess of the Lake of Serpents, and had made the acquaintance of its Lady, Neambis, the head of the Gray Sisters. It was Neambis who had convinced the Mother at the House of Kissare that whatever her personal opinion might be of where Clea had been and what she'd been doing for those two days, it would probably be better for all concerned if she keep it to herself.

During those two days, she had heard nothing, not even rumors, of the zai, or of the things called Night-Gluttons that had killed poor Kingfisher—or of whatever it was she'd glimpsed outside the House of Glass last night.

Behind her in the canoe, Clea heard one of the rowers exclaim as a seven-foot gar-fish rose from the canyon's depths and attacked one of the oars, biting the wood clean through. The men had to strike at it repeatedly, and she recalled, as if at a great distance, how on their way through the Dockside last night, rats had scuttled from an alley, to race to her and bite at her boots. She'd broken their necks with a couple of hard stomps—rats, even attacking, didn't impress Clea.

But the scene returned now to her mind.

Rats don't usually attack like that in the open . . .

The memories of the Reedmire were clearest, perhaps, of all the crowding recollections of those two very crowded days. Uncounted watery miles of reed-beds and sedges, unknown islands and isolated shrines. Birds, fish, and enormous eels. The portion of the Marshes that bordered on her father's concession of the Mire had barely been explored. To her knowledge, no one knew if it contained adamis or not.

Yet her father was guarding it. That meant sending not only troops, but food and supplies—and mages for each camp, something he had never done before.

Guarding something . . .

Does he know what?

Or is he just doing what Heshek tells him to?

Another memory, dark as nightmare in her brain.

The grotto in a deep canyon near Turtlemere, where the dredger Pikefish had told her the zai had risen. With the smoke and death-stink of the village still in her clothing, the sight of the bodies still coming back to her as if branded on the back of her eyeballs, she'd taken a canoe and gone out to the place, knowing she'd better see whatever was there. The grotto had been cold, and colder still the dread she felt when she saw the smashed barges, the ruin of the machinery there, the pulverized sheds where the adamis had been stored. The spoor that marked the thing's size and strength. There'd been a smaller grotto beyond, and she'd paddled cautiously through its low entrance, prey to a curious horror at not knowing how deep the water was beneath her, or what might be in it.

Then the greater horror of hearing Himelkart's unmistakable drawling voice in the outer grotto behind her.

Himelkart kneeling on the overturned canoe, thin as some otherworld creature himself, with his dark, wet hair hanging like seaweed over his shoulders. Darkness rising from the water before him. Then the screams of the guards, and the young man's eerie stillness as he concentrated on his spells while their blood splattered his clothing.

She opened her eyes, putting the memory aside.

If he can't control it yet, at least he could keep it from attacking him.

And it comes out of water.

Star was watching her, the Ghoras warriors also. Ithrazel's eyes were half-open, like a man still on the edge of a doze, but in them she saw, not his usual watchful hardness, but concern, as if in her silence he sensed the horror of visions as dreadful as his own.

"Either my father wants to control this thing," she said softly, "to use against his enemies, or the Crystal Order wants it, to use it—and him—against theirs. But who called it up, really? Or did it rise up of its own accord? Is it part of the same thing that's brought the Night-Gluttons? That seems to drive even the rats and the fishes to strike out without meaning. And *why*? Do they really think they can learn to control it? Whoever bridles this thing is going to control the emperor, either through fear or through his greed."

"But what *is* it?" whispered the shepherd.

"Nothing that we know of." Ithrazel raised his head from where it had been sunk on his breast, blinked a little at the chill glitter of the new morning on the water as the fog burned off. "It could be a god, for all we know. Or it could be but the littlest mouse that runs before the coming of a lion. Your father is a fool, girl."

"No argument there. He sees what he wishes to see—what he thinks will further his House."

"And what about you?" He regarded her with a kind of sleepy malice. "Evidently your father isn't the only member of your family who thinks it's a good idea to bridle the lightning in pursuit of your cause."

She met his gaze. "I'll take my chances."

"As he thinks he has the skill and the strength to take his."

"I deal with a man," said Clea softly. "He with a beast."

The wizard sighed. "I wish I knew," he murmured, "whether either of those propositions is actually true. But the New Mages aren't fools. That's what frightens me."

Twelve

Star's village was called the Place of a Thousand Frogs. It lay a day's long paddle into the Mire, so closely surrounded by canyons that it amounted to little more than a table-land ringed by a deep, uneven moat. As they climbed the ladder from the canoe to the clifftop through gathering dusk, Clea could glimpse, far down the blue gloom of the canyon, something pale that looked like the ruins of a stone bridgehead. "We're only a few miles from the City of Butterflies," said Ithrazel, and his glance shifted up to Star, who climbed ahead of them. "Aren't we?"

And, when she nodded: "Is it still there?"

"It's a city of butterflies now in truth," she replied. "They bask in the sun on the broken pavement of the Great Temple. The bitterfruit vine cloaks the walls of men, and wild pigs root for food where the markets used to spread. Those who weren't taken away to the dredger-villages by your people fled deeper into the Mire, Mud-Grubber, and the fields of potatoes and corn have long since gone back to the trees. Are you proud of the glories your civilization has wrought?"

She stepped clear of the rope and held down her crippled hand to help Clea scramble the last foot or so to the top. Hamo cried from further down the ladder, "My lord had nothing to do with—" and Ithrazel signed him quiet.

"I have paid a price," he returned in a tired voice, "for some of my sins. If the gods ask more from me, I have no argument against them." Star stepped aside and refused to help him. He dragged himself wearily to the thicket of laurel and sapling-oak from which the ladder dangled, and glanced around sharply, taking in—Clea saw—what she had already

noted: that the dense foliage around them concealed twenty-three Ghoras warriors in hunting-paint, amulets around their necks to ward off
the notice of other tribes. As far as Clea knew, the Crystal Mages could
see straight through these Darklander spells. Telmayrian slaving-parties
often took mages with them.

Clea took Ithrazel by the elbow and steered him deeper into the trees,
where there would be shelter against the thin rain that had begun to sprinkle
down. She could feel him shivering with exhaustion. Graywillow stumbled
when she got to the top of the ladder, and Clea caught her.

"I'm all right," the novice whispered. "I'll be fine."

The hell you are—

"She needs to get warm," said Clea. "And something to eat." She realized
she herself was famished, having had only scant field-rations of pemmican
and parched corn at noon.

"We can see no one following," said the leader of the warriors who had
met them, as Hamo and the rowers scrambled off the top of the ladder and
men came forward to draw the canoe itself up out of the canyon. Eagle, his
name was, Clea recalled. Star's cousin. He tapped his left pectoral with his
right hand, in a greeting that Clea returned as well as Star.

And, she noticed, Ithrazel did as well.

"Obsidian Shield of the Lion Family, and Green Jade of the people of the
Three Straight Canyons, came into the camp this afternoon," the man continued as the party moved off into the darkening woods. "Also Blacklamb of
the Reed Family. They ask to see the Iron Princess." His eyes went to Clea,
and in them she saw the hope that she saw in the gaze of nearly every one
of the Twilight People. The hope that looked on her as the granddaughter of
Greenshield the Wise. One of their own, who had learned the ways of the
dark-eyed Easterlings without forgetting the pride in her own blood.

And I can do it, she thought, her heart stirred as always by what she
knew of them, past and present. *I can free them . . .*

*If they don't get me killed by calling me their Deliverer where my father
can hear them. Or the Crystal Mages or my father's spies or anyone who might
want those ten silver pennies Liver-Eater talked about . . .*

Tired as she was—and she realized she was exhausted, after three days
of constant travel at the highest pitch of alertness—she knew she'd have to
speak to these men before she slept. She'd dozed a little in the canoe, but had
not dared to lower her guard enough for real sleep.

Yet they'd come a long way to see her. If her father's troops were moving
about the canyons, they had come at the risk of their lives.

And in fact, once she'd sat down across the fire from them, in the low, makeshift longhouse that was all but invisible among the trees—the weariness fell away. When she'd gone out for a big robbery as a child or, later, for a kill, it had been the same. The Ghoras of Star's kindred brought stew of fish, seeds, and berries, thickened with the wild yams that the Twilight People still gathered from the fields around their abandoned towns. Rat Bone had always advised, *If you can't eat, sleep; and if you can't sleep, eat.* The food made her feel better. She found she had no trouble giving the whole of her mind to the accounts of the chiefs Obsidian Shield, Green Jade, and Blacklamb, not only of the iniquities of the Bright Lords upon their people, but of the movements and position of her father's men . . .

And of stranger things besides.

"We have seen these creatures, too," affirmed Green Jade, when Star spoke of the Night-Gluttons that had killed Kingfisher in the attack on the camp two nights before. "The size of a wolf, or of a young bear in its first winter. But round, like a severed head. It has a great mouth all fringed with arms that can pull a man to pieces almost before he can strike back."

"There are smaller things, too," added Eagle. "No one has seen them, but we've found their tracks." He leaned forward and drew in the dirt of the fire-pit marks that reminded Clea of smashed scorpions, claws pointing all ways. "And we've seen the blood of their kills. They can climb trees, and they make webs, like the webs of spiders but larger."

"There are others, too," said another of the warriors. "Like stoats, but with many legs, many eyes . . ."

"Have you tracked them?" Clea recalled with a shiver the thing she thought she'd seen in the gardens of the House of Glass. "Can you tell what direction they come from?"

He named the places where the marks had been found. It took only moments to mentally locate them within a day's journey of Turtlemere. And the Three Straight Canyons—the territory of Green Jade's group—lay only a day's journey farther into the Mire. It was all within the area encompassed by her father's new guard-posts in Sand Canyon and the Orchid Maze, and along the edge of the Reedmire . . .

He's guarding it. Whatever it is, it's in there.

Rage stirred in her heart. *You irresponsible bastard . . .*

And no, she thought, *my bringing Ithrazel back into this world isn't the same thing.*

"It is like nothing we've seen before," said old Obsidian Shield. "Like nothing our ancestors saw."

Graywillow had retreated to a bed of blankets and brush at the far end of the longhouse: like all the dwellings of the Twilight Kin these days in the Mire, easily dismantled and scattered when they moved on. Clea had seen the ruins of their towns—cities, almost—with their temples and shrines, the school-halls where their children had been taught and their men and women had studied the deeper arts of lore and medicine and the interpretation of the stars. Many of these shrines had even been built in stone. She'd seen where the forests had grown over the fields that had surrounded those places, fields where they'd cultivated corn and potatoes, pumpkins and beans—vast meadows where flowers had grown for their ranked hives of honeybees.

Now the insatiable demands of the Bright Lords' mines and refineries had turned them into a fugitive people, hiding like animals in the Mire.

No wonder Ithrazel hated them.

Hamo, too, had fallen asleep, under a couple of deerskins against the autumn cold. Ithrazel sat near him, wrapped in a bearskin and listening in spite of his fatigue. Firelight glinted beneath his shaggy brows. The Ghoras kept their distance from him: Easterling, Bright Lord, slave-master of these lands. If he hadn't been with Clea, they'd have cut his throat.

Far off in the forest a lynx screamed as it struck its prey. Chill wind splattered raindrops on the makeshift roof of leaves overhead.

The world of the Twilight, her tutors in Morne termed this place, though the sun shone here in the daytime, even as it did in the Bright Islands of the east. A world of benighted people, savages compared to the glories of Telmayre.

This land. Silent in the rain and the night.

"I'm going to have to go in and have a look at it if I can," she said quietly. "At least see if I can find its lair, or something that will tell me where it came from. Any information is better than this ignorance." She cursed herself for not having studied old Khymin's books more thoroughly when she had the chance—not that the old man would have let her touch them.

If they caught him, they'll have seized his books. And they might very well have left somebody to watch the place where they'd been, to see who came looking.

But those books might have said something about this.

"It has no lair," attested young Blacklamb of the Reed clan, from deep in the Mire. "A thing so huge would have left marks, and it has left none. Nor have these other things."

The other hunters nodded their assent.

"You are learned in the ways of the Easterlings, Princess," said Eagle softly. And you know that our people in the towns are ready to follow the blood of Greenshield the Wise. Can *we* learn to use these creatures, these zai, against *them*? To drive them utterly from our land. To return the world to the way it was before their coming."

"The world is never going to go back to the way it was." Clea looked up with the embers of the fire gleaming in her tawny eyes. "And the Easterlings are never going to go away. We need to learn how to meld with them, to ally with them—"

"Which we could do," the hunter urged, "if we could *tame* these things—"

"*No*," said Clea. "Not ever. You didn't see the village." And for a moment she turned her face aside.

The thinning rain dripped a little at the entrance of the longhouse, then ceased.

"So why did it arise?" she asked softly. "Why now? What changed? Maybe the Crystal Mages know, and maybe they don't. Or maybe," she added grimly, "one of the older orders—the Black Mages, or the Red"— she deliberately avoided adding the Brown Wizards to that list, Ithrazel the Cursed having once been their Archmage—"brought it into being, either as a weapon against the Crystal Order or as the result of some other spell, some great spell, going wrong, as their spells now often do."

The warriors looked sharply at one another. Ithrazel's brows pulled down over the bridge of his nose and he looked for a moment as if he would speak. Then he let the matter go.

"We've asked Neambis the Gray, the Hand of Farrawen," spoke up Star, "whether this zai, these creatures, came here through the anger of the gods. The zai after all attacked the diggings of the Mud-Grubbers, and the village of their slaves." Her troubled green eyes went to the chiefs on the other side of the fire-pit. "The hunters speak of all these things, in the Orchid Maze. Have any of you heard of any shaman, or any priestess, say anything about what the gods have felt or thought? It has been a long time since they've spoken at the Serpent Shrine."

"I've heard that they don't speak anymore." Obsidian Shield folded his hands. "Even in the farthest shrines, out in the Blue Marshes and the Salt Deeps, they are silent, and the Ladies pray their prayers in vain."

For a time there was only stillness: the red flicker of the fire, and the smell of the forest and the night.

Young Blacklamb glanced across at Ithrazel. "Can the Easterlings drive out even the gods? Is that what they next intend?"

Everyone else looked, too. Clea said, "It's the same in the cities. My sister"—she nodded toward the shadows where Graywillow slept, and used the Ashupik word that meant *sister of the heart,* not of mother's blood—"is of the Shrine of Nyellin in Morne. The gods are silent to all."

"That doesn't mean their silence isn't because of what these sea-robbers have done to our land."

"Whether this is true or not," returned Clea, "we do not know. Nor, I think, do we have any way of finding out right now. And we would be fools if we ran about making up stories without learning what we can of this thing. Are you camped in this place for a little time, Star? Can I and my friends impose on you for a day's hospitality while we rest?" At the chief's nod, she looked around at those gathered about the fire. "Then the day after, I'll need at least a few with me, if we're going in the direction of these things. I can't fight the Night-Gluttons on my own, and maybe these web-weavers you speak of are more dangerous than we know. And we know not how thick they'll be, the farther west we go toward the Reedmire. But this is going to be very, very dangerous—"

Hamo sat up sleepily, and lifted a hand. "I'll go."

Two or three of the Ghoras warriors—as if miffed that they'd been beaten to volunteering by a shepherd—added their voices at once: "And I." "And I . . ."

Her eyes met Ithrazel's and she almost said his name, then remembered and only said, "Uncle?"

A corner of his scrubby mustache lifted at the designation. "Have I a choice, my dear niece?"

He dreamed of the Night-Gluttons.

Dreamed of walking through the streets of the City of Butterflies: bright clear daylight and the gaudy oceans of marigolds in the city market. The smiles of the market-women greeting him, the thump of looms from the weaving-houses and the voices of children playing. Second Ox, the greatest of the Ashupik shamans, dwelled there, in a sort of swallow's-nest of reed and bamboo built halfway down the side of the canyon at the northern end of the town. A long, dizzy stairway of rickety bamboo descended to it, but it was exquisitely quiet for his studies of birds and the stars. Ithrazel saw himself pacing those winding streets, those tiny squares, a slight sandy-bearded man in the brown robes of his order. Now and then hunters or craftsmen would look at him twice and make the sign against evil. Even this far into the Mire, the Twilight Kindred knew him for an Easterling.

He knew he was coming to find Second Ox.

He knew that in his satchel he carried the rolled-up parchment on which the Sigil was written, that terrible circle that he meant to draw on the Hill of Oleanders that overlooked the Marble City of Dey Allias. He knew the words of the spell whispered back and forth in his heart, though his dreaming mind refused to hear them. His dream-self refused to think about what it was that he was going to do.

In his heart—as if from a terrible distance—he saw again the few pale stones of the broken bridgehead, which had once guarded the way into the City of Butterflies.

How long had the place been deserted? In the damp climate of the Mire, even stone buildings perished fast. What had happened to those market-women and craftsmen, those weavers and their children? Even as he walked it was as if he could see the shadows of slave-raiders flung against the walls by the fires of burning buildings and burning books. Though he tried to shut his ears, he heard, beneath the happy singsong of the children's' games, their screaming.

Around him, the temples and marketplaces of the City of Butterflies turned to charred jumbles of stone. Lizards basked on broken hearthstones; burned rafters lay like jackstraws in the weed-grown streets. When he reached the edge of the canyon the house of Second Ox was gone. Only the stumps of its supports projected like broken teeth from the cliff's edge, sprouting with resurrection-fern. . . .

Dear gods, what did they do to those who helped me? To Second Ox, to Khoyas White-Eyes. . . ?

Are they, too—my friends, my colleagues—screaming for eternity on some crag with eagles ripping their entrails out?

Did my daughters get away?

They must have, they lived well south of the city . . .

But sudden dread sickened him. *Akuhare . . . Chiviel . . .*

Then darkness. Darkness and the harsh metallic stink, like hot metal. The screaming of women and children.

Ithrazel turned around and saw the streets of Morne. The shabby slums of its waterfront, wreathed in darkness thicker than the darkness of night. Women fled through the narrow ways, children clutched in their arms, screaming—the whores he'd seen outside Liver-Eater's broken-down stable, the skinny children who'd fought over dog-turds in the gutters, the rat-skinner Gerti and the hulking Pig-Face . . . All fleeing, as the Night-Gluttons rolled like monstrous pillbugs through the street. Their lashing tentacles caught men, women, children, dragged them into the darkness that surrounded them.

The air stank of blood and burning metal, and flared with the searing presence of magic.

His own magic . . .

He shouted, "STOP IT!!!" and woke, with Hamo shaking his shoulder.

"It's all right . . ." The shepherd's voice was gentle, as if speaking to a child. "It's all right, it'll be all right . . ."

"It won't!" Ithrazel shoved him away, clutched his own arms tight around his chest, the pain worse, inside, than it had ever been when he'd been chained on the crag for the birds.

At least on the crag he had known there was nothing that he could do. And that he was the only one who was going to suffer.

He pressed his hands to his face, fighting to stop his tears.

In a small voice he repeated, "It won't."

The zai is only the start.

He knew that.

All those creatures—he had seen them come out of the earth in his dreams. Night-Gluttons. Blood-Thieves. Silvery ghaist-spiders . . . Over and over again.

Hamo scootched over to a gourd that hung from one of the bent saplings that supported the low roof: it was half-full of the sort of spruce tisane that Ithrazel remembered Darklander herdsmen would make. *What happened to their sheep and goats?* Tiny creatures, some of them barely bigger than good-sized dogs: they'd grazed the woods around the Ashupik towns. Clearly they weren't keeping herds now. They kept nothing that would lead Telmayrian slave-takers to them.

Morning light filtered through the thatch of leaves close overhead. *Early yet . . .* The world smelled of last night's rain. For a moment, if he closed his eyes, it was as if all the long nightmare had never been.

"Are you hungry?" asked the shepherd, as if Ithrazel hadn't thrust him away a moment before. "I was, when I woke up—after yesterday I could have eaten a whole sheep. There's stew from last night."

"Thank you." Ithrazel felt drained, like a man after a long sickness. The flesh of his wrists still smarted, where the chains had burned when they'd been in the grounds of the House of Glass.

The echo of the screaming was like a burn, too, inside.

"How's Graywillow?" he asked at length. "Those spells of fog—even if she was being helped by the Lady of Farrawen—are no joke to keep up for that long."

"She's well, she says. She was up before first light, helping with the cooking." Hamo smiled affectionately at the thought of her. "She's insisting that she wants to go with Lady Clea to look for these—these monsters. At least we'll have a day to rest before going, may the Good God be praised! And of course—"

Outside the hut, there was a small commotion, one of the village dogs barking and a child crying, "Fairies!" in delight. Then Clea's voice, and the creak of boot-leather as she scrambled to her feet: "My lady!"

She sounded impressed, even awed.

I have GOT, thought Ithrazel, *to see what would impress HER* . . .

He pulled on his clothes and the wolf-skin coat, for the morning was cold, and ducked through the hut's entry-hole to the outside.

Thirteen

G ray Sisters.

Graywillow, who had been helping to sand-scrub the gourd bowls near the new-built fire, rose in order to turn and then kneel again in a deep obeisance. The hunters and warriors, the women and children of the Ghoras camp, bowed deeper still, their heads to the ground. It was worth getting up, reflected Ithrazel, kneeling himself and yanking Hamo down beside him, to see Miss Damn-Your-Bones Clea on her knees, her head inclined to the three women who stood at the edge of the camp's little clearing.

Their gray robes, though much faded from washing, were of good quality, and their hands were the hands of women who didn't scrub their own dishes.

The Shrine of Farrawen? It was still evidently the biggest and most powerful in the Mire. *Is the village of the Coiled Serpent still there?*

The smallest of the Sisters—white-haired, straight as an arrow-shaft, and her head would barely have topped Clea's shoulder—went to Star and helped her to her feet, the signal for everyone else to rise. Her sharp eyes—the dark blue of the ginger-haired Setuket tribe—went to Ithrazel for a moment and she frowned. She didn't look quite old enough to remember him, so she must have sensed the spells on his wrist-shackles. Or maybe it was just the cast of his features and the sandy color of his hair.

"Clyaris . . ." She turned then to Clea and spoke the name that Sister Shumiel had used. *Presumably the one the girl was given at birth.* "Clea," in his own time, had been Ashupik street-slang for a baby rat, and he thought that probably hadn't changed. The old woman then smiled at Graywillow, asked in a surprisingly deep voice: "Did your hidden journey prosper, child?"

"It did, Lady of the Serpents. Thank you for helping me."

The Lady's eyes narrowed again and she glanced once more at Ithrazel.

"We would have come to the Shrine, my lady," added Clea, "at our first opportunity, had not word reached us here about . . . *things*, to the north and west, near the Reedmire and the Orchid Maze. Evil things."

"I have heard"—the Serpent Lady's gaze returned to Clea—"of these evil things. It's why I came here seeking you."

Does everybody in the Mire know where Clea's putting her feet up today? Ithrazel noticed two women—Lhogri, not Ghoras—with the tattoos and the bearing of chiefs, who hadn't been in Thousand Frogs last night. He knew how swiftly word traveled among the Twilight kinships. Presumably more swiftly still, as rumor of zai and Night-Gluttons and what-all else spread, not to speak of Papa Stylachos's guards traipsing all over the woods. Star's hunters were already bringing up branches to the fire, for their new guests to sit on, and someone else fetched a gourd of tisane.

"You've heard of these things in the Mire, then?" Clea asked, standing respectfully until the Gray Lady motioned for her to sit. "It sounds to me like my father is sending his guards out into the Mire to keep outsiders away from where these creatures are hiding."

"Your father is a fool."

"About some things," agreed Clea, "absolutely. But the Crystal Mages aren't fools. They're helping him—or more likely using him, because they think they can control these things. And I think the first thing we need to do is find out how right they are. Have you heard anything, Lady? Either from the hunters who come to the Shrine, or from the gods themselves? Or is there something in your lore, some tale, maybe—maybe even just a name—that speaks of things like this?"

"It has been fifteen years," said the Lady quietly, "since any of the gods appeared to any of their servants. And before that, three."

Clea visibly stopped herself from swearing by God's braies.

Ithrazel nearly joined her in the oath. *Eighteen years!*

"Some of us are going tomorrow into the Orchid Maze," Clea went on after a moment, "and on into the Reedmire, to see what we can see. And if we find ten of them, dead around a patch of mushrooms, we'll know that all we need to do is feed them mushrooms." Her brief smile was wry, and then vanished in darker possibility. "Maybe we'll find their eggs, and at least destroy those before others are born. If you would give us some . . . some spell of protection . . ."

"Any spell I could lay upon you," returned the Hand of Farrawen, "this thing, I think, would cut straight through, as it cut through those cantrips that protected the village of Turtlemere from wildcats and wolves. But I tell you now, you will find no eggs, no nests." She lifted a wrinkled hand, tiny as a child's.

"Our hunters have searched. Nor is Sand Canyon the only place, where hunters have sometimes seen things rise in darkness from the deepest waters of the earth. No scat, no bones, no tracks. These child-faced mages who have your father guard this place, they have sought for months now to hide the knowledge of these things—to keep it to themselves—but they are no closer to making them do their bidding than they were when first the villages began to whisper of the zai."

"So what *are* they?" And for the first time Ithrazel saw the shadow of doubt in her face, the shadow of fear. He had thought that it would please him to see this cocky young sword-blade of a girl realize that she faced a darkness beyond her own strength—but he found that this was not so.

The old woman shook her head. "The kin of the Night-Gluttons. The kin of the Blood-Thieves that come on sleepers in the night. Like the zai, these other things also have a magic in them that sheds the spells of humankind, as if they came from a world other than our own."

Clea was silent for a time, and the old man could almost see what was in her mind: the winding walls of that great flood called Sand Canyon. The tangled morasses of the Orchid Maze. The whole of the Reedmire, hundreds of square miles of marsh and pond and lakes of problematical depth, and below them, twisting miles of clay.

We don't even know what adamis IS, thought Ithrazel. *Not really. Maybe even the Crystal Mages don't know.*

How many weeks—how many years—could you wander in the Mire, not even truly knowing what you seek, while the zai, and the Night-Gluttons, and these other things—these things I thought were demons—multiply in the land?

In time Clea touched her chest and said, "Thank you, Lady. But if the rising-place of these things can't be found, what is *your* counsel? My heart tells me to stay wide of the Crystal Mages—tells me also, that my father and my brother are deep in peril, having anything to do with them. But the answer lies with them. Or at least part of the answer. . . ."

"We know not where the answer lies."

And Ithrazel thought, just for a moment, that the Lady of Serpents cast him another quick, calculating glance.

"But there is another question, out in the Reedmire—and this is why I have sought you out, Greenshield's child. It may turn out to be part of the same question, for the days are now full of strange things, as if they all grow together out of the same root. Even if it is not . . ." She made a small gesture with her wrinkled little hand.

"It is still a question, and one that in seventy-seven years I have not encountered—itself no small consideration. You have been schooled in the lore of the Easterlings, Clyaris; in the knowledge of the Bright Islands. And you have walked in the Tunnels below Morne, and heard the whisperings of those that see what others do not. It is *your* counsel that *I* seek."

"We first saw him—or it—at the beginning of summer." The Serpent Lady's voice was soft, and now and then she would pause in her speaking, and pass her hand across the surface of the water, as the canoes bore the travelers northwestward, deeper into the Mire. Ithrazel was aware that as she did so, she was renewing the spells of mists, the light haze of Disvisibility, that lay over the long vessels, and marveled at the way she could move back and forth between the trance of enchantment, and waking life.

"There is a magic that surrounds him that we do not understand, like the magic that surrounds the creatures that have been seen. None of us can descry his whereabouts, neither in water, nor in dreams, nor in fire or crystal or ink. But whether this is because of a power in him, or because the Goddess no longer speaks to us, I do not know. What is it, child?" And she turned her eyes back to Graywillow, on the narrow bench behind Clea.

"The Lady Anamara . . ." began the young woman hesitantly.

And, when the Serpent Lady raised her brows:

"The Goddess Nyellin appears to her in dreams sometimes."

"Anyone can claim to have dreamed about the goddess," said the lady as Ithrazel bit his tongue not to pronounce exactly those words. "Only the goddess herself knows to whom she speaks." Then she closed her eyes again, briefly, and the silence of the Mire settled on them again: endless green calm, and the line of sunlight moving slowly down the faces of the east-looking canyon walls, as the day rose above them.

They traveled in two canoes, swift as water-striders and unerring as they passed from canyon to canyon, leaving the world of the Bright Lords, the world of merchant houses and diamond-sands, behind them in the mist. Like the Black Order, the Brown, and the Red, Ithrazel was aware that the magic of the male shamans was stronger and potentially more violent among the Kindred. But it was the subtler magic of the women that not only surrounded the canoes, but seemed to permeate the air, thicker and thicker as they moved into the Mire, until he could almost feel it, like silk against his skin.

The Lake of Serpents—and the miles of marshland that surrounded it—formed the first frontier of the Reedmire, a great zone of circular depressions within the Mire, like a succession of freshwater inland seas. Whereas the endless plateau of the Mire was crossed with a labyrinth of flooded canyons, the Reedmire, stretching west and slightly south in what seemed to be a huge curve, lay at the level of the canyons' water-table, and its meres were studded with tiny islands, lost in forests of head-high sedge and cattail where the lakes were shallow. Over a hundred round zones of deep water had been charted—many of them by Ithrazel himself. He wondered as he watched the flights of birds that appeared and vanished into the mists, and heard the far-off bodiless voices of the Green Children, how much more of this strange land had been explored since last he'd paddled these mazes . . .

With Anaya, he thought.

With his friend Second Ox of the Ashupik.

One of the voices calling out across the marsh sounded like that of his elder daughter Akuhare. An illusion, he knew.

But even knowing, it hurt.

"The hunters of the Reedmire bands will see him sometimes," the Lady went on in time. "Or they'll find the marks of a single bare foot that might or might not be his. They'll find the remains of kills, eaten raw, but no sign of traps. Nor are their traps robbed, which says magic to me. Sometimes at night they'll hear him screaming."

Clea didn't flinch, but Ithrazel saw by the movement of her head exactly what was in her mind: it was the image that leaped to his own. The square stone bulk of that building in the House of Glass, dark in the dense fog of the night. The spiked iron grille over its doors, double-spiked with the invisible glitter of spells.

The screams that burst from its windows like splattering blood.

"Does it look like a man?" she asked softly.

"It looks like that was what it once was."

"And it has been in the marshes. . . ?"

"Four months," said Neambis. "That we know of."

"And the Night-Gluttons let him alone?"

"It may be only that they have not caught him yet."

The shrine of Farrawen stood on a cone-shaped islet in the center of the Lake of Serpents, ringed by deep water nearly two miles wide. Between the deep water and the shore lay another mile or two of reed-beds. To the west stretched the Reedmire; to the north and east, the plateau of the Mire with its cloaking woods. The Lhogri town of Coiled Serpent had once stood on its shore, shrunken now—to judge by the sparse prickle of its lights through the foggy darkness as the canoes emerged from the long, sloping woods—to barely a village. *Slave-takers,* guessed Ithrazel. Fury stirred in his soul again, like prodded embers.

All my hatred of them then—back in my lifetime, my real lifetime—was for pin-pricks. Baby-slaps, compared to what they have made of this land, these people, now. For the sickening obscenity that is Morne.

Did I somehow look into the future, back then seventy-five years ago, when I decided to do it? Was this what I saw? What decided me?

Did I really think destroying Dey Allias would help?

He shut his eyes for a time, at the thought that he had been that foolish.

But with his eyes shut, he saw the ground beneath that city split, and the fire gush forth.

And in the fire, the rolling balls of tentacles and eyes—demons, he had thought then—the spider-like horrors that had crawled and crept up the hill. The slimy, glistening red many-legged devourers . . .

When he opened his eyes again, the lights of Coiled Serpent had vanished in the mists. A light shone ahead, an apple-seed of gold in the cindery dark, in the place where, long ago, Farrawen had first shown herself to the women of the Lakes.

The shrine itself was a round building, like all such places having four doors, all open to the misty night. The wizard's night-sighted eyes made out three priestesses sitting beside the little stone fountain-house where the goddess's spring bubbled out of the rocks. It hadn't changed.

I've never heard Nyellin speak, Graywillow had said. *It's as if the gods themselves are drawing back . . .*

Drawing back from what?

From the things that first came from the split river-sands that night? The things that seemed to be appearing now, again, in the wake of the zai?

From the rising of the zai?

Can that thing of darkness devour gods? Or only cloud the vision of them?

What kind of faith would it take, to worship a deity who might or might not be there? Whose small, subtle magics might as easily be the result of a spell, as a gift from a god?

A line of meager huts stretched to one side of the shrine, with the steep-pitched roofs characteristic of Lhogri dwellings. Lamplight outlined windows and doors. Ithrazel tried to think of a way to ask if villagers still crossed to do shrine-duty—cutting wood, weaving, working in the gardens, grinding wheat—without revealing the length of time he'd been away, and his question was answered in any case when two women in ordinary dress emerged from the long weaving-room nearby and made their way to the huts, laughter sweet in the gloom.

"Are they slaves?" whispered Hamo. "Like the poor people in Turtle-mere?"

Ithrazel shook his head, and caught his balance on legs long cramped from a day in the canoe. "In my time, at least, the Sisters would ward off mosquitoes and rats from the town, and summon fish from the lakes, and birds from the air. The council of the town voted them a certain number of workers every month, but there was never a shortage of volunteers. In Brownwaith," he added drily, "the settlement where we came into this world, the merchant council in Dey Allias used to contract with us for the same services, but they'd pay us in silver. We used it to buy slaves. I understand that at the beginning—before my time—the Archmage would free those slaves, and then keep them on as paid workers. But too many of them were kidnapped by the refiners and the dealers in the city. We found it easier to sue for their return if they were still slaves."

He remembered Sina, the slave who'd been assigned to his hut and that of Goerk, the wizard who'd lived closest by. Sina had been a quiet little Placne woman from the north coasts who had adored his children, taught his girls the elaborate quillwork in the designs of her people . . . had spoken with hope of her own two sons, who worked—somewhere—in the diggings . . .

And what became of HER?

Out of the darkness—far, far across the lake, like a breath of some terrible disaster—he heard the screaming, and the sound froze his blood. Clea whipped around, eyebrows suddenly dark against a pallor that only Ithrazel could see in the gloom. Graywillow, who had not accompanied them to the House of Glass, clutched at her arm. Madness, despair, agony, like the marrow squeezed from crushing bone . . .

Clea whispered, "Since the coming of summer? Four *months*?"

"Not every night," murmured the Serpent Lady, stepping from the canoe—*she* seemed to feel no cramps, observed Ithrazel drily—and shaking straight her faded robes. "We used to go out seeking him, thinking we must find . . . I don't know what. Bones, blood, shredded remains." She shook her head. "Sometimes he'll scream for hours. Then two days, or a sennight, later, some hunter will glimpse him . . ."

"If it *is* him," said Clea, "making the sound."

"It's him." Ithrazel knew it, to the bottom of his soul. When the others looked at him questioningly, he added, "You'd be surprised how much pain a man can endure, and live."

Clea frowned, thinking he meant the birds.

But he didn't.

Fourteen

They set forth in early morning: Clea, Graywillow, Ithrazel, and a young Lhogri guide named Cat-Tail who knew every inch of the marshes around the lake. Clea had sat up far too late in conversation the night before, first with the chiefs of the Orchid Family and the Pelican Family and other friends among the Kindred, then with young Cat-Tail and with the Lady Neambis. She had spoken little, but had listened to all the Lady—and Cat-Tail, and the other hunters and herb-gatherers of the Mire—had to say about those who had seen the zai, or where it had come from. The deep waters of the canyons and grottoes. The darkness unplumbed, and underlain with the glitter of adamis in its clay-beds.

Clea guessed, in her skin, in her bones, that as Neambis had speculated, she was looking at not several puzzles, but one.

This morning her eyes felt heavy and scratchy, but she noted it only as something to be taken into account and worked with.

Look for the pattern, Rat Bone would tell her, when she'd help him prep for a kill or a heist. *It's always there if you look for it*. And since her visit three nights ago to the House of Glass, she had felt as she'd felt as a Thief's Brat: that she was seeing some pattern whose meaning she couldn't yet quite make out.

The memory of her old mentor made her smile. *Who comes and who goes, and when? What time of the morning do they light the fires? How often do they buy butchers' scraps?* Sitting up on her low pallet bed in one of the servant-huts, she thought about her father, as she had seen him last. Dinner, that had been. Eleven nights ago? Twelve? Dinner before she'd gone up to her rooms in the north wing of the Griffin House, to be helped out of her red velvet gown and its golden over-robe by her ladies—Gabbie, Pennylips, and Slurper, she had privately named them—and put to bed. The moment they were out of the room, of course, she had taken the black and red hose and doublet of one of her father's pages from inside her pillow, armed herself from assorted hidey-holes behind the paneling and under the hearth-bricks, climbed out the window (sliding the bolt into place with a thread behind her—Rat Bone had taught her that trick before she was ten years old), and found one of the palace attics to sleep in. It was little more than a slip of waste-space above the ceiling of the palace armory, but for the past several nights—as the weather had grown cold—she'd been sleeping in attics and cupboards near the palace kitchens, and was wary of setting a pattern.

You never could tell who was watching. Or who was in whose pay.

It was there she'd waked from that dream of her mother's trial, to the knowledge that Graywillow was waiting for her in the stable yard.

Her father had seemed like a golden idol in the lamplight of dinner: gold hair, gold robe, gold and crimson doublet beneath. The black griffin of the House Stylachos embroidered on the breast. More like a prince of one of the noble families of Telmayre than a common-born—albeit extremely wealthy—merchant "king." Ganzareb tar-Azazris, his Master of Swords, who actually *was* of genuine noble blood, sat perforce at the upper table in the hall, clothed in the archaic formal robes of his rank (and the silly hat that nobles of Telmayre were required to wear), the red jewel of the Azazris winking on his brow. The two other Bright Islanders of noble blood who had also been at table that night regarded the Master of Swords as they would have a sister who'd saved the family fortunes by going to work at the Courtyard of a Thousand Ecstatic Cries in the Dockside, and Minos Stylachos with the forced congeniality of the girls there themselves. Their families, Clea knew, were nearly broke and they were negotiating for Shumiel's hand, provided they could get assurances from her father that his controlling interest in the Nightshade Maze diamond-clay concession would pass to her when he died, and not to the mageborn Pendireth.

Did you know about this? Clea wanted to scream at her father across the distance of space and time. *DO you know about this? About Himelkart clinging to the overturned canoe, making signs above the water with the zai hanging in darkness before his eyes? About Pendri lying in the House of Glass?*

About whatever it is, screaming its lungs out in that prison surrounded by spells?

And she heard Rat Bone's voice again in her mind: *Just watch out that you don't go seeing patterns where none exist.*

How do you tell the difference? she had asked.

And he'd grinned at her, bright, broken teeth like his namesake's. *You smell it.*

And she smelled something here, in the tales of things seen and things heard in the mazes beyond the Reedmire.

In the cool light of morning the marshes were silent. The fog had whispered away overnight. Skeins of geese passed overhead, a soft honking and a winnowing of wings. Once she thought she heard the soft voice of a Green Child—whatever those beings actually were—calling what seemed to be her name.

They were in two canoes, barely bigger than a pair of slippers. The waxed leather of their hulls clove the water without a sound. Clea wielded her paddle expertly, following Cat-Tail through the maze of green and buff reed-stems—she was a little surprised to see how adept old Ithrazel was in the little swamp-craft behind the young guide. With a mage in each canoe, their quarry—even if he had magic of a sort—shouldn't be able to sense their coming. In any case he, or it, had been sighted by hunters from time to time.

So he was real, unlike the Green Children, or other illusory things that haunted those flooded lands.

There was a place where he fished, Cat-Tail had told her last night. A shallow pool near the shore of another islet in the marsh. They drifted past the place among the reeds and saw nothing. Moved on, and disembarked on five or six little "oakers," as the former sandbars were called when they built up soil enough to host thick tufts of trees and swamp-laurel. When they came back to the fishing-place again around noon, Clea saw him.

Since the beginning of summer, Serpent Lady had said. Four months. Whatever his coarse, knee-length blue tunic had looked like back in the spring, it was so dirty now, and so tattered, that it seemed more like an animal's faded pelt on the man's bony back. Twigs and mud matted his dark hair and beard. But he was a young man, Clea realized, freezing motionless in her canoe near the pool where he crouched. And he'd been clean-shaven before . . .

Before what?

She watched him, barely breathing. He knelt beside the pool, whispering and muttering, and behind her Clea heard Graywillow's stifled gasp of surprise. *That's how he's survived,* thought Clea as the Wild Man reached unhurriedly down into the pool and took out a fish. He whispered a word to it and wrung its neck as a farmwife would have wrung a chicken's. *He has magic. He uses it to catch them.*

His arms and legs, and the flesh of his lean sides where she could see it through the rips in his tunic, were covered with scabs, old cuts, and gashes, some quite substantial. *Infection would have killed him months ago if he weren't using spells of healing on himself.* But he didn't look healthy, or as if he were taking even the most rudimentary steps to keep himself clean. Animals—even pigs—will be clean if they can, and this man had the look of the dreamsugar-ghosts who wandered the grimy alleyways of the Dockside, the ones whose minds had almost ceased to function. He'd used magic to heal his cuts, but hadn't bothered to wash the blood from the original wounds off his arms and legs. He didn't even brush at the flies that were drawn to it. When he turned his face a little in her direction she saw his eyes were hollow, bruised underneath and the lids stained brown with sleeplessness and fatigue.

The overhanging leaves of the willows along the shore nearly hid the canoes, but the Wild Man jerked his head around with a gasp and ran for the deeper trees of the island. For an instant Clea thought he'd simply disappeared, and perhaps, she thought, if she hadn't been with a White Sister, she would have lost sight of him entirely. But Graywillow called out something, and made a movement of her hand, and Clea drove the canoe to the shore with one stroke and leaped out, and in that same moment the guide Cat-Tail did the same. Cat-Tail and Ithrazel sprang from their canoe, circling to cut the Wild Man off from the side of the islet nearest the main shore; the Wild Man turned, raised his hand, and Ithrazel flung himself at Clea, knocking her sideways off her feet as the damp tangle of creeper and jewel-weed beneath her feet burst into a smoky roar of flame.

"Stay down!" yelled the wizard as she struck out the burning sleeve of her shirt and would have rolled to her feet. "And keep moving!" Then he dodged aside, as what looked like thin blue lightning seared up out of the earth where he had stood. "And get out of the boat!" he shouted to Graywillow, who still sat, paralyzed, in the canoe. "Keep your distance, damn you!" he added, when she would have run, floundering in her wet dress, to Clea's side. "MOVE!"

Clea dodged from tree to tree, keeping low and shouting at the Wild Man to draw his attention away from Graywillow, who had only a very rudimentary notion of evasive action. "Over here, idiot!" she yelled. "Your brother turns tricks on the wharves!"

"Look over there!" shouted Cat-Tail, catching on to the strategy, and the Wild Man, confused, turned his head in the new direction. "There's a dragon behind you!"

"You got your spells wrong, toad-sucker! Water, not fire!" She dodged a spear of blue earth-lightning that burned a gash in her boot. "My sister's dog can do better than that!"

Ithrazel dodged nearer, and Clea could see he'd pushed the adamine shackle down close to his hand, where he could use it to strike the mad creature's flesh.

"Sheep-biter!"

"Cot-quean!"

A roar of flame consumed a tree directly behind the wizard as he dodged, the blast of the spell throwing him to the ground. He rolled, barely evading the lightning.

Clea leaped in, only feet from the Wild Man, dodged back: "Snail-head!"

"Rivan!" shouted Graywillow, emerging suddenly from behind a tree—not dodging, standing still, her hands held up. "Rivan!"

The Wild Man froze, staring at her. Clea and the guide halted where they stood, knowing at once that to startle the creature would call down his next spell on Graywillow, standing before him now, her face pale with shock. Ithrazel, halfway to his feet, seemed to have been turned to stone.

Softly, Graywillow repeated, "Rivan. You are Rivan, aren't you?" She moved a step toward him.

The Wild Man stood as if in a dream, staring at her from those eyes that had not closed in sleep in . . . *How long?*

"We won't hurt you," said Graywillow. "Do you remember me? I'm Graywillow. Eluriel of the White Sisters . . . We used to meet in the marketplace—I was only a novice then. The White Sisters would send me for milk and peaches. Do you remember the peaches, old Miss Didi who sold the peaches that you liked so much? You bought me one, and showed me how to make the wasps dance when they buzzed around over the barrows . . ."

The Wild Man lowered his arms. "Ri . . . van . . ." The words dropped like formless chunks of clay from his lips.

"That's it." Graywillow took another step, held out her hand. "Do you remember now?"

"Ri . . . van . . ." The Wild Man reached out a hand as if to touch her fingers, then stood looking at his own hands, broken nails gummy with filth and fish-blood, as if he had never seen them before.

Then he fell to his knees, clutched his arms around himself as if he feared that if he did not, his bones would wrench themselves apart, and screamed.

And screamed.

And screamed . . .

Graywillow made a move to reach him and Ithrazel flung out one hand, warning her off. Three strides took him to Clea: "Get these off me." He held out his shackled wrists.

She produced her pick-locks and had one of them off in moments, and before he could speak—and she knew he was going to—she sprang to the Wild Man's side and had the spell-saturated blacksteel locked around his wrist before he was aware of her, so great was his agony. When the shackle clicked shut he whirled on her, shrieking in rage, in horror, in fury, seized her by the throat in a maniac's grip. Clea swung her arm over his wrists and dropped her full weight, and even so it was barely enough to break his hold, the filthy nails tearing the flesh of her neck like claws. He struck at her head, still screaming, and Ithrazel and Cat-Tail grabbed his arms, holding with all their strength as he fought them like a roped bull. Clea was about to help them but had to leap back and grab Graywillow, to prevent her from getting into the fray, it being obvious to everyone but herself that the Wild Man—or Rivan, as she had called him . . . as he had called himself—was far past recognizing her.

"Don't!" Graywillow was sobbing. "Don't hurt him!"

Ithrazel swore like a muleteer as Rivan bit him. Clea thrust Graywillow back, said, "You *stay there!*" and sprang into the melee. With both Rivan's arms pinioned it was a matter of moments for her to hook one arm around his throat from behind and choke him into unconsciousness. "Bind him," she ordered, gasping, when he went limp in her grip. Cat-Tail ran back to the canoe for rope.

"Here." Ithrazel thrust his left, still-shackled wrist toward her. His right wrist was ringed with scabs, bruises, and raw flesh left by the blacksteel band. He'd carry the scars for years—*if any of us live that long. . . .*

"One's enough." Clea met the wizard's eyes and saw the flush of rage stain his cheekbones.

But he said nothing. No *I saved your life.* No *Isn't it about time we trusted each other?* No *What do I have to do to prove myself?*

She saw he understood that there was nothing that he could do that would win her trust.

There was nothing anyone could do. Ever.

If in fact his goal simply wasn't to win her trust enough to get an opening that would let him flee.

This was too important. Shifting her glance across to Graywillow's tear-streaked face, Clea had the feeling of having been handed a piece to the puzzle . . . or maybe a piece of another puzzle altogether. "Get him in the canoe," she said. "And let's see what we've got."

Fifteen

H e was one of the Crystal Order," explained Graywillow, later that evening in the Serpent Lady's quarters, when she finally emerged from the small strongroom that had been hurriedly converted into a cell for the man she had called Rivan. Her eyes were reddened from crying and one of them was blacked where Rivan had struck her, when she had insisted— once they had him in the cell—that he be released from all his bonds but the blacksteel shackle on his wrist. At that point, while the small group of men from the village had subdued (and re-bound) the screaming wizard, Clea and Ithrazel—despite the furious silence the old man had maintained toward her all the way back to the Shrine—had traded a single look of perfect understanding: both of them thinking, *I told you so*, but neither about to say it to the weeping Graywillow.

The strongroom lay a foot or so below ground level, all that was possible in these soggy lands. Its walls were stone, low arches supporting the floors above. Across the Shrine compound in the Serpent Lady's quarters, where they now sat around the small stone hearth, they could still hear Rivan's howls.

Night was closing in.

The Lady Neambis poured out tisane for Graywillow, whose hands trembled as she took it. Clea, kneeling behind her friend's low stool, kneaded her shoulders, and felt them tight as twisted rope.

"When I was fourteen—when I first came to the Goddess's shrine in Morne—the Lady Anamara used to send me to the market, as I said," Graywillow went on. "I was new to the city and scared. The district down by the fruit market can be pretty frightening. And I missed my parents, and my sisters, and my village. I missed the sound of the spring behind our house, and the voices of the birds before dawn. Rivan was kind to me. He was from Morne, he said, but he knew what it was to miss all those who were dear to you. He tried to adapt some of the spells of his Order so that a woman could do them, so that *I* could do them, to cheer me."

"Did that work?" Ithrazel sat forward on one of the carved stools, his own small pottery bowl of tisane steaming gently between his cradling hands.

"I've never heard of any of the Crystal Order showing any of their magic to anyone," added Neambis in surprise.

"Not really." Graywillow smiled wanly at the memories. "We did work out a spell to summon butterflies, and to make crickets sing, but they didn't always work. The spells I learned at the Shrine to do the same things actually worked much better. But we did talk about magic, and why men's magic is different from women's. That was seven years ago—just when the magic of the other Orders was beginning to . . . to not work so well . . ." She glanced apologetically at Ithrazel. "Rivan was about twenty-five then, maybe a little older. I asked him why the gods had ceased speaking—he said he didn't know. And he seemed troubled about it. When I learned a little more, and spent more time in study, I didn't go to the market so often, and so we no longer met."

She fell silent then, and looked for a time down into her tea. Grieving—Clea could see it in her eyes as she came around and took her own stool beside her friend—for the man they'd literally dragged up from the canoes to the strongroom that afternoon. On Clea's other side, Ithrazel rubbed absently at the blacksteel shackle still locked around his left wrist. He had, she saw, begged a scrap of linen cloth from somewhere, to poke between the metal and his flesh. His right wrist, freed now of the bond, was bandaged, though Clea had seen far worse galls in her own days in her father's dungeon. At least he didn't have to worry about rats—or the huge brown roaches of the sewers—sneaking up to chew on the raw flesh while he slept.

One reason they'd tied Rivan was to keep him from tearing at the black metal circlet on his wrist. He'd already ripped open the flesh of his fingertips doing that, and of his lips, biting at the metal as well. He hadn't even pleaded—as would any person she'd ever encountered in her life—*Get it off, get it off . . .*

Just shrieked like an animal.

CAN he speak? He had seemed to know his name . . .

"Going by the length of his hair," she said after a time, "and by his beard, he looks like it's been since spring. That's shortly after the first attack of the zai on Sandmire."

"Could this . . . this *zai* . . . have done that?" The Lady glanced across the hearth at her. "Eaten his mind?" Her eyes went to Ithrazel as she spoke, to the blacksteel spancel still on his right wrist.

Another question, Clea guessed . . . which her own look of query would only have made more puzzling to the old priestess. *To say nothing of whatever Cat-Tail had to say about this afternoon's adventures . . .*

Ithrazel growled, "What're you looking at me for, girl? I know no more of this thing than you do." But there was a slight hesitation in his words, and after a moment he added, "It doesn't seem to have snacked on anybody else's wits at Turtlemere."

"The people at Turtlemere weren't mages." The Serpent Lady folded her small, thin fingers like a stack of ivory spindles and studied him with narrowed eyes.

"No, but Himelkart is a mage," said Clea. "And a Crystal Mage at that, of the same Order as Rivan. He didn't seem to have his mind stripped away, from facing this thing down . . . from sending it away . . ." She frowned. "Although it's true I haven't seen him since."

"But your brother has." Firelight made gold points in the wizard's eyes. "And he didn't notice anything amiss."

His head turned slightly, still listening to Rivan's shrieks as he rubbed his own galled wrists.

"And the thing obviously doesn't eat *magic*, as such," Clea said thoughtfully. "Rivan still has power."

"Magic lies within the flesh," murmured Ithrazel. "In the blood, in the bone-marrow . . . Teaching—spells—sourcing power from the earth or the stars or the gods—merely focuses it."

Neambis' faded gray-gold glance shot across at him again, then back, questioning, to Clea. "Or it did," the old woman said. "Before the magic of men—of *most* men—began to shift and change."

"Could it be . . . shock?" Hamo, who had up till this moment sat without speaking on the ground beside the hearth, spoke up now. "Something he saw? Something that happened to him? Star of the Ghoras said that sometimes wizards come out to join your father's men." He glanced up at Clea, and in his blue eyes she saw that he'd been listening to all the talk, taking it in and sorting it in his mind as he'd have sorted any peril faced by his herds back home. She realized with a little flush of shame that because he was a shepherd, and in love with her, she'd assumed he was stupid. Now she saw that this wasn't the case.

"It might not have been these zai, you know," he added. "Those things—those Gluttons—that attacked us on the road . . . people say they've never seen such things before. Other creatures—the web-weavers Green Jade spoke of, the ghaist-spiders . . . or others that no one yet has seen. They might eat minds like that. Eat souls, and leave the magic in the flesh, so the man becomes like . . . like a child playing with a sharp knife."

"And it could be," suggested Graywillow, "that Rivan is in such pain from the blacksteel's spells on his wrist that he can't tell us what's going on, or what he knows . . ."

"I am *not*," retorted Clea, "going to have an insane wizard free to throw fire and lightning around at whatever happens to frighten him."

Ithrazel said "Hmph," so softly that only she—and perhaps the Lady Neambis—heard.

"Will you try to talk to him tomorrow?" She turned to look at the old man. "He's got to quiet down sometime."

"What makes you think so? I'll try," he added, in a kinder tone. "But judging from his behavior before you got the shackle on him, I'm not sure there's anything there to speak *to*. And I'm not at all certain," he added as they rose from their finished tisane and took up candles to guide them to their huts through the dense, coal-black fog that had risen outside from the marshes, "that the answer is as simple as some creature—this zai, or the Night-Gluttons—or indeed the things your boyfriend Liver-Eater hinted at in the Tunnels—devouring Rivan's mind. I think there's something else going on. I just don't know what."

Having stood in the foggy darkness of the House of Glass and listened to the shrieks drifting from the barred windows above her, Clea felt inclined to agree with him. Yet the thought of a creature—either the zai, or something akin to the Night-Gluttons, or something unheard-of—that could rip away the mind and leave the body to live on, mindless, terrified her. *Worse than mindless*, she thought, lying awake in the darkness of the hut she shared with Graywillow. She saw again the filthy form hunched over the pool, crusted with mud and blood, twisting the heads of the fish that it was going to eat raw . . .

God's braies, what if they've summoned something at the House of Glass that does this?

But he'd known his own name, for a few moments at least.

That, she thought, *was the worst . . .*

Is that what they feed the zai? she wondered. *But Himelkart wasn't taken that way. How much do THEY know about the zai, if they're still looking for them here?*

What has changed? she asked herself for the hundredth time. *Why hasn't this happened before?*

In the morning Rivan was still screaming, the sounds hoarse and raw. Near noon his cries sank, but when Clea and Ithrazel descended the stone steps to the shallow strongroom beneath the Shrine's tower they could hear, through the door, a kind of endless, keening whine on a single note, like the wail of a dying dog. The watcher outside—volunteers from the village, at the Serpent Lady's request, had sat through the night to make sure Rivan did himself no harm—got to his feet looking pale and ill. "I had to bind him close, m'lady," the man said, touching his breast in respect, "to keep him from beating his head on the wall. It went to my heart to do it, poor soul. But I truly think he'd have killed himself, else."

Rivan lay trussed on the floor, hands bound behind him and ankles tied, and still there was blood on his forehead and glistening in his black hair. Spots of it blotted the stone floor all around him. His eyes moved with the lamp flame Clea carried in, and went to her face, then to Ithrazel's. His wailing didn't stop or change.

Ithrazel knelt, and laid a hand on the bound man's shoulder. Rivan jerked and twitched, and the older mage immediately withdrew his touch. "Rivan?" he said gently. "Rivan, can you hear me?"

Clea shivered. The man huddled before her on the floor reminded her horribly of the men and women she'd seen in the deeper cells of her father's prisons, the ones who'd been down there for so long they no longer recalled their own names, or how to speak when she'd try to whisper comfort to them. Why her father—or her grandfather before him, who by all accounts was ten times more uncaring and cruel—didn't simply kill them, she'd never understood. Did he—or his father—think the political situation might change, and they might have to produce the prisoners at some time in the future? Or was continuing alive in that state part of their punishment, for whatever it was her father considered they had done?

Quietly, she stepped to the cell's doorway and whispered to the watcher, "Is there water?"

The man handed her a gourd. "I tried earlier and he wasn't having any."

"I'll try again."

Ithrazel glanced back as she re-entered the little room and his eyes thanked her for getting something he'd been about to ask for. Together they knelt by Rivan's side. "Can you hear me?" asked the old man. "Do you know where you are?" He held Rivan's head and put the gourd to his lips; the water dribbled out untasted to the floor. "Can you tell me what happened? What you saw?"

But Rivan bucked violently against his touch, and when Ithrazel tried to use a little of the water to wet the young man's face, tried to roll and scooch himself away. Patiently, with infinite care, Ithrazel remained at Rivan's side until the sun was halfway down to the tops of the western trees, seldom speaking now but occasionally making the effort to give him water, or to bathe his face.

Rivan never stopped wailing, a sound that grew weaker as the afternoon wore on. "You don't have to stay," Ithrazel said to her at one point, and Clea, sitting against the wall with knees drawn up, shook her head.

"I'm all right."

When they finally left the strongroom, and climbed the few steps to the tower's outer door, Clea asked softly, "Do we let him go?"

"I hate to." For the first time, she heard doubt, compassion, and pain for another in the old man's voice. The man he had been, she thought, seventy-five years ago, before he had done what he did . . . "If he stumbles into any of the New Order, out in the Mire, I think they'll just drag him back into captivity in the House of Glass, don't you?"

"That's who's up there, isn't it? In the House of Glass?" They stopped in the low doorway, the shadow of the stumpy strongroom tower falling before them halfway across the shrine compound to where the shrine itself stood, shabby and weathered in the westering light. "Others like him?"

"I don't really see who else it would be," said the wizard. "I can't see them keeping a non-mage alive. Probably not even one of the other Orders. It sounds horrible to say so but I'm deeply curious as to what would happen if the zai came on him in the Mire. Whether it would devour him, or . . . or what. But I can't . . ." He hesitated.

A woman—a lesser novice, by her gown—emerged from the shrine and hurried across to the line of huts where the priestesses lived; through the open archways of the shrine itself Clea could see two others bending over the waters of the fountain, their heads together. At the Shrine of Kissare, she'd seen the Ladies of the White Order talking to one another through the waters of the goddess's fountains. *News from somewhere?*

"I know," she answered him. "I wonder that, too. Seeing the way it killed in Turtlemere—wildly, as if maddened itself. But I wouldn't do that to a dog, or a goat. I could bring myself to do it to a cage full of rats . . ."

Ithrazel grinned, an expression that quickly faded.

"I think he'll die if we keep him," she finished simply.

"I think you're right."

Neambis emerged from one of the huts, crossed back toward the shrine while the novice hurried toward the refectory.

"Do you have any spells that would help him?" she asked, meeting the old man's eyes. "Bring him back? Or that would at least tell whether he's . . . he's alive in there, or not?"

It was a long time before Ithrazel answered her. Then he said, "No. Looking into his eyes—looking into his mind—I see nothing. And I doubt I would see more were I free." He gestured, slightly, with his chained wrist.

"What about drugs? I don't mean dreamsugar, or magic mushrooms, but poppy, maybe, that would dull his mind down to the point that if he's merely . . . merely being held prisoner in there by something, he can see past it . . ."

"We can try." The old man sighed. "At least it might numb him to the point where he could be fed and given water. The Lady—"

He broke off as Hamo and Graywillow emerged from the refectory—the novice behind them—and hurried across the open ground of the shrine compound toward them, Graywillow's white gown a billowing cloud behind her in the sunlight.

"Clea—!"

"My lady—!"

It was news. From one of the other Shrines.

Or someone is seeking me . . .

Pendri . . .

Clea cursed, and crossed the compound at a run.

Sixteen

The woman who came to the shrine of Gingul, on the Gray Hills above the Denzerai, was masked." The Lady Neambis sat on a stone seat in the circular shrine, and held her hand out over the waters that bubbled in the little basin of the fountain-house, the place where Farrawen had once been wont to speak to those who served her. The other two priestesses had brought up kneeling-mats for Clea and her companions. The smell of cooking fires drifted through the open archways, and with it the green pong of the marshes, the clammy scents of mist and vegetative decay. The stillness there was like the blessing of the gods.

"She gave the Lady there—Winterflower, who is of our order—a great deal of gold, and asked that she seek among us for word of you. A matter of great urgency, she said."

"Did she give a name?"

"Snowball."

And Clea said, "Ah."

"She said that the emperor has sent an embassy, concerning a child you spoke of at the bedside of your brother." The Lady half-closed her eyes, her head tilted a little as she brought back the words. "The Darkland Council has been summoned to see this child's powers, on the day of the full moon, on the meadow of the Tarnweald, at the hour of noon."

Clea cursed, and the Lady half-raised a finger, for silence.

"The Shrine of Nyellin—this Mistress Snowball said—was yesterday offered half the profits of the Cottonwood Canyon dredging operations—"

"I take it the dredging concession on this Cottonwood Canyon belongs to the House Vrykos?" Ithrazel inquired.

"Pigs eat his children. He's trying to buy their help—"

The Lady lifted another finger. "That same day mages of the Black Order, the Brown, and the Red, in different parts of the city, paid their debts and closed up their houses—"

"Pigs swallow them all sideways. The Vrykos are planning a fraud."

Neambis's sapphire eyes opened under the white fringe of lashes. "She asks your counsel," she concluded. "She is in the Gray Hills, she says."

"That'll be at Sunmist," said Clea. "That's the manor my father gave her when he decided she was legitimate after all. It used to be my mother's. It's only a few hours' ride from there to the Gingul Shrine." It was like Shumiel, she reflected wearily, to go through the whole charade of masks and false names and then practically announce who she really was by her location.

"And she said that your brother is safe, and has returned to your father's house."

"Thanks be to Nyellin." Graywillow kissed her knuckle in Blessing.

"For all the good that's likely to do anyone," remarked Clea, "if Heshek and his minions are free to walk in and out of Father's house as if they owned the place. Thank you." She rose from her mat, knelt again at the Lady's feet, and touched her forehead to the ground. "Thank you more than I can say. The more so because I know this isn't something you usually do— and I want to slap my sister, for treating you and your sisters like messengers, and the goddesses like pageboys."

Neambis smiled, and reached down to touch Clea's bowed, red-gold head. "Many years ago," she said, "I asked your grandfather if there was anything I could do for him. For him, and for those that he sought to help, in Morne, and in the dredging-pits, and all through the coasts of the Twilight Land where the Easterlings have put their feet. He said, 'Only stay true to the ways of our people, that the Kindred may have a refuge that no magic of the Bright Lords can touch.'"

Light and strong as a cat's paw, the small hand moved to Clea's shoulder, raising her up before the stone seat carved with serpents, the whispering water of the fountain in its basin.

"I have watched you, Clyaris. Here in the waters of the Reedmire, I have heard how you have helped our Kindred in Morne—how you've tried to talk your father into making laws to protect the dredgers, how you've hidden those who escaped and arranged to give food to those who are hungry. How you've met with the councils of the Kindred in the Dockside and the barracks, and then sworn to your father that no such councils exist . . ." And she smiled, at Clea's startled look.

"That's nothing," protested Clea, as embarrassed as if she'd been caught kissing a baby. "I *lived* on the Dockside. I know what it's like down there. Anybody would—"

"Not anybody," returned the old lady. "Not your father, certainly. Or the merchant lords of the Darklands Council, whose wars with one another can bode only ill for those they enslave. This is the favor I owe to your grandfather. Go with the blessings of the Lady of the Rain and the Waters."

"You're not really going to walk into the lady Shumiel's house to 'counsel' her, are you?" asked Graywillow worriedly as they stepped out into the gold slant of the misty afternoon.

Clea shook her head. "So His Majesty's looking into the possibility that there's a mage afoot whose magic hasn't gone askew, is he? One who's *not* one of the Crystal Order? I wondered when that would happen." She thrust her hands into her swordbelt, estimating how long it would take them— with good rowers—to return to Morne. "And the Darkland Council as well, by the sound of it. The Lady is right: whatever the Vrykos are up to, buying the help of the older orders, it's not going to be good for anybody who works in the dredging-pits. To say nothing of what it might push Heshek and Himelkart into doing with Pendri." She turned to Ithrazel. "Would having three wizards of three different orders working the same spell preclude it from going awry?"

"Why ask me? I'm only your old Uncle Iohan, who can't be trusted off his chain. I should think it would." His scrubby brows drew together. "It's a deuced clever idea, anyway—not that I think for a moment the New Mages will be far away. There's sure to be a hell of a crowd, and even if your father's enemies have got members of the Old Orders watching for them, there'll be just too many people to keep track of. Some will slip through. If your sister's telling the truth," he added, with a glance back toward the shrine.

"Why wouldn't she be?" Hamo looked disconcerted at this display of mistrust.

"You speak like a man fortunate in his sisters." Ithrazel frowned, considering. Clea wondered if it had crossed his mind—as it had hers—that 'Mistress Snowball' might not be Shumiel at all. Or that Shumiel might be working for her father . . . or the Vrykos . . . or Heshek.

She'd certainly sell me to the diggings for a chance to go back to Telmayre and marry into the nobility there . . .

Maybe Pendri as well.

The wizard went on, "I'm not sure how our baby-faced friends can disrupt the demonstration without it becoming obvious that that's what they're doing, but if the emperor—who would that be, now?—thinks they're getting too big for their boots, it might explain why they're so eager to tame this zai."

"Mesismardan son of the Holy Uthu—"

"*Mesismardan?*" The old man's brows shot up. "Mesismardan had just been enthroned—son of *Uthu*? I was at the ceremony! He must be . . ."

"He's over ninety." Clea's voice was dry. "His son Nadinahi is sixty-something, and getting impatient, I expect . . . The Crystal Mages are unsurpassed healers—you saw that when they cured Pendri. Half the Great Lords back on Telmayre are being kept alive by their spells, into their tenth and eleventh decades. No surprise they're popular with His Majesty, and own more adamis concessions than any merchant house. But if Father's letting himself be used as a catspaw in a war between the orders of the mages—"

"It will be no more than he deserves."

Clea's lips tightened as she met the old man's tawny eyes. Less than an hour ago, in the underground cell with Rivan, and standing in the doorway of the stumpy tower, she had felt a sense of unity with him, almost friendship, seeing for the first time his gentleness. Now the ruin of Dey Allias returned to her mind, the remembrance of death that still clung to that charred desolation. "Nevertheless"—her voice was like steel—"you will come with me to Morne and help me."

"I'll come with you," he returned, "because I can't very well do otherwise, can I?"

"And you'll help me for the same reason."

"So that your father can win the squabble over who gets to make slaves of people whose magic can't stand up against the wizardry of the Bright Islands?" Contempt gleamed in his tone.

"So that my brother doesn't get killed. So that I don't get killed. That's usually what happens in power struggles like this. And so that maybe I can figure out what Heshek and his . . . his *minions* . . . are up to, before a whole lot more people get killed, if it turns out they can't actually control the zai as well as they think they can."

"I agree that this Heshek sounds like a dangerous fool," retorted the wizard. "And your brother seems to be a perfectly nice boy whom I'd be sorry to see come to harm. But myself, I'd hand your House Vrykos a stick of firewood to brain you with."

Turning, he stalked away across the compound toward the line of huts where the Shrine's guests were housed.

To pack, Clea hoped, fighting down the urge to throw a rock at his retreating back. They had a long night's travel ahead.

She sought out the Lady of the Shrine two hours later, the goddess's pool now ringed with a circle of candle flame, gold in the indigo dusk. The Serpent Lady's thin body rocked gently back and forth with her silent prayer, murmured in the ancient language of the Ancestors of the Ancestors, who held the Twilight Lands before the Lhogri and the Ghoras, the Placne, and the Ashupik, and all the other kinships of the lands moved down from the north and west. *Eighteen years . . .*

Standing under the open arch of the shrine door, she wondered which god it had been who appeared that last time, fifteen years ago, and to whom?

And how long had it been since the old woman before her had even heard the voice of Farrawen in her dreams?

Are the gods dead? The magic of women was supposed to come from the gods—it was their gift. So they had to be alive somewhere. *Don't they?*

On the other hand, the blacksteel sword she wore at her hip, and the blacksteel pick-locks that jingled softly in her pocket, had been gifts from Rat Bone before he'd been hanged. And when the hangman had cut that poor skinny body from the gallows in the Gatehouse Square, where had Rat Bone—the real Rat Bone, the man who'd fed her with scraps from his own food and taught her a trade (as he'd said) *that you can make your livin' at*—where had Rat Bone been then?

The White Ladies at the shrine of Tianis, cold-faced god of the dead, in their hollow in the Gray Hills, had had no answer for her when she'd gone to ask them. From the age of six she'd lived around corpses, spoken daily with the wounded and sick whom she knew would never recover, first in the prison, then in the Dockside. The comforting stories that Shumiel, and her own ladies-in-waiting at the Griffin House, told about Nie the Mother Goddess taking the souls of the dead (but only the good ones) into her arms and heart, meant little to her.

The pick-locks, and the sword, still worked perfectly well, though the maggots that had eaten Rat Bone's flesh had long ago themselves been devoured by birds. His bones were mixed with river mud. *There is no Rat Bone anymore.*

So why do I feel what I feel?

And why can't I put it aside?

He'd tell me to.

"Lady," she said, when Neambis turned in the candlelight. "Thank you for putting a canoe at our disposal, and rowers—the more so since I think the way will be very dangerous back to the city. I already owe you so much it's ridiculous to suppose I'll ever be able to repay you. But if I live to come into any inheritance whatsoever, I swear to you I'll try." She knelt in a deep obeisance, and again touched her shining head to the earth.

"The waxing moon will look down on you tonight." The small hand, short-fingered like a wrinkled child's, rested on her hair. "You have the reputation of caring for those who serve you, Clyaris, daughter of Rethiel. Your debt I transfer to the people of the Mire. See that you pay as much of it as you can to them. Is there anything else that I can help you with?"

"Just to ask that your rowers take us first to the shrine of Gingul, above the Denzerai—"

"Where you left all that money?" The old woman smiled as Clea looked up at her in surprise and some annoyance. She thought she'd hidden the gold better than that. "The statue you contributed to the shrine last year is a lovely one, but our sisters at the shrine all remarked on its weight. I have that much gold, and more, here in the Lady's treasure-house—the strong-room that we cleared for your poor guest. He sleeps now under poppy, they tell me, but even as he dozed away he would not or could not speak. I fear the mind is gone. I see nothing in his eyes."

"Care for him," said Clea, "nevertheless. If we set him free, I fear what would become of him, should the Crystal Order find him."

"I will care for him. And I will pray for him to Farrawen of the Rains, under whose care he now rests." And, when Clea made no reply to that, the Serpent Lady added, "Because she has not spoken to me—because no god has spoken to any of us, in either Sisterhood, for many years now—it does not mean they cannot hear our prayers. Nor does it mean they do not answer."

Morning dawned foggy, after a night that remained clear until just before dawn. By then they were in the worked portion of the Nightshade Maze, as that tract of the Mire was called, a vast network of narrow canyons that lay so close together that the lands in between seemed like islands, the largest barely a dozen square miles in area and the smallest scarcely bigger than a good-sized farm. Farther south the canyons were fewer, and the land between them wider, useless for the purposes of dredging. It had been

farmland once, before the slave-takers struck the little towns and villages of
the Ashupik and carried them off to work the canyons. This less-valuable
land had been consigned to the Vrykos, the Shiamat, the Othume.

"But none of it comes up to what the Stylachos have," she whispered to
Ithrazel, while the paddlers guided the boats like floating leaves between
the walls of vine-draped rock. "And my father and grandfather bought up
the debts of so many of the Great Houses of Telmayre that Father wields
incredible power back home, for all that they won't admit it. It may be
another reason the emperor's looking for some way to strengthen the
Vrykos."

"And so your father's looking for a way to fight back." Ithrazel sniffed.
"Using Heshek and the Order—maybe using the zai. This is sounding better
and better."

Sometimes they passed through canyons that Clea could have spanned
with her arms, and the trees on the land above them twined their branches
seventy or a hundred feet over their heads; sometimes the waterways lay like
shining roads in the moonlight, fifty yards from wall to wall. Clea couldn't
suppress an inward shiver every time they passed a cave-mouth, like eyes
ten or a dozen or two-score feet above the surface of the water, or round
black mouths at the waterline, grottoes like the one in which she had seen
the zai rise from depths incalculable. She kept her tone brisk and her man-
ner off-hand before the paddlers, and before those who depended on her:
Graywillow, Hamo, the old man who sat cynical and largely unspeaking on
the bench behind her, watching the banks.

The destroyer of Dey Allias.

The man who had so hated what his people—*their* people—had done
to the Kindred of these lands that he'd apparently been willing to kill thousands of Darklander workers and slaves in the Marble City in order to stamp
out the power of their enslavers.

And there was nothing to tell her—in eight days of travel at his side—
whether he'd do so again.

That horrifying spell of destruction spoke of tremendous power . . .
seventy-five years ago. *Is that power in him still? Enough to go up against the
Crystal Mages?* And though he spoke of his willingness to track down the zai
and solve the terrible riddle of their arising, she sensed within him deeper
secrets, deeper power, impenetrable as a nodule of blacksteel. It was as if
she carried an enchanted dagger, like the heroine of one of the romances
Shumiel was so fond of, a weapon that, once drawn, would unleash events
unpredictable and unthinkable.

But now and then the moon would catch in his eyes, or outline the furrows that seamed his tired face—bitterness, anger, and the unfathomed loneliness of a stranger in an utterly alien land.

Like myself.

And she didn't know what to think.

In the small hours of the morning, as the fog began to rise from the waters to conceal the boats, they began to pass the wharves, bucket-chains, and treadwheels of Stylachos dredging-stations. Lines of barges, each bearing the sign of the Black Griffin, tied under dozing guards. Cressets burned like bleared eyes through the darkness. More lights, high at the top of the canyon, showed where villages stood, like Turtlemere surrounded by wooden palisades and guarded by locked gates. Clea saw Ithrazel's glance pick those out, and his nostrils twitched, as if he smelled even here the stink of Morne.

At sunrise they rested, in the deserted diggings in an enormous grotto that had been one of the first underwater sites claimed by House Stylachos under Clea's grandfather. It had yielded thousands of tons of diamond-clay over four decades, and had only given out a few years ago. The dredging platforms there were permanent, built on pilings from the grotto's relatively shallow floor. The paddlers set guards and spread their bedrolls in the little buildings that still remained on the platforms; ate cold pemmican and cornbread, lest even a whiff of smoke issue from the cave's mouth and alert the local garrisons to their presence. Clea walked the entire platform, made sure that sentries were posted at the grotto mouth and a dozen yards up the canyon outside, and ate a sparing meal with the paddlers, joking with them to keep everyone's spirits up.

Ithrazel, she saw, had lain down to sleep not in one of the buildings, but near the edge of the platform, overlooking the black water. She recalled the dark surge of the zai passing beneath her feet underwater and shivered at the sight.

"I've tried to get him to come indoors," murmured Hamo's voice at her elbow. She glanced over her shoulder at the tall young man who had walked up to her so softly on the creaking old platform boards. "After what the Serpent Lady said about the zai rising out of the waters of a cave like this, and what you've told me . . ." He winced, as if the thought of it made him grow cold. "He said he wants to listen, down into the water, for the coming of such a danger."

"He needs to sleep."

"He doesn't sleep," said the shepherd. "Not very well, anyway. Sometimes he cries out a name—I think his wife's. Sometimes he weeps." He folded his arms, a heavy swell of muscle under the muted gold leather of a Ghoras hunting-shirt. "I know the spancel hurts him," he added, and touched his wrist, but Clea made a slight gesture, *We're not going to argue about that now.*

"Did he ever speak to you of who he was—of what he did—before? When you were a child?"

The shepherd shook his head. "I didn't . . . People in the village said he was a god, being punished for some horrible deed by the other gods. Usually by the time I'd get up to him—in the evening, when the birds were gone—it was almost dark, and I had to get my father's sheep back to fold. And he was so badly . . . badly torn, almost ripped to pieces . . ." His face tightened with horror and pity at the memory. "Many times when I got up there, I thought that he was dead, until he would move his head a little, and try to speak. Father would beat me, for bringing the sheep back late," he added, as matter-of-fact as Clea was when she'd speak to Graywillow of living in her father's dungeons, or learning to burgle houses. "I told Father why once, and he beat me worse, and said I must never go up there again. He said that the man on the crag was bad luck, and he didn't want the bad luck coming down on himself or his sheep."

Clea gave a little sniff of laughter. "He was sure right about bad luck coming to *you* from it."

And Hamo half-smiled, his eyes on her face, and shook his head. But all he said was, "What will your father do if his men catch us?"

She looked up at him—he stood half a head taller than she, a rarity among men. The daylight outside reflected in the water and glimmered in his blue eyes. "Don't let his men catch you," she said. "Run away and hide in the woods. If we're taken on the water, go overboard and swim for a cave like this one. *Do not* be taken . . ."

Hamo shook his head again, dismissing that whole aspect of the subject. "What will he do to you?"

It was in her heart to say, *Nothing. A few days under house arrest, is all* . . . because she saw in Hamo's eyes and the way he stood, and heard in his voice, that Graywillow's wretched love-spell was as strong as ever. *If I tell him, he'll get himself killed . . .*

But she guessed, too, that though he was illiterate as his own sheep and had clearly never seen a city before, he was a judge of people. He would hear the lie in her voice.

So she spoke the truth, the real truth. "The truth is that I don't know," she said. "My father fears the tribes. He knows they look on me as one of them. He knows that some of them hope I'll unite the Twilight Kindred and lead them against him, against the Bright Lords. I've sworn to him a dozen times that I'm loyal to him and to the emperor, and it would be madness—total insanity—for the tribes to rise against the Lords of the Bright Islands, with or without me leading them. They'd be wiped out and I know it. The magic of their shamans could never stand up to . . . to ours."

Ours? Theirs? She almost couldn't speak the word.

"But he fears it. And the Crystal Mages fear it even more."

"Why?" His brows knit. "They're . . . *mages*. And the Crystal Mages are the only mages whose power is still reliable. Everyone—even the tribesmen in town—depend on them for healing. What do they have to fear?"

"Disruption," said Clea promptly. "Not getting shipments of adamis. They own some of the mines in the Bright Islands, but not nearly as many as they do here. I suspect—and I haven't any proof of this except the huge increases in everybody's shipments over the past six years—I suspect that most of the adamis mines in Telmayre and the islands around it are played out. It's mined there, deep in the rocks—they have to pump constantly to keep the mines from flooding. And all but a few of the islands have been deforested from refining the ore to blacksteel or white-steel or adamine. Up in Aktas, the Vrykos make about a quarter of their revenues shipping tim-ber back to the islands, as well as adamine. Timber just to burn."

The young man gazed at her, as if struggling to believe. "They can't use anything else instead?"

"Beats me. I don't think so. Both Graywillow and the old man have told me that their power is *sourced* from adamine, the way Ithrazel's is sourced in the earth, and Graywillow gets hers from the gods, wherever and what-ever the hell *they* really are. I'm not a mage and I have no idea about these things, but I do know that the Crystal Order's spells *depend* on adamine. It may be the reason their magic hasn't begun to fail. Sometimes I wonder if it's the reason that everybody else's *has*."

"Even that of the Ladies?" His big hand moved a little, as if he struggled even to find words for the idea. "Is the adamine the reason that the . . . the gods are in retreat?"

"I don't know. But what I do know, is that even a short disruption of shipments of the stuff might leave them open to some kind of counterattack from the mages of the other orders: the Black, the Brown, and the Red."

"Would they *do* that?" He sounded aghast. "Attack other wizards—"

"Again, beats me. But the Crystal Order *can't* let the tribes rise here. If they can get rid of me by marrying me off to some noble house in the Bright

Islands, they'll do that. But the Great Houses there—the real, land-holding aristocrats—are pretty snooty. They won't even offer for a legitimate, well-bred, brainless poppet daughter of a Merchant House unless they're really hard up for cash, much less the might-be bastard of an Ashupik witch."

She shrugged. "So to answer your question," she concluded, "I really, honestly don't know whether my father would believe me if I told him I didn't come back because I'd been warned that people at his court were trying to have me killed. And at this point I don't know if Ganzareb—his sword-master—and his guards are working completely for him, or for Heshek. If I were captured, I honestly don't know to whom I'd be taken. But whoever it is," she added, "I'm pretty sure that whoever I'm captured *with* is going to be put to the sword out of hand. So if we're outnumbered—you run for it."

"I won't desert you."

"You'll desert me because that's an order, soldier. I'm giving it to you now, since I'll probably have other things on my mind if it happens. I might survive. You won't."

"I don't want to survive you." He looked into her eyes as he said it, and though he spoke quietly, he said it with his soul.

You damn silly lummox, it's a SPELL . . . Don't get yourself killed over a cantrip that I was stupid enough and vain enough to turn to because I needed muscle!

"Ithrazel has the same orders," said Clea—a lie, but a safe one, since she knew damn well the wizard wasn't going to die on her behalf. "So does Graywillow. Together the three of you can get me out of whatever mess I might be in, *later*. But not if you're dead in a ten-to-one fight. And not if someone can get to me by threatening you. This is not about loyalty, Hamo. It's not even about love. It's about timing. All right?"

She moved her head as he tried to turn his eyes aside from hers.

He mumbled unwillingly, "All right."

Seventeen

S ee anything?"

Ithrazel leaned his elbows on the projecting root of the tree behind which they lay. To the west and south, the ground dipped away toward the meadows where the Tarn River flowed into the Greenflood. He adjusted the focus on the mariner's glass Clea had lent him. "Yes," he murmured. "Oh yes."

The open meadowland called the Tarnweald had been chosen, presumably, because, as he had said to Clea three days previously at Farrawen's shrine, there would almost certainly be an enormous crowd gathered to watch this miracle-child, this mage-baby, of the House Vrykos—*Wonder what had happened to oust them from the stranglehold they'd once had on the Darklander Council?*—demonstrate that reliable magic was not the sole province of the Crystal Order. Eighty years ago, the Tarnweald had been the chief grazing-ground for the herds of the half-dozen little Ashupik villages strung out between the little river and the great one, situated as it was above the usual level of the winter floods. Clumps of water-laurels grew along the margin where the land dipped to the river's thickly wooded bed itself, but the oaks that had dotted the meadow—and the woods that had cloaked the Gray Hills beyond it—were gone. Sacrificed to the insatiable fires of Morne's refineries, and to the hearths of its teeming population. The land looked shorn and scrubby in the cold blue-white moonlight, like the dishonored and beaten corpse of a woman once beautiful and loved.

This made it almost impossible to hide in, unless one happened to be a wizard—or at least a wizard who didn't have a ring of spell-soaked blacksteel locked around his left wrist. It would be equally difficult for whoever might want to sneak up and observe the meadow without being seen. Approaching the Tarnweald through the hills on horses they'd acquired from the very small shrine of Gingul, goddess of mice, above the Denzerai, they had seen no one in the meadow in the gathering twilight. Nevertheless, Clea had insisted on the long process of circling the area, scouting for tracks.

They had found them. Fresh, three men who moved over rough and muddy terrain with the lightness of the young. By that time it had been too dark for those not mageborn to see accurately by moonlight.

The sky was clear, the new-risen moon bright, but Ithrazel doubted that either Clea or Hamo could have seen the men moving about the meadow. Something about their movements—kneeling, rising, moving a little distance; kneeling, rising again—said *Wizard*.

Even with the glass he could discern little beyond dark cloaks.

"It looks as though they're putting spells into the ground."

"They can't think that Heshek isn't going to have Himelkart come out and check the meadow beforehand," objected Graywillow.

"It's certainly what I'd do," agreed Ithrazel. "Spells may have changed since my lifetime here—before this twisting, this mutability, set in, I mean." He lowered the slim brass tube. "One of the Old Orders may have experimented with magics to circumvent this . . . this whatever-it-is . . . and come up with a means of hiding a spell-mark or sigil from the eyes of other wizards. It may be how they mean to fake reliable magic to impress Mesismardan's ambassador."

"Could that work?" Graywillow edged nearer, looking like a pretty boy in the hunting-shirt and leggings of the Mire tribes, her dark hair braided down her back.

Ithrazel shrugged. "I shouldn't care to try it. In my own day, the great mages of the New Order—Gerodare Starknife and Tarronis Zartoreth— were gifted with deep sight indeed. Machodan Indigo could tell which mage had drawn a sigil by passing his hand over the signs. Sometimes only by touching the walls of the room. If there's fakery being done, I shouldn't like to get on the wrong side of the people who wrote the spells that defend that prison of theirs in the House of Glass."

They fell silent then—the brief discussion had been conducted in whispers less noticeable than the rustle of the laurel-leaves above their heads— and Ithrazel went back to watching the three men moving in the meadow. In the center of the open space, a sort of pyre was half-constructed, a framework to be filled with wood that would then, at a guess, be soaked with water. It was a common test of wizardry to light such a beacon on fire. Racks, like a very high gallows, stood nearby, on which cages would be hung, containing live beasts—or possibly men—upon whom the mage in question would cast spells of pain or fear or whatever else they thought would most impress an emperor concerned to enslave the population of a continent. It was difficult to tell at this distance, even with the aid of a spy-glass, but by the look of it the shaggy meadow-grass had been scythed short over a space about a quarter-acre in area, and what looked like pens had been erected along one side.

More animals, probably. He wondered if the great, slender griffins still haunted the mountain woods of the Bright Archipelago's many islands, and if one would be killed for the edification of the emperor's envoy.

On the other side of the meadow, wooden stands were half-built, with stanchions for a canopy. *In case of rain? Or will our little magelet summon rain, to soak the groundlings while the Council and the Bright Lords sit under shelter?*

The three wizards moved about in the scythed demonstration-ground, standing and kneeling, standing and kneeling, under the cold glimmer of the gibbous moon.

They're fools if they think they can put sigils—even hidden marks—in the ground. To Ithrazel's mind returned the image of Machodan Indigo's beard-less face—a teacher of the New Order at twenty-two, those chilling dark eyes without pity or concern for anything except the perfection of his spells. Gerodare Starknife, Machodan's inseparable companion, had by then taken over as head of the Mages' Council, but it was Machodan who'd actually led the Council wizards, of all the orders combined, in the hunt.

And though his mind shied from the circumstances of his capture, he wondered with a grim inner smile whether that had been the last time all six Orders had worked together. *Did I really have the distinction of being the only cause that could get the New Mages to work with the Old, for the only time in the Order's history?* He wondered who he could ask about that, and if he'd get a truthful answer.

He did remember that it had been Machodan Indigo who had ruled that death would be too easy and merciful a punishment. Too final. That there were worse hells to plumb for a guilt like his.

Something told him that the New Order had not changed their attitudes in the past seventy-five years. For all their skills of healing, and their spells to add years to man's life.

The three mages had horses, concealed in the trees where the ground rose toward the Gray Hills. By that quicksilver moonlight, Ithrazel saw the animals walk from the scrubby remains of the woods, reins trailing, and knew that they'd been summoned by a word. "Will they know if we enter the marked ground?" breathed Clea as the riders vanished into darkness of the road back to Morne.

"I shouldn't wonder." Ithrazel got to his feet and folded up the seeing-glass with a snap. "They can't have put down warding-spells, if magic has become unreliable. It would give the game away if every rabbit in the countryside were irresistibly drawn to the marks made to keep intruders off. But they could be watching through a scrying-bowl."

His eyes narrowed as he scanned the wide meadow before him, the long grass now hiding the scythed area where the wizards had moved. *They'd be fools to mark the ground . . .*

So what were they doing?

"If they did plant marks," whispered Clea, "could you tell who they were from those marks? What order?"

"Of course!" Graywillow sounded surprised. "The magic of the Brown Mages, for instance, feels nothing like that of the Red. And no wizard-power feels anything like the spells of the gods."

"Hamo—Clea—you'd better remain behind," Ithrazel murmured. "Willow, my child . . ."

They advanced slowly, a step at a time. The wizard extended his hands, fingers spread, seeking the scent—only it wasn't really a scent—of magic. The whisper that wasn't a whisper. The invisible color that clung in the air around wizards' marks. He felt nothing, sensed nothing. If the marks hadn't been activated, they'd be very hard to spot even for an experienced mage. *Is it the full moon that will activate them?* Quite a few of the Black Mages' spells were sourced from the power of the moon. But the gods only knew how teaching might have deteriorated in the Old Orders, once spells started to go astray.

He thought of the crowds that would be gathered here on the day of the demonstration. They'd have to be working fairly powerful spells, these conjoined mages of the Old Orders, in order to win over the Darklander Council. The lesser cantrips were still fairly reliable, according to Graywillow, and the subtle magics of the gods. But he'd heard enough, from Graywillow and Clea, from the Gray Sisters at the Shrine and from the rowers who'd borne them with such steady speed last night and the night before, about even moderate spells, to make him break into a cold sweat. Spells of healing that had ruptured the patient's lungs. Mouse-wards that set thatch afire . . . but not every time. Rain songs that killed whole herds of cattle and sheep. A house-blessing that drew swarms of ants and lice. Babies found dead in their cradles a week after a healer had cured grandma's arthritis in the next room.

Thank the gods poor Hamo only fell in love with our Iron Princess, instead of finding himself transformed into a donkey. The astonishing thing was that the love-spell had worked at all.

The Corridor of Mirrors returned to his mind, black abysses beyond its paving-stones. Hamo's voice crying desperately from its darkness. The night in the Ghoras hunting camp at Thousand Frogs when he'd waked from his own nightmares to the muffled sound of Hamo weeping in his blankets. *For love of the Iron Princess?*

Or merely because he misses his family, and his sheepdog, and the friends in the village where he was born?

How much experimentation, how much practice, did the mages of the Old Orders perform, he wondered as he picked his way toward the scythed ground, to be sure that the three Orders working in conjunction could keep their spells true? In his own day, faced with such a problem or in fact with any problem, the masters of any Order would have poked for years at the edges of the issue, reading endlessly in their arcane libraries, seeking advice from ancient sources on Telmayre. Testing every step, every source, every limit, every word until he—and half the young mages he "came up" with through the years of teaching—were ready to scream with impatience.

A thought snagged at his mind, and he stopped in his tracks. As if he'd caught his sleeve on a rosebush. *Something . . .*

Graywillow halted at his side. Looked at him inquiringly, the mists of her spells—of Insignificance, of Invisibility—drifting almost palpably about them, like chilly unseen mist.

Something . . .

The thought dissolved. But it left a stain like the taste of a forgotten nightmare, and he found his heart was pounding.

He'd almost touched it, that time.

Whatever it was, that he'd forgotten.

Something about Machodan. About Gerodare . . .

He was aware of that thought itself trying to disappear.

Would the younger mages coming up in the Old Orders, the students of the students of his contemporaries, seeking the training in modes now discredited . . . Would they have the patience their elders had? The patience that would take years to test limitations, to study the ancient lore, before proclaiming an answer to the problem that bore so deeply into the core of their being? The core of their pride?

He didn't think so. With age, that was what wizards learned. Patience.

The New Mages—he supposed he should stop calling them "New"—had none. They were boys.

And the older mages were aware that their own time was running out.

They were still over a dozen yards from the scythed ground. The half-built seats and pavilions were no more than jumbled lattices of blackness in the moonlight. Stanchions and gallows stretched skinny fingers against the velvet sky. But he was trembling, cold through to his heart. No shred of magic whispered on the moonlight, but he knew that to move forward would be their undoing.

Like a good little soldier, Graywillow waited behind him, her own hands moving gently, seeking any trace of the spells he himself couldn't find.

He knelt in the rank grass and spread his hands out over the earth. The Brown Mages sourced their power chiefly from the earth, and despite the spell-riddled blacksteel that burned his wrist, he could feel that magic still. The life of the dirt that fed the grasses' roots, like flavors on his tongue. The stones that formed it, granite and flint and schist, like the faces of childhood neighbors. The dreams of moles. The acrid smell of ants. The music of water in the soil. Earth-magic . . .

Adamis.

Silver, sharp, and bitterly cold.

He reached forward, arm's-length from where he knelt, without rising.

They'd sprinkled the ground with adamis.

He edged forward, a foot, two feet. Smelling the night air, mentally erasing the odors of grass and earth.

Yes. The scythed ground. The whole quarter-acre must be dusted with it, like the floor of the boy Pendireth's sick-room . . .

He edged back and rose; signed Graywillow to follow him back to where Clea and Hamo waited in the darkness by the roots of the trees.

"They've seeded the ground with adamis." It astonished him that he could speak quietly. That he could speak at all, against the terrible sense of shadow, of cold, that crept through his thoughts and flesh.

Something . . .

The sense he sometimes had, that he was going to return to his nightmare of standing on the Hill of Oleanders, watching the streets, the houses, the temples of Dey Allias burst into molten flame.

Pain, darkness, demons great and small that poured glistening through dark glittering holes in the air . . .

The blackness like a concealing cloud that had streamed out with them.

"What, that whole area?" In the shadows of the few remaining trees she must barely be able to see his face, to see that he was shaking as if with fever . . . "That would cost a motherless fortune!"

"The demonstration is obviously worth a motherless fortune to somebody. Listen." He held out his left arm to her. "You have to free me from this shackle. I have done everything that I can," he added, cutting off her protest, "with my magic limited. We have reached the point where I will need more power than our Lady Gray can either conceal or provide. The point where you will have to trust me."

She was silent for a moment. Then, "Do *you* trust *me*?"

"No."

"I need to know—to *know*—that you will not disappear, or turn against me. You're the only weapon I have. I can't loosen my grip. Not for one second."

"Young lady, I am a hat-pin," said Ithrazel quietly. "You need a sword."

"What can they do with adamis?"

"*I don't know.* But I think we're all going to find out. And I think when we do, you're going to want a sword in your hand. And at that moment, you may not have the time to pick the lock."

Clea stepped closer, and stood for a moment, looking across into his eyes. Trying to read, though she could barely see. Putting together every moment, every conversation, every word and deed since first she'd come upon him lying on the rocks, weighed against what she'd heard of the destruction of Dey Allias. What she'd seen of him, in two weeks of travel in his company. What she knew of the threats that surrounded her, of the Crystal Mages, of her father . . .

She took his wrist in her hand and paused again, and he knew it was because she could feel him shaking. Without turning her head, she asked, "Graywillow. *Was* there adamis on the ground?"

"I don't know," said the young priestess. "He drew me back out of there too quickly for me to search."

Her mouth tightened. But after a long moment she dug in her pocket, and brought out her blacksteel pick-locks.

It was midnight when they reached the little shrine of Gingul again. Down the hill, on the canal, the lamps of the barges twinkled, orange and gold.

From the shrine in its tattered grove, they could hear the men cursing the rising fog, and the barking of the little black barge-dogs, sharp as knives in the night. After thanking old Winterflower—her Telmayrian name was Irusin—for the use of the horses, and ascertaining that yes, the woman who'd come to her at the quarter-moon was in fact Shumiel (with Snowball in tow), they slept in the stable. This place had no such guest-houses as the goddess's holy place in the Lake of Serpents did, and lived only by renting out its lands to a Placne woman named Porcupine who lived two hillsides away and raised sheep and cattle for the city markets. Clea spread her blanket closest to the stable doors, but knew this to be a useless precaution. Even before the blacksteel shackle had been removed, she guessed Ithrazel could have slipped past her unseen. Only the threat of exposure to the Crystal Mages had kept him from doing so, the threat of being taken and returned to his crag and his eagles . . . or to something worse.

You have reached the point . . . where you will have to trust me.

She turned her head, hearing his breathing deepen. He was right, she knew. She needed a sword, not a hat-pin—a blacksteel sword redly ablaze with every spell of victory in every grimoire in the world, and then some—if she were going to take on the Crystal Order and her father's suspicions. Not to speak of the Vrykos clan and whatever tame mages *they* had from the Old Orders, and whatever the *hell* it was lurking out there in the Reedmire, the hideous dark Thing that her father was helping the Crystal Mages try to tame.

Khymin knew about the Corridor of Mirrors. She turned what she knew over in her thoughts, knowing she should sleep and unable to put down the puzzle-pieces in her mind. *He knew what had been done to Ithrazel. He'd read it, in those moldy old scrolls of his. Did he, or any of the Black Mages, know about the zai as well?*

The thick scents of hay, and the far-off voices of a barge-crew on the Denzerai, smaller than the chirp of summer crickets. Closer, Hamo murmured something in his sleep.

Does ITHRAZEL really know? Has he been lying to me all along, just for this moment?

Am I *the one who's being used as a catspaw, to bring him back. . . ?*

Is THAT what this is really all about?

She could kill a man with a hat-pin. The blacksteel sword that was needed in this circumstance would not be in *her* hand . . . and could be turned against her at any moment.

Or at the very least, could simply disappear, leaving her weaponless to her foes.

Sleep, dammit . . . This isn't helping you.

Clea tried to remember the last time she'd given her trust without a backup or an escape route in place. Even the fact that Hamo, back in that other world among his flocks, had willingly agreed to lead them to the chained god on his crag and had obviously been nothing more than a good-natured young shepherd, hadn't been enough. She'd had Graywillow slip the strongest love-spell at her command on him, just to make sure he wouldn't betray them.

Betray us to who?

If you know WHO, Rat Bone always said, *it wouldn't be a real betrayal.*

She certainly had never trusted Rat Bone.

Graywillow, she thought. *I trust Graywillow . . .*

Would I trust her if she had greater power? The power to harm me?

She didn't know.

Pain sliced her at this awareness: as if she could look into her own opened breast and see that her heart had somehow been turned into a diamond. Like her father's . . . Or that her heart had been taken away when she was a child in her father's dungeons, and a diamond put into its place.

Or maybe that she'd pulled out her own heart and traded it for a diamond, impervious alike to both love and error.

She recalled a time when she'd have traded it simply for food.

Mother had a heart of flesh. Nevertheless her throat closed briefly, and tears she had forgotten how to shed burned her eyes. *Would I have been hurt less, had hers been diamond? Or more?* She didn't know, and didn't know from whom she might find out the answer to that question, or if she really wanted to learn it.

Useless, she thought, and turned her mind away. *Useless now, anyway, and for the foreseeable future.*

Silver and smooth, like the waters of the Greenflood. *If you feel anything inside, your hands will shake. The strong don't shake.*

The strong don't cry.

She shut her eyes, seeing again—briefly—the open Tarnweald in the moonlight. Through the mariner's glass Graywillow had said she saw something moving in the long grass, but hadn't been able to make out what it was. She herself had seen nothing. As was to be expected, she supposed, if whoever was out there dusting the ground with adamis—Brown or Black or Red—wore spells of Invisibility strong enough to fool a novice White Sister's eyes.

On the day of the full moon—five days hence—her father would almost certainly be sitting in those seats they were building. The Griffin banner—black, red, and gold—would be flying from one of those jackstaffs behind the seats, with the emblems of the other Merchant Houses—the Sun of the Vrykos, the Sea-Snake of the Othume, the Brazen Head of the Shiamat, which a thousand years ago had uttered prophecies. And above them all, the Heart Pierced with Three Swords, the emperor's guerdon, to mark the presence of his ambassador . . .

Her father, and Pendri, and Shumiel the Golden Princess her sister. *And how am I going to arrange to meet HER in circumstances that preclude a trap. . . ?*

She was still puzzling this out when she fell asleep.

When she woke at first birdsong, Ithrazel was gone.

Eighteen

He rode his borrowed horse fifteen miles south of the Denzerai canal, then turned it loose, knowing that the Gray Sisters would have long ago woven spells of safe return into its heart and hide. A farm wagon took him as far as the fishing-town of Etha, where he spent the night. The place had barely changed, save that every boat in the little harbor was marked now with Crystal Order spells and the glimmering silvery wink of adamine. The old gray stones of every house whispered of ward-spells and safe-spells written in the same silver runes, overlying the earlier marks of the Brown Mages who had chiefly come through the town. He even saw a few of his own.

When he slept—again in a stable, for he had no money, though he'd stayed at the inn across the courtyard a hundred times when the grandmother of its current proprietor had been a toddler collecting kindling—he dreamed again of Second Ox's house, halfway down the cliff below the City of Butterflies. Dreamed of that big, rosy man in the embroidered shirt of a common merchant among the tribes, his faded hair—the characteristic red of the Ashupik paling slowly to white—braided up in a topknot, pacing as he listened. Light fell through the windows at his back, glimmering with the water far down in the canyon below.

Tasted, in his dreaming, the tea brought in by Second Ox's wife and beautiful daughters. Heard the laughter of Second Ox's young son.

Dear gods, what happened to THEM . . . afterward?

White Jade. Hummingbird. Ten Sparrows.

And for a moment the faces of his own daughters returned to him. *And what happened to THEM?*

When the women were gone Second Ox turned to him, and his green eyes were grave and filled with pain.

Because of what we were planning to do?

Because he feared for his wife and his children? Dreaded the consequences of failure and even more the consequences of success?

Ithrazel couldn't remember.

He saw the images in his heart as if they were painted on silk, every tiny detail exact. But he could not remember a single fragment of what he had thought or felt.

In his dream he took the rolled-up parchment from his satchel, and spread it out on the table between them.

It was blank.

Ithrazel opened his eyes and saw the rafters of the hayloft above him, the furtive glimmer of the eyes of rats in the dark.

He slept no more that night.

The Faithful Harlot was a rambling tavern on the Street of the Broken Loaf. It backed onto the alleyway that served the refineries and seemed to float in a constant dirty murk of throat-catching smoke. Clothed in a slop-market dress and a mended petticoat, and with her bright hair loosened from its usual knot and dyed brown with walnut juice, Clea explained to its pro-prietress—in accents and vocabulary she'd picked up from Liver-Eater and Gerti the Rat-Lady—that her mistress had escaped from an unkind family and would pay well for nobody in the inn to mention her presence there with her handsome new husband. Hamo wasn't enough of an actor to por-tray a blackguard, but he could look sulky and aloof and that would suffice, at least for the next four days. With her hair dyed a tawdry yellow, a cheap new gaudy gown, and enough face-paint to put her mother into a seizure, Graywillow was a fairly convincing adulteress.

Mistress Kamine had seen it all before.

Together the three of them rode out to the Tarnweald, and as Clea expected were turned back by blue-clothed Vrykos guards—who offered to procure them front-rank places in the crowd on the day of the demonstra-tion ("And if you believe *that*," remarked Clea as the "loving couple" and their "maid" rode back to town, "I have a selection of the imperial crown jewels to sell you . . ."). Their outing that day took them past the small manor-house of Sunmist, where they drew rein to watch the Lady Shumiel's household ride in after a day of hawking, the Golden Princess like a little pink and gilt doll in their midst.

"That's your sister?" asked Hamo as grooms in red and black livery scurried to take the party's horses and two footmen pushed forward the mounting-steps to enable Shumiel to descend. "The one who asked you to come to her?"

"She is my sister." Clea sighed, and reined toward the nearest clump of woodlands along the road, some two hundred yards from the house.

"Will you go to her?"

Will I go to her? Clea's earliest memories were of her beautiful mother drawing and re-drawing, all around her bed, the signs of the goddess Nie, who protected children, to guard her against whatever magics Shumiel might be able to hire. And *would* hire, to revenge upon her tiny half-sister for what had been done to Shumiel's mother.

A groom handed Snowball tenderly down from the padded basket attached to Shumiel's sidesaddle. Ecstatically, the little dog licked his mistress's face. Clea hoped her sister's cosmetics were at least reasonably digestible.

No sign of Pendireth in the hawking-party. He would barely be recuperated from the yellow sickness, and in any case Clea couldn't imagine her father letting his precious only son (*and mageborn at that!*) out of his sight. *If he was here, there'd be half a hundred guards at least.*

"I don't see guards in her party," the shepherd added, as if that made a difference. In the blue leather doublet and white shirt they'd purchased for him with the Lady Neambis's gold, Hamo no longer looked so much like an ignorant country boy, and she'd seen Mistress Kamine back at the inn eyeing him with approval. Ithrazel's disappearance, Clea knew, had hurt him deeply, and he still insisted that the wizard would return.

Clea dropped from her mare's back within the shadows of the grove. "That doesn't mean my father's men—or someone else's—aren't watching the house. Graywillow, I'm afraid you'll have to come with me, in case somebody's put mages' marks around the place. If anyone comes along and asks you, Hamo, you tried to steal a kiss from me, Graywillow ran off in a huff, and I went after her . . . but I doubt anybody will ask. This isn't a very frequented road."

Graywillow obediently kicked her feet free of the stirrups, dropped down in a great flurry of blue and gold skirts, and wrapped herself in the anonymous cloak of misty gray that she'd brought along. Clea loosened cinches and took the bits from the horses' mouths. The saddles the Sisters had lent them were the type in use for women all through the Bright Islands, with the stirrups politely on one side only. Clea had been taught to ride thus as a tiny child on a pony. In her training as an assassin, Rat Bone had insisted she continue that method as well as learn to ride like a man: *You have to be able to pass for an idiot girl, see, if you're going to get close enough to a customer to slit his weasand.*

"We should be back in an hour . . ."

It took them a little longer than that to circle the grounds, but Clea found no trace that the place was being observed, at least by the usual methods. "I'll have to come back tonight, to have a look at the stables to be sure. Anyone come while we were gone?"

Hamo shook his head, and gallantly if clumsily helped the girls to mount, Clea cursing at the man who had invented sidesaddles and the other man (*"It HAS to have been a man . . ."*) who had decreed that a woman who didn't ride thusly must be an irredeemable slattern.

"You truly think your own sister would betray you?" By his tone, Clea guessed he had a sister, or sisters, whom he loved dearly.

She sighed again. "My own sister," she said, "whose father put *her* mother aside—who accused her of adultery, and declared their daughter a bastard—so that he could marry *my* mother, in his quest for a mageborn son. My father exiled the lady Sylmayne to a house in the Mire in the dead of winter, so cold and damp that she caught her death."

"Why didn't he just let her go back to her family?" asked Hamo, shocked. "In my village, if a man and a woman don't agree, she simply goes back to her parents' house."

"Because Sylmayne Shiamat was the daughter of Dorvazin Shiamat, the greatest of the merchant ship-owners of the Bright Islands—*and* related to the Shiamane Family, who are real nobles of one of the Great Houses back in Telmayre. If it was Father's fault the marriage ended, Father would have to return the dowry. With the evidence he procured that she was an adulteress, he turned her own father against her—turned the whole of the House Shiamat and the nobles of the Bright Islands against her. He had Shumiel sent home from Telmayre in disgrace and labeled a bastard. That judgment was later reversed, but it meant that Shumiel, Golden Princess or not, has never been able to wed—she'll be thirty this year—and probably *will* never be able to wed because of the lingering questions left by so many lies."

His dark brows pulled together over that small, straight nose. "But that's no reason to hate *you* enough to betray you. You weren't even born!"

"I expect she hates my father also," returned Clea as the horses turned their heads back toward the distant smear of smoke in the south that was Morne. "But he has power, you see. She can still use him. And I have none."

* * *

She returned to the manor of Sunmist that night. She debated about trying to slip into the Tunnels—there were half a dozen entrances to the old drainage system within a few minutes' walk of the tavern—to see if she could find Khymin's books, or some trace of the old man himself, but guessed that the Crystal Mages would have spies there. With the Vrykos's demonstration coming up, she didn't even trust her friends in the Dockside. Liver-Eater—or the Ashupik merchant Kulchan, who headed the strongest of the Darklander councils in the city—would protect her in a pinch, but there were simply too many people down there who were too frightened of the Crystal Order, or too desperate for a silver coin.

So instead, the "illicit lovers" retired upstairs early at the Faithful Harlot, and spent a giggling half-hour pounding the bed-heads against the chamber's thin walls, moaning and howling and shouting endearments, before slipping quietly out the window and through the ankle-deep muck of the yard to fetch their horses. Beyond the mists that usually covered the low-lying town, chill starlight washed the land, and waxing moonlight showed them the road into the hills. With Graywillow at her side to cover her—to listen and sniff for magic around the house while Hamo was left holding the horses again—Clea counted the mounts in the stables and the stocks of fuel and flour in the bakery, then ghosted into every building in the little manor's grounds, to make sure there wasn't a contingent of guards on the premises.

Through a window she saw Shumiel, wrapped in a fur-lined velvet robe, peering nearsightedly at a scholarly text while her maid brushed her shimmering hair. A beautiful woman still, reflected Clea, and felt a stab of sadness, and pity. Relaxed and at peace, Shumiel's face had a gentleness to it, a symphony of soft ovals: beautiful dark eyes, a soft mouth with just a trace of firmness to the pink lips, a perfect, slightly retroussé nose. Clea noted that without daytime cosmetics, slight lines had begun to appear between nostril and chin, and in the corners of the eyes. The tiniest ghost of a second chin flawed the perfection of her throat.

It had been twelve years since the Golden Princess had been called unceremoniously back from the emperor's court. The days of her greatest beauty were passing, sterile because of the accusations raised during the divorce. The scandal was long over, but its shadow remained.

How can she not hate me for his sake?

On the following evening, the three rode out earlier, and once clear of the town Clea changed her maid's garb for the red and black hose of one of her father's pages—part of the outfit she'd worn when she escaped her father's palace on the night almost three weeks ago when Graywillow and the men of Turtlemere had come to tell her of the rising of the zai. With these she wore a Ghoras hunting-shirt with quillwork on the sleeves. A close-fitting cap concealed her dyed hair. It was what she would have worn had she been hiding in the hills rather than in the town, and when Shumiel came from supper into her own bedchamber and found Clea sitting there by the fire and asked, startled, where she had been, Clea had only to shrug and say, "Where those who may have lied about me can't find me." Shumiel would assume, she knew, that her guess had been correct and that Clea was hiding among the tribes.

After Shumiel had assured her, with every appearance of earnestness, that the manor wasn't being watched and that—in spite of the reward he'd offered—their father's sole concern was for his younger daughter's safety—"I promise you, Clyaris, no one has spoken lies about you, or poured poison in Father's ear . . ." Clea asked, "How is Pendri?" and, laughing, held off Snowball at arm's length as the little dog licked her face. "And will he be at this demonstration, when the moon comes to full?"

"He will," said the older princess. "Shall I send for wine? Or cocoa? Have you eaten?"

"I have," said Clea. "And no, no wine or cocoa, but thank you. I've been a bit indisposed, and have a long way yet to ride tonight." In truth, Clea had the digestion of a shark, but since Shumiel suffered from an assortment of gastric ailments, her sister didn't press her. She would have, Clea guessed, if she really had the intention of drugging or poisoning her.

"Pendri's much better." The Golden Princess sank into a chair and bent to pick up Snowball, who begged to be taken into her red velvet lap but was too stout to leap up there himself. "But I do think even Lord Himelkart was frightened there at first. And yes, Father's bringing him along, to see what the Vrykos have up their sleeves." She had had far too many lessons in deportment to squint or peer at Clea's face, but Clea saw her eyes narrow as she tried to focus them across the purple marble of the tabletop.

"According to the man Father pays in the Vrykos household, the boy Vervaris is indeed being taught by a Red Mage named Dalmin Zhodel. This Dalmin studied in Esselmyriel, but hasn't worked magic of his own in years. Nobody's ever heard a word against him, Father says. I've heard—though no one tells me much—that the child is a skilled mage already, but if somebody's been paying the mages of the older orders, and even offering money to the White Sisters, doesn't it seem to you that . . . well, that the whole thing may be a plot? Or a hoax? Could they . . . could they *do* that?"

"It does," said Clea grimly. "And they could. And if you don't think House Vrykos would hoax the emperor into thinking they have some form of magic separate from that of the Crystal Order—magic that works the way it should—I suggest you think again. Thank you," she added. "Thank you for sending me word."

Her sister frowned a little, and shook her head. "I know you're better at plots and politics than I am," she said. "I heard about it almost by accident, from my hairdresser, who also works with that stuck-up hussy Linvinnia. And it didn't sound right to me. Especially not if the Darklander Council was meeting over it, and the emperor sending an embassy. Though how anyone could be so wicked as to even *think* of hoaxing the Lord Emperor . . ."

For a moment she looked aside into the fire, dainty jeweled hands toying with the somnolent Snowball's fur. "But there *are* wizards who can work magic as children. Lord Himelkart is always saying that Pendri shows such promise . . ."

"You're asking the wrong person." Clea shook her head. "Snowball's probably got more magic in him than I do. And I keep my distance from it. But I've never heard of any child working real magic before the age of about fifteen, except the Crystal Mages."

"Might it be that the gods are now starting to speak to male children? To work through them the same way they work through women? Pendri's able to work a little now, since he's been taught by the mage Master Tsorkesh. And everybody knows the magic of women hasn't changed."

It was an intriguing idea, but Clea shook her head. "If that's really the case—if it's magic given by the gods—old Tashthane Vrykos is in for a rude surprise when his little mage-baby won't be able to do things like cure yellow sickness or blast a man with fire at thirty feet. Women's magic—gods' magic—isn't fighting magic, or blasting-your-enemies magic. I've seen the demonstration grounds, and they've set up for things like lighting wet wood on fire and turning aside charging bulls. Women's magic is mostly about making your crops grow and keeping bugs out of the flour barrel—which doesn't always work—and making people fall in love with you . . ."

Shumiel's eyes flashed to her face, and Clea—who had (and she cursed herself for it) relaxed enough not to guard her every word—realized what she'd said and felt herself flush from her collarbone to her ears. For a moment, it had seemed, in the quiet of the firelight, she had been able to talk to Shumiel as a sister, a genuine sister, as she had on those occasions in her earliest childhood when the older girl had, at their father's command, made sincere attempts to care for her tiny sister . . .

God's braies, don't I have ANY sense. . . ?

For she'd been thinking of poor Hamo, and not the accusation that her father had leveled at her mother. The accusation that Shumiel had all her life believed.

"I'm sorry," she stammered. "That was a stupid thing to say—"

"I'm sure you only spoke your thought." Shumiel's tone could have peeled the gold veneer from a nobleman's fingernails. "It's quite all right. Think nothing of it. I assume, from your lack of formality in this visit, that you will not be staying . . . Will you attend the demonstration?" She rose from her chair and made as if to conduct Clea to the door, indicating quite firmly that the interview was done.

"I'll probably have some people watching from the sidelines." Clea rose also. Too late, she reflected, to gain points by asking her sister what she was going to wear. "Tell my father—if you'd be so good—that my loyalty has always been to him, and to our house. Tell him that I've heard only that there are those close to him who wish me harm. That more than anything else, I fear that he will have a poor opinion of me."

"You won't better it," retorted Shumiel with a sudden flare of temper, "by hiding in the Mire with savages like a bandit. Or by dressing like one," she added, her glance raking Clea with scorn. "What is he, or anyone, supposed to think? But I assume you'll suit yourself. You always do." She moved another step toward the door and gestured as if she would have taken the handle, then paused, curtsied, and asked, "Or would you rather depart through the window?"

"Window," said Clea airily, thinking she'd be damned if she left the room the way she'd come in, which had been through a secret stair that she'd learned of as a child, when her mother had briefly owned this house. The stair wound around the room's chimney from below and was concealed in the gaily painted oak of the paneling, its lower doorway opening behind the vines that cloaked the north wall of the garden. As Clea opened the casement and took hold of the vines outside, she whispered a prayer to Chellis, the guardian god of tame plants, that she wouldn't fall and break her ankle.

That *would* be an embarrassment.

Once safely on the ground (*Thank you, Chellis! I owe you a chicken!*), Clea lost no time in getting over the manor's outer wall (more vines), finding Graywillow, and hastening back to where they'd left Hamo with the horses. She'd hoped to learn from Shumiel the truth of a couple more rumors she'd heard in the Thieves' Market that day about the doings of the House Stylachos—including Shumiel's possible return to Telmayre in quest of a noble husband—but it had *not* seemed the proper time to make further inquiries.

If Shumiel vented her irritation to her maidservant (*Does Shumiel confide in her maids?* She couldn't imagine her sister doing anything so undignified), the gods only knew where information about her visit would end up.

Nineteen

Ithrazel the Cursed stood on the middle slopes of the Hill of Oleanders and looked down on what had been the city of Dey Allias.

Even from here—two-thirds of the way up the hill—the memories were nearly unbearable. Worse still was the sense that there was something that he did not remember, that he *must* not remember, like a steel drill-bit being twisted in his brain. *If I see it I'll die. If I remember doing it, braiding my own magic and that of the other mages to summon the fire and the demons and the darkness, to swallow innocent and guilty alike, I'll . . .*

What?

His heart was pounding and he felt as if his bones would dissolve, as if he'd shatter and wake to find himself on his mountain crag again, watching the sun rise with newly re-born eyes and waiting for the first of the eagles to appear.

He'd dreamed again, the previous night, of Second Ox—of playing tigers with little Hummingbird while Second Ox looked on. Had dreamed, too, of Khoyas White-Eyes hobbling on his stick, Eketas in his billowing brown robe—Eketas who'd trained with Ithrazel back on the Bright Isle—helping the old Black Mage over the rough spots in the road . . .

He'd dreamed of all the days he'd spent seeking out each one of them—in the City of Butterflies, in the little Brown Mage settlement in the coastal woods, on the tiny island five miles over-sea from the headland of Doomrock beyond Morne, soaked with spray in his little leather cockleboat . . . Dreamed of telling them, asking them . . . begging them . . . *What?*

In every dream, when he unrolled the parchment scroll he carried, the scroll was blank.

His heart was blank. He could not hear the words he said. Sometimes in his dreams he wept in his desperation that they help him, lend their power to his. Sometimes, instead of words, blood came out of his mouth, spilling like a river down onto the table or floor or hearth, wherever it was that he sat.

What became of them?

He lived in terror that another night's dreaming would unmask that information.

The Marble City had been built on the Dey River, which flowed sluggishly out of the Mire in a wide estuary between the Gray Hills and the Dark. From the Hill of Oleanders—the tallest of the Dark Hills, and the furthest north—everything still had the precision of a map: the palaces of the great merchant houses, their wide gardens overgrown now in twisted riots of weeds, their stables and storehouses and banqueting-rooms cracked open to the sky. The maze of silted-up trenches raked for miles what had been the beaches around the estuary, where the diamond-sands had been dredged, and the refineries and wood-yards down by the two harbors were now barely more than huge rectangles and circles of foundation stones choked with sedges and saltbush. On the higher ground some oak trees even grew, sturdy after seventy-five years.

By the moon's pallid gleam the streets near the harbor could barely be traced, even by mageborn eyes. The garrisons still stood out as thicker rectangles of broken stone, blanched against the crowding gloom of laurel thickets. The slums he could only locate by memory, where the barracks of the workers had stood. The shabby huts of the camp followers and slaves that had stretched for miles had vanished utterly under hackberry, salt pines, swamp elders. It was as if they, the innocent, had never been.

Ithrazel wondered if anyone had ever gone into the ruins to clear out the bodies. If the things he'd seen crawl from the earth haunted those thickets still.

The islets that dotted the estuary, where the merchant lords had had summer houses and little pleasure-palaces, were gone entirely. Waves glimmered over a rock or two, but nothing else of them remained.

He took a deep breath, closed his eyes, shuddered in his wolf-skin coat. Autumn was giving way to winter. He had done what he did in midsummer; the stink of the city had risen to him even at this distance. The memory, vivid as yesterday, smote him almost to his knees. Now all he could smell was the sea.

Opening his eyes, he could see with a wizard's sight what, seventy-five years before, had been a bed of dimly glowing ember, ten thousand lamplit doors and windows, the lamps just going out for the night. There had been much sickness in the city then, he remembered that. Summer fever and flux, the growing price of overcrowding. The smoke of the pyres had been a sort of gritty veil on the lights. He and the other Brown Mages had gone into the city to help. From up here, it had all looked quiet. Men, women, children, rich and poor, slave and free, guilty and innocent, going to bed.

He remembered clearly thinking at the time, *Anaya is down there . . .* But the memory carried nothing with it. No terror, no dread, no hope that she'd get out in time. Nothing.

Anaya and Ios . . .

What the hell was I thinking?

He did not know.

Turning his back on the ruins, he climbed toward the top of the hill.

"What is it?" Clea raised herself on her elbow. In the shuttered black of the room even the indigo glimmer seemed bright where Graywillow had opened the shutter a crack. So silent was this dead hour before dawn, when even the taverns were relatively still, that she'd heard the older girl's soft footfall, the creak of the leather hinge. The dark shape that was Graywillow moved a little in the window. The sinking moon was nearly full.

Above the stink of the street below and the choke of refinery smoke, trapped and held by the fog, drifted the faintest whisper of the sea.

"Just thinking." She and Hamo had put on their usual performance for the benefit of the neighbors, jumping on the bed, pounding the pillows, gasping and shrieking extravagant love-cries and collapsing into giggles. Hamo had retired to the tiny room in the attic, which Clea was supposedly occupying, only an hour ago. Clea, lying awake at Graywillow's side wondering where the hell Ithrazel was and how she was going to deal with the Crystal Mages without him—not to mention her father and his enemies—had been aware that Graywillow, too, lay waking.

Wondering the same thing? She was now the only mage in Clea's little band, and it was almost a certainty that even if they weren't taking bribes from the Vrykos, neither the White Ladies nor the Gray would challenge the greater power of the Crystal Order.

"About Rivan."

Clea shuddered at the memory of the mad wizard's emaciated face, of the blood gumming his hair and beard where he'd tried to beat his head on the stone walls of his prison. Of his screams lacerating the air.

Of other screams.

Of Khymin, dragging himself about his cluttered lair by the light of a single grease-lamp, fumbling through his scrolls.

Of whatever it was she thought she'd seen—thought she'd smelled—in the shadows of the foliage near the walls of the House of Glass.

"What happened to him, Clea?" Her voice sank and she closed the shutter again. Clea heard her shift rustle as she crossed the little room, felt the weight of her on the bed and the heavy susurrance as she dropped her cloak back across the bed's foot. "Does the magic of the Crystal Order drive its practitioners mad? That prison you spoke of, there in the House of Glass—"

Clea whispered, "Yes—"

"Children don't work magic. It comes to us like . . . like games. Like dreams. No reason and no lists to memorize, just . . . magic. Some of what I remember about it—about calling birds down to my hands, and making the plants in Mama's garden sprout in the moonlight—it may have *been* dreams. I didn't tell Mama because nobody really wants their daughter to be one of the Sisters. It means she'll have to leave the household, and there won't be someone to help with the cooking and cleaning and the garden . . ."

Outside, the dawn-sounds of the city were stirring: the first clattering of the carts whose din made the days in the poorer quarters unbearable, the bells in the refinery towers, clanging to call the workmen to their labors.

"Then it went away," murmured Graywillow. "I thought I really *had* dreamed it all, until it came back when I was thirteen, and started dreaming about the Goddess.

"But Rivan—"

"Yes," murmured Clea. "The Crystal Mages watch for mageborn boys. They'll sometimes approach their parents, if they hear of some child making flowers bloom or scaring away the rats in the attic with just a word. Or they'll pay parents, for the loss of a child who's taken into the House of Glass. And they start teaching them when they're little, like Pendri. And their magic *doesn't* go away. Or when it does, it comes back earlier, and stronger. Like a hothouse flower, or strawberries forced to early ripeness. I've wondered about that, too. How they do that . . . and what it does to the child."

Would it be better, or worse, Ithrazel wondered, if he hadn't known Dey Allias as well as he had? If he hadn't lived there, when first he'd crossed from Telmayre to the Twilight Lands?

Would this pain be less if his daughters hadn't been born there? He saw their faces again in his mind—dark, thin Akuhare and blonde Chiviel, both married and gone before that night . . .

Had the Mages' Council gone after *them*? He didn't even know how he could find out.

He and Anaya had had rooms in the strange, domed compound of the Brown Mages near the North Harbor in those days. He'd walked those streets, visited the shops where books and paper came in from the Bright Islands, chatted with shopkeepers and market-women and stepped out of the way as lines of slaves—Lhogri and Placne, mostly, they'd been then—were marched through the streets to the refineries, each man stumbling under the weight of straw baskets of raw diamond-sand from the flats south of the city.

He'd always hated the stink of the place, from the moment he'd set foot ashore that first time. In the fifteen years he'd lived in Dey Allias, the stink had grown as the city grew, as the crowds thickened and new refineries were built. There were more barracks, more poor, more slaves. The adamis trenches and pits along the shore-sands had stretched out of sight down the estuary, a wasteland of crudely rigged towers and pumps and waterwheels. Most days the smoke of the refineries made the air unbreathable, so that his girls were always sick. By the time his son had been born, he and Anaya had shifted quarters to the little settlement of Brownwaith in the hills by Sweet Creek. But by that time, he'd been Archmage of the Brown Order and was often called to the city on its business.

One of his only memories of climbing the Hill of Oleanders on Mid-summer's Night had been that he'd known that Anaya was in the city that night, with little Ios. He remembered he'd put marks on them both, to keep the sickness at bay.

And . . . something else . . .

He was almost sick with dread by the time he reached the top of the hill, shaking as if with fever. But there was nothing really to see. Even the land had changed. Seventy-five years previously, the Hill of Oleanders had been—like most of the territory around Dey Allias—deforested, the trees cut down to feed the refineries. Even the brush had been cleared away, for the convenience of those who came up there to scan the eastern horizons for the first sight of incoming sails. At one time, one of the merchant houses—the Othume, if he recalled correctly—had built a sort of tower at the hill's summit. It had burned down a few years before the destruction of the city, due to the carelessness of a couple of drunken guards.

The oleanders for which the hill had been named had grown back, dark-leaved jungles of them on the south and east sides of the hill. The north side, where the cobbled track from the city had lain, was choked with brush and overgrown with elder and ash. The top, when Ithrazel reached it, was wooded. Only by standing at the edge of the small northern escarpment, where the trees thinned away from the rock underfoot, could he look down on the ruins as he had looked that night. The thought of doing so almost nauseated him, but the sensation of having briefly caught his sleeve on a thorn—the sensation that there was something he half remembered, should remember—forced his steps to the place. Sweat ran down into his eyes, as if he faced some terrible peril, the monstrous zai of which that brat Clea spoke, or the floating horrors of the darkness beyond the Road of Mirrors. The things he saw pouring out of the torn earth just before the flames roared up . . .

But the night was still.

All he could hear was the sea.

He opened his heart. Opened his mind. Opened his senses, as if finally welcoming the vultures of the Desolate Mountains.

The pain in his skull loosened, for the first time in days.

There are no night-birds.

It's winter . . .

No. It's autumn. The refineries and diggings were gone. The estuary should be alive with geese and cranes, whippoorwills and ducks, birds of passage . . .

And even the few thin coppices left by the woodcutters—when he'd walked out from the city with his friend Eketas in the evenings, all those years ago—those had rustled with the movement of foxes, shivered with the lonely cries of owls and killdeer.

They were silent now. He knew in his soul they'd been silent for seventy-five years. They'd never come back here, even when the city was gone.

Adamine.

With his heart still and listening, the night glittered with it. Faint and dim, as it had been in the boy Pendri's room in the House of Glass. As it had been in the rough-scythed stubble of the Tarnweald. But everywhere . . .

Ithrazel turned, looked back into the woods behind him, then down at the ground beneath his feet. He called the thought of it, the spells to perceive it, back to his mind.

A silvery glimmer flickered among the dead roots of the grass.

He paced back to the center of the wooded hilltop, the place where he had stood. The place where he stood nearly every other night in dreams, lifting his hands to the sky, shouting a word . . .

What word?

There was adamine underfoot.

He knelt, ran his hands over the thin undergrowth of fern and dying loosestrife. Dug his fingers down into their roots. He felt its echo, ground into the soil, though the rains of seventy-five winters had mostly leached it away. The roots of the grass had absorbed it. The roots of the trees that had grown tall since that night.

And as if someone outside himself was asking—but he knew it was himself that asked—the question came to him:

What word did I shout that night?

Inside him his heart turned perfectly cold.

The ground was sown with adamine.

I didn't see it then because I wasn't looking for it. I had less experience with it in those days. No one had experience—only the New Order. Machodan, Gerodare, Tarronis. It was less in use—far less had been mined, less had been refined. It was still hidden, diffused, in the earth . . .

But it was here. Concentrated, refined . . . Underfoot, while we were weaving our spells, drawing our sigil, calling power . . .

WE WERE TRYING TO DO SOMETHING ELSE.

The adamine had changed the spell.

The adamine LET someone reach into our circle, and turn our power to another end. Turn our spell of . . . of . . . of whatever it was—healing? Because of the plague? Turned it into horror and destruction and death to fifty thousand people.

The realization took his breath away.

And then:

And that's exactly what they're going to do in two days' time, in the Tarnweald.

The ground there is sown with adamine. It will let SOMEONE turn the spells of that poor little boy—of whoever those wizards are who're trying to work in concert—into another holocaust of death that will discredit everyone who wields magic . . .

Everyone except the New Order of Mages.

He stood, trembling, a shadow in the chill shadows of the woods. As a wizard he was nearly always aware of where the heavens stood, of how long it would be before moonset, sunrise, morning. It had taken him longer than he'd thought to reach the Hill of Oleanders from the Tarnweald. But if he walked through the night—and for most of tomorrow night—if he could manage to get a ride from a carter on the way to the city—he might still make it back by the morning of the demonstration.

He descended the hill at a run.

Twenty

The merchant lords of the Darklands Council turned out in their splendor to meet the *Varthyriel*, the flagship of the emperor's representative, when it glided to the end of Stylachos Pier. Named for the Great Goddess of the Bright Islands, it was a giant vessel, large enough to carry a dozen pieces of siege artillery on her decks beneath a cloud of sail. Smaller vessels trailed her, settling at the lesser piers and wharves of Morne and crowding the adamis-ships: tenders, merchants, transports for horses and servants. Music from the *Varthyriel*'s decks flashed gold in the damp morning air.

"It's like a mountain!" Hamo whispered, at Clea's elbow. On their first afternoon in Morne, three days ago, the shepherd had stood transfixed beside the harbor, staring at the huge, tubby adamis-ships in stunned disbelief, for he had never seen a vessel larger than the fishing boats that plied the lakes of his home world. When he'd entered Morne for the first time eleven nights ago—under cover of darkness and impenetrable fog— Clea had had to explain to him what the sea was, and how much water and food was needed for those who would cross it. But she knew he didn't understand.

Now he stood dazzled anew, wondering and aghast at this world into which he had come. "How many men does this ambassador bring?" he asked, turning from the flagship's painted and gilded sides to gaze at the lesser fry of the fleet, then looking back toward the tiny figures that swarmed the rigging, the red-gold and blue banners that streamed from the masts, like blood and morning glories. "For what would anyone *need* a ship so large?"

"For war." Clea stood with folded arms, calculating the capacities of the vessel, offensive and defensive. "Look at those things on the deck. The ones like giant bows shoot arrows longer than you are tall. Those bronze tubes shoot fire. The slings can lob stones, or fireballs, over the walls of any city that defies the emperor. And that's to say nothing of the mages a warship would carry, whose spells can spread plague or fog or black rot on all the bread in a city. No one defies the emperor. Not even our peoples' gods."

She stepped back half a pace behind the big shepherd's shoulder as the first of the trumpeters marched past. She'd paid their landlady's son to hold a place for them, just where the Street of Ships emerged onto the wide apron of land above the sea-wall, and had paid an equal sum to a man their landlady had recommended, to remain at the inn and guard their possessions. She'd already recognized a dozen of Liver-Eater's "boys" from the Dockside, and knew that most of her old acquaintances from her pocket-picking days were shoving and slithering among the crowd: *those who haven't been hanged by this time.* It might have been better, she reflected, had she remained back at the inn herself. Despite her dyed hair and servant's clothing, there were far too many people in the city who knew her, and who desperately needed those silver pennies her father would pay.

But she wanted to see who was in town, and who was riding in whose train.

Yes, there he was. The bitterness that soured her mouth couldn't entirely quell the stir of her heart at the sight of him: Minos Stylachos, with his golden hair and his curled beard like short-clipped golden fleece. President of the Darklands Council and the most powerful man in the Twilight Lands.

My father.

Save for a little thickening of his waist, a broadening of his jaw, and a brassiness where his hair had been dyed to cover its fading, he looked as he looked in her dreams. Those terrible dreams of him standing before the assembled Councils—the Darklands Council and that of the Mages—and accusing her mother of laying spells on him to cause him to set aside his true and beloved (and regrettably already deceased) wife, Sylmayne Shiamat.

My blood. Whose heart of diamond I seem to have inherited . . .

She drew her breath deeply, forcing her feelings smooth. Smooth like the Greenflood, smooth like a silver mirror. *If you feel anything inside, your hand will shake.*

Pendireth rode beside him, ashen-pale under rouge skillfully applied. In his black, red and gold velvet tunic he looked like a doll that had been made up from his glorious father's scraps. Ganzareb tar-Azazris, just behind him, likewise wore the colors of the House Stylachos, but in addition sported a jewel on his forehead the size of a double silver-piece, as if to remind the world (in case his five-lobed silken hat didn't make it clear) that although he was a younger son and obliged by this fact to seek employment, the man who fed him, clothed him, and commanded him was in truth less than the dirt beneath his elegant boots.

Beside Ganzareb, stylish in blue and violet velvet beneath a beautifully cut white surcoat, rode Himelkart of Thourmand, calm assurance sitting oddly on that narrow, youthful, oddly epicene face. His dark eyes, profoundly old, were the eyes of one who has received imperial ambassadors a hundred times.

And why shouldn't he look so? reflected Clea. *If he's destined to step in— when Heshek retires back to the Bright Isles—as commander of the most powerful Order in the world? And where IS Heshek, anyway? Today of all days, he should be here.* Throughout her childhood in the streets, Clea had always seen them together, the golden, blue-eyed gargoyle Archmage and his faithful, mocking twin . . .

All that power, at the age of eighteen?

What does that do to you?

And add to that the promise that the scion of the House Stylachos is going to become one of the Order himself?

But the only mage with him was Tsorkesh the Librarian, Pendri's teacher—only a year or two older than Himelkart himself, a man of the dark-skinned people of the great Southern Isle, with those same boyish features, those same ancient eyes.

Her glance went back to her father's profile as Minos Stylachos drew rein at the head of the Pier, golden on his snowy horse. Beside the image of the man who'd stood before the Darklands Council to denounce her mother, she saw the man who'd held her, a tiny child, in his arms and had sung songs that he'd made up for her. Who'd listened to her lessons and made sure she had the books that, even at the age of four, she'd craved. Made sure she had teachers who would give her the skills at reading, at music, at dancing . . .

Wanting to hate him and not being able to do so. Not entirely.

Wanting him to be someone she could love, as she had loved as a child.

The other members of the Council, the merchant princes Clea had met over the past two years, emerged from the wide street onto the open ground that had been cleared last night of its food-stands and beggars and barrows of fish. She whispered, nodding, to Hamo, pointing them out: white-haired Igilsand Shiamat, Shumiel's grand-uncle and the only one of the merchant princes qualified to wear the jewel of nobility on his brow. (Rumor had it that his grandfather had paid a staggering price to the Shiamare family for the privilege of wedding a minor princess of that house and assuming their name.) Dour, hook-nosed Momus Othume, with his four sons grouped about him like bodyguards. Tykellin Stylachos, her father's broad-faced, yellow-bearded cousin and ferocious rival: "He'd sell his loyalty to any of the others, in order to get a dozen acres of Father's land," Clea whispered.

"That's Tashthane Vrykos," she added as the last of the merchant princes rode into position, dark-haired and dark-eyed like many of the people of the Sea Islands east of the Bright archipelago, bending his head to the crowd with a suave graciousness. "The boy with him must be Vervaris, their child-wizard—Sons of Hell, he can't be seven years old!"

The child was trying hard to look haughty, but his wide brown eyes were clearly filled with terror. He kept glancing back at the riders ranged behind him: a handsome, grizzle-bearded man in the red robe of a mage, and two others, white-haired, in the robes of the Black Order. He looked about to cry, *and no wonder*, thought Clea, outraged. She remembered Graywillow's words last night, and what others had told her about mageborn children: that the powers that came to them when they were four or five disappeared at six or seven, not returning—if they returned at all—until puberty. *How DARE they turn that poor little mite into a pawn, even if it IS to snatch power from Heshek and his filthy gang . . .*

"The gods know what will become of that child," whispered Graywillow, "if it comes to fighting between the orders of the mages."

"The gods know what will become of any of us," murmured Clea back, "if the Crystal Mages get control of the zai . . ."

Like the single sweep of wind across a barley field, every rider on the waterfront dismounted and knelt beside the heads of their horses. The music from the deck of the *Varthyriel* changed, the bright gold fanfares of the trumpets yielding to the sweeter, more magical melodies of wood-winds and psalteries. A sort of archway had been erected at the top of the gangplank, carven and gilded like everything else on that enormous vessel, and through that arch now rode a tall man in the archaic, many-layered robes of the noble families of Telmayre. Cloaks of thin silk lay one over the other upon the rump of his horse, so that they fluttered like a many-petaled flower, gold and maroon and white. Men riding before him (*One false move and they'll be off the side of that gangplank and into the harbor*, reflected Clea, amused) bore the banners of the emperor, the bleeding heart pierced with three swords. Upon reaching the bottom of the gangplank, they turned to each side and remained mounted, like a second gateway, through which the ambassador himself rode.

In unison (*How much practice did they have to put in?*) they cried, "Apsunahi tar-Alordan, son of Burnharian son of the Holy Uthu, speaker for our Lord Mesismardan."

"Rise"—Apsunahi extended one white-gloved hand—"Stylachos."

Peeking around Hamo's shoulder—because everyone in the crowd was kneeling, too—Clea studied the ambassador's face, long and rather horsey under its formal paint. Beneath his official hat, with its jeweled tassels swinging from its four corners, his hair was light brown, oiled to gleaming slickness. He looked like one of the statues of the gods in the Griffin House's shadowy pantheon shrine. In puffy rings of flesh, his tawny eyes were very bright.

Her father went immediately and held Apsunahi's horse while the ambassador dismounted, then—according to the protocol lessons with which Clea had for two years been tortured—knelt again, and was told to rise again. Learning to kill armed guards with a hatpin had been easier than being drilled in appropriate reverences to the complex imperial ranks, but Clea was well aware that in his sleazy heaven of willing houris and never-empty wine-cups, Rat Bone would be rubbing his hands with glee: *Not everybody can get manners that'll admit them to palaces for the asking!* She could almost hear him chortle.

The men of the Darklander Council came forward one by one, to kiss the ambassador's hands. Precedence was supposedly governed by date of the House's charter in these western lands, but Clea knew it was actually determined by substantial bribes. And of course, after her father, House Shiamat went first by virtue of Grandma tar-Shiamare way back in the day. Then Himelkart stepped forward to kiss the imperial hand as well, and after him, Lady Anamara of the Shrine of Nyellin, the white wool of her gown spotless and her gray hair a lacquered tower of interlocked braids. Clea was aware that behind his façade of statue-like calm, the emperor's representative was regarding both Pendireth and poor little Vervaris Vrykos with calculating curiosity.

Then everyone mounted up again, the music switched from ethereal flutes to martial trumpets once more, and the imperial banners led the entire procession, in reverse order, back up the Street of the Ships toward the Griffin House, where Apsunahi tar-Alordan (and his entire suite, which poured down the gangplank like a very stylish invading army) would be housed. Clea was aware, around her, not only of every pickpocket in Morne (save the ones who'd forgone the ceremony to rob every house and inn whose servants had sneaked out to watch the spectacle), but of mages, moving through the crowd. Brown robes, black robes, red robes—faded as the spells that helped keep the colors bright failed— caught her eye as, after nearly an hour of slow jostling, the press around the wharves finally loosened up.

"Mages are people like everyone else," replied Graywillow, when Clea commented on the fact. "It's not every day you see Emperor Mesismardan's representative come in, or a ship that size. Wasn't it beautiful?"

"It was." Clea held up her striped skirts to hop over a gutter. "But if I was planning to hoax the Council, and the emperor's nephew, into believing that a poor little child is working major magic, I'd sneak down to the harbor, too, and get a look at how the land lies. Did you notice that nobody in the ambassador's suite was a mage? I don't think I've ever heard of His Majesty sending out a representative without one. I'll be curious as to whether mages are even going to be permitted in the Tarnweald on the day of the demonstration."

"Surely they can just hide in the woods, or the hills," protested Hamo. "If they have seeing glasses . . ."

"The other orders may have arranged to set up some kind of ward-spells around the grounds." Clea's eyes narrowed. "If the magic of the gods isn't affected by this mutability . . . but whether the magic of the gods can stand against the Crystal Order I don't know. Graywillow?"

The older girl shook her head. "There has never been a conflict between the orders like this," she said unhappily. "They have always worked together . . ."

"That we know about." She stepped back to allow a chattering party of shopkeepers' wives to pass—already their talk, as far as she could hear it, was of which of their neighbors was committing adultery, and with whom. "Pox blister it, I wish I could attend the council at my father's this afternoon, to get some idea of what's really happening. If there's a serious movement against the Crystal Mages in Telmayre—and who's behind it, Mesismardan or his Heir. And what's happening with the other Orders there. And I wish," she added grimly, "that I'd followed my instincts and kept that shackle on that old man."

"He'll be back." Hamo's brows drew down over his nose. "I know it. Even without the shackle, he has nowhere to go."

"We have no idea," returned Clea, "*where* he has to go in this world. Things that existed seventy-five years ago could be forgotten now, like that cellar passageway in the old Brown Mage settlement, or half the Tunnels in Morne. Now that he can work magic again, we have no idea what his intentions are."

Hamo repeated stubbornly, "He'll be back."

Twenty-One

The following morning of the full moon dawned chill. Rank fog clung to the moldy walls of the Faithful Harlot and its neighbors like a winding-sheet. "It'll be clear away from the harbor," predicted Clea as she laced Graywillow into her tawdry finery, and so it proved. Although they had once again paid young Dakdak to hold a place for them along the wooden barricade around the demonstration area, Clea thought it wise to set forth at first light, to the city-wide clanging of the refinery bells. Even at that hour, half the city seemed to be on the road north to the Tarnweald, and they reached the shaven portion of the meadow to find their landlady's son in a heated altercation with a fishmonger's numerous family over how much space along the railings one person was entitled to. Hamo showed signs of taking violent exception when the fishmonger's son described the two young women as "some fancy-boy's whores"—the first time Clea had ever seen the good-natured shepherd lose his temper—but a fight was the last thing she wanted with her father's guards among those keeping order along the rails. A silver half-coin dispensed to the fishmonger solved the problem. It was rather more than they could afford, but, Clea knew, they couldn't afford *not* to have a view of the demonstration.

The sun put its head above the hills. The clammy chill abated. Jugglers, dancers, acrobats spread out their blankets, passed the hat, and kept the crowd amused. Market-women circulated with baskets of pasties and jugs of beer. After a time, men in the blue and gold livery of the House Vrykos came down the "processional way" that had been likewise barricaded to keep it clear, with carts of wood for the traditional Wet Pyre test of firelighting skills—watched by men in the red and black of the House Stylachos, to make sure barrels of oil weren't being concealed underneath. Two bulls were led down by the same route and put in the cages; a wheeled cage containing a lion from the Southern Isle was dragged in, and another followed filled with rats.

"The bulls and lions look good," whispered Graywillow to Hamo. "But it's the rat-ward spells that really count. That's what first lost the favor of the Black Mages, who had a contract on the city granaries." The shepherd looked startled at the information, as if he'd never thought of the matter before.

"Have you no cities, in your world?"

"None. At least I've never heard of such things. Each man grows grain to feed his own family, and shares with his neighbors if their crop is bad."

To Graywillow, Clea whispered, "Was Ithrazel right? Is there adamine on the ground?"

Since they'd been at the Harlot they'd ridden out twice to ascertain this, but there had always been guards near the grounds. Yesterday—while the emperor's ambassador was being entertained by every merchant prince in the city—the guard had included Imperial Marines, armed with white-steel pikes. This was the closest the three companions had been able to come. Graywillow glanced both ways to make sure no guards were near (they were ordering venturesome spectators back behind the railings, in one case enforcing their commands with cudgels). Then she pulled her veil from her hat and let it drift on a breath of wind onto the shaven grass of the demonstration grounds. With a little cry of distress, she ducked under the rail and hurried to pick up the errant square of pink silk.

A Vrykos guard started immediately for her. Graywillow gathered up the veil, made a placatory gesture toward the man, and scurried back to Clea and Hamo. "He spoke truly," she breathed. "It's all over, not just adamis, but refined adamine, gallons of it. Underfoot, ground into the dirt . . ."

"Is that important?" whispered Hamo. "I thought it was just something wizards use to make spells."

"It is," said Clea. "But it holds magic, far longer than even iron or silver."

"And it holds more complex magic," added Graywillow, trying to tuck her brassy curls out of sight under hat and veil. "Including spells that conceal it."

"So what the hell are they up to?" muttered Clea. "Magnifying whatever spell they'll work for that poor kid? Getting around Crystal Mage watchdogs?"

Graywillow shook her head. "The older orders all use adamine these days, but it's sort of grafted into their older spells. They don't source their power from it, like the Crystal Mages do."

Clea glanced toward the brushy woods on the hillsides above the meadow, where she and her friends had lain five nights ago. "If that's what they're doing, it'd be a whole lot safer than trying to hide in the crowd to work their spells. Look at the number of guards they've got here. And I've seen half a dozen informers in the crowd already, just around where we're standing. That fellow over there in the yellow cap is one of the regular police spies down at the Blossom Garden. That's Thunder-Thighs over on the other side of the ring, near the grandstand, in the green skirt: she works the waterfront and sells whatever she hears to whoever'll pay. Watch how they're looking around. I think they're looking for mages in the crowd."

Unless they're looking for me . . .

In the striped petticoats and leather bodice of a servant woman, she felt reasonably safe. Still . . .

"Is it just adamine scattered on the ground, or in a sigil or something?"

"Just scattered. A sigil would give off magic of its own, and be easier to spot. You can't really sense adamine unless you're looking for it."

"If they've got a couple of mages up in the trees—of different Orders, no less—they'd almost have to be in line of sight. Even a mage here on the rail with a scrying crystal would be slow—and obvious . . ."

Hamo followed her gaze toward the thin trees. "Shall I go up and look?"

May rats devour Ithrazel . . .

Clea raised an eyebrow at Graywillow, who spread her hands helplessly and shook her head. *I have no idea,* rather than, *No, don't.*

Damn him back to his damn birds . . .

Clea looked back toward the road, where the people were shoving and stirring now as the music of trumpets and hautboys colored the air. Her prickling sense of danger deepened. *Even if Hamo catches a three-color squad of wizards in the act, what then? There's only three of us here. If he leaves, there'll only be two . . .*

As Rat Bone had said, danger had to be smelled.

And she smelled it here.

She shook her head, and the first of the Council guards marched down the processional way and into the open field.

The riders who'd preceded Apsunahi tar-Alordan ashore from the *Var-thyriel* two days ago still led the procession, bearing the banners of the Bright Empire and of the House of Uthu. The ambassador himself followed, on a white horse led by Minos Stylachos on foot, in the purple of the Council. The other members of the Council followed, in their official robes and hats: *Serious business*, reflected Clea. Tashthane Vrykos walked among them, solemn as a priest. *Pretending he's only a witness to a demonstration that could shift the foundations of power and overthrow our House.*

Only after they'd taken their places in the first row of the grandstand—established, as it were, in their official capacity as witnesses—did the kindred of the Council members file into the meadow. The hooves of their horses, the shoes of their litter-bearers crushed that faint dusting of adamine powder deeper into the trampled grass. Clea watched Pendireth ride by on a black horse too large for him, peaky with fatigue under his rouge but with his head held high. A six-man litter carried Linvinnia Lyonis, Minos Stylachos' most recent bride: slender, dark-haired, and—when Ganzareb tar-Azazris helped her reverently out—clothed in a billowing rainbow of varicolored silks and glittering with jewels.

"She was a novice in the White Sisters at the Shrine of Nyellin," murmured Clea to Hamo. "My father has informers there, too, among the servants. They said Linvinnia was considered the strongest of the girls—in terms of magic, I mean, she probably can't pick up her own shoes off the floor, not that she'd ever try. There's her mother, in the next litter. Those pearls she's wearing were one of the things I remember my father giving to my mother. Linvinnia's always begging jewels from Father and then somehow they get turned into town properties in her mother's name, or investments in ships. Father won't hear a word against either of them. Look, there's Shumiel—"

Ganzareb, gorgeous himself in armor like jeweler's work, turned from assisting Lady Lyonis to her seat and bowed as he took the hand of Minos Stylachos's elder daughter. If the Golden Princess felt any offense at being outranked by her father's latest mother-in-law—or at being relegated to a four-bearer litter instead of a six—she didn't show it. Dainty as a golden-haired doll, cradling little Snowball in her arms like the child she'd probably never have, she took her seat at Pendri's side.

"Those are her two waiting-gentlewomen behind her, and those other two are *my* waiting-gentlewomen, the Lady Gabiel tar-Kinzaru and the Lady Nikhtu atar-Daisum. My father didn't grudge a copper spangle in hiring true Bright Islands nobility to wait on me, and on Shumiel and Linvinnia. On ordinary days they sit around their private chamber and drink tea and talk about what a waste of time it is to try to teach the likes of me and Linvinnia the first thing about true manners. *Blood will tell*, Lady Gabbie's always saying. I'm surprised Father let Gabbie and Nikhtu come, with me in disgrace."

Around these ladies, the wives and progeny of the other Council members were being likewise escorted to their places by swordmasters or chamberlains or minor scions of the great Houses. Clea picked out her cousin Tykellin, like the lord of one of the lesser Houses in his own right, in the midst of a swarm of his wife's gentlewomen and the young men who hoped to marry his daughters. The crowd behind the railing was now packed like curds in a cheese-hoop. Even the sellers of fried bread and salted plums had been squeezed out.

"I don't see any wizards in the grandstand," said Graywillow quietly. "Or—no—there beside the lord ambassador, in white . . ."

"Do you know her?" Clea studied the stout, motherly form in the white robe.

Graywillow shook her head. "She must have come ashore later . . ."

"When people wouldn't see her. Does the emperor mistrust *all* the Orders, to send a White Sister to keep an eye on things?"

The music reached its fanfare, then ceased. Far back in the press, a child screamed that he couldn't see. Silence then, in which the angry bellowing of the penned bulls came loud as a trumpet.

Clea turned and craned her head, trying to see what might be movement in the trees, or the blink of pale forenoon sun on window-glass. Wizards couldn't see other wizards in scrying-crystals: *But if I know Heshek, he's got about a dozen of the Crystal Boys planted in the crowd. And Pendri's here, too . . .*

From a small booth only a few yards to Clea's left, just within the rails, a man and a child emerged. The man was refulgent in crimson velvet, lined with silk the hue of blood. The child, in the blue and gold of the House Vrykos, looked even tinier and more scared than he had on the wharf the day before yesterday. At a finger-twitch from Lord Apsunahi, the White Sister rose from among his party and crossed to the booth in which the child Vervaris Vrykos had sat, and passed her hands over all sides of it, outside and in.

"Will she be aware of the adamine?" whispered Hamo.

"Not unless she knows to look for it."

"My Lord Ambassador." The Red Mage—the same grizzle-bearded man who had accompanied little Vervaris to the wharf—bent low in a bow to the grandstand, sunlight catching on the gold of his rings. "My lords of the Council. I beg the indulgence to present my student, this boy, Vervaris

Vrykos, already a mage of extraordinary ability despite his tender years. The nature of magic is changing, my lords. We are all of us aware of it, though none have yet fathomed why this should be. Yet in this child are the old spells—working in the old way—reborn."

Lord Apsunahi spoke without moving ("He has to have rehearsed how to sit that still," whispered Clea), hands resting on the arms of his chair like those of a sculpted god. His voice, like a god's, was beautiful, a light baritone trained to carry to the far edges of the field. "The Lord of the Bright Islands, the Emperor of East and West, Prince of the Sunrise, Mesismardan Son of the Holy Uthu, grants you indulgence." He made another slight gesture with a finger, and one of the council guards stepped forward, carrying two pairs of blacksteel manacles.

To one of these, the White Lady stretched out her slender wrists. Clea felt Graywillow flinch in sympathy as the chains were locked in place. The Red Mage ("I think that's Dalmin Zhodel," whispered Graywillow into her ear) drew back protestingly as the guard came to him, but after a moment straightened his shoulders and allowed the spancel to be affixed. "You are wise, my lord," he said, turning toward the ambassador as if he'd thought of this precaution himself. "Yet I can assure you, Vervaris's magic is all his own. At an age when most mageborn children lose their powers, his have remained, and multiplied. Make your obeisance to His Lordship, child, and to the greater Lord whom he represents."

Little Vervaris stepped forward and made an elaborate court obeisance, of the sort reserved for the emperor. "I ask only your leave to serve you." His voice quavered, and if he'd been trained to project it so that all could hear—as Clea had no doubt whatsoever that he had—the lesson was gone from his mind now.

Her eyes went to Pendri, and she saw her brother's expression of sympathy and pity, that anyone should have to go through this. Their father leaned back and whispered something to him, gesturing toward the younger boy as Vervaris walked back toward the center of the open field.

Sons of Death, thought Clea, *I wouldn't want to have to make a thirty-foot spell-circle with my father, my father's enemies, the emperor's nephew, the whole Darklands Council and three quarters of the population of Morne looking on. . . .*

A low murmur of approval ran through the crowd as the child began to draw a Sigil of Power, first with iron filings, then with salt from a spell-marked gourd. Dalmin Zhodel and the White Lady both stood well back, and the dark-haired boy looked very tiny in the midst of that open space.

According to old Khymin, in the Tunnels the power circle of a Sigil had to be perfect; Clea wondered if someone had come out last night by moonlight and scratched guidelines for the child in the dirt.

Her mind went back to the first time she'd picked the pocket of a hanging dummy covered with bells, before the watching eye of old Snaggle-Fang the head of the Thieves' Guild. It had been nearly as unnerving, given the severity of the beating she'd been promised if she failed. Graywillow whispered, "He's very good."

"Doesn't matter how good he is," returned Clea shortly. "If this little scheme of the Vrykoses doesn't work—if three spells can go wrong just as easily as one—there's no telling what—"

Her words cut off as a man leaped lightly over the rail and walked to the center of the ring, and a harsh, powerful voice cut through the silence.

"My lords, you are being deceived!"

Twenty-Two

Ithrazel had picked up from somewhere the black robe of one of the Old Orders—much patched and faded—and the red tabard and cloak of another, and looked, Clea thought, sufficiently like a wizard to command the ambassador's attention, at least for a moment. Tashthane Vrykos yelled, "Get that man out of here!" and his guards—and those of the Council— sprinted to obey. But Ithrazel swung around on them, holding out the staff that bore the appearance of something he'd picked out of a hedge, and they all skidded to a stop.

To the ambassador, the old wizard called out again, "You are being deceived, my lord! The ground underfoot is dusted with adamine! It will twist whatever magic is done in this place!"

At Ithrazel's first words, Clea's gaze had darted from the ambassador— she already had a good idea of what his reaction would be—to sweep the rail and the crowd behind it, so she saw eight men shove their way to the fore and scramble up onto the fence as if they would leap over it and complete what the guards dared not. She recognized Himelkart's dark tousle at once—as she'd suspected, he wore the simple brown and blue doublet of a townsman, and a black velvet cap—and the grave, dark face of the librarian Tsorkesh, likewise clothed as a simple artisan. Three of the others—graybeards—she knew as practitioners of the three Old Orders of wizardry, whom she'd seen over the course of the past two years at her father's court or in the streets of Morne: Manzardath of the Brown Mages, Amil of the Red, and Kenzag (Graywillow had told her that his original name among the Loghri had been Bear Fishing) of the Black.

None of them, nor any of the other cold-eyed youngsters who clustered around Himelkart and Tsorkesh, were attired as mages either.

Himelkart shouted, "That's a lie!" and Manzardath knelt and spread his hands out over the ground. His dark eyes widened with shock and outrage.

"What he says is true, Lord Ambassador!" He straightened up. "There's adamine all over this ground! No spell would work as it—"

"And what are *you* doing here?" demanded Himelkart in his Sea Islands drawl, "when the High King has forbidden any mageborn to interfere—?"

"What am *I* doing here? How came *you*, and your colleagues, to be in this place? What trickery have you plotted—?"

Unnoticed in the midst of his half-writ Circle, the child Vervaris burst into frightened tears.

"And what trickery have *you* plotted?" yelled old Amil the Red. "It wasn't *we* who spread adamine far and wide here—gods above, the cost of it alone could only have come from the House of Glass!"

"Or the House of Vrykos!" retorted Himelkart. "Who is this man—"

He swung around just as Ithrazel, retreating without a sound, had almost reached the safety of the barrier, and at a sign from the ambassador the council guards closed in on him. The old man tried to wrench free and was dragged to the grandstand, Himelkart striding forward, like a young and furious god.

"Who are you to—"

He stopped, facing Ithrazel, still in the grip of the guards.

Clea was close enough to see his face change, his eyes widen in shock.

Close enough to see Ithrazel's stunned horror as their gazes met.

Himelkart whispered, "You—" He seized the old man's hand, shoved up the grimy black sleeve and stared at the telltale burns the blacksteel had left on his wrists.

Ithrazel said nothing, but it was as if some impact had driven all the blood from his face. As if he saw, finally, the thing that he had been made to forget.

"Ithrazel—" Himelkart swung back around to where the ambassador had actually risen from his seat in offended dignity. "My lord!" cried the young mage. "Ithrazel the Cursed! It is Ithrazel, destroyer of Dey Allias, murderer, renegade, and—"

Ithrazel's eyebrows shot up. "Sonny," he said patiently, but in a voice that carried effortlessly to the whole of the crowd, "your *grandfather* wasn't born when the New Mages put that old bastard to death. You expect the imperial ambassador to believe that you'd just know Ithrazel by sight? And that he just happens to be the person who's accusing the Crystal Mages of throwing three hundred pounds of adamine all over this field on the day of the demonstration? What's the adamine for? To pull the power Brownie, Blackie, and the Crimson Sorcerer over there"—he jerked his head toward the three mages—"are raising to fool the ambassador, and use it maybe to do something else?"

Himelkart stammered, "Pull their . . . What do you mean?"

"Adamine," retorted Ithrazel succinctly. "Twisting spells awry. Turning their hoax into a bigger one. That's a good try," he added, "saying I'm Ithrazel . . . but the only way you could recognize Ithrazel is if the Crystal Order had decided not to kill him after all. If they just put him away someplace in case they needed his power for some other little job they might want to do in the Bright Islands someday."

"That's ridiculous—"

"Of course it is. As ridiculous as my saying—"

"Silence!" roared Lord Apsunahi. "Himelkart of Thourmand, who is this man?"

"I am Iohan of Caith Isle"—Ithrazel named one of the farthest islets of the Bright Archipelago as he bent in deep obeisance to the ambassador—"if it please Your Lordship. I am at the service of the Emperor of Light, Mesismardan, and of Your Lordship."

"He's lying!" Himelkart whirled to face the ambassador. "This is Ithrazel the Cursed—"

Ithrazel rolled his eyes.

"He has returned to bring destruction—"

WHAT'S THAT SMELL??? Clea's hair seemed to prickle straight up in the same instant that she realized that the sun had darkened, as if eclipsed by a smoked lens. A wet smell, a cold smell, the smell that had clung to the charred timbers of Turtlemere village . . .

And at the rear of the packed crowd in the meadow, a man screamed.

Twenty-Three

S he saw its eyes before anything else: bodiless, gleaming, in the darkening air above the crowd.

The wall of heat struck her, as if she stood in an undertow in deep water, rocking her back while all around her Council guards cried out and looked wildly around them. Others dashed with reflexive defensiveness toward His Excellency (*as if they'd be able to protect him from any danger*). In the crowd, people screamed, pushed—*In another minute they'll be in the arena . . .*

Eyes caught the light—*No*, she thought, *the light is from within it . . .*

It came into being, like the amorphous, impossible darkness coalescing. Shadow first, then flesh, that great smooth bulk that moved in the dark of her nightmares. The mouth on its rubbery proboscis that she'd seen break the surface of the black waters of the grotto in the Nightshade Maze, to bite Himelkart's guards in half, blood spreading in the water . . .

It swooped down onto the crowds now and the mouth uncurled itself, swallowed up a woman—or the top half of a woman, leaving the legs to fall, kicking, in a fountain of blood and entrails tangled in green petticoats. Clea yelled, "Clear this ground! It'll come here first!" Clear as daylight in her mind, she saw the burned sheds in Turtlemere, the melted adamis puddled in the dirt. "Make for the trees—"

Like those will offer any concealment . . .

And above the shouting all around her she thought she heard Pendri's shrill voice cry, "Clea!"

While the Red Mage Dalmin clawed at his blacksteel shackles, his Order-brother Amil stretched forth his hands toward the thing—forty feet it was, from tip to tip of those weirdly billowing, rubbery wings (*the*

Turtlemere villagers were right)—and the lightning that flashed from the air was thready and nearly invisible against the spreading dark. Clea saw the blue flare of it run sizzling over the dull-gray glittering hide, like spit on a hot flatiron. The creature dipped, swooped up, lashed with the silver club at the end of its whiplike tail. But whether its shriek was pain or triumph or madness no one could tell; it was more like the blast of a discordant metal horn than anything of flesh. It swooped down again, caught up another man—the ground below seethed with people running frantically to get out from under the shadow of those stinking wings.

The wizards Manzardath and Kenzag grabbed each others' hands and like the Red Mage made the long swooping gestures of spell-casting, but the fire—if it was fire they were casting—burst on the testing-ground's wooden railings rather than on its target, then ignited the roof of the grandstand. Glancing back—though she was certain that the grandstand was empty, and indeed it was—Clea saw for an instant Himelkart standing alone before it, his hands upraised.

As she'd seen him in the grotto in the Nightshade Maze, kneeling on his overturned boat. Hands forming the signs she'd seen then, as the zai surged from the water and swallowed up his guards.

The zai swerved in the air, silvery hide flashing in the smoke. Then it plunged straight toward them again, and Himelkart turned tail and ran like a rabbit. Clea reached the knot of imperial marines around the ambassador in three long strides: "Adamis draws it! We're standing on bushels of it here!"

The ambassador bolted, holding up his robes around his thighs like a housewife in a stampede of mice, his marines around him. Clea grabbed the pike from one of them and the fleeing woman didn't fight her for it—*Pigs eat their children, not one of them brought a bow!*

"Adamis," croaked Ithrazel's voice at her side. "Look at its hide, what does it look like—"

"No wonder the lightning wouldn't strike—"

Vervaris Vrykos screamed like a kitten in a trap as the shadow of the dripping wings fell over him, and a woman in the plain frock of a servant dashed from the crowd to scoop him up.

"Clea!" Hamo dashed to her from the direction of the grandstand like a man fleeing through a rainstorm, two swords in his hands. Two other guards followed him, House Vrykos bodyguards who'd probably get their pay docked for abandoning their employers. The shepherd flung her one of the weapons—Ithrazel wrenched the other from the young man's hand.

"Get out of the way, you fool, you don't know how to use one of these things!"

Manzardath and Kenzag had another try at a spell—the gods only knew what it was, because it didn't work—and the zai plunged straight at them, screaming that horrible metallic cry again. Clea stepped in under it and slashed at the rubbery throat as its mouth came down, felt the hot sear of saliva burn her hand as it veered again, swooped up—

Vanished.

For an instant they all just looked at each other. Shocked, stunned ...

The smell of it smote Clea again and she yelled, "Watch out!" instants before it appeared, on the ground now, balanced on its single huge hind leg and stumpy forearms, only feet away. She hacked at it as it snapped the nearest guard, tore off his sword arm, shoulder, half his trunk. Then it launched itself into the air again, vomiting yellow acid mixed with blood as the guards scattered.

She was aware of Ithrazel slapping his hand down to break the grasp of the Brown Mage's hand on the Black's: "Don't cast spells, you idiots, the gods know what it'll do!" at the same moment the two Red Mages attempted (presumably) to fling fire at the zai as it swerved back. (*Dalmin must have had the spancel keys on him*, she thought.) Their own robes, and the tabard of a nearby guard, blazed up like candles—the men ran burning, screaming, as Clea caught up the guard's seven-foot blacksteel halberd, unable to spare them even a glance.

It's drawn to the adamis. She saw it gyre in the air, plunge back—

"Get out of the test-ground," she yelled. "I'm gonna cut its hide."

Ithrazel had a wizard's acute hearing and caught her words over the din. He and Hamo were stripping Dalmin from his burning garments, but he grabbed the shepherd by the wrist, dragged him to the rail where Graywillow—*thank the gods!*—waited alone, the only one standing among a dozen wounded. Clea followed, slower, watching the movement of the zai as it plunged down again. It vomited fire this time, huge swathes of it searing across the adamis-dusted ground, its movements erratic, circling and diving in to smash the roof of the grandstand—

It's mad, she thought. *It's striking out at everything and anything, as it did at Turtlemere.*

She yelled, stepped forward, brandished the sword she still held in her right hand. Leaped aside from a sticky gout of acid, blood, and fire, swung the sword, the blacksteel that veined it flashing in the glare.

She ran forward as it came in, dropping the sword, catching the halberd-shaft in her right hand as she plunged straight in under the zai. The blade slit its underbelly and it swooped up, raining blood that burned her skin like droplets of acid.

And I hope to Nyellin Ithrazel can aim . . .

She heard a crack like thunder, the sizzle of lightning. Almost over her head she saw, for a flashing instant, the bolt of his power sear like a blazing needle into the open wound.

That scream was pain. She knew it. The zai faded, vanished, but she saw where the blood still dripped, spattering from the sky—saw the hell-yellow glare of its eyes. The stink was appalling. She snatched up the sword, looked around the test-ground—near the corpse of a guard was an ornamental dagger of blacksteel, probably the man's pride and joy. She grabbed it, shoved it into her belt. The ambassador's staff, pure white ada-mine . . . she caught that up, also, never letting go of the halberd, watching the zig-zag splattering of the blood. From the corner of her eye, she saw Ithrazel linking hands with Graywillow, with old Manzardath and Ken-zag, amid the trampled ruin of the half-made Sigil. Hamo, disobeying her orders, had run back behind her, was helping the two burned Red Mages toward the rail—

That glimpse lasted the flash of a second, and she put it from her mind in the next needle of time. *Can't think of that . . .*

The zai faded back into view, shadow first, then flesh. She raised the blacksteel dagger, the white staff, and it plunged.

The wave of its heat thrust her back and she braced herself, dropped the bait, sidestepped and cut.

The blistering sizzle of lightning . . .

The zai burst into flames as it fell. Flames and darkness swirled around it, and where it struck the ground great clouds of silver dust—adamis dust—billowed into the air, a blinding fog that caught firelight and sunlight like a rainbow made of whirling razors. Ithrazel caught Hamo's arm, for the young man would have plunged straight under the rail and into that blaze. By the time the first explosion of light and fire died down, guards had surged in from around the grandstand.

Someone shouted, "It fell on her!" and Hamo snatched up a halberd lying on the ground, thrust it into the hideous blaze and tried to shove the mass of burning flesh aside. *As if,* thought Ithrazel, backing away, shielding his eyes, *she could yet be living under that conflagration . . .*

Then he saw something on the halberd-shaft in the shepherd's hands, and turned his head in time to see the little knot of guards, the flash of dark straight hair under a black velvet cap, disappearing into the crowd beyond the ruins of the grandstand. The grandstand, too, was in flames. *When had that happened?*

More guards were moving in from beyond the testing-ground.

Graywillow was beside Hamo, probing also with one of the guards' ornamental spears. The bright glare of the adamis mist still surrounded them, though it was fading. The wizard tried to imagine any kind of natural process that would have caused it. The zai hadn't hit the ground that hard, and though it was huge—its collapsed body made a waist-high mound among the flames—adamis in general didn't produce this sort of dust.

But even as he reflected on this he was striding into the glare, catching the two young people by the elbows. "Let's get out of here," he said. "Now."

Hamo braced his feet. "Clea—"

"NOW." And when he'd dragged them to the edge of the testing-ground—the burning rail had been knocked down—he said, "Dockside. Great Pool. Full dark. Get back to town now, immediately, and don't let anyone see you. We can't afford hostages right now."

"Clea might be—"

"Clea was ten feet behind the thing when it fell," said the old man, and even as he spoke, he was stripping out of the red tabard and cloak he'd worn in the test-ground, rolling them into a bundle with the cloak's dark lining outermost. "Where you picked up that halberd." He handed the bundle to Graywillow. "The New Mages got in behind the glare of the fire, the second the thing was dead. They've got her. Lose that," he added to the girl. "Don't let anyone find it. They'll look for someone in red for a while, anyway."

Shivering a little—his black robe was threadbare and the autumn wind had kicked up—he thrust his hands through his sash and hurried away, pausing to kneel beside the dead two or three times, like a man who is not escaping for his life. Aware of the guards scattering around the fringes of the field, where the dead lay—men, women, children who had been struck by the zai's flame, or the acid it had spurted, or who had been bitten by that gaping, froglike mouth.

Hoping that Graywillow had the sense to get Hamo someplace safe and keep him with her until dark, not heeding whatever harebrained plans the boy might come up with.

Hoping that he himself could come up with some kind of a plan to get Clea away from the House of Glass, that didn't involve going back into it himself.

Twenty-Four

The man called Pig-Face (*a gross slander on pigs*, reflected Ithrazel) sat on a broken chair before the shut doors of the broken-down mansion's stable. By the clamor and chatter of the men and girls around him, Ithrazel guessed that the first of the pickpockets hadn't beaten him to the place by very much. Two he half-recognized, from the crowd on the testing-ground: a skinny straw-haired boy with the sharp features of the Setuket, and a massive-bosomed woman in a blue-striped skirt. They, and the half-dozen others with them, were trembling, hands jerking. Dust-covered faces still ghastly with shock.

And no god-cursed wonder . . .

Striding through the streets in the wake of the old water-seller he'd paid to guide him to the shrine of Rycellis—Ithrazel had remembered that place, at least, and knew he could find Liver-Eater's house from there—the wizard had seen no other sign that word had reached the city. Only when they'd gotten close to the waterfront had he been conscious of the first commotion: a man pounding on a door with the same shaky desperation of these people here in the court. A young boy in the garb of a servant running from another court and dashing toward the city gate with a look of horror and dread on his face. *Sent running to see if it's true . . .*

Ithrazel was through the group and in front of Pig-Face before anyone took notice of him.

"I need to see Liver-Eater," he said.

The big man stood: unshaven, stinking, three hundred pounds with a core of brutal iron under the flab. "The Boss don't see no one."

"Don't be an idiot, man, his only chance to save himself is if he acts *now*."

The beady dark eyes shifted uncertainly; Ithrazel could almost hear the rusty clank of unused wheels turning in his skull. Impatiently he stepped around the man and flung a spell at the door. The lock was adamine and heavily spelled, and as things were, Ithrazel had no idea whether the lightning he summoned would strike the door or not—it had taken him four separate spells to get it to sear into the zai, and for a hideous moment he had feared that no spell would summon it.

Certainly the spell that had called it forth on the testing-ground didn't work now.

It did, however, cause the wood of the door to bleach and crack (*Hmm, now THERE's an effect I've never seen*), and the fire-spell he threw the next second, with a scornful air of triumph, did work, the suddenly desiccated wood of the door almost exploding with the heat. As everyone cried out in astonishment and awe (and Ithrazel heaved a well-concealed sigh of relief), he strode forward, being careful to pull the skirts of his too-large black robe close about him as he ducked through the narrow, flaming hole in the door.

"Now, wait just a—" Pig-Face bellowed at his heels, but providentially, the clear gap in the midst of the flame was barely large enough to admit a man of Ithrazel's slight stature.

Behind him, as he crossed the stable court, the wizard heard yells of panic as people ran about to put out the fire.

The guard posted next to the door of Liver-Eater's chamber—the first of the stable's box stalls—fled inside as Ithrazel approached and left the door open.

Probably to wake him . . .

The bandit chief was, indeed, sitting up amid a tangle of dirty silk quilts and furs in an elaborately carved louse-farm that had formerly been a rich man's bed. The guard—who probably owed his position here today to a lost card-cut—hovered nearby, a fighting-ax in either hand. Ithrazel barely glanced in his direction. "You can go."

The man left. Ithrazel supposed Liver-Eater would have some words for him later, but didn't much care.

"You, too," he said to the woman sitting up beside the bandit chief: fortyish, not pretty, with a hooked nose and wise, wary eyes. She slid her hand under the pillows—presumably for a weapon—and glanced questioningly at Liver-Eater.

"Run along, darling." The thief patted her shoulder. "Leave the knife."

Ithrazel fetched a gaudy silk robe from the nearest chair and held it out to her as she got out of bed; she snatched it from him, spit at him—not out of respect—and walked away down the darkness of the smoky, filthy dormitory, nude, trailing the robe behind her. Ithrazel bowed after her, then turned back to Liver-Eater.

"A zai attacked the demonstration on the testing-ground," he said. "The Lady Clea and I managed to kill it, but in the confusion the Crystal Mages took her. She'll be in the House of Glass now. I need your help to get her out."

Liver-Eater's mouth opened as if he would have made some observation, then closed, and his dark eyes shifted as the information sank in. He got out of bed, wrapped himself in a robe as gorgeous as it was dirty, and took from beneath the pillows a sheathed dagger the length of his forearm. "Don't be silly." He thrust the weapon into his sash. "If they have her, she's dead now." His voice was level, but his eyes glinted dangerously. "Is it true all the adamis from the refineries is being moved up to the warehouses? This zai—"

"If they wanted her dead," replied Ithrazel, ignoring the question, "they'd have killed her on the testing-ground. The zai fell nearly on top of her. Himelkart ignited its flesh with a spell—at a guess, the moment it was dead and unprotected by its own magic. It went up like a bucket of lamp oil. They don't know what they can get in trade for her—thank you, dear," he added as a young boy came tremblingly in with a tray containing a steaming beaker, by the smell of it a potent mix of coffee and brandy.

There was only one cup—gold and shell. *If you're going to steal, by all means steal the best . . .*

Ithrazel took it, filled it, and handed it to Liver-Eater with a bow. He'd already noticed a couple of cups—of the same set, it looked like, presumably left over from last night—on the small table beside the bed. He took one of these and poured it full for himself.

He rather felt he'd earned it.

He waited for Liver-Eater to drink, before he sipped his own.

"Not only don't they know what they can get in trade for her," he continued, "they don't know what she knows. I know Himelkart." The words were poison in his mouth. *Dear gods, I know Himelkart. . . .*

He hid the shudder that went through him and went on. "I think I know Heshek, too. They're far too wary to kill a potential bargaining chip." Even speaking of them turned him sick with shock, recalling that first cold horror as he'd met the eyes of that dark, sardonic youth and knew him.

Knew him for who he really was.

Recognized him.

Someone else's face. Someone else's body.

Dear gods . . .

He remembered. He remembered everything.

He was aware of Liver-Eater's eyes on his face.

He began to say, "At the moment they'll be in a panic. Within hours they'll be in council with the merchant lords and the ambassador. They won't—"

His voice faltered, and he was aware that the blood had drained from his face, from the shock and reaction he had, till this moment, kept at bay. Walking—running when he could—back to Morne, he had forced it from his mind, forced everything: the adamine ground into the earth of the old spell-circle on the Hill of Oleanders, Machodan Indigo's eyes looking at him from the face of an eighteen-year-old boy.

Machodan Indigo . . .

And who was he before that?

Don't think about it, he had told himself. *Figure out a way to get Clea out of there first . . .* That had been enough—almost—to drive the panic and shock from his mind.

For a moment, Liver-Eater regarded him in silence. Then he got up, put a surprisingly strong hand under his elbow, led him to one of the black-wood chairs and drew up the other for himself. After another long minute of quiet, he said, "What's really going on?"

Gods . . .

What's really going on?

His hands were shaking and he forced them still. Liver-Eater raised one end of his bar of eyebrow, reached across the little table between them and put his hand on Ithrazel's. By the heat of the bandit's flesh, the wizard knew his own extremities were still icy with shock.

Liver-Eater considered him for a moment more, then said with a sort of kindly off-handedness, "Drink your coffee." Rising again, he walked on into the flophouse, picking up his scythe-handle as he went. Ithrazel saw his shape moving through the darkness of the old stalls, prodding bunks and cursing in a conversational tone. Three or four dim shapes staggered and rolled from the beds, and the bandit kicked, beat, and harried them out through a small doorway at the far end of the dormitory.

When he'd flung the last of them out by the scruff of her neck, he came back, neatly replacing the scythe-handle beside the first of the stalls. Then he sat again, and sipped his coffee. "You take sugar?"

Ithrazel shook his head.

"Had anything to eat? I shouldn't have let Gula and Sugar-drawers go—"

"I'll get something later."

Liver-Eater nodded, and folded his hands. "What's going on?"

Ithrazel drew a long breath. "The New Mages are trying to come up with a way to control the zai."

"So those rumors are true? About Darklander water-monsters . . ."

"They're true. If you go outside now, the city's probably in a panic, with the stories coming back from those who fled the testing-ground. It's not just zai, either. The things your little friend Quillet spoke of that have been seen in the Tunnels—"

The bandit-chief nodded again. "If it was just one or two, could have been a bad batch of dream-sugar. Sometimes you'll have half a dozen hallucinate the same thing. But—"

"No." Ithrazel shook his head. "The zai are drawn to adamis, in all its forms. Drawn to it—and driven mad by it. I watched it, when it came down on the testing-ground." He shut his eyes for a moment, sickened. The images seemed burned on his sight, even as the horrors had been when Dey Allias had gone up.

For a man who supposedly killed fifty thousand people, you're damn squeamish . . .

"No wonder everybody's rushing to get all their adamine locked down in the warehouses. In half an hour, you won't be able to cross the street because of the carts."

"It wasn't hungry," the wizard said. "It wasn't hunting. It bit, tore, then spat the bodies out, like an animal bites and tears at things when it's in pain. It moved as if it were mad. Yet it kept circling back to the testing-ground, which the New Mages had covered with raw adamis dust—" He lifted his hand as Liver-Eater's eyebrows flared upward, probably at the expense involved.

"They were going to do something, divert the power summoned by the wizards who were faking the Vrykos boy's spells. Possibly strike the ambassador dead. That's what I'd have done, to discredit the other orders . . ."

"Or kill the whole crowd," suggested Liver-Eater casually. "Ten thousand people? Fifteen?" Ithrazel turned his face aside, from the echo of nightmare screams. "Go on."

"Adamis draws them. It's how Clea got it to come in on her, close enough that she could cut open its hide. She surrounded herself with the stuff, held it up in her hands. It had to come in, though the stuff drove it mad—"

"Like those poor stiffs in there." The bandit nodded back toward the bunks of the opium-den.

"They volunteer to get started," returned Ithrazel. "I'm not sure the zai do. A zai attacked a village called Sandmire six months ago. The New Mages got House Stylachos to hush it up. Three weeks ago another village, Turtlemere, was destroyed. The adamis sheds were battered to pieces and burned. The creature—or creatures—had rolled in the stuff, like cats on catnip. That was hushed up as well. After Turtlemere was destroyed, Himelkart went out looking for the thing. Not to destroy it, but to see if he could control it by spells."

"I heard something about that," murmured Liver-Eater. "So they didn't summon it? Or breed it, or manufacture it . . ."

"No. From what the Gray Ladies say, out in the Reedmire, these things seem to have begun to rise up out of the deeper canyons, out of the waters, or the diamond-clay itself. The gods only know how long they've been sleeping down there, cozied in with their dreams. The Crystal Mages wouldn't be trying to learn about them, trying to find some way to control them, if they'd created them. Or if their rising had ever happened before. Don't you see?" he went on, leaning forward across the little table.

"For a century and a half, men have been mining adamis. They came here to the Twilight Lands looking for it—digging it out of the rock back on Telmayre, dredging it from the river-sands along the Dey, scooping it up out of the beds of the canyons. . . . Raw dust, that they concentrated and refined, and that they've used for *everything*, every form of magic and spell—weapons, mouse-wards, healing, longevity, finding lost dogs. And all the while it's been accumulating, more dense, more strong. I suspect that its aura permeates the very air now. It foxes other magic. Distorts it. Changes spells that *don't* use it into something else. And it calls to those things that fed on it, that nested in it—back when it was diffuse and harmless. That went to the beds of it in the canyons to die, maybe. Only they didn't die."

"Like poppy." The bandit-chief's voice was neutral. "Harmless enough, when it's only a flower."

"A hundred years ago," said Ithrazel softly, "a new order of mages started sourcing their spells entirely from the magic within refined adamis—adamine. Their spells were so good—especially spells of healing—that more and more was dredged and mined and scooped and triple-refined. Seven or eight or ten or maybe twenty years ago, there was enough refined adamine that it began to interfere the working of ordinary magic. Began to interfere, I think, even with the ability of the Sisterhoods to speak with the gods. The effects grew stronger, and worse. Then six months ago, there was enough of the stuff refined, soaked with magic and twined with the spells of every order of mages in existence, that it began to call to . . . whatever was down in the canyons. Not just the zai, but the smaller horrors as well. Giving them life. Drawing them forth. Driving them mad."

For a time the two men looked at each another in the dim glow of the lamp. From beyond the doorway, Ithrazel was now conscious of voices in the courtyard: first calling out questions and rumors, then the rumble of frightened talk. Evidently they'd managed to tear away the burning ruins of the gate.

And beyond them, the rising clamor of carts being driven along the Dockside, toward the higher ground where the palaces of the merchant houses stood, and the long ranks of their fortresslike warehouse compounds.

He could see, in Liver-Eater's dark eyes, the working-through of what it meant, if it were true.

How much adamis IS there in Morne?

At length, Liver-Eater remarked, "Shit."

"Yes. The Crystal Mages have to stop this." Ithrazel moved a finger, taking in the clamor outside. "Control panic and rumor, until they're ready to come up with some kind of explanation. Keep anyone from knowing that the whole foundation of their magic—the whole foundation of everybody's wealth—is now poison. Is now deadly danger. They have to know who else knows, and silence them. It's why they've been after Clea. And they have to know what to say to the ambassador and to the council."

Liver-Eater nodded. Like thieves guilds everywhere, the Morne organization worked on exactly the same lines as the Merchants' Council, *except*, reflected Ithrazel, *with gentler methods and more compassionate hearts.*

Liver-Eater said, frowning, "And we have a shitload of adamine down in the Tunnels."

"Good," said Ithrazel. "We're going to need it."

Twenty-Five

Though she had been blindfolded, almost from the moment that Himelkart and his guards had surrounded her in the glare and the dust and the billowing smoke of the testing-ground, Clea knew where she was.

She had heard the noises of the waterfront as they'd passed it, the guards—professionals, for all they wore the rough garb of city laborers—keeping silent, presumably because Himelkart had some kind of spell of concealment over them that wouldn't stand up to excessive noise. Even in her exhaustion and terror, her mind noted the rattle of carts clogging the greater avenues, the fear in the voices of the drivers. *Somebody clearing out? Not leaving the city already . . .*

Once she heard Himelkart curse the traffic, in his nasal Sea Islands drawl.

The creak of the kitchen gate had been familiar, followed almost at once by the woodsmoke of baking-ovens and the stench of latrines.

Kitchen courts, she thought. *It's the House of Glass, all right.* The mulch of kitchen gardens. The lap of the sea beyond the walls, even when the gate closed behind them and the guards muttered back and forth among themselves. Clea kept her mouth shut, and faked a stumble or two, like a woman still too stunned—and she almost was—from the battle with the zai to be quite steady on her feet.

Her heart hammered in her chest, as it had all the way back to Morne, buried under blankets at the bottom of a swift-moving cart. One of the guards had kept a knife-point under her ear, until they'd gagged her before thrusting her into the cart. She had no doubt whatsoever they'd kill her before Himelkart would risk being unmasked as her kidnapper.

She wondered what her father would say.

What her father *had* said, about her disappearance on the night of the last moon's waning, when Turtlemere had been destroyed. He had been hunting her, had offered a reward for her . . . but *why*?

If they were sure they want me dead, I'd be dead. It would have been easy as tripping on a stair . . .

Dreamlike, the iridescent bulk of the zai seemed printed on her mind with the terrible clarity of a vision. Glittering silver, seemingly plated all over with adamis dust. Shedding the sparks of the spells that had been thrown at it, everywhere save the gaping slits left by her halberd-blade in its hide.

Pulpy red flesh, a horrible glimpse of yellowish organs moving within, blood streaming down.

Red blood, like creatures of this world. Her arm still stung from the burn of it.

Then the searing blue flash of Ithrazel's lightning bolt.

The zai had buckled in the middle, had already been falling for half a second before it burst into flames.

Did the old man get away safely? Was Graywillow able to hang onto poor Hamo and keep him from dashing in . . . or is he dead, too?

And if he isn't, will they use him to get at me?

The grief and guilt she'd felt at using Hamo—using him shamelessly and casually, without a thought as to what might have happened—turned her sick, for about one second before she returned her mind to the sounds and smells outside the room where they'd thrust her. *If you feel anything inside, your hands will shake . . .*

You can weep later.

The window was barred, the shutters on the outside, not to be opened from within. Through them, she still smelled garden mulch and the sea. Thin slits of light through the cracks added to the even dimmer glow of daylight that came in under the door: There must be windows in the hall outside. It was only a few hours past noon. She'd been in darker tunnels, navigated in blacker corners of her father's prisons.

Someone screamed again, close by. An animal sound, or like the cry of a terrified child, over and over again. But the timbre of the voice was a man's.

She knew perfectly well where she was.

Many voices. Her trained ear picked them apart, one from another. All men. Two or three screamed, turn and turn about. Others moaned like injured beasts. The sound swelled and ebbed, as if the men paced back and forth in some room where they were kept, possibly across a hall from her own.

Ithrazel, staring at Himelkart, ashen with shock.

You—Himelkart had whispered, like a man who'd taken a spear in the chest.

Himelkart knew him. Recognized him.

And Ithrazel recognized Himelkart, whose father couldn't even have been born when the New Mages had chained the old man to that rock.

The only way you could recognize Ithrazel is if the Crystal Mages decided not to kill him after all. If they just put him away someplace in case they needed his power . . .

The way they seek to bring the zai under their dominion, rather than save peoples' lives by killing them . . .

But it isn't only that. She groped her way back to the floor beside the pallet that was the room's only furniture, where a jug and a covered latrine-bucket stood by the wall. She sniffed the water in the jug, and detected a faint, musky odor, like decaying flowers.

Pigs eat your children. She covered the jug again and set it down. Blue sleep, a soporific much favored by assassins when it was necessary that members of the household be seen to be moving about rather than sprawled asleep where they fell. She wondered how long it was going to be before someone came in, held her nose, and poured it down her throat.

It isn't only that. Himelkart knew Ithrazel. Recognized him—had seen him before.

So how old does that make Himelkart? But she knew the answer: her own age. Eighteen. She'd seen that dark, cocky child riding in procession, the day the infant Pendireth had been taken for the gods' blessing, only months after she'd gotten out of the prison. She'd seen him dozens of times since, growing as she grew. *So how could he know Ithrazel? How could Ithrazel know* him?

Another scream from the room across the corridor made her flesh creep. Why keep madmen? This was clearly where the mad Rivan had escaped from, but why keep him in the first place? And why were there others? Was there something about this New Magic that drove its practitioners insane? Was that what adamine did, if you used too much of it in your spells? She remembered how the zai had moved, drawn to the glittering dust on the ground, to the blacksteel and the gleaming adamine staff in her hand. *Drawn, yet in pain. Savage, like a rabid dog.*

She tried to remember other Crystal Mages she had seen. The older ones, men Rivan's age—twenty-five? Thirty? An age when the wizards of other orders were still novices, learning to source the powers of earth, air, their own blood . . .

Are they even going to tell Father they have me here?

And what kind of questions will Father—and the ambassador!—ask them about what happened?

She leaned her head back against the wall behind her. *Plaster*, she thought. Wattle and slats between supports, not the stone of the building's shell. *Don't sleep*, she warned herself, though with the shock of the fight that morning it was all she wanted to do. *You don't know how long it'll be, before . . .*

Before what?

She moved across to the door again and put her ear to it, to listen to the screaming and the moaning of the mad wizards—*How many of them* are *there?*—across the corridor. *That should keep me awake . . .*

In fact, it didn't.

She woke sweating, shivering, at the sound of shouting somewhere in the gardens. The light was gone. Only the thinnest breath of glow shone beneath the door beside which she sat—*corridor lamps?* But with little fear of tripping over anything—since the cell was almost completely bare—she crossed to where she knew the window to be, found it with her hands.

Dampness and the smell of river fog. Thick, by the chill breath that seeped through the cracks. It muffled the voices in the garden below: "How could he get in?" and "It's impossible! It has to be illusion . . ." "Don't be daft—" Surely that was Himelkart's twanging Sea Islands accent? "He couldn't hope to use an illusion on us . . ."

"When will Apsunahi be here? How the hell could he have known about us—?"

"You imbecile, that letter was a bluff. Any thief in town could get hold of a messenger's uniform—"

"It was addressed to you," insisted another. "Not to Himelkart of Thourmand. To Machodan Indigo—"

"It's a bluff!" Himelkart's voice was suddenly sharp and hard as a kitchen cleaver. "It's a god-cursed bluff! No one knows—"

"My lord!" Shouting from a distance, and with it, as the air shifted, the sudden smell of smoke. "My lord—!"

Running feet.

Machodan Indigo. Who had said that name? Machodan Indigo.

Ithrazel. He'd spoken of the mage—the Crystal Mage—who'd woven the spells that had crushed him at last. Who'd led the mages who captured him . . .

Machodan Indigo.

It was addressed to you . . .

Illusion? Making himself look like a young man? The spells the Crystal Mages wove with adamine let men live hale and healthy into their nineties these days; the emperor was said to look like a man of sixty . . .

Does the adamine eventually drive its users mad, like the zai? Is that why they're trying to cover everything up? Are ALL the New Mages really old men who look young?

But I've watched him grow up!

Feet on the stair. Wood, like all the partitions within the building, shuddered under pounding weight. Clea rolled to her feet, caught up the water jug in one hand, the clumsy length of the pallet in the other, wadding it around her left arm, the best she could do for a shield. Stood behind the door as the bolt was shot open—

"Clea!" It was Hamo. In one hand he held a sledgehammer that would have brained an ox.

With him were Star of the Ghoras, and the dredgers Rediron and Pikefish. Scar-faced Second Rabbit the Ghoras hunter, and others she knew who moved back and forth between the Mire and the city. She saw runaway dredgers she'd met when she lived in the Tunnels . . . Not the thieves, assassins, scavengers who lived on the pickings of the Bright Islanders. These were the sons and daughters of the Twilight. Laborers, runaways, tribesmen . . . Men and women she knew from the secret councils that met in every Darklander alley and slum, men and women who hid weapons, helped runaways.

The men and women her father and the other merchant lords whispered of, and feared.

"Run!" said Star. "Now, while they're dealing with the fire—"

What fire? She didn't ask.

Instead she crossed the corridor in a stride, stopped before the door there—

"It's got spells on it," she said. She couldn't even see a bolt. "How'd you get in?"

"Drainage tunnels under the baths." Star caught her arm. "This way—"

"Break a hole in the wall," ordered Clea, and reached to seize the nearest of the hallway lamps. "I have to see."

"We don't have time—"

"I have to see."

Hamo obligingly put the sledgehammer through the thick wattle and plaster of the wall a few feet from the door.

The screaming on the other side stopped.

Clea held up the lamp, ducked her head, and stepped through.

And let's hope none of these fellows retains enough of his wits to direct a magic defense . . .

Most of them had drawn back to the far end of the long room. Some of them clung together like terrified children, hiding their heads in their comrades' clothing. At least a dozen simply sat along the walls, gazing blankly at nothing.

The stinking darkness glittered with eyes. You could have cut with a knife the smell of excrement, of spoiled food, of dirty bodies and dirty garments.

Clea stepped forward, lamp raised. Counting first, as she always counted—thirty-six . . . *thirty-six!*—then looking from face to face. Some were no more than thirty. Others, men in their sixties, dirty white hair lank around faces as unlined as those of five-year-olds. Uncut beards straggled down, streaked with food. Uncut nails so long that they twisted like tree-limbs. She recognized, as she had seen on the faces of simpleminded beggars in the Tunnels, where some of them had scratched their own faces. Uncut toenails clattered the wooden floor. The coarse blue tunics they wore were the same as Rivan's.

Thirty-six . . .

"Come on—" Star thrust her head through the hole in the wall. Some of the prisoners drew back in fear.

Behind her, Pikefish said, "Ziran?" his voice blank with shock. He slipped past Star in the impromptu entry-hole. Beside her, one of the prisoners, a round-faced, dark-haired man in his thirties, turned his head at the sound of Pikefish's voice, blinked as if trying to recall something.

"Ziran?" said the dredger again, staring at the man. Then he looked quickly at Clea. "He used to come in and put rat-wards around the barracks. He was good to the children, always friendly—he'd bring sweetmeats sometimes." He turned to the prisoner. "My lord, don't you know me? I'm Pikefish." And to Clea, "They said he was going back to Telmayre."

"When?"

Pikefish shook his head. "Five years ago."

Another Loghri stepped in after Pikefish: weathered skin and deep-scored sun-wrinkles of a fisherwoman. Heron, her name was—one of the most efficient organizers of the city's northern slums. "And that's Tredian Malgennin." She went to one of the men seated by the wall, passed her hand before the man's eyes. They moved, under their golden shelf of brow, but returned to that dim, puzzled stare almost at once. She looked at Clea. "He was quartermaster of the House of Glass, oh, six years ago? Ten years ago?"

"I remember," said Clea suddenly, and stared in her turn at him. She recalled the man going among the market stalls on the waterfront with a purse the size of a cantaloupe dangling temptingly from his baldric. Rat Bone had clipped her one on the ear and hissed, *Don't even* think *about robbing a wizard, girl*—

She'd seen him almost daily in the markets, a man in his thirties . . . and then she hadn't. But she'd returned to her father's household about that time and hadn't thought more about it.

"I always thought he was so young, to be quartermaster," said the fisher-woman. "But they're all babies, aren't they? And he haggled like a man twice his age."

A man twice his age . . .

Clea felt short of breath, as if another moment would give her the answer to this riddle. But she knew that Pikefish and the others, who had risked their lives to get her, would die if they were caught. She wheeled, ducked back through the hole in the wall: "Which way out?"

They started to move, and Hamo said, "No."

She turned and saw him standing beside the hole he'd hammered in the wall.

"We can't leave them."

The thought of trying to get out of the compound—with the most powerful order of mages in the world buzzing behind them like infuriated hornets—made her toes curl, never mind shepherding thirty-six stumbling scarecrows . . .

"There's nobody in there," she said. "Nothing. They're like Rivan back in the Serpentmire. They're gone."

"Rivan could look for food," Hamo pointed out. "He knew his name. My sheep do that."

Fire was taking hold somewhere—Clea could smell the smoke, mingling with the fog. From everywhere came a clamor of voices, shouting and cursing. They had minutes, if that, and the price of getting caught would, she knew, be considerably worse than hanging. "This isn't the time . . ."

"It is." Hamo met her eyes, his own hard now, like a wall of rock. "The mages will kill them, now that everyone knows about them. Their lives are in danger. That makes it the time."

"You're an idiot," said Clea.

"We cannot leave them. *I* will not leave them." He handed Pikefish his sledgehammer, pulled his belt from around his waist, and turned back into the room.

Clea saw him make a loop in the belt's end and fit it gently around the man Zirdan's wrist. Then he untied Zirdan's belt, to bind the empty man's other wrist to the wrist of the old man next to him.

She said the worst curse she knew of from Rat Bone's considerable vocabulary, then turned to the group gathered in the corridor, who watched her with eyes filled with terror. She'd already counted—it was second nature to her to tally first thing what she had to work with. *Fifteen.*

"All of you," she said. "Each of you take two. Star, Rabbit, you keep your-selves free and scout ahead, Rediron, you watch behind. Those who have three sleepers"—she kept herself from saying *dummies*, as any scavenger in the streets would have said—"tie them in a line, like Hamo's doing . . ."

Is it really *worth it to risk our lives herding them out of here? Sons of Death, they'll be more trouble than a flock of geese and a lot less useful . . .*

She hoped that grimness in Hamo's eyes meant that that triple-damned love-spell was finally wearing off . . .

"Did my brother get away?" she asked as she moved to the back of the line. "Does anyone know?"

No one did.

A back stair. Another hole in another wall to a storeroom, and thence through to the bath-house where yet another hole had been hammered in the wooden floor, up from the drains below. Clearly, nobody was about to touch any door or trap that might bear wards or curses.

What if the sleepers themselves had a spell of some kind on them, the way farmers would sometimes pay to have spells put on valuable stud horses or prize bulls, that could be traced if they were stolen?

But if they still had magic in them, as Ithrazel had said, it was impossible for a mage to scry another mage.

The bath-house windows were open, onto a night so thick with fog as to be nearly impenetrable. Yet fires blazed in two or three places—she won-dered if it were possible to put a spell on a fire, to counter magic intended to quench it. *Is that Graywillow? Or Uncle Ithrazel?*

As she'd feared, the former mages had been shut indoors for so long that being outside terrified them. They began to cry and pull on their leading-strings, one or two of them flailing their arms. Blue ground-lightning crack-led among the garden shrubs and three trees caught fire. . . .

Sons of . . .

She moved back along the line, letting Star lead. Touching this man's arm, that man's shoulder, speaking soothingly, gently: "It's all right. You're going to be safe. No more pain . . ."

She saw Hamo was doing the same thing, and whispered to Pikefish and Heron and the Eagle, "Keep moving. Don't stop. Keep them moving . . ."

The Crystal Mages go mad. Commonly, it looked like.

How can they teach their skills to the boys they take? Do ANY of them return to the Bright Island, the way they're said to?

There was a clear-out entrance to the sewer line in a corner of the garden, and Hamo and Pikefish moved aside its bronze cover. *Thank the gods somebody had the sense to cover it when they came in. . . .*

The shouting was coming nearer in the fog and the smoke, and of course all the former mages—sleepers, sheep, stumbling remnants of the men they'd used to be, the children they'd used to be—took one look at the hole in darkness and began to cry and wail and balk, and Clea fought the urge to tell her company, *That's it, cut 'em loose . . .*

She knew they'd all be killed if they were found now.

Their voices, their sobbing, resounded from the low brick of the arched roof as they fell and stumbled and had to be dragged and picked up and thrust onward, dripping with slime. Some of them screamed and tried to run away from the gleaming red eyes of the rats.

Adamine drives them mad, as it drives the zai. How long have the Crystal Order been using it? Since Grandpa Tethys's day? Probably not much before . . .

Is that *why we haven't seen Heshek?*

Sometimes it wasn't only rats. Once the lantern-gleam showed her what had to be a Night-Glutton, rolling away into the black of a side tunnel. Webs unlike those of any spider she'd ever seen glistened with wet: snagged bones. Not all of them merely rats'.

Once they passed a cistern, and though the brick-lined tank was smaller than a peasant's hut, she thought she saw a darkness hanging over its water, as darkness had hung over the grotto where Himelkart had confronted the zai. The air there seared with the thin, penetrating, metallic fetor of the Night-Gluttons, the Blood-Thieves, the slimy red thing she'd glimpsed in the gardens of the House of Glass.

They come out of water, like Neambis said.

Or water opens ways for them to come through from . . . somewhere else . . .

Sons of Death, are the zai *going to start rising here in Morne?*

Don't think about it now, she told herself. *Follow where you are*— for the drain quickly fed into the tunnels that she knew, drains and old smuggler-holes and the sub-crypts of merchant palaces that had been deserted and let fall to ruin. But as they passed holes that led into long-forgotten wine cellars, where beggars camped or old women operated cut-rate opium dens, she glanced behind her again and again, to those bearded faces, those vacant eyes . . .

Stop it. Keep an eye on where you are, in case something happens . . .

And she was prickling with the awareness that something very well might.

"What the hell's going on up there?" she whispered to Star as they passed near an open drain-hole in—she calculated—the Street of Ships. "It sounds like they've got every cart and wagon in town on the move."

"They do," returned the hunter. "The Vrykos, and the Othume, and all the lesser fry—*and* your honored father"—she put a twist of sarcasm in the title—"heard something about needing adamine to fight that creature, and that started a panic. Everybody in town is moving it to safekeeping in the warehouses—"

Clea groaned. "No! *Damn* it—!"

Mingled with the stinks of sewage, the smells of smoke and cheap cooking, now she smelled the metallic reek of the creatures everywhere. Twice they were attacked by rats—*Does the adamine drive* them *mad as well? Or some side effect of its magic?*

"It's what I hear," put in a blacksmith named Three Arrows. "Everybody figures they'll be making weapons of it, or something. That the prices will go up. Everybody from the street-corner moneylenders on up is afraid theirs'll be stolen— You should see the caravan they're putting together at the House of Glass, to store with your dad, girl!"

"*No*—"

"First time anybody can remember," added Rediron, "that the Mud-Grubbers have worked together—"

"*Damn* it!"

As they passed a sort of cavern in the tunnel wall that had at one time been occupied by the Monkey King and his abominable mother, she thought she saw movement within its absolute darkness: the glint of eyes, too close to the floor and too far apart to be human, or to belong to any beast she knew.

Of course they're down here. Everyone in the city steals adamine. It's the most valuable thing there is. Dear gods, Liver-Eater has tons of stolen adamine stashed in the crypts under his headquarters, the purest pickings of the refineries . . .

The thought of what could happen with all the adamine in the city concentrated in one place turned her cold.

She knew where she was now: in the maze of old sub-cellars and drainage tunnels in back of the Dockside. Khymin's lair had been somewhere hereabouts, though Clea had known from her childhood that she never could find it. Nobody could, not even his particular friends and protectors among the thieves. Behind her she heard Hamo whisper, "Are we safe now?"

Pikefish replied with grim quiet. "We're never safe."

"Nor shall we be," said Clea softly. "Not until the Crystal Mages are banished from the Twilight Lands, and from the Bright Isles east of the sea. Thank you." She reached back and grasped the old dredger's shackle-scarred wrist. Looked around her at the men and women, dark and fair, as they slipped through a broken archway into what had been another cistern, knee-deep in stagnant water and smelling of piss and mold. Put out her free hand, and touched them one by one as they came through, herding their sobbing, terrified charges. "Thank you all. Thank you. Do any of you know what Heshek planned for me?"

Heads were shaken. Heron, the gray-haired fisherwoman, said, "The Boss sent out word, that you'd been taken. Your old uncle"—it took Clea a moment to realize she meant Ithrazel and not Tykellin Stylachos—"said as it was the Crystal Mages that called the zai. That they'd kill you, for knowing it. He's a deep old bastard," she added, following Pikefish to the ladder of rusted iron rungs in the opposite wall. "Here you go, darling, that's right—" she added, to the one she'd called Tredian Malgennin. "Hands on the rungs . . . and up we go. . . . He's one of the witch-born, isn't he? Your uncle, I mean."

"Said he'd get himself into the House of Glass," affirmed Pikefish, shifting the bent, white-bearded, sewage-soaked old man he'd been carrying on his back for the past three quarters of a mile. "Your father, Lady, and his pimping excellency the pimping ambassador have been at the House of Glass since just before sunset." As he spoke, he set the old man down, used his own belt to tie the confused ancient's wrists together, then slipped his head through the resulting circle of fragile arms. "There you go, Grand-dad—legs around my waist . . . That's it . . ."

Behind him, Rediron guided Pikefish's other charges up the ladder.

"Went there all in procession they did, on white horses and with His Excellency's band walking before him playing music all the way, just like as if they hadn't run all the way home from the Tarnweald like scared pigs. I don't expect he'd have done that if aught had befallen your brother—"

"You don't know my father," retorted Clea grimly.

"Well," agreed Pikefish, "there is that. Old Uncle Iohan said he'd go in and let himself be seen. Said he could disappear, keep them stirred up and looking for him." The dredger gripped the rungs of the ladder that led to the tunnel above, then as an afterthought pulled on his passenger's long beard, to bring the old man's head forward so it wouldn't scrape the narrow sides of the ladder-hole. "Myself, I thought it was just asking to be took—"

"Did he get out?" Clea called up the ladder after him.

Pikefish's voice drifted cheerfully down to her. "Not the foggiest."

And well he should be cheerful, reflected Clea. *We all got out of the House of Glass alive. That's something I'd have bet money against, if I could have found anyone willing to wager . . .*

Rediron climbed the rungs, nudging the last of the numbed, stumbling sleepers before him.

Beside her, last of the party in the cistern, Hamo said softly, "Thank you, Clea."

Clea shook her head, looked up into his face. "No," she returned. "Thank *you.*"

She knew if she'd left the sleepers where they were, she would have seen their faces—some so young, some so old—every night when she shut her eyes, for the rest of her life.

She'd known it in the corridor outside their prison, when she'd said, *Which way out?* and prepared to leave them there.

Hamo regarded her for a long moment, then put his arms around her, and for an instant, held her tight.

She knew there was not a reason in the world that she should feel safe—not coming from where she was coming from, not going into what she knew was ahead of her.

But she did.

Twenty-Six

The crypt at the top of the ladder led into a huge room beneath brick groining crusted with white crystals of niter, where damp had seeped from the porous clay all around. At one point in the past, it had held a nobleman's considerable stocks of wine, but at the moment it was occupied by two separate camps of thieves. The air was thick with the stinks of smoke and cooking; thicker still with the language used by the women clustered around the tiny fires.

"I see you got her safe," said Mama Sugarplum from the smaller of the two groups. A one-time whore, she now, Clea knew, made her living kidnapping children for sale to beggars. "Good to see you, Princess . . ."

She spat ceremoniously before Clea's feet, then held out to her a boiled-leather beaker of ale and a chunk of bread smeared with the soft cheese of the Gray Hills farms. Clea took barely a second to devour both.

The larger encampment included thirty of the Twilight Kindred whom she knew were not thieves but, like Pikefish and Rediron, escaped dredgers or wood-haulers. With them were a half-dozen Ghoras hunters, unmistakable by their tattoos despite the rough laborers' clothing they wore: men and women who'd slip into town to sell rabbits or birds in the markets, then slip out again before the recruiters for the processing mills could catch them. With them also she recognized two of the leaders of the Darklander Councils: Kulchan of the Ashupik—scarred like an old tree and the fixer who mediated between the tribal neighborhoods and the thief-gangs—and the Placne woman Porcupine, whose cattle range near the Denzerai was a favored refuge for runaways.

Star was already giving instructions to the tribespeople, to find food—and wash-water—for the cowering, weeping men who huddled together, clinging to Hamo as if they understood it was he who would care for them. Licking sheep-milk cheese from her fingers, Clea walked among them again, touching arms and shoulders, speaking gentle words: "It's all right. You're safe now—" *There's the biggest lie of all! We'll all be lucky if we see morning . . .*

Particularly given the amount of adamine Liver-Eater's got stored in every crypt and tunnel for two hundred feet around . . .

"Hamo, would you stay here with them and keep them from panic? Remember they still have magic. Kulchan, does anyone know if my brother got away?" And, when the sturdy little fixer gestured his ignorance: "Listen, you need to get word back to the Kindred! My father and the merchant lords . . . Pig-Face," she called out as the door at the far end of the vault opened and the massive form of Liver-Eater's bodyguard lumbered down the steps. "Could I beg you to brew an opiate—quarter-strength should do it, I think—for these poor bastards? Enough to calm them down—"

The big thug stared at the milling, sobbing, unspeakably befouled group and said, "Looks like they've had enough of *something.*"

Clea shook her head. "I'll explain later. They have magic but their minds are gone, they need to be kept calm. They need to be taken care of," she added, meeting the man's steely eyes. "Your boss is going to want to see them. Maybe my father as well. There are thirty-six of them."

And I'll know damn well if the count is short when I come back later.

Pig-Face's eyes shifted from hers. "Oh, all right."

"Don't bind them unless you have to. Hamo's in charge of them."

He looked the shepherd up and down with ill-disguised contempt, and said again, "All right. Brute!" he called out, to one of the thieves around the second fire. "Sly! Get some half-and-half dreamsugar brewed. Red Flower mixture should do it." And, to Clea, as he gestured back toward the narrow door, "He wants to see you upstairs."

No need to ask who *He* was.

"I'll ask about your brother." Kulchan touched her arm, disappeared back among his followers.

"What about the boy Vervaris?" she asked Pikefish as the bodyguard walked ahead to open the door for her. "Who was supposed to be a wizard? Did he get away all right?"

"Lord, I hope so." The dredger shook his head. "Poor little tyke. But with that thing tearing and spitting and belching fire, and you out there calling it to you, and everyone running and screaming, I couldn't have found my own wife in the uproar, nor said what became of her. We'll be here when you need us, Princess."

He saluted with a mockery of the military reverence as Clea ascended the stair to Liver-Eater's house above.

What had been a small servants-hall in the original Dockside mansion had been cleared and was lit by a couple of smoky grease-lamps. Clea knew the place. The rest of the building had been reduced to a ruinous warren of beggars camps, whores' cribs, rat-nests, and dens where Liver-Eater's favored bravos and their partners slept. Four chairs had been drawn up to a much-battered work table whose top was graced with four cups of gold and shell-work, two bottles of rum, a small silver bell, and an opium pipe, still drifting smoke. Liver-Eater, at the table's head, glanced up, dark eyes calculating. A look, Clea knew, which never boded well. . . .

Beside him—next to the pipe—was an empty seat. Ithrazel slumped in the next chair, wrapped in two silk shawls and a noblewoman's sable cloak and shuddering as if with deadly cold. From the table's foot Graywillow watched him, haggard with fatigue, concern in her eyes.

Clea knew the pipe.

Her eyes went to Liver-Eater's. Then she stepped forward, bowed, and ceremoniously spat at his feet. "My lord," she said. "Thank you. Have you had any word of my brother?"

"I understand he's well, and at his father's house." The hard eyes went to Graywillow. "Little lady, why don't you go downstairs and sit with Studly True-Heart for a while?" His finger, with its polished red nail, flicked dismissively toward the door. "But thank you," he added. "If any of us gets through this alive, I'll remember your help. You, too, Uncle Grumpy." His glance moved to Ithrazel. "I stand in your debt. Tell everyone"—he turned back to Clea—"that I won't forget them. And do please let them know that if one word of any of what happened tonight gets back to me from any source besides yourselves, I'll remember them as well. Every single one of them. They didn't see us here. They didn't see you, Princess."

"I'll tell them." Clea wouldn't have given more than even odds on ever seeing Hamo, or Graywillow, or Star, or Pikefish, or any of the others again. Ithrazel gave no sign of having heard any of this. His eyes were shut and he looked like a man in the deeps of a long sickness.

She drew a long breath, and addressed the wizard. "Nice fire."

"Thank you."

"My father and the ambassador get out of there?"

"Like startled bunny-rabbits, dearest Gloriana," purred Liver-Eater. "The moment the fun started."

"They back at the Griffin House?"

"As of half an hour ago." The pockmarked face beamed in a smile.

"I'll need to go see him," said Clea. "Now, tonight."

"I hope you brought along a change of clothes."

She looked down at her striped skirt, soaked to the hips with sewer-water, her tattered petticoat and shit-caked boots. Then she raised her eyes to the thief's again.

"I brought thirty-six prisoners from the House of Glass," she said. "Crystal Mages—or men who used to be Crystal Mages. The ones who're supposed to have gone to the Bright Isles. They're mad, their minds are . . . are gone." She turned to look at Ithrazel. "Just like Rivan at Serpent Lake."

Ithrazel opened his eyes then, a thousand years older than they had been in the little shrine near the Denzerai. "I know."

"You know?"

His sigh had a whisper to it like bones dissolving within his flesh. "Dear gods . . . I knew it couldn't be anything else."

After a long moment, she went on, "Somebody brought Himelkart a message. One of the Crystal Mages in the garden said to him, *The letter was to you, to Machodan Indigo, not to Himelkart of Thourmand. And you knew him, at the testing-ground . . .*"

"I wrote that letter." The old wizard's glance flicked to Liver-Eater and a wry smile pulled the corner of his shabby mustache. "Dictated it, rather—I gather Apsunahi wasn't ashore two hours before samples of his handwriting were available to every forger and confidence artist in Morne."

Clea opened her mouth to speak, then closed it again, knowing.

Angry. Not knowing what to say. *If you feel anything inside, your hands will shake . . .*

"Yes." Ithrazel's sunburned brown hand stirred in the fur around his shoulders. "Yes, Himelkart is Machodan Indigo. I knew that implying knowledge of it would guarantee every New Mage over the level of novice would be tangled in council while I sneaked in through the kitchen gate and kept everybody distracted chasing me.

"Pig-Face and his men set the fires, and Graywillow and our friend"—he nodded toward the narrow door of what had probably once been a boot-hole—"called down fog."

The door opened, and a desiccated bundle of black robes and white hair crept forth, like a very old spider covered in dust.

Ithrazel got to his feet. Clea stopped herself from crying "Khymin!" knowing that there was no place where they might not be overheard. She took one withered claw in her hand, and Ithrazel took the other, between them guiding the octogenarian to the table where Liver-Eater still watched with interested, cynical eyes.

Clea said, "Thank you. All of you." She turned, her glance taking in Ithrazel and Liver-Eater. "I owe you both more than I can say. More than I can ever repay . . ."

Ithrazel, wrapping his silks and furs around old Khymin's shoulders, murmured, "Oh, I'm sure our friend will think of something." His eye slid sidelong to the robber chief. "Won't you?"

Again Clea started to speak, and again stopped herself, as if at the sound of steel sliding free of a scabbard, in a dark room that was supposed to be empty. Then she said carefully, "With your permission, Lord—" Another bow to Liver-Eater. "I need to get my brother out of my father's house. Out of anyplace where the Crystal Mages can get to him. Tonight. If what"—she barely remembered to use the right name—"my uncle says is true—if the Crystal Mages are . . . are taking the bodies of mageborn boys—"

It sounded fantastic even to speak the words, but Khymin said in his creaky disused voice, "It is."

"That's why they want Pendri. And the minute they get themselves sorted out—the minute they realize the . . . the Sleepers, the husks of the boys they took and used up and moved on from . . . The minute they realize they're gone, they'll go after Pendri. Probably go after every mageborn boy in the city they've had their eye on. If I can beg you for something to wear . . ."

"That's an interesting conclusion to jump to." Liver-Eater picked up the silver bell from beside the rum bottles and shook it, once. Both the door to the crypt, and the door that Clea knew led into the house's old kitchen, opened, guards framed in them in the makeshift armor of hired bully-boys. Their host smiled, made a small gesture—*Just testing, boys and girls. Seeing if the bell works . . .*

The doors closed again.

"They'd immediately think their game is rumbled because—how many did you say there were? Thirty-six dribbling-mad old crocks missing and not able to remember their own names nor who they might have been ten years or twenty years or forty years ago . . . Why would they keep them around anyway? Surely not from sentimental altruism!"

"Because magic is magic." Ithrazel spoke up from where he'd sat down again at Khymin's side. "Because magic inheres first in the flesh, then grows

in the mind. They may well be trying to come up with some way of extract-
ing even that, the way far-gone addicts will soak and boil the wrappings that
dreamsugar is shipped in, if they can't afford the sugar itself. The way the
refineries will sift the ash when they clean out the adamis kilns, to get the
residue—the way the poor will go through the ash-piles again . . ."

"It's why they kept you." Khymin turned his head to regard him, spoke
in his faint, scratchy croak. "All those years."

"You were the one who knew where I was?"

The white head bowed slightly.

"Who knew what had been done to me?" And when Khymin again
nodded in assent: "Do you know—did you learn—what became of my
daughters?"

The broken hesitancy of his voice went through Clea's heart like a knife.

"Seventy-five years," murmured the old Black Mage. "It's enough for you
to know they are dead. And their children."

Ithrazel made no sound, but after a long time, Clea saw his lips form the
words, "I see."

Liver-Eater raised his brows. "And did they keep you . . . Uncle?"

Ithrazel made no reply.

"They would have done the same with me," Khymin went on, looking
back at the robber-chief. "And they'll need it. Magic that isn't tainted with
adamine . . ."

"Ah, yes," said Liver-Eater. "Adamine." He returned his attention to Clea.
"Do you know what it's going to do to every city in these lands—to every
city in the emperor's realm—if people start believing that it's dangerous to
use anything that has to do with adamine?"

"*Start* believing—"

Clea stopped, seeing in the dark eyes the glitter of calculation: of fig-
uring how to get the greatest advantage out of the situation, and from
whom. She knew, suddenly and to the bottom of her soul, that Liver-Eater
was going to have them killed. *He can't possibly afford to let that happen.
Nobody can.*

Including Father.

Not until they have some other plan in place.

She took a deep breath and made her voice casual. "Do you know what's
going to happen if they don't?"

"It might not," he reasoned. "Or not in my time, anyway."

"Let me take you down," said Clea, "to the cisterns and collect-basins
between here and the harbor, and we'll have a look at the ones that the

people who live down there don't go near anymore. The ones where darkness hangs over the water, even in daytime or torchlight. You can see tracks sometimes on the bricks that aren't made by human feet, or rats, or anything that you've ever seen before the past few years. Webs of slime that could catch and hold a lion—or a beggar . . ."

"You've seen that, have you?" murmured Khymin. "They come out of water, yes." The old mage's creaking voice fumbled on the words, as if long unused to even the normal tones of speech. "Night-Gluttons. Those horrible spider things—you've seen them, too, Princess? And the rats, and the very cockroaches, that drink that water. I thought . . ."

His hand groped automatically for his opium-pipe on the table, and Ithrazel laid a hand for a moment on his wrist. The pale eyes met the hazel ones; Khymin folded his hands. "I thought I was dreaming. But some nights the darkness collects above the water—"

"Nights when you've had a pipe or two?" Liver-Eater's dark brows rose.

"That's what my father's going to say." Clea made a gesture, letting go of her father, her mother, everything she'd wanted from them. *Smooth as the Greenflood . . . a diamond for a heart. Rat Bone would be proud.* "And people will probably believe him, the same way they're going to believe that my uncle"—she nodded at Ithrazel—"summoned the zai this afternoon . . . yesterday afternoon," she amended, knowing it was nearly morning. The night felt like it had gone on forever. They'd be hearing the bells on the refineries soon.

"And they'll probably believe Himelkart," added Ithrazel, "when he tells them—for the gods know what reason—that I'm old what's-his-name that destroyed Dey Allias."

"Later we'll get into why they'd do that," remarked Liver-Eater, his clever, cruel eyes studying the old man's face. "Particularly if Himelkart really is this other mage. Wasn't Indigo the one who finally nailed the Cursed One's hide to a tree? If he is Indigo, wouldn't he recognize Ithrazel?"

"I'm sure he will," retorted the wizard. "That doesn't mean he wouldn't lie about it to shut me up from identifying him—and to push the blame onto me, for calling the zai."

"And wouldn't old Ithrazel recognize *him*?"

The old man said nothing.

"*Did* you call the zai?" Liver-Eater's voice was conversational. "To cause panic, maybe, and a drop in adamis prices? Or to convince me to turn my own stockpiles over to you? Or drag them to the warehouses of our Gloriana's dear father for safekeeping? Maybe even to get hold of concessions on lode-bearing canyons?"

"Those concessions are going to be worthless," said Clea quietly. "Your stockpiles are going to be worthless. Six months ago the village of Sandmire was destroyed by a zai. Another village, Turtlemere in the Nightshade Maze, was torn to pieces and burned less than three weeks ago, the store-sheds ripped apart, rolled on and melted. Then there was an attack on the Tarn-weald. Does it sound to you like these attacks are getting more frequent?"

"It sounds like you're a young lady who has an answer for everything."

And, when Clea turned impatiently toward the door that led to the crypt, "And don't think old Khymin, or dear old Uncle Iohan, are going to try any tricks for your sake, my dear. I am very well warded." He fished into the neck of his gown and brought forth a half-dozen Crystal Order amulets, very expensive and probably very effective. "And from all I've heard, the spells of the Black Mages—and of whatever order you actually belong to, Uncle—are just as likely to set the house on fire, or kill every man and woman down in the crypts, including your friends True-Heart and Willow-Girl, as they are to make me keel over in this chair. They might even have the effect of letting our friend Himelkart know that someone here is working magic."

"This city"—Clea took a firm hold on her patience—"is going to be destroyed. Like Sandmire. Like Turtlemere. Maybe every city, since every city of the Bright Lords is based on accumulating as much adamis as the Great Houses can possible wring out of the earth. In every city—maybe in every grotto—there are almost certainly patches of darkness, where these things are . . . maybe materializing, maybe just waking from an ancient sleep. Waking up rabid. Not just the zai, but the Night-Gluttons, ghaist-spiders, Blood-Thieves . . ."

"You know she speaks true, Sythenes." Khymin spoke the name that Clea recalled Rat Bone had said was the one the robber chief had borne as a child. "Ask Mama Sugarplum, whose child was eaten in its cradle by these things, the year before last. Ask Ballygore, that was found torn to pieces in the crypt of the old Othume refinery, and the bites on his throat and belly, made by teeth unknown to any hunter from the Mire."

"Ballygore was a drunk." Liver-Eater waved the name away. "And if you can find me one of the people who sleeps in the crypt of the Othume refinery who isn't pickled to his hairline in dreamsugar, I'll give you a cookie."

The old mage simply regarded him for a time, like a mummy preserved in dust, or a thousand-year-old parchment upon which has been written the true name of Darkness. Then he said, "You know I speak true."

"All that tells me is that I need to keep this quiet—"

Ithrazel sprang to his feet, hand outstretched toward the robber-chief, who half-rose from his chair—

—and sank down the next second when Clea smashed him over the head with one of the bottles of rum.

Ithrazel was around the table in seconds and tying the unconscious Liver-Eater's hands with the man's belt while Clea shoved as much silk shawl into his mouth as would fit. "That was very good," she said, and Ithrazel nodded acknowledgment.

"Thank you, Princess. You as well."

Rum had spilled everywhere. Clea picked up the second bottle and took a long swig, passing it on to the wizard. Ithrazel drank and handed the bottle to Khymin.

"Can you get us past the guard on the stair?" Clea asked.

"My dear girl—" Ithrazel helped himself to all the amulets from around Liver-Eater's neck and divided them between himself and her. "I may be a hundred and forty years old, but there are some things one never forgets."

He corked the rum flask and dropped it in his pocket. "Your father will have to make the best of your appearance."

Clea shrugged and slung the amulets around her neck. "He's seen worse."

Twenty-Seven

Ithrazel tapped gently on the door to the crypt. When the guard opened it a crack, the old man kept his body between the man's line of sight and the crumpled shape of Liver-Eater lying on the floor. In the dimness of the dark chamber, Clea guessed it didn't take much magic to complete the illusion. Ithrazel whispered, "He wants to see the lady Star."

And, when Star duly came up, Clea gave her instructions in an undertone.

Star went back down the steps. As she shut the door, Clea murmured to the wizard, "Thank you for coming back."

"Thank you for taking the shackle off me. You actually brought the prisoners away out of the House of Glass? That couldn't have been easy."

Past his shoulder—and the guard's—Clea had seen that most of them were sitting up, huddled together but no longer in fear. Pig-Face must have followed instructions about how much dreamsugar to give them. Red Flower was one of the mildest mixes. Mother's Milk, some called it.

"Not something I ever want to do again. Is that true what you said about the Crystal Mages trying to find a way to . . . to pull magic out of their flesh?"

"I think so. I wouldn't put it past them. But they would have killed them rather than risk having anyone see them, anyone who might recognize them and guess the truth."

"That's what Hamo said."

Behind them at the table, Khymin was staring into a fragment of crystal he'd taken from his pocket, pale eyes losing their focus. In his soft, scratchy voice he said, "Now," and Ithrazel tapped at the door again.

"He wants to see you," he informed the guard, whom Clea garroted the moment the man stepped through the door.

Rat Bone had been a competent professional, but when Clea was fourteen, and had developed sufficient arm strength for the exercise, he'd paid (*in the gods only knew what currency*, reflected Clea) Loti the String to give her advanced lessons in the delicate art of the silken rope. She supposed Liver-Eater's door-guard would be no loss to society, but her years as a professional had given her a distaste for killing anybody she didn't need to.

She guessed he wouldn't be singing love songs to anybody for a while, though.

As she tied the man's hands with his own belt and shoved the other silk shawl into his slack mouth, she heard the quiet scuffle as the Darklanders overpowered the thieves in the larger camp—and those in Mama Sugarplum's camp prudently took to their heels.

There were plenty of niches and corners in the old wine vault. Neither Liver-Eater nor his guard would be found anytime soon.

"Where did you go?" she asked the wizard quietly as he drew rat-wards around both men.

"Dey Allias." He didn't look at her. "To see the place. See the Hill of Oleanders."

"Did you?"

He nodded. "The spell-circle we made there—four other mages and myself—is long gone, but there's adamis ground into the dirt of the hill where it was. Gallons of it, like there was in Tarnweald yesterday afternoon, it must have cost the Crystal Order a fortune—"

"They have barrels of it," said Clea shortly. "They own three refineries and the gods only know how many concessions. Every merchant house in town has to deal with them over the rights."

"It was a trap." His voice was barely a murmur, but she saw his hand shake as he drew the signs of the ward with his forefinger in the dust of the floor, sprinkled them with a crumble of salt he'd taken from Liver-Eater's cupboard. *As he'd drawn them*, she thought, *that night seventy-five years ago*.

"The power we raised—Second Ox, Khoyas, Dershin, Eketas, and myself . . . They'd heard about our plan somehow. They were only waiting for us to do it. Machodan Indigo, Gerodare Starknife, Tarronis Zartoreth and the others. They used the adamis to turn the purpose of our spell, and used our power to another purpose, a terrible purpose. To destroy Dey Allias, knowing that the blame would fall on me."

"Fifty thousand people?"

He turned, still squatting on his heels, and his eyes met hers.

After long silence, she whispered, "Why?"

Voices in the crypt, soft echoes. Hamo striding toward her, and past him she saw the Darklanders—now some fifty strong—had coaxed the sleepy and confused former mages to their feet. She rose, leaving Ithrazel in the small invisible circles of his spells and went to the shepherd, knowing what he would ask her. There were two or three archways leading back into the tunnels. Kulchan was nowhere to be seen, but among the tribesmen Clea recognized Second Gecko and Blue Gecko, the sons of Porcupine and active themselves in the secret Kindred organizations. Good men, she knew, trustworthy and kind.

"Can you take these men to your mother's cattle farm near the Gingul Shrine?" she asked quietly. "You can see they're helpless, and frightened, but they'll need to be watched carefully. They do still possess magic. Graywillow . . ."

Blue Gecko shook his head. "You'll need the Lady Willow with you, Princess. Mother will get our aunt Winterflower from the shrine to help."

"Thank you." Recalling the three old priestesses who'd given them shelter on their way back to town, Clea grasped his hands, then his brother's. "And thank your mother, and your aunt. I am deep in your debt already." She glanced in the direction of the last of the bound thieves being tucked away into the vault's darker niches. "Are there others of the Sisters willing to help?"

"More than you know, Princess." The young man smiled. "Kulchan's gathering them now. Word went out throughout the city when we heard you'd been taken. All the Kindred—all the councils, all the dredgers and slaves. This is what we've been waiting for. This . . . and the blood of Elannin Greenshield. Your knowledge of how their world works. We're ready. And we're armed."

"We better be." Clea gripped his hands again. "We'll need to be."

Pikefish came up on her other side, with the guard's sword-belt and Liver-Eater's largest dagger in his hands. "They're saying you go to your father tonight."

"I have to." Clea belted on the weapons, and wished she had time to change clothes (*and take a damn bath, as long as I'm wishing* . . .). "Aside from getting my brother to safety—because Heshek will be coming for him, as soon as they get their fires put out at the House of Glass. Heshek needs his power. And he needs the power of my father's House. I have to convince my father that the zai will come again. That they're being drawn up from the waters beneath the earth, that the Crystal Mages are lying about them. That more will come . . ."

The brothers looked at each other, and at Pikefish, then back to Clea. Second Gecko's voice was low. "Do you know this?"

"I know it," she said. "I've seen them. And my father needs to ready the city for the next attack."

"We'll follow you," said the dredger. "There are a hundred of the Twilight Kindred within two streets of this place. Three hundred more can be gathered in the time it takes to skin a hare. We'll be within call."

His glance went to Ithrazel, conscientiously drawing rat-wards around all the places where the thieves who'd been camped in the crypt had been stowed, bound and gagged.

And will rat-wards work against Blood-Thieves? Clea shuddered at the recollection of the thing she'd glimpsed near the House of Glass. Of what she'd heard about those fat, glistening red sausages with legs like centipedes and mouths like toothed maggots.

"Get somebody to keep an eye out down here against things like Night-Gluttons," she said to Pikefish as she strode toward the ladder that led to the sewer tunnels. Ithrazel, Hamo, Graywillow fell into step behind her, Star and her hunters bringing up the rear. "As soon as we're clear of the neighborhood, somebody go tell Pig-Face where his boss is . . . I owe the old bastard for helping me get into the House of Glass in the first place. Tell him I'll make it up to him."

"Oh, he'll forgive you anything if you say you're sorry," retorted the dredger with a grin.

She stooped, and lifted the bronze cover of the tunnel. The smell from below was deadly, metallic, and evil. Night-Gluttons. Blood-Thieves. She would a thousand times have preferred rats. "And you probably better get Khymin out of here as well. Liver-Eater's got a soft spot for the old man, but when he wakes up, he's not gonna be thinking straight."

She looked past him, at the crypt, now almost completely engulfed in blackness. Lantern-light picked out the dazed faces of the Sleepers, the brisk movements of the Darklanders. From a pocket of darkness behind a couple of ruined barrels, Liver-Eater could be heard, making mooing noises around the gag of the silk shawl.

He did not sound pleased.

There was no sign of Khymin. The old mage had melted like smoke into the darkness.

After almost three weeks away, Clea Stylachos entered the house of her father as she had left it, through the stable courts. The Darklanders who followed her divided, moving like water down the mews and minor courts of the wealthy neighborhood behind the compound, and though it was not yet dawn, the clamor in the streets and courtyards all around the compound walls sounded like bright forenoon and a damn busy forenoon at that. Drays and carts, torches and shouting. All streaming toward the line of warehouses on the Street of Ships, crowding thicker and thicker as the panic spread.

Men-at-arms in scarlet and black, others in blue and gold, surrounded each cart and massed at the gates of the warehouse yards. As Clea and the core of her party crossed an alleyway under the scrim of Ithrazel's spells, she caught a glimpse of Ganzareb tar-Azazris's blond hair, framed in cressets in the gateway of the Stylachos yard. He was shouting at a knot of town merchants, each with covered barrows of their own private stocks of adamine, gesturing frantically, demanding space within and the protection of the Griffin House's guards. Further along the great thoroughfare where the merchant houses had their headquarters, ornamental wagons and litters jostled and swayed, the women and children (and nursemaids and handmaidens) of the Othume and the Kinnesh and all the various branches and ramifications of Vrykos and Stylachos struggled against the tide of the adamine carts, making for the ships or the roads out of town.

And around the fringes of the growing mob on the Street of Ships, she recognized every thief and pickpocket she'd ever encountered in the Tunnels and the Dockside, swarming like bees in a hot springtime. Watching. Waiting their chance.

Graywillow gasped—rather unnecessarily—"Oh no!"

"God's braies . . ." Clea gritted her teeth, and Ithrazel let out a crack of bitter laughter.

"I see it's not going to be long before our theory gets tested."

"Another word out of you"—she jabbed a finger at the old man—"and I'll brain *you* with a bottle. Brue!" she added as one of her father's grooms shoved his way to her through the press.

"Stable gate's open, Princess," the man said, with a clumsy bow. "If you can get through the carts coming out. Your dad's in conference with the Crystal Boys."

"Heshek there?" She tucked her bedraggled, striped skirt higher into her sword-belt as she followed him, working their way to the edge of the mob—and glanced to one side and another, counting Pikefish's men around her, catching their eyes. Brue was a Loghri, one of the informers who kept

Kulchan apprised of what went on in the Griffin House . . . But at Clea's signal, her followers drew close.

You never know . . .

The great sea-gates of Griffin House lay ahead of them, facing toward the waterfront. They had left behind the squalor of the Dockside, and the stinking district around the refineries, but the crowd here seemed little less. By the leaping glare of torchlight, Clea saw the gold and crimson wagon that her father had given his bride's mother, one wheel broken and its eight horses plunging and kicking wildly in their traces as grooms tried to free them and servants (and pick-pockets) milled around them in an ever-tightening maelstrom of shouting and confusion. She turned out of the mob, and into a cobbled and muddy mews, flattened against the wall to avoid being trampled by the stream of carts coming out the stable gate.

Carts, servants, porters bearing bundles, men and women yelling questions. She reflected that she could have walked past them in her ordinary court clothes with her hair un-dyed and gleaming in the wild flare of the gate-cressets, and not one of them would have paid her attention. It was better than a spell.

As they stood to let a wagon-load of fuel and the Lady Lyonis's furniture trundle past, drawn by a twelve-horse hitch, Ithrazel asked quietly, "And does this Heshek have a habit of tugging on his lower lip when he's thinking? Like this?"

He demonstrated. Graywillow looked puzzled but Clea said, "Yes. I saw him a dozen times, when he was still coming out to visit the White Ladies' shrines."

"Yes." Ithrazel's brow creased in sudden pain. "Yes. Gerodare Starknife did that—Machodan Indigo's favorite pupil, his chosen successor. Only I'd known Gerodare when he was a child. I knew his family. They were kin of my own master, Brancas, on Telmayre. He came out to these lands on the same ship as me." His shaggy brows tightened with remembered pain.

"At that time the Archmage of the New Order here in the west was Cheyan ar-Silterian—of one of the highest families in the realm. He did that, too . . . tugged his lower lip, like your friend Heshek. And like Heshek he was being seen less and less—getting ready, they said, to go back to Telmayre. I wondered if Machodan would go with him—they were inseparable, like brothers, finishing each other's sentences, clowning about the way lovers do. Then one day Cheyan was no longer around, and Machodan was Archmage—Machodan, who had the worst Sea Islands accent you've ever heard off a comic theater stage. And Gerodare . . . changed."

Very quietly—feeling as if she saw through fog and darkness a shape she'd half-guessed was there all along—Clea said, "Rat Bone told me that Heshek and Himelkart were said to be lovers."

"I think that's when I started to wonder," murmured the old man. "All those years ago. And started to ask . . ."

With the confusion of wagons and horses and grooms in the stable court—no guards (*They're probably all around the warehouse gates . . .*) —they were able to slip through the gate and cross the court to the quieter, empty dark of the kitchen garden beyond. No ambush: in thanks for that, as much as for anything else, Clea gripped Brue's hand in gratitude. Star, Eagle, Rediron—she counted them behind her with her eye. Graywillow, Hamo, Ithrazel . . .

Others following, spreading out through the corridors and gardens to watch their backs . . .

A short stair. A walkway along Linvinnia's private garden, every window dark. Clea tried to estimate what time it had to be, and failed. The sky was like tar above the turreted roofline, but she could have walked any corridor, found her way to any corner of the Griffin House compound, blindfolded. It was the first thing she'd practiced, when her father had brought her back.

A bronze door, standing open, somebody's dropped cloak lying half out of it. The broader corridor that led to the family quarters, and to her father's conference chamber beyond.

Lamplight in the doorway ahead of them. Guards would be in that room. Clea entered one of the smaller chambers of the suite, passed through the darkness to the wide windows that looked toward the sea, torchlight reflecting through them from the terrace outside.

"I don't know how many years it takes," Ithrazel went on softly, "for the mind of a usurper—an intruder—to wear out the physical brain, the physical flesh, of its victim. Indigo—Himelkart—is, what did you say, my dear? Eighteen? And he took over the body of the real Himelkart, the child Himelkart of Thourand, when that child was eight."

In a hollow voice, Clea said, "Pendri is eight. And he says his powers have begun to come, under the Crystal Mages' training." She felt cold inside, her heart hammering as she walked along the tiled terrace, where she'd used to run in the wake of her mother's billowing veils.

Run to meet her father. With the queer double vision of memory she almost saw him at the end of the walkway, laughing as he held out his arms for his beautiful Rethiel Elannis, his Dark Jewel . . .

If you feel anything inside, your hands will shake, she reminded herself. *You need a heart like a diamond.*

But when Hamo touched her arm to steer her around a chest of blankets that someone had dropped on the terrace—Hamo with his sledgehammer over his shoulder like the god of blacksmiths—she felt as if she'd had a steadying glass of brandy and six hours' sleep.

Beside her, Ithrazel went on, "And Heshek—Gerodare—is, what? Ten years older than Himelkart? How old would your friend Rivan be, Willow? About that?"

She whispered, "He was twenty-four when I was thirteen. I'm twenty now."

"They used to last longer," murmured the old man. "They used to not disappear—not 'retire to their meditations' or 'go back to Telmayre' until they were in their forties. They're wearing them out quicker."

"Pendri," said Clea again. And then, "Gods of Death . . ."

Through the triple window that she knew to be her father's private audience room, she heard Shumiel's voice. "Thank you!" said the Golden Princess, tears behind that sweet soprano. "If we can do that, it is truly all I wish for . . ."

Clea signed to the others to stay back. Graywillow's hand moved, as if to lay on her the veil of a spell, and Ithrazel caught her wrist.

If Himelkart's there, he'll feel the magic . . .

"That's a damn big 'if,' girl," said her father's beautiful, unmistakable voice. "Myself, I'd rather have that peacock in a cage in my house before I go around selling its feathers."

Edging forward alone in the dark of the terrace, Clea saw the shoulder of her father's doublet, the calf of his leg in the black silk stocking, the glint of gold embroidery on his shoe.

He was sitting near the door.

The deep voice would be in her dreams, she knew, 'til the end of her life. Calling her Honeycomb.

Calling her mother *my Twilight Lady*. Their hands twining as they stood on the terrace in the dusk.

If I had a knife, I'd cut that memory out of my heart.

She moved a little, so that she could better see into the room.

His profile was pure and strong as that of a marble god, carved by the finest artists of the Bright Islands. Lamplight glittered in his golden beard. He wore a short velvet robe as if for riding, as he often did when not in audience: black, over a doublet of daffodil silk. Heavy with rings, his hands were strong, the hands of a sportsman and a fighter.

Shumiel, exquisite in gold and pink, had just risen from a deep reverence, her hands clasped before her breast as if to contain the leaping joy in her heart. Ecstatic, Snowball stood on his skinny little hind-legs and pawed at her skirt and whined his delight.

Minos Stylachos turned back to the men standing before him, his dark eyes hard. "You say your Order can make me Bright Emperor in Esselmyriel, Lord Himelkart. I suspect Mesismardan's going to have some words to say about that; his heir as well. Not to speak of eight or ten of the Great Houses, the real nobles of that land, who're related to the Imperial House . . ."

Himelkart smiled, and spread his hands. "Do you think we can't, Lord?" His dark gaze shifted momentarily to Shumiel—almost, Clea thought, he would have winked at her. "With the men of my Order behind your claim, which of those Houses will gainsay you? They'll be too busy scrambling over each other to wed your daughter and invite you to hunt on their lands."

Stylachos's beautiful voice turned light as a steel blade, neatly pushing aside any hint—any thought—of anger. "I'm not going to sell you my son for the pleasure of going hunting in the Soldukarian Woods." *Just a jest, a funny exaggeration* . . . His gold-brown eyes twinkled.

Duly, the young wizard laughed. "I understand your concern about the succession, my lord, once young Master Pendireth joins our Order. But you will beget others, you know. We"—his graceful gesture took in Tsorkesh the Librarian beside him—"can assure you of that.

"And your *next* son," Himelkart went on, "Master Pendireth's brother, will sit on the Throne of Light."

Or Heshek will. Clea felt as if her breath would stifle in her lungs.

"But we must have young Master Pendireth *now*," the young mage went on. "Tonight. He must be initiated into our Circle—become one of our Order—at once, because frankly, we're going to need every gleam of power we can muster. You've seen our resources . . ."

His gesture was a graceful reminder of the carts moving into the Stylachos warehouses, whose clamor and torchlight drifted on the night outside. "And of course the Order is now deep in your debt . . ."

But Clea was already stepping back into the deeper shadows of the terrace. "That's it," she said softly. "We need to get him out of here now. *Right now.*"

As they strode off, silently, down the tiled walk again, she heard behind her the dark-faced librarian saying something about ". . . combined with your own. Pendireth and his brother will command . . ."

"That's what this is about, isn't it?" she asked quietly as the others fell into step. "To put Heshek—your friend Gerodare—or old Cheyan tar-What's-His-Name—on the emperor's throne?"

"It is now, yes," said Ithrazel. "Seventy-five years ago, the other orders—mine, the Black, the Red—were stronger. Seventy-five years ago, the Crystal power was newer. There was less adamine in the world for them to work with. The Mages' Council could still enforce their rules, had they known what was going on." In his shabby, dark robe, with a gaudy, stolen shawl around his shoulders, for the first time, he looked every inch an Archmage. "Seventy-five years ago, my anger was only for the sake of the boys they took."

The Sleepers, she thought. *Screaming night after night in their stone cell. Not even remembering who they'd been, or what it was they'd lost.*

They had reached the dark colonnade that flanked the other side of Griffin House. More hunters had joined them, slipping like ghosts out of the dark. A guard stood beside the door. There were usually two. (*Guard-duty at the warehouses?* Clea guessed.) Ithrazel made a slight gesture with one finger, hidden by the shadows of the colonnade. The man fidgeted where he stood, muttered a curse, and walked off behind a buttress, the place men on watch, Clea knew, usually went to piss.

With two men on watch, they usually did this as a matter of course. The servants would clean it up before morning.

Ithrazel put his hands on the door's great lock and turned them, whispering words of power . . . Instead of the door opening, a dozen rats emerged from all corners of the court and ran toward them as if someone had dropped a cheese.

The wizard cursed. "Damn spells . . ."

Clea pulled her bundle of picklocks from her boot—ignoring the rats, which turned tail and fled when Hamo lunged at them—and nudged the pins neatly aside. It was far from the first time she'd picked the locks in Griffin House.

"Minx," grumbled the wizard, and followed her in.

Twenty-Eight

Pendireth's tutor, Berosale, emerged from a room at the top of the stairs and was halfway down when he saw the invaders ascending from the vestibule below. Star reached him with her knife before he even gathered his wits to speak—though Clea had never had much of an opinion of the man's wits.

"Anyone else up there?" she asked softly. She knew the young scholar was a man of great learning, but no ability whatsoever to lie.

Berosale shook his head in terror. Eagle and another of the hunters bound, gagged, and escorted the tutor to the nearest clothes-press; three more retreated into the shadows at the foot of the stair to keep guard. Clea took the steps two at a time, Ithrazel and the rest at her heels.

Despite the dead hour of the night, and the cold sea-fog that breathed through the open casement, Pendri sat on the sill gazing out. The clamor from the warehouses was audible from here, the orange flare of torchlight from over the wall reflected on the branch-tips of the garden trees. The boy said, "Is Ruggidan back yet, Bero?" without turning his head. "Will we have to—?"

His thin face lightened when he saw it was Clea.

"Clea! And Uncle Iohan!" He sprang from the sill, ran to embrace her, thin as a little bundle of twigs wrapped in his linen night-rail. "What's happening? Bero said you slew the dragon—the thing . . . He said you were killed—!"

Then, turning to Ithrazel, he bowed, held out his clawlike little hand—still so thin from his illness—in greeting. "It's good to see you again, sir." And his eyes—traveling past the old man's shoulder to Hamo and Star, Rediron and Eagle, all smutted with soot and grime and fearsome as demons from the Pits of Hell—grew huge with admiration and delight.

"I damn near was." Clea ruffled the boy's gold curls. "And we'll all of us be in for it, if we don't get you out of here right now, this minute, tonight—"

Hamo was already gathering Pendri's clothes from the cupboard, tossing them onto the bed.

Pendri looked back at the flame-glow beyond the wall through the window. "Are more of those things coming?"

"More and worse than more," said Clea as her brother pulled off his nightshirt, grabbed shirt and breeches.

"Bero said he was attacked by two of the kitchen cats. He says even the spiders in the cellars seem to be crazed. Will Father—?"

"A moment." Ithrazel knelt before the boy. "With your permission, Lord?"

After a quick glance at Clea, Pendri nodded, and Ithrazel put a hand under that pointed little chin and looked into Pendri's eyes.

Clea thought, *God's braies, what if the Crystal Mages have got to him already?* Molten anger flooded her, blind hatred for Heshek and all his crew. *Will they be able to find us by reading his thoughts?*

"Did Lord Himelkart teach you a spell while you were sick?" asked the old man softly. And when Pendri shook his head, "Or did you dream that he did?"

Pendri nodded at that. "It was a magic gate," he explained. "I was in a garden, but there was a gate in the wall, and outside was the sun and the sea and the air. I'd be able to fly."

"Was there a sigil on the gate?"

"Five sigils. Two on each gate-post . . . No," the boy corrected himself, frowning a little in concentration. "Two on the right side, one on the left. One on the lintel, one on the threshold. And I heard his voice saying, *These will set you free.* I've been practicing them."

Clea saw the old wizard's lip twist, as if he'd bitten rotten fruit.

His voice remained gentle. "Listen, son. That dream was a lie. Do not ever, *ever* make those sigils; not if I tell you to make them, or your father or Clea tells you, or Himelkart or any of the mages tells you. Not waking, not in a dream. No matter who tells you, or why they say you should."

His shirt in his hands, his thin bare shoulders trembling with chill, Pendri asked, "What will happen? Lord Himelkart said—"

"Lord Himelkart doesn't know the secret behind them," said the wizard. "A terrible secret. Terrible things happen to those who go through that gate seeking that freedom. And things more terrible still to those they love."

From the look on Pendri's face, that obviously wasn't what Himelkart had told him, but the boy nodded. Clea came forward and helped him on with the garment. Tried to keep the blinding wash of fury out of her own voice as she said, "It's not something you need to worry about now, Pendri. We've got to get you out of here." She held the doublet for him, passed him his boots, boy-size, new and costly. While he was pulling them on, her glance crossed Ithrazel's. *DAMN them! Pigs eat their flesh, and trample what's left into the muck. . . .*

She was almost shaking with anger.

He'll write those sigils half in a trance, thinking they mean something else . . . and when in his trance he runs through that ensorcelled gate, it's Heshek Paramos—or Gerodare Starknife—or whatever that monstrous bastard's name originally was—who'll step into that garden and lock the door behind Pendri, lock him out forever.

As surely as she remembered her days in the prison, as surely as she remembered her first kill, she knew that. It was as if she'd seen her brother's dream. Seen for herself whatever it was that burned in Ithrazel's eyes.

They give him the knife, to kill himself. And tell him it's his heart's desire.

"Will Father come with us?" asked Pendri. "Or stay to fight? What *was* that, Clea? It didn't look like a dragon—"

"Father's staying behind for right now. It's called a zai—"

"Like the water-monsters Nursie Cat-Fox used to tell us about?"

"That's the one. But it's drawn to adamis, like bees are drawn to honey. And adamis drives it mad."

"Then the Mages—" His head turned toward the window again, the torchlight, and the clamor of the carts.

"That's why we have to get you out of here," she said, to the look of shock and horror that filled his face. "Father'll take care of the problem here, but we have to go—"

"Bero's down there," said the boy, aghast. "He went to see if anyone knew anything—"

"Uncle," said Clea firmly, "you go look for Berosale, and meet us at the stables in ten minutes if you can't find him." *And you'd better make up a good story about how safe he is . . .*

From the hallway she heard the swift, soft stride of feet—not her father's domineering step, nor the clank of his guards—and at the same moment a thin, frantic voice from the bottom of a clothes-press in another room wailed "Help! Assassins! Help!"

Damn it, I knew we should have cut that sissified pen-pusher's throat . . .

She said, "Not a word—" as Hamo scooped the boy up in his strong arms. Star shot the bolt on the door (*Not that THAT'S going to do us any good. . . .*) and Ithrazel bent to scrawl signs on the floor. (*Like those are going to work any better than the one he used on the door-lock outside. . . .*) She'd heard no sound of struggle from the foot of the stair; the three hunters they'd left on guard must have known themselves outnumbered and vanished. Graywillow was making flustered passes with her hands. (*And how much good'll THAT do against the spells of the Crystal Boys?*)

Clea shoved Hamo and the half-dressed Pendri into the dressing room, thrust open the window there that overlooked the garden and didn't (*Thank the gods for THAT, anyway!*) have to tell Hamo to spring to the boughs of the nearest elm tree, which almost brushed the wall at this point. She reached back through the door, grabbed Ithrazel by the back of his tattered robe and dragged him into the dressing room as Star and Rediron hustled Graywillow after them.

"Jump to the tree," breathed Clea, crossed the room in three strides to the window by which Pendireth had been sitting and shoved the casements wide, then strode back (*Can they hear me?*) to the dressing-room, just in time to see Star—the rearguard—vanish through the narrow window. Clea hooked her thread around the bolt on the shutters, slipped through, and pulled the bolt shut after her.

Sprang to the tree branch. Down two branches, then dropped to the ground. *And with any luck pursuit will follow us out the wrong window and head for the wrong quarter of the grounds. . . .*

"Run!" she said, and they ran.

Ithrazel had already marked the garden gate. "Bath-house," gasped Clea as they ducked through. The gate was unguarded—she wondered whether the guard who usually stood in that corner of the kitchen courts beyond the garden wall was helping keep thieves from the warehouses or had been seized with a sudden attack of dysentery moments before. "Drainage tunnel . . ."

Pendri, she saw, had switched over to riding Hamo piggy-back, thin arms clutched around the shepherd's neck and eyes huge with fright that was half wonder. He made not a sound as they dashed through the kitchen courts, down the laundry-yards, behind the armory. Though they were farther now from the warehouses the voices of guardsmen grew louder, calling out. Ithrazel strode a pace behind her, stopping now and again to write sigils with his fingers in the air—she saw Pendri's eyes follow the movements, wondered if the boy could see the marks written on the darkness in light.

Once, as she led them a roundabout way behind one of the compound's many shrines, she saw her brother gasp and turn his head to bite the thick cloth of Hamo's collar, eyes squeezed shut.

(*Of course, they're casting a spell after him, forcing him to cry out . . .*)

Then someone in the shadows that surrounded the wide scriptorium court yelled, "There!" and the air *hrush*ed with the whapping of bowstrings.

Ithrazel spun like a swordsman and spoke a word that might once, Clea reflected, have worked at making arrows fall out of the air . . . and in fact a dozen of them clattered on the brick pavement all around them. (*Not that it would take a magic spell to make some of those idiots in the guards miss a target*, Clea reflected.)

Graywillow cried out and staggered as an arrow went through her leg just above the knee, and she would have fallen had not the hunter Rediron sprung to her side.

The delay was enough. Clea saw the glitter of lamplight from a high window on the curved blades of white-steel halberds, the pointed domes of blacksteel helms. There were deep shadows behind them where buttresses supported the compound's outer wall, but the blue-white flare of witchlight behind them, the way they had come, told her concealment in the darkness was useless.

And there he was. Himelkart of Thourmand, thin and angular in a gold-stitched blue doublet that would have drawn sighs of admiration from any one of those young scions of nobility who orbited her father's court, a white cloak of exaggerated cut billowing like wings behind him. Ganzareb and twenty of his men followed, swords flashing white in the witch-light and sweaty faces grimed from wrestling carts and barrels of adamis and boxes of blacksteel all night.

It must be dawn, thought Clea. The night felt that it had gone on forever. But above the stumpy towers of House Stylachos the sky was black as soot even yet.

Himelkart said to the Master of Swords, "Get me the boy. Kill the others."

Clea stepped forward as the men—all except for Himelkart—advanced. "Did my father give you the order to obey him?"

Ganzareb stopped, scowled—at being questioned, she thought. "You going to tell me you didn't kidnap the prince?"

"Answer my question," said Clea, in her most reasonable voice. "Did you get any order from my father?"

The big man hesitated, as if trying to remember. *How many guards between us and the bath-house drains?* Clea wondered . . . *And where's the librarian?* She saw Himelkart make a tiny gesture toward Ganzareb with his fingers and say, "Come here, Master Pendireth."

Pendri let go of Hamo's neck, wriggled his way from the young man's grip. But he looked doubtful, and when Hamo rested his big hands on his shoulders, he stood still.

In a firmer tone, Himelkart repeated, "Come here."

Pendri looked at the archers, still clustered on the other side of the court. At Graywillow, clinging to Rediron as the hunter bound her thigh with a tourniquet. At Himelkart. "Promise you won't hurt them?"

The young mage inclined his head. "I promise."

Pendri looked up at Clea.

She said, very quietly, "He's lying." And, more loudly, "Did you even see my father, Ganzareb? Or did Himelkart just come running up to you and say my brother was being kidnapped, and call out the guards?" Though she kept her eyes on the Master of Swords, she was aware of his men looking at one another. Of their whispers.

"The bitch is lying." Anger edged the young wizard's voice. "Of course you saw Lord Stylachos, Ganzareb. He was with me. He spoke to you."

Ganzareb stammered, his head moving a little so that the ruby on his brow flashed. Groping for memories that eluded him.

"He's the one!" snapped Himelkart suddenly, pointing to Ithrazel, who stood silent at her side. "He's the one who's making you not remember! Do you know who that is? Ithrazel the Cursed, destroyer of—"

"Oh, are we going to start that again?" sighed Ithrazel. "If the man was alive, he'd be a hundred and forty years old, and how would you know him anyway? It's not like you were around . . ."

"Get the boy!" Himelkart ordered, losing his temper and his patience. "Get over here, boy—"

But Pendri turned his head sharply, listening.

Listening in the darkness for what Clea was hearing as well.

The bells in her father's refinery. In every refinery along the curve of the sea.

Calling the men to their work.

Pendri asked, "Why is it still dark?"

Twenty-Nine

The wind shifted. Even to the stillness of the courtyard it brought for a moment the weird metallic smell of evil. Night-Gluttons. Blood-Thieves. Zai.

"Damn it!" Accoutrements rattled in the gate behind Himelkart and his men. Witch-light flashed on gold. "I thought I told you potion-peddlers to be off," rang the deep voice of Minos Stylachos. "I said you'd get your answer by sunset, and the sun isn't even—"

"Father!" Pendireth broke from Hamo's grip and ran, and at Clea's quick gesture, Hamo, Ithrazel, and Star followed Clea so close behind the boy that it would have been impossible for anyone but a trained assassin to shoot them without hitting him. It was certainly, Clea reasoned, beyond the skill of any of those wobble-fingered chowderheads in her father's guard.

As she passed Rediron and the half-swooning Graywillow, she touched the hunter's shoulder and signaled with her eyes: *They're not looking, get the hell out of here . . .*

A tumble of leaves fled across the courtyard, and Himelkart's white cloak lifted a little in the wind.

The smell of the zai came on that breeze.

The smell of the darkness they wrapped around themselves . . .

All the adamine in the city is within five hundred yards of us . . .

Minos Stylachos strode to meet his son, reached out his strong right arm.

"Damn you!" Himelkart shouted, and flung his hand in a long sweep toward that golden merchant prince.

The air cracked with ozone. The guards fell back as both Ganzareb and Minos Stylachos cried out and dropped, like men struck by the bolts of catapults in battle. Clea was within a few yards of her father and saw the blood burst from his mouth, saw Ganzareb's shirt, beneath doublet and armor, stain with red, as if under his clothing his flesh had split in a dozen places. Saw him grab weakly at his throat. Pendri screamed "Father!" and tried to run toward him, but Himelkart caught the boy just as he reached his father's side.

Ithrazel stepped forward with a gesture almost like the young mage's and from his hands, Clea saw the skeletal flicker of lightning—lightning that Himelkart flung back on him with a word and a stroke of his hand. The old man staggered under the blast, raised his hand again, and Himelkart, face transformed with hatred and rage, strode toward him. Fire seared from the ground. Ithrazel rolled clear of the flames but Himelkart's sweeping hand called another blast of light. As the old man cried out in agony, Pendri dropped to his father's side, grasped his hand. "Father—"

Clea scooped him up, and her eyes met those of the man who had killed her mother. The man she had never quite been able not to love.

They were bloodshot wells of shock and pain. But he knew her.

"Save him—"

She hoisted the boy to her hip—he didn't weigh as much as a fighting-dog—and turned to run for the gate. Ithrazel scrambled to cast some other spell, some other attack, but all it did was ignite the roof of the scriptorium fifty feet away. Himelkart's counter-blast crushed him once more to the ground, bleeding from mouth and nose. He raised his hand as if that would ward off the strength of the Order that had broken him all those years ago, and as he did so the earth between them split, spewing up a wall of flame. The next second, wind screamed down out of the darkness, hurling Himelkart back like a rag-doll.

Hamo and Star were on either side of Ithrazel, dragging the old man to his feet. Pendri, for all his frail appearance, struggled against Clea's hold like a tiger, shrieking "Father! Father!" and making her stumble as she ran. More fire blazed up between the broken courtyard flagstones behind them, and she could hear Himelkart screaming orders. But something else was moving in the night, she could feel it, smell it, passing in the blackness overhead, as once she'd felt it pass beneath her feet.

Eyes in the shadow . . .

Damn it, RUN . . .

They reached the bath-houses as greenish-yellow flame ripped from the sky above the warehouse courts and the screaming of horses and men split the night like world's end.

Was it like this when Dey Allias went up?

Clea was last across the courtyard by the baths, and Hamo came running out of the low, long building to snatch Pendri back under one arm, grab Clea's wrist with the other hand. His strength was the only thing that got her under cover as the zai passed overhead. Bigger than the one she'd killed—much bigger.

Star had the cover off the big drain at the end of the baths; Rediron was just lowering Graywillow down into the chilly dark of the tunnel below. In Hamo's arms Pendri was crying. Clea wondered for half an instant where Shumiel was in all this chaos—*the thing'll attack the main palace*—and then her mind was on what Kulchan had said, about gathering all the dredgers, all the tribesmen, all the hunters in the city. She heard Pikefish's voice again: *We're ready. And we're armed.*

And they're probably the only ones in town who AREN'T guarding the adamis . . .

I have to get to them.

Now is the time. The guards will be in confusion . . .

Sons of Death, was that PENDRI who called that fire?

Something moved on the rafter overhead and looking up, she caught a glimpse of the fat red greasy thing that she thought she'd glimpsed in the garden of the House of Glass. *Was that only two weeks ago?*

Pale light glimmered below her in the tunnel. She dropped through, pulled the cover back into place; the dim glow showed her Ithrazel's craggy face as he bent over Graywillow. The young woman's eyes were already open, her face taut with pain. "How is she?" Clea whispered, bending—as they all had to—to walk beneath the low brick arch of the drain-tunnel.

"She'll live." The old man didn't look like the same could be said of him, though Clea was aware now that he was far tougher than he looked.

"Are you all right?"

"Besides needing a mad-doctor to tell me how I managed to get mixed up with you? How's the boy?"

Pendireth, face ravaged and slick with tears, edged his way through the adults, knelt in the wet muck of the tunnel floor to take Graywillow's hand. A little hesitantly, he said, "They taught me healing spells. The easy ones. And to take away pain." His huge dark eyes raised to Ithrazel. "I can—I'll help her, if you're tired, Uncle. I mean—" He hesitated, trying to be polite to an adult and a wizard at that.

"Himelkart beat the crap out of you." Clea pulled the scarf from around her neck, handed it to Ithrazel to wipe the blood from his face. "I honestly didn't think you were going to get up again. And those counter-spells you called. . . ."

"Those weren't my spells." Ithrazel put his hand on Pendri's head. "I had nothing in me. Thank you, Pendri, that's good of you and I appreciate it. But you can't, not at the moment. A spell that strong would draw them to us. The arrow that struck her had a spell on the head of it, can you feel it? What they call *k'aasthu*, a spell of the Crystal order . . ."

The boy nodded quickly. "I know *k'aasthu*. But they only use them against the enemies of the gods, the enemies of the emperor . . . That's what Lord Tsorkesh says, anyway." He pressed his small hands against Graywillow's bandaged thigh and winced.

"We have to move," said Clea. "They'll figure out where we've gone the minute they have a second to catch their breath. Hamo, can you carry Graywillow? Are you all right to walk, Ith—Uncle?"

"I'm not in my dotage, girl." He tried to rise, and Star put her shoulder under his when his knees buckled.

"Here." Clea dug in his pocket for the flask of Liver-Eater's rum. "We have to get out of these tunnels as soon as we can."

"I'd say your friend Liver-Eater has other things to think about," replied Star grimly, "besides hunting for you."

Something sloshed in the blackness nearby; the acrid stink of abominable creatures momentarily rode over the human pong of waste and rot. Clea edged past the others, orienting herself by the marks scribbled, half invisible under grime and mold, on the tunnel's brickwork. "Liver-Eater's thugs are going to be the prettiest little flowers we're likely to meet down here tonight. This way."

There were wells in this part of town, descending to lower levels of tunnel and eventually to the water table. Where the main drainage-line touched the first of these, Clea leaned through the opening and listened. Clamor and shouting, screams of terror human and animal, the clatter of flight in the courtyard at the top of the shaft. Rags of torchlight. Snatches of despairing prayer.

Clea cursed, and remembered what the zai had done to the village of Turtlemere in the madness of its pain. "This one must be ripping through the whole district of the great houses," she said. "We can get out through the Baths of Othume—Pikefish said he'd be gathering the Kindred from all over the city."

"The hunters we left by the stair will find them," affirmed Star, and Clea nodded, knowing well that the men had more sense than to take on the palace guards. And it was not the guards, she knew, who were the chief danger in the darkness. She pushed from her mind the recollection of the body fragments she'd seen in Turtlemere, the nature and size of those appalling wounds. The awful remains of Kingfisher—what the Night-Gluttons had left of him. *If you feel anything, your hands will shake . . .*

If I feel anything, I'll start screaming like everybody else, and won't be able to stop.

I can't let them down.

She took a deep breath. "Baths of Othume this way."

The public baths built by Momus Othume were the largest in the city, and built for the convenience of the Bright Lords, not the children of Twilight who served them. Rat Bone had stolen only the most fashionable of dresses for Clea—and had had one or another of the girls from the Dockside dress her hair—when she'd slip up through the main maintenance tunnel to loot her way through the women's changing-room in the middle of the afternoon; she knew the way in the darkness as easily she knew the route from Griffin House to her father's kitchens. Even the air in the ramp that led from the main tunnel to the maintenance shaft was familiar, warm with the heat of the furnaces, banked for the night but glowing like ovens. *Who in Morne guessed at sunset last night what morning would bring?* The bricks of the tunnel smelled of dampness but not of mold: the great pools were drained and scrubbed one day in five. The gods forbid all those second-rate relatives of the noble houses of Telmayre who came to Morne to make their fortunes should go home saying, *Really, those bumpkins of the House Othume can't even keep their baths clean! I was never so disgusted in all my life.*

She was halfway up the ramp when she smelled, behind her in the dark, the alien fetor of the Night-Gluttons. "Watch it back there!" Her hand touched the iron rungs of the ladder in the dark—*Do the Gluttons hunt by sight?* She recalled they had eyes . . .

Well, Shumiel has eyes, too, but hers don't work worth a . . .

She pushed aside the pain that gripped her heart. Her mind stumbled on the thought of her near-sighted sister. The Golden Princess, her face aglow with the thought of going back to Telmayre, of being treated as a great and valuable lady again. Of wedding into the old nobility at last.

Shumiel in pink and gold, scooping up faithful little Snowball in her arms . . .

Not both of them. Not her and Father, too . . .

Dagger gripped between her teeth, Clea scrambled up the rungs, listened for a moment beneath the cover before pushing it aside. The noise of attack, of terror, was still audible up here, but fainter. Buildings were burning in the neighborhood, but nowhere near the baths. Distant reflections from the windows played across the water in the main pool. Presumably the caretakers had fled, and who could blame them? Under other circumstances, she would have cautioned the others to wait while she made a patrol of the whole huge room, but there wasn't time. She'd seen the Night-Gluttons strike. Dagger in one hand, she whispered, "Pendri—" and her brother came scrambling up, Rediron just behind him. Getting to her feet, she turned to scan the darkness around her, glanced back now and again as Ithrazel was lifted up through the shaft, then Graywillow, handed up into Rediron's arms. The smell was stronger from below, sudden and terrible—

"Keep watch!" she ordered Rediron, and dashed across the open, tiled floor to the niche where the caretakers sat during the day.

She heard Star curse, as someone—probably Hamo—hurled her bodily up from below. The stench of the Night-Gluttons breathed up after her . . .

Hamo's still down there . . .

His head and arms appeared, the others dragging at him as he half turned, kicking at something below . . .

Clea yelled, "Hang on!" and slammed over the lever that controlled the drains from the pool, and she felt the vibration of the water as it roared down into the ramp. Plumes of it splashed up through the drain, soaking Hamo as they hauled him to safety. *Unhurt, no blood . . .*

The bellow of the water beneath the floor momentarily deafened her, but those around the shaft must have heard something, because they all clustered close about the round aperture, reaching down . . .

And dragged up a young man. Drenched and gasping, he clung to their arms in the sudden flare of pale light that Ithrazel must have called. A short blue robe stuck to his body like a wet sheet, a white tabard half torn from his shoulders, a crystal amulet—like those she'd taken from Liver-Eater, but larger—gleaming on his dark breast.

"God's braies!" She crossed the tiles in three strides, sword springing as if by itself to her hand. *If I strike him fast—*

"Don't!" The young man fell to his knees, spread his pink-palmed hands to show them empty—*as if one of those vermin with spread and empty hands isn't as dangerous as a housefire, and a lot harder to deal with . . .*

"Lord Ithrazel!" The newcomer grabbed Ithrazel's arms and clung to him in desperation. "I swear I'm a friend . . ."

Clea raised her sword, every nerve in her shouting *kill him NOW . . .*

Ithrazel moved his fingers, and she fell back, breathless. Furious and unable to strike, as if she had been frozen in amber for ten thousand years.

"You *were* a friend." Ithrazel looked quietly down into the young librarian's haggard eyes. "What was it . . . seventy-five years ago, Tarronis? Eighty years ago?" His grief-scarred face was hard as stone, and deeply sad. Clea fought to scream at him, but even her voice, for the moment, had been stilled. "Have you come for the boy? Are the others outside?"

Tsorkesh the Librarian shook his head. "They're coming for him. Searching for him."

The old man was silent for a long time. The immobility seemed to pass off and Clea lowered her blade, but found she still could not step forward.

He said, "Was that you, who kept Himelkart from killing me? Who sent the lightning, and the flame?"

The young mage nodded.

"And you've suddenly decided you want to betray your comrades who've helped you from body to body to body over the past . . . how many years has it been, Tarronis? Or whatever your name originally was . . . how many decades? And now you want to join up with us, who just happen to have a mageborn boy with us—"

"It isn't like that." Tarronis's voice cracked on a sob.

Clea opened her mouth to snap, *And what IS it like?* And then closed it.

Very softly, Ithrazel asked, "And what *is* it like?"

The younger man—only Clea realized he was probably older, much older, than Ithrazel—turned his face aside.

Memory? Shame?

Acting lessons from Himelkart. . . ?

When he looked back it was not at Ithrazel, but at Clea. "You saved the old men," he said simply. "The Dead Mages, who are no use to you. They can do nothing for you, they could have got you killed at every step getting away from the House of Glass . . ."

He looked at Ithrazel again. "Gerodare—Machodan—they started talking about taming the zai. When the first reports of them came to us, Gerodare never so much as mentioned destroying them, or defending against them. He didn't even send word to Nhubansar, the Grand Archmage of our Order on Telmayre."

"Wanted to keep it all to himself, did he?" the old man murmured.

Tarronis averted his face again, as if he'd been struck. "He said it was better so."

"And you obviously wanted to believe him. When did he suspect that it was adamis that drew them?"

"Almost from the first. They—and the other things—rose up first out of the canyons in the Orchid Maze, where the adamis lies thickest beneath the water. This was a year ago. They'd attack dredging-parties, melt the diamond-clay into adamine. By the signs, they'd roll in it, and then they'd go mad, and tear to pieces everything they could find. People, animals, houses, trees . . . Adamis, or something like it, crusts their skin, and there's a magic in it that we cannot pierce. Machodan has tried, since first we knew of these things."

"And you didn't think to mention any of this to anyone?" asked Clea, surprised to hear her own voice so calm. "Or maybe let my father—oh . . . *warn* the people who worked the canyons?"

"He wanted to," the librarian whispered. "Gerodare forbade it. He promised him a special . . . a special *arrangement* . . ."

"Yeah," said Clea dryly. "We all know about the special arrangement."

Tsorkesh—Tarronis—though the boy named Tarronis, Clea reflected, the actual boy born and named that, had ceased to exist decades ago—looked aside. "I tried to talk to him . . ."

"I'm sure you did," murmured Ithrazel. "But you always listened when they said, *Keeping our power is the most important thing.*" His voice held just the faintest trace of Himelkart's drawling Sea Islands vowels. "*We're doing all this to help humankind.*"

"Yes."

"*Look at the lives our healing has saved,*" he went on, still mimicking Himelkart.

"Was that how it went? *As the magic of other mages begins to fail, ours remains strong. As the gods fall silent, we are the only ones who can help hold famine and plague and old age at bay. Surely that's worth a few boys who, when they grew to manhood, would gladly have dedicated their lives to helping in any case . . .* I heard him make that argument once. He didn't know I was listening, of course. It might even have been to you."

"Don't . . ."

"*If those boys wanted to be wizards to help people, surely they wouldn't object—once they'd grown up a bit—to helping other wizards who have greater wisdom, greater skills, greater power to continue helping, rather than have all that power for good set back, time after time, by a wizard dying of old age just when his wisdom and his learning and his power are coming to true fruition."*

"Stop it." The words were barely a whisper.

Clea glanced beside her, saw her brother's eyes fill with tears.

"And surely it was worth killing fifty thousand people in Dey Allias—well, most of them only Darklanders—to get me out of the way? To keep the light of your wisdom and your power blazing and growing for the betterment of humankind at large?"

"I can help you."

"Of course you can."

Clea stepped forward, conscious of the shortness of time. Of the zai circling the city in the darkness. "The zai—can they think? Do they have minds?"

Again Tarronis shook his head. "None that we have ever been able to touch, or even detect."

Bitter weariness returned to the old wizard's voice as he sighed, "And I'm sure you've tried."

"Their minds—like the minds of the Night-Gluttons, and the Blood-Thieves—are . . . different. Of a different order than those of humankind, or even of animals." His hand closed briefly around the amulet he wore.

Something to guard him from the zai? she wondered. *And how well did THAT work?*

"No spell, no wards, no symbols or signals—it's as if they don't even perceive them. I'm not certain they even perceive the world as other animals do."

Clea was aware of movement in the darkness behind her. Aware that the darkness itself had grown thin and strange, as if the bright midmorning were faintly struggling through the shadows that the zai—*How many of them are there nearby?*—seemed able to draw around them. Her head whipped around and she saw Kulchar, and the other chiefs of the neighborhood councils, those secret organizations that had kept the Kindred strong. Saw Pikefish, and the young chieftain Blacklamb; old Obsidian Shield, and the red wizard Dalmin, with his face and hands blistered, his splendid curly beard half burned away. And behind them, more shadows gathering. The dim glow of Ithrazel's witch-light slid along the edges of bows, axes, billhooks and threshing-flails.

We're ready. And we're armed.

She even thought she glimpsed Pig-Face, and old Mother Sugarplum horrifically armed with a club studded with razorblades. . . .

The Twilight Kindred moved nearer, but hesitated to come into the ring of mage-light. Clea could almost hear the whisper of Tsorkesh's name, and who he was, passed from man to man. One of the Crystal Order. One whose magic was deadliest.

A white-robed woman, queenly and beautiful even with her gray hair a half-unbraided dirty snarl, broke from the group and ran to Graywillow's side. Clea recognized the Lady Anamara the White. Recognized, too, the movements of her hand as she made the signs of healing magic.

Quietly, Tarronis said, "Gerodare—Heshek—wouldn't listen to me. He wouldn't even listen to Himelkart. He was starting to go mad by then. It's what happens to us."

"Is that from taking the bodies of children?" asked Ithrazel, and there was no surprise in his voice. "Or is it just the adamis?"

"The adamis, I think," said the young man, after long silence. "Or maybe it's only that a mage's brain can take only so many transferences. I've tried to find out, but nothing was ever written down."

"No surprise there." Ithrazel sniffed.

Tarronis flinched. "Seventy-five years ago—when we silenced you— such spells of transference would be good for twenty years, thirty years. . . . I used to be able to take over the body of a lad of thirteen or fourteen, and it wasn't until he was a man in his prime—thirty or thirty-five years, when a man's magic matures and settles—that the dreams would start, and the pain, and the rages. That I'd start to hear voices, and see fires and lights that weren't there . . ."

He wrapped his arms around himself, as if his wet robes grew suddenly cold.

"I'm hearing them already. Seeing them already. So is Machodan, and it's less than ten years since he took the body of Himelkart of Thourmand. Sometimes the men—the boys—start to go mad within the week. They didn't used to. Last year when we formed a circle to carry Zarabant Uthri over into his next body, something went wrong, we still don't know what. The child went mad, screaming and struggling and unable to speak, but Zarabant's former body stood there, emptied of its occupant—"

He shook his head, unable to bear the memory.

Ithrazel opened his mouth to speak, closed it. At length he said, "I would say it served him right, if I hadn't seen the Sleepers." Then for a time he stood, staring into the shadows of the vaulted room as if he, too, couldn't bear the memories he saw.

"My lady . . ." Kulchan stepped softly to Clea's side. He wore the old-style quilted armor of the Ashupik warriors, and carried a pike and a bow. Hamo laid a cautionary hand on his arm.

"What became of them?" Ithrazel asked, his voice very calm and distant now, like a man willing himself not to feel unbearable pain. "Second Ox, and Khoyas, Shalzaib and Eketas . . ."

"He had them hunted down and killed."

All heads turned at that new voice, crumbled and creaky out of the shadows. In the patched, uncertain twilight that filled the great marble chamber of the baths, Khymin more than ever seemed like a tattered ghost, the corpse of someone he once had been. Clea guessed he'd come up through the auxiliary drain—the hem of his black rags was wet, and his bare feet were crusted with the particular grayish mud characteristic of the district through which those drains ran. But the others, even Pig-Face, gazed at him as if he'd materialized, like the zai themselves, out of shadow and darkness.

"The emperor sent his marines," Khymin continued. "In the Dockside and the villages they said that the mages forced him to do it, because without their spells he would grow old and die . . . or worse, grow old and not die. As I myself have grown old . . ."

When he shook his head the long white weeds of his hair clattered, like dried vines on a cliff-face in winter. "But that wasn't so, was it, Tarronis? My father killed himself, rather than be taken by the men Gerodare hired . . ."

Ithrazel startled, stared at the withered form before him. "Hummingbird!"

"It was my name," agreed Khymin, "yes. Hummingbird, son of Second Ox. Gerodare and the others—Tarronis, you were one of them, weren't you? And your friend Zarabant another . . . They hired a score of Sea Island mercenaries and came into the City of Butterflies by night, under the cloak of Gerodare's spells. While the city was burning, Father showed himself to them, and lured them to our house, then kept them fighting—he barricaded within—for nearly an hour, with Machodan's spells of pain and spells of blood and spells of delusion and madness all chewing at him—"

Tarronis winced again, as if at the cut of a whip.

"—because Gerodare wanted to take you all alive. Ithrazel, and Father, and the others, before the emperor's men killed you. Many of the imperial marines had kin in Dey Allias, and families who had died there. The emperor had thousands of crowns invested in the diamond-sands of the Dey."

The old man frowned, as if he had lost the thread of his tale, as Clea had seen him do many times before. Lost it, and feared to seek for it, like a man fearing to grasp a burning coal.

Gently, Ithrazel said, "And you escaped."

The white head nodded. "Father held them off long enough for Mother to get us out of the city," he said. "Then when he could not hold on longer, and they had stripped all the magic from his bones and broken in the door, and broken his body with spells, he set the house afire, with oil he had poured about him when first he fled there. From the forest we watched it, Mother and I and my sisters, break off the cliff and fall burning, two hundred feet into the canyon below. Gerodare and the other wizards had sent the mercenaries ahead of them, so they were not killed—"

"Three of us were," said Tarronis quietly.

"Were they?" Khymin regarded him with raised brows. "Good."

Tarronis looked as if he would have replied to this, but didn't.

To Clea, Khymin went on, "The spells of the mages sent to catch Father poisoned the croplands of the city, and the forest for twenty miles around it. You would have kept him," he continued, turning back to the damp, shivering man in the soaked blue robe, clutching his crystal pendant. "As you kept poor Ithrazel, wouldn't you? In someplace where he would be alive and in pain forever . . . until such time as you found a way to drain away his magic from his body, to use for yourselves. To add to your power. The way you kept those poor outworn shells of the little boys you possessed, when you were done with them. Hoping to find a way, to drain out the magic that had been born in their flesh."

The filmy eyes went from Ithrazel's stone-hard face—shocked, appalled, but, Clea observed, not surprised in the least—to her own, and then to that of Tarronis, taut with sickened misery. "Were you one who tried to invent such a spell, Tarronis? Tried to find one in your books?" At last his gaze found Pendireth, clinging to Hamo's arm.

He smiled, with horrible toothless gums. "They're not nice people, little prince."

And at once his wrinkled claw reached into the depths of his rags, forestalling Kulchan's urgent, "*My lady . . .*" by bringing forth a roll of parchment, brown now with age and spotted with a black leprosy of mold.

"It's why I've brought you this." He held it out to Ithrazel, and Clea saw the old man's eyes widen, with shock and disbelief. Struck, as he'd looked when he'd first seen Himelkart on the testing-ground of the Tarnweald, and remembered who and what that young man was.

"Destroy them," Khymin said softly. "Do what you would have done on the Hill of Oleanders, seventy-five years ago. Call on the power of the earth, and the power of the night sky, the blood of magic in our veins and the spirits of the living and the dead. Breathe a wind like fire and star-storm through the world and drive the souls of the New Mages from their stolen bodies, blown away like spiders into eternal dark."

Ithrazel's hands trembled as he took the parchment. He moved like a man who wakes from a dream to find the flowers he picked in his vision spilling through his fingers.

"Where had you this?"

"Father gave it to Mother," replied the man who had been Hummingbird. "And she to me, when she died. I will help you, to raise the power to accomplish the spell."

Clea thought old Ithrazel genuinely looked as if he would faint. Under his sunburn his face had turned ghastly, his shaggy brows seeming almost black against his flesh as he stared at the sigils written on the page; four sigils, and the diagram of a circle of power. She said, knowing it for truth, "That's what you were trying to do at Dey Allias that night, isn't it? That's the spell you were trying to bring about."

The old man said nothing.

"That's why it was worth it to them, to destroy a city and its people to stop you."

Tarronis got to his feet, slowly, and took a step closer to her to reply. "Machodan got wind of it somehow," he answered her quietly. "I don't know how. Maybe just because he heard Ithrazel was gathering mages to help him: Second Ox, and Shalzaib, men who had also begun to suspect what the Crystal Order—what *we*"—he corrected himself, his face pale with shame—"were doing. Who we really were. One of Shalzaib's nephews was taken by the . . . by Gerodare . . . by *us*. I was there when Shalzaib met the boy afterward: I saw his eyes."

The muscle of his jaw twitched, with the clench of his teeth.

Clea said slowly, "So you dumped adamis all over the hilltop where you knew the spell-circle would be laid out." She heard her own voice, calm as if discussing the theft of grain by a stableboy, but within herself she felt it: a red inferno of rage. Not blind, and not hot: cold and clear-sighted, as if she indeed had a diamond for a heart.

Remembering Machodan Indigo in the body of some poor dark-haired eight-year-old boy, riding in obscene triumph in procession to Pendri's dedication. Remembering old Heron the fishwife in the marketplace, sobbing behind her little baskets of whelks and shrimp, and when Rat Bone had asked, *What's the trouble, Auntie?* the woman had sobbed that the Crystal Mages had taken her boy. Had paid her man for the child and just taken him, and what was she to do. . . ? How could you fight the mages?

Remembering the screams of Himelkart's guards as the black horrible thing had passed almost beneath her feet and risen from the waters of the grotto, and Rivan trying to beat his own brains out against the wall of the strongroom in the Temple of Serpents.

Tarronis, Heshek, Himelkart . . . all those other mages of the Crystal Order . . . they had seen the threat. To their lives, to their power, to their position as deathless shapers of the world.

Of course it was worth a city.

"Did you know what would happen?" she asked, still in the who-stole-the-grain voice of calm.

"I knew that it was a spell of great destruction, laid on Dey Allias. We'd just begun to learn that adamis could make the spells of other orders go awry. We knew if there was adamine mingled with their spells, it would let us work a magic of our own, with the power they raised against us. I thought . . ."

He stammered. "At the time I thought it would be a matter of . . . I don't know, roofs catching fire, everybody's chickens dying, machinery breaking in the refineries. The diamond-sands around the city were nearly played out, you see. Machodan and Gerodare—and Nhubansar the Grand Archmage—had sold out the order's holdings around Dey Allias and were already buying up concessions in the Mire."

Still clinging to Hamo's arm, his tears now running down his face, Pendireth whispered, "But you're *mages*. You *help* people. Heal them . . ."

Tarronis appeared not to have heard. He went on after a moment, "Everyone knew Ithrazel hated us—hated the Bright Lords. They'd believe he would do such a thing. No one would raise a hand to keep us from killing him. Not even his own order."

Kulchan moved forward again, urgency in his voice. "My lady—"

Ithrazel looked up from his scroll, still speaking like a man in a dream. "Magic has changed," he said, and there was a note in his voice, cracked and hoarse, that pierced Clea's heart.

For the first time he looked old. Old, and defeated.

Had he looked that way when they'd caught him? She didn't think so. Even chained to his rock, he had been ready to fight them still.

"Adamis—refined, pumped from the ground, scattered everywhere as dagger blades and hairpins and dust in every corner of every stable and kitchen that needs mouse-wards—has eaten at the magic that isn't founded

in it. Eroded it for seventy-five years. Its vibrations permeate the air. I doubt
I could raise the power to do this."

"My magic hasn't eroded," returned Tarronis quietly.

Ithrazel looked sidelong at him. Steady and questioning: *You know what
you're offering?*

The young man quietly returned his gaze.

"Enough of mine remains," put in Khymin, "to draw the sigils, and
frame the circle . . ."

And Pendri, slipping his hand from Hamo's and stepping between Clea
and the librarian, added, "I can help. I don't have a lot of power—just a little—but I've . . . they've helped me learn. It's Crystal magic. It should work."

"What will you need?" Clea asked, and at that moment, Pikefish thrust
his way forward, and knelt at her feet.

"Lady." She saw there was blood, and soot, mixed with the grime on his
clothing. Was suddenly aware again that the clamor outside had fallen, the
distant voices of men no longer crying out, but grinding, like the waves on
a rock beach, speaking of a storm far out at sea.

"Forgive me," said the dredger. "Jeweled Hand, the Lady of the Shrine of
Rycellis in the Dockside, sent me to find you. Winterflower of the shrine of
Gingul in the Denzerai spoke to her through the smoke of the altar—as did
Neambis, the Hand of Farawen. Both say they have seen zai, rising in darkness from the canyons. They sent warnings to the villages—your father's
men tried to keep the workers from fleeing, then fled themselves when the
things attacked, destroying everything. They say they are coming this way."

Thirty

They can be killed," said Clea. The smell of the thing returned to her, the huge darkness of it, the splattering burn of the fluids of its body as she slashed it open. Her bones ached at the thought of trying to do that again. "How many are there?"

"I'll find out." Graywillow spoke faintly, sitting up in the Lady Anamara's arms.

"Child, hush," whispered the Lady. "Rest."

A small, stout woman in a Gray Sister's robe pushed through the crowd to Pikefish's side. "Jeweled Hand said there were two, one great and one small. They are hard to scry, in crystal or ink or water."

Clea was aware of voices murmuring at the far ends of the great hall, of more people coming in and word being passed along to them. Anamara unpouched a chunk of purple crystal from her belt, stared into its depths.

"And one more already here," said Clea. "It was tearing apart my father's house—probably all the great houses—"

"I can see those houses." The White Lady looked up from the crystal in her hands, and her voice had the dreamy note of a woman half in a trance. "No trace of the thing now, though there is great ruin and fire—"

"It'll be back." Clea glanced around her, counting weapons, tallying her forces. "The adamis will draw it. And the others on their way. . . . No way of telling how much time we've got before they arrive?"

"If they are maddened with what they can sense in the villages on the way," said Tarronis doubtfully, "they may turn aside to destroy, e're they get here."

"But they'll be here." Clea took a deep breath. "And when they come, we'll need to concentrate the adamis. Bring it from all the warehouses along the waterfront, to a single area—"

The White Lady looked up from her scrying-stone with a gasp of dismay; the Red Mage Dalmin cried, "That's madness!"

"It is," said Clea firmly. "Their madness. How would you capture all the addicts and drunkards in the city?" She looked around her at the shadowy shapes, hundreds of them now, crowding in the gloom. "You make a big pile of dreamsugar and booze."

"We need blacksteel, and white-steel," cut in Ithrazel. "Pig-Face—" He turned to address the bodyguard, looming out of the mob. "I assume you know where your boss keeps his stockpile? We need mounds of adamis topped with at least two feet of pure blacksteel or white, and yes, yes," he added as Pig-Face opened his mouth, "I have a reasonably good idea of what your boss is going to say about it—if he, or you, or anyone in this part of the city is alive at sunset today. And if those creatures reach us, you won't be, you know."

The tawny brown eyes held his, and Clea heard in his voice—and knew the big ruffian could see in those eyes—the absolute truth in those words. Even a man whose intelligence was limited to the cunning of a killer, she thought, couldn't step aside from that certainty.

In a tone of sweet reason, the old man added, "I'm a wizard—supposedly a very evil one—and both Khymin here and Tarronis are pretty powerful." He looked around for them, but both had vanished into the crowd. He went on with a smile nonetheless, "You can tell your boss we forced you."

"Or you can help me of your own free will," said Clea. "My father is dead. The power of Telmayre may not survive this day. But if we do survive it—if I live—I will owe you a debt. And you know I won't forget."

Pig-Face inclined his shaven head. "I know you don't forget things, Princess." And he spat formally at her feet. "Boys," he then yelled at the top of his lungs. "You heard the old goat! Get to the strongrooms and get out the blacksteel—and any man even *thinks* about puttin' a bar of it in his pocket's gonna be eatin' his own tripes for breakfast tomorrow mornin'!"

"And the gods only know what that much adamine underfoot is going to do to your magic," murmured Clea as Pig-Face and several score of the assembled rabble poured down one of the drains and back into the Tunnels like a murky army, "when I open that zai's hide for you to blast it."

"It worked at the demonstration!" protested Graywillow, shocked. "You—"

"It worked barely," said the old man. "We were lucky. How much difference it will make to be standing on top of a mountain of it . . . I suppose we're going to find that out."

Clea sprang onto a marble bench, then scrambled from there onto the plinth of a statue of Elynnia, the love-goddess sensuously nude and combing her long hair. From there, Clea's words carried to the end of the hall—which she saw now, in the weird smoky twilight of the cursed morning, was crowded almost to the walls with men and women, bearing whatever makeshift weapons they could find. "We need to open the creature's hide. Bare its guts. Anybody there know where I can get a halberd? Blacksteel, or white-steel . . ."

One of her father's men-at-arms came forward—the hook-nosed Placne Sarpellis, who for two years had taught her the finer points of military weaponry. His clothes were fouled with blood as well as smoke and dirt. He held out to her the seven-foot white-steel glaive used by her father's honor troops, deadly as lightning and woven with spells of death. "Will you need us around you, Princess?"

She saw now that over a score of his fellow Griffin House guards stood behind him, Bright Islanders as well as the Twilight Kin, bloodied, acid-burned, with the bleak eyes of men and women who have seen their world collapse. Watching her as the others watched.

Ready to follow. Needing to be led.

As their fingers met on the shaft of the glaive she asked, very quietly, "Did anyone get out? Shumiel . . ."

Very slightly, Sarpellis shook his head.

Damn it.

Stupid of me to hope. . . .

"I will," she said. "Others, too. Thank you."

She looked around her, identifying those she could most trust. "Kulchan, can you take a gang to the warehouses—Sarpellis, go with him to talk some sense into the guards there. The courtyard of my father's compound is the largest. Bring all the adamine from the others there as well. Build it into four hills, one at each corner of the main yard. Blacksteel on top, when Pig-Face gets here with it."

Her voice echoed in the tiled vaults of the baths, above the murmur of voices. From the top of the plinth, she could see that word must have gone across most of the city that resistance was being organized here. Ragged, bloodied clerks and small traders—Telmayrians—stood shoulder-to-shoulder with the Kindred; in one place there was a whole squad of sailors from the harbor.

"I need a couple of blades on each hill," she called out. "Strong arms, people who know how to handle a pole-arm. The zai is going to come right down on top of you. Slit its belly—open its hide. Mages—"

She looked around for them. Saw old Manzardath the Brown in a doublet and breeches clearly borrowed from some shopkeeper, black-robed Kenzag clinging to Mother Sugarplum's arm. Dalmin the Red, also in a tradesman's smock and hose, holding—to Clea's surprise—the child Vervaris by the hand.

"Stay under the gateway, or between the warehouses, where you can see the halberdiers on the hills but as far from them as you think you can throw lightning."

Where the hell are Khymin and Tarronis?

"We don't know how badly that much adamine is going to affect your magic. Team up, work together if you can. You have to blast lightning straight into the open wounds. Sarpellis, split your troops up. That whole area's going to be crawling with other things as well, Night-Gluttons and the gods know what else. You've got to protect the halberdiers—"

Men and women crowded forward: pikes, halberds, scythes.

Sarpellis saluted her, and she crouched on the corner of the plinth to speak to the Lady Anamara. "Can you throw lightning?" she asked. Other Ladies had joined her, with their satchels of herbs and dressings. At the foot of the plinth, her white robe stained with soot and blood, the motherly Lady who had come in the train of the ambassador studied a scrying-crystal cupped in her hand.

Anamara shook her head. "That is not our skill," she said. "We do not kill. Not even such as the zai."

"Can you fool them, then?" asked Clea. "I know the magic of the gods isn't—hasn't warped the way the powers of the other orders have. Can you make these things not see us, standing on the hills of adamine?"

The White Lady looked startled at the thought. "I have no idea," she said, for the first time sounding like an ordinary woman and not the Lady of a Shrine. "We have no knowledge of their minds—"

"They have none." Pendri tip-toed, to reach up and touch Clea's boot. "Tshorkesh—Tarronis"—his voice caught on his teacher's name—"said to tell you. To give you this." He held up—to Clea's surprise—Tarronis's crystal amulet. Shutting his eyes, as if calling back instructions, he went on: "He said give it to the Lady Anamara or the Lady . . . the Lady Fyliaris . . ."

The Telmayrian lady looked up quickly, stood, cast a quick glance at Anamara. Clea started to say, "You don't know what spells—" but both women closed their hands around the jewel. The Lady Anamara's eyes flared with surprise.

"It's what Tsorkesh—Tarronis—had read of the minds of the zai." Leaning on Rediron's arm, Graywillow limped to the side of the plinth. "I've heard of spells like that—of using scrying stones for that—but I've never seen it . . ."

"Let's hope it helps." Clea glanced at the high windows around the dome of the great chamber, gauging the queer silvery light there, like a stormy morning. *How soon does the darkness come, with the coming of the zai?*

How much time do we have?

Damn it, she thought, her eyes going to the golden-haired boy gazing up at her. *Damn it, damn it, damn it . . .*

"Can you throw lightning, Pendri? Did they teach you that?"

"A little bit." His voice was steady.

"Could you focus it," she asked, "if another mage . . . sent his power through you? I've heard of that being done—"

"It's dangerous," said Ithrazel quietly. "To both the focus and the source. The focus risks burning out his power completely, killing that part of him that can source power—especially if the disparity between their powers is great." He glanced across at Dalmin the Red. "Was that what you planned to do, at Tarnweald?"

"Absolutely not!" The Red Mage, shocked, drew little Vervaris against him protectively. "We were going to execute the spells from a distance—"

"You'd have been lucky if you didn't ignite the grandstand—"

"I can do it," insisted Pendri. "We can't think about what happens . . . after . . ."

Damn it, you shouldn't have to be doing this. . . .

"Can you focus power," asked Hamo, coming up quietly behind the boy, "through something like an arrowhead? If you put a—a spell of some kind on it beforehand?"

The mages looked at each other. Ithrazel said, "The lightning follows the arrow."

Hamo nodded. "Yes. Can you?"

Kenzag and Manzardath looked at each other—having clearly never heard of such a thing in their lives (*and why would they?* reasoned Clea)— but Ithrazel said, "Yes. Yes, I can."

* * *

We can't think about what happens after, Pendireth had said.

Or maybe what came before, either.

A barricade of carts had been set up before the gateway of the Stylachos warehouse compound on the Street of Ships. Men still surged and struggled before it: not only her father's soldiers, but those of the Vrykos and the Kinnesh, and of her cousin Tykellin, hacking at the vanguard of the rough-armed Kindred.

Damn it, they think this stuff is still valuable. If they knew what was going to happen here, they'd be running like hares . . .

But Sarpellis (*May the gods crown him with flowers!*) had already done his work: Clea saw that the Kindred had been joined by contingents of the Griffin House guards, by the sailors and hunters and by squads of Vrykos and Othume and Kinnesh troops as well. Above the jammed, shouting mob, she glimpsed the standards of the Kindred, hidden for years by those secret councils, as Kulchan and his men poured into Merchant Street from every alleyway and lane in the city.

And behind them, carts jostled and lurched, hemmed in by men of the Tunnels, men of the Dockside—porters, dredgers, stevedores—already dragging in adamine from the other warehouses, the other compounds. Kinnesh fighting Kinnesh, Vrykos struggling to move them on and to drag them back, and the sky overhead cloudless but eerily patched with drifting veils of darkness.

Clea yelled, "Stop!" and sprang up onto a foundered wagon, bellowing above the din. For one whose childhood had been spent in silence, Clea Stylachos had a battle-yell that could split tree stumps. "The zai are coming!"

Hamo leapt up beside her, blew the signal-horn he'd seized from a fallen sergeant. Sarpellis followed him a moment later, thrashing a tattered Stylachos banner scooped up from underfoot.

"The zai!" he bellowed. "The zai!"

Some men turned. A lot kept up the fight.

Damn imbeciles . . .

"Flying V," she commanded her followers, in a more normal voice. "We'll have to push our way through—"

"Oh, for the gods' sake—" she heard Ithrazel mutter. The next second, white light burst within the gate, violent, blinding, with a crack like thunder. The old man sprang forward at a run, Clea following and her mixed squadron of Darklanders and Griffin guards streaming behind. The defenders—Clea heard the hoarse shrill voice of Tashthane Vrykos screaming orders—closed ranks in the gateway, and this time the roar was the roar of fire, springing up out of the ground as it had in her father's courtyard, driving the merchants' forces back.

Himelkart was waiting for them, just within the gate.

He smiled as Clea stopped short before him—smiled as if she wasn't armed with a white-steel halberd in one hand and a blacksteel sword in the other. Smiled as if he hadn't killed her father three hours before.

"Truce," he said reasonably. "You need us."

Clea shut her jaw hard on what she really wanted to say and settled for, "What I don't need is wondering whether you're going to aim lightning at the zai or at me."

"You have nothing to fear, Clea," he assured her.

Liar.

"We can't control them . . . yet." At his gesture, the guards defending the gateway fell back; soldiers dragging wounded comrades clear of the aperture, blood mixing with the debris of overturned carts, scattered ingots and blackly silver dust glittering on the ground before him. Those thin, elegant hands motioned toward the jam of carts that had stopped in the gate, then moved to take in the chaos of the wide yard behind him: more carts, piled bales, ingots dropped from burst sacks. Shockingly, the corpses of three porters who had clearly been torn apart by Night-Gluttons.

Over everything, the dark gleam of adamine dust.

"I think we're going to need all of this," he said, "to find a way to bring these creatures to our bidding. For now, what we need to do is defend, and I don't think any of your friends have quite the skill of old Ithrazel. . . . Where did the old liar get to, by the way? He was here a minute ago."

Turning to follow his gesture, Clea saw that Ithrazel was gone.

Good, he had that much sense. . . .

"He took an arrow in the back," she said, "coming through the gate. Hamo?" She turned, praying the shepherd had the wits to support her improvisation.

"They took him back." Pendri stepped forward, pointing behind him through the mob crowding in the gateway. "The White Lady, and the others. I did what I could for him—"

Hamo pulled the boy to his side again, but Clea saw, like the focused lance of sun-glare through a crystal, Himelkart's eyes go to him. Saw the way his body tensed, as if he would leap forward and seize her brother there and then. Hamo leaned down and said to Pendri—loud enough for the wizard before them to hear—"You did well. He'll be all right."

And as he said it—Clea could have kissed him for knowing how to play the scene back to her—he met her eyes, and shook his head.

The young mage seemed to catch himself, to recall where he was and who was watching him, and what might be at stake. In an elaborately casual voice he said, "I never thought he could have pulled together that effort at the last."

Old mage, Clea thought. *Centuries old.* Again she saw the cast-off husks shambling helplessly around their prison, saw Rivan screaming on the strongroom floor. The hair prickled with rage on her scalp.

And he doesn't realize it was Tarronis who saved us. . . .

IF all that eye-wash back at the Baths wasn't part of Himelkart's plan. If HE wasn't the one who told Himelkart where to find us . . .

"Whatever his fate," said Clea grimly, "the zai are on the way. The one who destroyed my father's house is still at large—" And she kept her voice hard, as if speaking of her father to the man who killed him were of no more moment than a piece of the strategy of the day.

"It's back up at the Denzerai." The slight movement of Himelkart's fingers dismissed the matter. "Tearing up the warehouses there, and attacking the barges."

"It'll be back. What we need to do now is bring them here, trap them, and kill them. We can do that by concentrating the adamine here, in this courtyard, and we don't have much time. A few hours at most."

The dark glance remained for a moment on her face, then went past her—scrupulously avoiding Pendri—to the carts that, all this while, had been drawing up in the gateway behind her. Vrykos drivers. The Quillet and Gerti the Rat-Lady on the seat of a wagon heaped with blacksteel halberd-blades. Loghri shopkeepers with sacks on their back that leaked threads of adamis dust. Stronger now, she smelled from the back of the crowd the acrid, metallic fetor of the Night-Gluttons. *Can the guards cope with those? I guess we'll find out. . . .*

And all the while, she was burningly conscious of the skinny, ragged little boy at Hamo's side.

"Well, well," murmured the young mage. "What a clever girl it is." And he glanced behind him at the yard, calculating—Clea knew as if he spoke his thought aloud—how many zai could be brought to the place for his own attempts at spells of domination. Then he bowed, almost mockingly low. "And you are quite right, Lady of the Tarnweald—do you know they've started to call you that? I think that for some time to come, we will all need to help one another." He waved the erstwhile gate-guards aside; Clea signaled the carts to come in. Withdrew a little as they poured past, Kulchan and the woman called Porcupine shouting orders: those carts to this corner, those carts to that.

More shouting from the fringes of the crowd—*Night-Gluttons?*

She looked around her, making sure that Star and Hamo and at least a dozen hunters still surrounded Pendri. Standing only a few yards from Himelkart, near the broken-open door of the nearest warehouse, she could almost smell the wizard's craving, his greed, focused on Pendri, though Himelkart never gave the boy so much as a glance. She noticed, too, that Pig-Face, Sarpellis, and the Telmayrian Lady Fyliaris kept unobtrusively closer to Himelkart than Himelkart was to her, the two men holding their weapons in readiness.

"As for the Cursed One," continued Himelkart casually, "if you should see him—if he still lives—please him we bear him no ill will. Though I will be very curious as to what his version is, of the events of seventy-five years ago. Right now—"

He turned quickly as a dozen young men slipped through the broken door of the warehouse behind him. Some wore the white doublets or tabards that the Crystal Order affected, with hose and shirts and sleeves of more stylish fashion; a few, the loose white trousers and tunics that she'd seen in the House of Glass. Some of them were very young—thirteen or fourteen. Behind them, keeping to the shadows, a skeletally thin man followed. Long blonde hair dirtied, gargoyle face haggard, but Clea recognized him by those great, crystal-blue eyes, and the wide shape of sensual lips.

Heshek the Fair. Heshek Paramos. Archmage of the Crystal Wizards, who had not left the House of Glass for years.

And no wonder, she thought, appalled.

The staring gaze went at once to Pendri, hanging back behind her, and the man stepped forward. She saw that his nails, like Rivan's, hadn't been cut or cared for in months. Himelkart went smoothly to him and took his arm, steered him tactfully back among the younger mages. When he glanced at Clea again, she made sure she was looking not at Heshek, but at the sky.

But she felt him as she had in her childhood felt it when a sewer-rat would come creeping into her cell.

The day was brightening toward a heatless noon. But northward and westward, where the Denzerai lay on the other side of the Gray Hills, darkness blurred it. Darkness and smoke. Closer, the Griffin House compound—the house of her father—was still in flames that nobody had had time to put out. Houses in the city were burning, too—they'd passed them, on their way through the streets from the Baths of Othume—and the men and women who streamed from the city to the warehouses bore the stains of soot and mud on their clothing and faces, and makeshift dressings covering wounds.

She glimpsed Liver-Eater's mistress Gula, yelling at a troop of thieves dragging goods-boxes of white-steel tools and ingots of adamine toward the gate. The Monkey King trundled his wheelbarrow full of the stuff. Wagon-loads marked with the Brazen Head of the Othume creaked past her through the gate, ingots and bales of adamis and adamine thrown down into the corners of the yard where the hills were forming. Four men in the blue and gold of the Vrykos carried in a lady's gold and crimson litter piled high with darkly glimmering metal: she recognized it as Linvinnia's.

What became of her? Of those poor silly ladies Father gave me, Gabbie and Pennylips . . .

Don't. Don't even think. Not now . . .

Someone shouted for Kulchan. Down near the Vrykos compound there was screaming, and Sarpellis and his guards moved in with their halberds and flaming cressets they'd pulled from along the wharves . . .

She heard someone call her the Lady of the Tarnweald. Someone else shouted something about "the blood of Greenshield."

In the compound yard, the hills grew to mountains, vast, darkly shimmering, with a lake of spilled dust between them, stirred by the swarming feet of frantic workers.

Was the sky darkening again? *It must be just past noon . . .*

Beside her, Graywillow said, "They're coming . . ."

"Get under the gateway," she said. "Mages—as far from the adamine as you can get . . . Bowmen!" They crowded forward: Stylachos men-at-arms, Darkland hunters, one man she remembered from her days with the Assassin's Guild. "Blacksteel arrowheads? Good. Each of you—" She turned, jabbed her finger at those fresh-faced mage-babies who had reappeared from their warehouse, with their hundred-year-old eyes. "Halberdiers are going to slit those things open when they get close enough, when they come in to kill. You, you, you, and you"—she pointed to four young mages (*who're all probably older than Rat Bone's grandmother, and would just as soon blast lightning at ME . . .*)—"you blast power, lightning, whatever you've got, into the wound. Your magic won't go through its hide." She wondered if Himelkart had already given them orders not to harm the zai.

More than likely . . .

"You, you, you, and you—" Her eye picked out the red mages, the brown, and the black who came pushing toward her. Men she'd watched, over the course of eight years, slip from respected spellcasters in the neighborhoods to little more than fortune-tellers, as their rat-wards lost their efficacy, their healing-spells brought other kinds of misfortune, their love-spells resulted in hives or infestations or derisive laughter. "You're backup. Same target. Lightning to follow the arrowheads, or fire, anything . . . Sons of death!" she added as, a dozen feet from her, two Night-Gluttons sprang from around the side of a broken cart and threw themselves at the nearest defenders.

Three women in the livery of House Kinnesh guards fell on the things with halberds, cutting them to pieces—two men of the Vrykos waded in with torches, to burn the pieces that continued to lunge and snap at everyone within reach.

"They're all over the warehouses," panted Pikefish, from among the bowmen. "Worse things, too."

Clea swore again, and shifted her grip on the long, single-bladed halberd she held. "Cover us," she ordered. It was definitely growing darker. "Rediron, get the porters out of here. Get everybody but warriors out of the street. Pendri . . ."

She glanced back, reassured herself he still stood at Star's side. "Halberdiers—"

Guards from every merchant house crowded forward, uniforms soiled, bloodied, filthy. Few assassins or hunters learned to wield pole-arms.

"Get to the top of the adamine mounds. The zai will come down on you. Slit their bellies, then stand back . . ." She clambered to the top of a cart, the better to be heard by the rest of the troops. "And watch out, their blood'll burn you. Don't drive them off the mounds. They've got to come down where we can get them—Damn it!" she added as a voice yelled from the top of the wall.

"They're coming!"

Thirty-One

She yelled, "Go!" and sprang down, Hamo stepping forward to steady her. She saw he had a bow, as powerful and heavy as the one he'd carried in his own world, in his idyllic little enclave of sheep and village girls and strange legends about tortured gods. . . .

She shouted to Star, "Watch Pendri." And, when the hunter came nearer to her, "The mages are going to try to take him while we're fighting. I think that's why they offered help. Kill them if they try."

The woman nodded.

"Hamo—"

As she spoke, they were striding toward the tallest of the hills of adamine, twenty-five feet gleaming eerily in the semi-dark, sheeted now with white-steel and black. She was aware, with detached clarity, of the other warriors—Vrykos, Othume, a few Ashupik mercenaries—heading for the other mounds. Her white-steel halberd threw back the silvery glow; Clea felt light inside, neither hungry nor thirsty though she couldn't remember when she'd last eaten or slept. She remembered her father, dying with his hand in hers. "Save him," he'd whispered. His last words, his last thoughts, for the son he'd sacrificed for, but she thought, *I'll save them all, if I can.*

To Hamo she said, "Go back."

"I won't—"

"That's an order, soldier," she said as she had said before, and this time he shook his head.

"I won't leave you."

She stopped, facing him. "It's a goddam love-spell," she said. "I told

Graywillow to put one on you, because I needed a strongman I could trust. That's all it is. Don't die for it."

"There was never a spell on me." He looked down into her eyes. "I felt it—like a headache, or an itch on my skin. For a couple of nights, I dreamed about you—" And he grinned, and shook his head. "Wild dreams, like the stories my sisters tell each other . . . You should never ask a virgin to cast love-spells, Clea. I knew what they were."

He put his hand to her cheek, and bent to kiss her lips. "I was never under a spell."

She said, "You're an idiot."

He grasped her shoulder, shoved her in the direction of that glimmering silver mountain in the darkness. "Who's the one who's going to be standing under that thing?"

Turning back, quickly, she seized his arm, dragged his mouth down to hers. When she let him go, she said, "You're still an idiot." She pulled off the protective amulets she'd taken from Liver-Eater, put them around his neck. Then she ran, filled with fire and light as a deer, ahead of her followers, Bright and Dark, then left them behind with her feet slipping and slithering over the stuff that had made her father and her grandfather what they were, that had lured her father's people into enslaving her mother's. That had cost tens of thousands of Darklanders their homes, their peace—the severed hands and ears of their hostage children . . . the world they had known.

For this.

The zai came down out of the darkness.

They brought the darkness with them, like a fog. Two of them, tearing and slashing at the men and women who gathered in arms around the warehouse quarters and outside its walls. Greenish fire blazed where they spit their vomit, and she saw the remaining roofs of the Griffin House go up in flame. Saw one of them dive on the crowd, come up with a man's legs kicking from the side of its mouth, before they were severed and fell. *Damn it I hope the halberdiers on the other mounds stay put if they all attack here at once . . .*

How many of them are there?

Out of the corner of her eye she glimpsed the guard Sarpellis. He'd gotten a poleax from somewhere, but was staying back, letting her be the target.

Tarronis said they have no minds. Are they smart enough to steer clear of attacking an armed crowd. . . ?

Evidently not. She heard shouting, shrieking, and felt the oily heat of flame somewhere nearby, behind her. Smelled pluming smoke and charred flesh. A wizard—*one of the Crystal Boys?*—flung lightning at the thing and she saw the zai outlined briefly in racing lines of blue flame that flickered over its glittering hide and vanished.

It was, as Jeweled Hand had said, huge. The other was smaller—thrice the size of a horse, she thought as it dove at her. She ducked aside as it spit its burning slime at her, and all those fragments of crates and bales in which the adamine had been contained flared up around her.

She ran a few steps to get farther from the flame, and the movement must have caught at it.

It plunged. And the larger zai dove with it.

Timing . . . she thought, and thought nothing else.

She slashed, felt the burning acid of the thing's body fluids splatter her face and arms in the split second before the halberd was almost jerked out of her grip. Pain seared her right arm and darkness covered her, but she knew she'd been grabbed, felt the ground drop from beneath her boots. Blue lightning raced over the thing's hide, burning her as well—it had her by the arm, and the heavy cornel-wood shaft of the weapon was the only thing that kept her arm from being severed.

From the corner of her eye, flame dropping away below her, the swooping shape of the other zai—

Without conscious thought, she pulled her dagger with her left hand and buried it to the hilt in the squishy flesh of the monster's lip, raked it, cut again at the gum—

And then she was falling.

She hit the ground hard and tried to roll. *Where's that pig-festering halberd?*

She couldn't breathe.

The smaller zai came down faster and the larger grabbed it by the wing, threw it aside—

More splattering of acid—

Lightning. The zai screaming above her. She rolled out of the way as it came down like the fall of a tower, and saw the smaller zai, its wing half severed, scrabbling across the silvery ruin of half-melted adamine toward her. The flare and flash of more lightning, someone running toward her, stumbling on the rolling jumble of ingots underfoot, and she was aware of flame everywhere around her.

She was looking at the smaller zai—*smaller, hell, the thing's as big as a house*—as its fanged mouth opened to grab, and she brought up her dagger.

Trailing lightning, trailing magic, an arrow struck it straight in its mouth. She saw light explode in that blue-black gullet—

DO NOT FAINT . . .

But for what felt like half a minute, she could only lie stunned, smelling the burning sacks and slats and boxes broken among the adamine. Smelling the nauseating stink of searing flesh and the stench of the burning green vomit. *I have to get up. I have to run before I burn, and there's still another zai or two on the way . . .*

It seemed a lot easier just to die.

Save him, her father had said.

Save them . . .

And, *I never told Hamo I love him.*

She rolled over. It felt like her arm had been dislocated. *Good, it's still attached . . .*

She'd just managed to get to her hands and knees when someone grabbed her shoulders, helped her up. She knew by the smell of his clothes who it was.

"You all right, darling?"

She managed to say, "Screw you, Liver-Eater."

"Two others came down on the other mounds. Both killed—"

Others crowded around them, helped her out of the way of the flame. But cautiously. The darkness was clearing, and she saw why they hesitated, still on the crest of that pile of heaped magic and wealth.

Hamo lay at the bottom, his bow beside him, clothes half-burned off him and the huge black mark of a lightning strike crossing the flesh of his back from nape to waist. Blood glittered on his nose and mouth. Pendireth knelt at his side, bowed over, his thin little hand gripping the huge, limp wrist.

Damn it.

The cold that went through her heart was very calm and small, but deep, a wound that carries poison to the core of the soul.

For one moment she saw all the nights of trusting sleep in his arms, the children she would have borne him. The gentle years stretching away.

Like a candle blown out, leaving only darkness behind.

It takes so little. . . .

Damn it.

Ithrazel stood above them, facing Himelkart and two of the other youthful mages. Half his hair and one eyebrow had been burned off; there was blood in his scrubby beard. The ground all around them still flickered with dying flame. Tarronis stood at his side.

Himelkart said in his calm, reasonable voice, "Don't be silly, Tarronis. This is not the time to be fighting among ourselves. You know the Darklanders would have rallied around the girl."

Tarronis said, "This is not the time to be killing our own."

His clothes were burned. Himelkart—and his two companions—all bore signs of the spells that would have maimed or killed other men: faces streaked with blood, charred lines traced on foreheads and burned into their garments.

"Our own?" Himelkart raised one brow. "The bastard daughter of a Darklander witch? The people need a hero and her memory will rally them, of course. But what the people truly need, now, is authority, and organization—"

"What people truly need, now," said Clea, limping forward and forcing her heart not to weep—*if you feel anything inside, your hands will shake*—"is for all this adamine to be loaded onto whatever ships are left, taken out to the deepest part of the sea, and dumped. The zai will drown themselves going after it. With any luck, the lesser monstrosities will, too."

She looked him up and down, and added, "Those that aren't pretending to be men."

"Don't be silly, girl." If nothing else convinced Clea that she was dealing with someone several hundred years old—with someone other than the eighteen-year-old boy that he looked—it was the fact that he didn't blink or startle or look disconcerted, though she did hear the edge in his voice. "I think the Vrykos, and the Othume, and even your uncle Tykellin will have something to say about that . . . to say nothing of the emperor."

"Yes, what about the emperor?" asked Ithrazel. "Or has he had nothing to say about zai appearing in the Bright Realm itself?"

Himelkart's eyes shifted. From long training in watching prospective marks in her pickpocketing days, Clea could see him stiffen, taken off guard. "That's absurd."

"Is it?" the old man pursued. "I should think that if there's any place in the entire world that contains more concentrated adamine than where we're standing now, it would be Esselmyriel itself. Hasn't your Grand Archmage in Telmayre anything to say about what's been going on here? Or haven't you told him?"

"You're—" Himelkart stammered. "You're raving . . ."

"I tried to reach the Brown Archmage Jodrofar, in Yellenyth in Telmayre," spoke up Manzardath. "Kenzag tried to reach the head of the Black Order, Egalvax, just after the attack on the Tarnweald. I thought it was just . . ." He hesitated, then shook his head. "The changes in our power—"

In the sudden, uneasy silence that followed, Tarronis said sharply, "These creatures . . ."

"They come out of the flooded mines where adamis was dug. I understand there are a lot of those on Telmayre—on all the Bright Islands—these days."

Himelkart said—quickly, "All the more reason that we need leadership. True leadership, leadership by men who understand magic. Men who have lived a score of lifetimes, who can see farther than street whores and soldiers and men who took it on themselves to destroy the innocent with those they claimed were guilty." He jerked his hand impatiently toward Ithrazel. "Those are the men whose lives must be preserved, whatever the cost."

He made a move toward Pendri, still kneeling beside Hamo's body. Ithrazel—and Tarronis—stepped in front of him.

Himelkart's lips thinned. "Think you have another fight in you, Tarronis? That last blast of pyrotechnics when the shepherd fired his arrow didn't drain your power? Especially since you know I'm right."

"At one time I thought you were right," said the librarian wearily.

"And I think, with time—as we unite our forces to defend these lands— you'll understand so again."

From the circling crowd of warriors, Heshek the Fair pushed his way— Gerodare Starknife, thought Clea. And what other names, and for how many lifetimes back?

Her hand moved toward her dagger and the pain almost took her breath away. Drawing it left-handed she started to intercept him, but Liver-Eater and Pig-Face gripped her arms, wringing from her a cry of pain that she changed into the worst curse she could think of. And then, "Pendri!" and Ithrazel and Tarronis raised their hands.

Face twisted with scorn, Himelkart swept his hand at them, and the two wizards, old and young, staggered, and in that second Heshek dragged Pendireth to his feet.

Stared down into his eyes.

"Pendri—" Clea screamed.

The next instant Heshek hurled the child to the ground, like a man who has snatched at treasure to find he's grasped a worthless stook of straw.

For a moment he stared at the boy, mad blue eyes bulging almost out of his skull. "You—" Heshek's voice was a whisper. Then he raised his hand, screamed at him. "You idiot boy! You spent it! All, all, every last fragment of your power . . . on *that*?"

He stooped to strike him again, the boy turning his face aside.

And Hamo, gasping, rolled over and lurched to his feet. He took a step toward the wizard and would have returned the blow, had he not fallen to his knees.

Pendri scrambled up, grasped his arm. Heedless of pain, Clea pulled herself free of Liver-Eater's grip, ran, stumbling, to his side. "Hamo—!"

His arm circled her waist but he turned toward the infuriated Archmage, who was screaming now, "You sacrificed your power for THAT???"

He lifted his hand, to summon lightning.

And the air changed.

It felt like dust, though there was no grit in the air. It felt like heat, though Clea remained cold right through to her bones—save for the warmth that flooded her heart. It felt like dryness, dryness a thousand years deep—save for the first spring rain, melting a diamond.

Heshek gasped, his hand clutching at his throat. Past him, Clea saw Himelkart double over, as if stabbed through the belly with a sword of flame. Tarronis—and the two young mages behind Himelkart—tried to cry out, though no sound would come. Staggered on their feet, like men suddenly struck blind.

Himelkart reached toward his friend, his partner, the companion of a hundred years. Managed to scream a name that Clea did not know, before his eyes went blank.

None of them fell. They only stood, staring before them, their faces emptied of thought or anger or fear.

As the Sleepers had stood, in their prison in the House of Glass.

Ithrazel turned his head sharply, as if he heard something else: a fading whisper, a wail of despair. Like wind that sweeps across the earth and is gone.

But Clea heard nothing.

She and Hamo helped each other to their feet, each leaning on the other like a pair of drunkards. Clea felt like she could have slept for a week—*Not that there's any chance of THAT anytime soon. . . .*

Beside her, Hamo rested a hand on Pendri's shoulder: "You all right, son?"

The boy nodded, staring at the men who'd been his teachers, his mentors. Frightened, Clea saw, but without tears. A few feet away, Tarronis gazed at nothing. His slim hands pawed for a moment at his face, then dropped to his sides. He would have fallen, had not Ithrazel—his face filled not with triumph, but with a curious grief—caught his arm.

Clea limped over to Himelkart, passed her hand before his eyes. They tracked the movement, and his mouth moved a little, but only a thin grunting came out, and a little dribble of drool.

She said softly, "God's braies."

And on her other side, Liver-Eater—shaken for the first time since she'd met him—asked, "What happened?" And then, in a more normal tone: "And where did Khymin get to?"

Thirty-Two

Just before dusk on the following day, Ithrazel the Brown came to the walled compound on the western slopes of the Gray Hills, from which Porcupine, the mother of Blue Gecko and Second Gecko, operated one of the largest meat brokerages and cattle-farms that had served the city of Morne. The gates were shut. Before them a pyre smoldered, the smoke stinking of the alien reek of creatures not native to the human world. The young man Blue Gecko stood beside it, raking at the last of the coals with a hayfork. When he saw the old mage emerge from the thin brush and second-growth trees on the hillside he strode toward him. Ithrazel saw his head and one arm were bandaged, but his shirt was clean and whole. Whatever had come out of the woods at them yesterday, they'd won.

"What happened?" the Gecko asked. "You're the princess's uncle, aren't you? The Denzerai is in ruins, mother says. . . ."

"The zai were killed." Ithrazel leaned on the staff he'd cut, glad for the rest and gladder still that he'd reached the compound before night set in again. He'd followed hill-tracks—wary of the quicker route of the Hidden River—after a night of tending to the worst of the wounded . . . and a brief stop at what remained of the House of Glass. He'd looked over his shoulder every step of the way—the gods knew whether things like Blood-Thieves and Night-Gluttons even noticed protective wards. *I see we're all going to have to do a lot of work, coming up with new spells* . . . "Whole districts were burned, but I think there was relatively little loss of life."

"And Greenshield's heir?"

"Safe." His mouth quirked: when last he'd seen her, the Iron Princess had been squared off against Tashthane Vrykos, asking him to explain to the other merchant lords just how keeping any quantity of adamine in the city was going to help the situation *when*—not *if*—more zai showed up. The Widow Kinnesh and Momus Othume and his boys had been lined up behind her, and what was left of the Griffin House was surrounded by five thousand warriors, hunters, and grimly angry former dredgers of the Twilight Kindred, but he didn't envy the girl her position.

She'd have her work cut out for her.

At a guess, she'll revel in it.

Insufferable Telmayrian hoyden.

"She's sending healers out into the countryside as soon as she can round up enough." He nodded at the remains of the pyre. "You had hard fighting here?"

"Hard enough. But Aunt Winterflower and the Ladies from the shrine of Gingul are here." He shifted the hayfork to his other hand, took from the wizard the heavy pack he had carried through the night, and steered him toward the little fortress.

"And the old men?"

The Gecko shuddered. "They seem well."

"And Khymin?"

They'd laid Khymin out in the tack room of the main stable, on a trestle table used, Ithrazel guessed, for cleaning harness. It was too late in the year for ants, but rat-wards had been laid out all around the makeshift bier: Gray Goddess work, sourced from Gingul, who was after all the Lady of Mice. He wondered whether, if by some miracle Clea did convince the merchant lords to dump most of the adamine in the ocean, the gods would begin to speak to their Ladies again.

By the empty jug, faintly smoking brazier, and crumbs around a bench in the corner, he deduced the votaresses of Gingul had left someone to watch the body, for good measure, and was surprised at the thankfulness he felt for this act of respect.

The old Black Mage had been covered with an embroidered pall, by its decorations one that had been used for every member of Porcupine's family for generations. The design went back to the days of the great cities of the Mire: spindly-legged horses, deer, and frogs lining stylized water. Under the scraggy wilderness of beard, the old man's flesh was darkened, fallen in on the bones of his face, as if he'd been drained of blood and smoke-dried. His eyes were shut, and the rag that bound his jaw looked as if it had been changed recently. His hands were darkened, too, folded around the parchment that Ithrazel recognized—that roll that was blank, in every one of his dreams. Every tendon, every finger-bone, every knuckle and vein stood out as if they'd been skinned.

Voices came back to him, echoes of a dream. Laughter. The child Hummingbird, leading cousins, sisters, and Ithrazel himself, all armed with cattails, in a tiger hunt, with Second Ox as the tiger, trapped in a corner of the kitchen. Shouting to him to get around to the left and be quick about it before the tiger got away . . .

Firelight, cooking smells, and the distant sounds of the City of Butterflies in the dusk.

Then the next morning, the boy Hummingbird looking down over his shoulder at the parchment he'd spread out on the table. *My father says I'll be a mage, too, one day. . . .* Hummingbird had said.

Ithrazel wondered from whom the Black Mage had learned where he was. And how to reach him. Khymin had not said.

Porcupine and her sons had made up quarters for the Sleepers in one of the barns. The harvest was in. Hay and wheat, pumpkins and peas had had to be shifted all around to make room for their blankets. Second Gecko and Porcupine herself joined Ithrazel and the younger brother as they stood in the doorway looking into the dusky, sweet-smelling cavern, but it was Blue Gecko who asked him, "What was that, that they did last night? That Lord Khymin did?" And, looking past him, at the men sitting on the bins and bales—old men, middle-aged men—staring at nothing or humming very quietly.

"Was Lord Khymin able to talk to them?" asked Ithrazel, feeling a thousand years old.

"I—I don't know. He came here soon after we got them settled. He must have come like we did, on the Hidden River . . . One can hire canoes and rowers, you know, if you don't have your own vessel and servants like our family does. I came out to see if these old men needed anything and found him here, drawing the Sigil on the ground out there in the big paddock."

The young man turned, and pointed, and Ithrazel flinched a little at the sight of the half-eradicated circle still visible on the ground. Drawn—yes, he recognized it—in silver and salt, iron and blood. Spells that drew their power from the earth and the sky and the marrow of the soul, rather than from the silvery dust of adamine that had been sweated and melted and siphoned up out of the ground. He recognized his own work, his own spells. Only the power sigils had been changed. Instead of the four marks—crimson, brown, black, shamanic—sigils had been made all around the rim of the power-circle, close enough that the mages—or the men who had once been mages, the boys who had once hoped to be mages—could grasp one another's hands.

Did they know?

Had they consented, to lose even that power they had? And maybe with it what few shreds of self had remained?

"When we saw them in Morne," the Blue Gecko went on, "I thought they were just . . . just prisoners who had lost their minds. Unable to understand anything. But he had them gathered into a circle, holding hands. Singing, or chanting . . ."

Ithrazel walked into the barn, looked at the hands of one of the Sleepers. A man of fifty—a man with a blank childlike face, dribbled food in his grizzled beard. *My grandson's age, had my children lived . . .* The palm and fingers were bruised and burned, and had some of the sunken look that Khymin's had.

A handsome man. Had this man been Machodan for ten or twelve or fifteen years, after the Machodan whom Ithrazel had known had begun to go mad and started seeing lights and fire? Was one of the other men here the Machodan before?

Or had this been Tarronis?

Tarronis who had said, *My magic hasn't eroded,* knowing what would happen when Khymin shouted the words of power. The words Ithrazel remembered shouting on the Hill of Oleanders, looking down at the lights of the sleeping city.

He must have helped him down to the Hidden River from the baths. Laid spells of speed on the canoe, strength on the arms of the rowers . . .

He took a candle from his pocket and held it up before the Sleeper's eyes. It was only this morning that he himself had been able to light it, after the destruction of the zai the previous day and the confrontation with Himelkart. He still felt it, like a string being pulled through a hole in his flesh, when he called flame to the wick once more. Then he blew it out.

The Sleeper's blank eyes merely moved a little, tracking the thread of the smoke as if the man had never seen such a thing before.

Second Ox, and old Khoyas, Shalzaib, and Eketas, had all known that when the spell took effect, their power would be crippled by it—perhaps burned out forever. In the horrified aftermath of the altered spell, Ithrazel had ordered them to flee. Promised—lying even as he said it—that they'd reunite when it was safer, determine what they should do from there. Their strength would not yet have returned, when the mages who went out with the emperor's marines came to take them.

As Ithrazel had been helpless, when the Council Mages had run him to earth.

Anaya had been dead. Ios as well. He'd sent them into Morne, to be away from the great magic being raised that night. When the New Mages had found him, half-conscious among the deserted huts of Brownwaith on Star-Back Hill, he hadn't fought them, hadn't struggled as he'd been carried in chains down the hill and taken to the compound that Gerodare and Machodan had arranged for their Order. A farmstead like this one, Ithrazel recalled, fixed up weeks before that Midsummer Eve. . . .

For a moment he saw them together, Machodan and Gerodare, in those stiff collars and puffed sleeves that had been worn by everyone back then. Talking with glances. Once Gerodare put his hand on his friend's wrist. Knowing what he had known then about them, how they'd helped each other, helped their little circle of friends find replacement bodies, replacement skills, and the power to find more, all down the years.

It was Chiviel, his daughter, he recalled—his fair-haired clever scholar—who'd told him about the New Order selling off its played-out holdings in Dey Allias and buying up concessions in the Mire. When she'd told him he hadn't thought much of it, save to curse them for their greed. But after the catastrophe, when he'd been brought before them with the ruins still smoldering a few miles off, he remembered the scorch of rage that had filled him, at those monstrous, brilliant friends.

"I've had my daughters fix up a room for you in the attic." Porcupine's deep voice, like smoky honey flavored with salt, brought his thoughts back. He saw she'd followed him in, stood gently stroking the shoulder of the Sleeper before whom he knelt. The man smiled, and patted her wrist like a child. "One of the boys will take your pack up there—"

"Thank you, ma'am." He got to his feet, bowed to her. "I'll hold on to it myself, without disrespect to you or your boys. There are things better kept in one's own hands."

She sized him up—a small, chubby woman, much of an age as the burned-out husk of a mage still clinging to her hand. *Did she know that man, once upon a time? Friends in childhood, when his mind had been his own?* She had a burn on her forehead, from the struggle before the warehouse gates yesterday, and a bandage on one wrist. "As you will . . . Iohan? The princess's uncle?"

"That's me."

"Did you know the Lord Khymin?" she asked as she walked with him out into the twilight. "All these years I thought he was only a rumor among the Dockside tunnel-folk. We'll send up supper for you, and a bath—and you'll excuse us . . ." She nodded toward the men and women—drovers and drivers, armed with hunting bows and makeshift pikes—moving about the compound and building fires on the tops of its walls. "I think those things'll be back tonight. Not the zai, may the Lady defend us. But those other things. The unholy brutes from the forest, and the very wolves and foxes and rats, that've gone mad and turned savage. Obsidian Shield and the Ashupik sent some hunters to help us last night. Tcha!" she added as someone appeared against the lighted door of the main house and called her name.

She started away, then turned back. "Stylachos dead, they tell me?"

Ithrazel nodded.

"Well—the Princess will lead us. The zai-killer . . . she's his heir. She and Lord Pendri. She knows the ways of the Bright Lords. She'll deal with them."

And she strode off through the gloom.

Ithrazel returned to the tack room, where Khymin lay. It was almost pitch-dark there now, and he heard the skitter of rats in the corners, but the wards around the body seemed to be holding. He wondered how long it would be before there was a full-scale rising of the tribes against his own people, the arrogant lords of Telmayre. And whether the emperor would be able to raise an army to retake these lands from them, once it became clear that adamine could bring danger to those who wielded it and those who dug it from the earth.

How far did that spell reach? he wondered. Did the Crystal Archmage—whoever *he* was and had been—and all his followers on Telmayre across the sea, cry out and collapse, as their souls were blown from the bodies they'd taken?

And if so, what would happen to the emperor, and all those hundred-year-old Telmayrian nobles, clinging to health and life and vigor through adamine spells?

Civil war? The heir—who had to be in his sixties at least, spells or no spells—accusing the nobles of the Great Houses of engineering the destruction of the New Order. The fighting would certainly spill over into this realm. Would the tribes take sides? Clea had spoken of sending all the adamine in her fathers' warehouses out to the deepest part of the sea and dumping it. *As if that will actually happen, zai or no zai . . .*

And there would be more zai. He knew it. And more Night-Gluttons, and ghaist-spiders, and the gods only knew what other abominable things, with all the adamine on the continent concentrated in Morne now. . . .

How long before the merchants and the Great Lords and everyone who makes their living from adamine even BEGIN to believe?

And if the spell DIDN'T destroy the New Mages back on Telmayre, with what magic will they return here, to crush the revolt? And how long will it be before they come for me?

He felt weary beyond speaking, looking down into the face of his friend's child.

And wept.

Torchlight fell across him. With the coming and going of guards in the stable yard he hadn't heard the approach of footsteps. "I hope you're going to tell me you've found something for me to eat," he said, before he saw who it was.

Then there was a little silence as Clea looked at Khymin's body on its trestle, the parchment still clutched in its skeleton grip.

"Would the spell have done that to you?" she asked at last.

"Yes."

She said, "I'm sorry about Tarronis. Rediron tells me he was the one who killed another of the zai, on another hill."

"You'll be less so when you've had another look at the men whose lives they stole."

She began to say, "We've all done things . . ." and then stopped herself. "Maybe," she agreed. "Probably." Though she'd changed her clothes at some point—she wore the uniform of a House Stylachos guard—she looked dead tired. Her bandaged right arm was in a sling and he wondered how she'd managed on a horse, as she must have done from the ruined Denzerai, to reach this place so quickly. "It doesn't change the fact that he saved us. Saved a lot of people."

Ithrazel sighed, and rubbed his forehead. He wondered how long he'd had a headache . . . *At least seventy-five years*, he thought. *Maybe longer.*

Maybe much longer.

"It's what wizards do." He took the parchment from Khymin's hands, thrust it into the pack that he'd set down on the floor at his side. "At whatever the cost to everybody around them. How did you find me?"

"Where else would you come? I guessed it had to be Khymin here— where else would he raise the power? When you couldn't be found this morning, I knew this was where you'd be making for."

He made a tired gesture, like a duelist acknowledging a hit. "And how did your meeting with Vrykos turn out?"

She shrugged with her good shoulder. "It was touch and go," she said, "until a messenger came up from the harbor. A ship finally came in from Telmayre."

The wizard frowned, adding up times and days in his mind. "Were the New Mages there destroyed. . . ? A ship couldn't possibly have crossed since yesterday. Even with magic to drive the winds, it takes weeks . . ."

"I don't know about the New Mages," said Clea. "But Esselmyriel, and Yellenyth, and the Sea Islands ports were all attacked by zai the night before last. . . . By other things as well. Things that came up out of the flooded mines, and from deep in the earth. There was a Crystal Mage on board, who had told the captain and the passengers of it—and was found yesterday in his cabin, with his mind gone. I daresay there'll be other ships from the Islands on their way here soon."

"They'll be fighting over food in the cities," remarked the old man. "And over croplands. And of course, over people to work those lands. And the other merchant houses will be claiming that you—and the tribes—were the ones who summoned the zai, and that they have nothing really to do with adamine. . . ."

"They are already," agreed Clea quietly. "That's why I want you to come back with me."

His breath went out of him in a sigh, and he said, "No."

Even the thought turned him sick.

She started to speak, and as she had before, stopped herself, and closed her mouth. Only regarded him in the light of the torch she bore in her good hand, hazel eyes shadowed, and tired, and old.

"I can't do it," he said after a time. "Not again. I put my power at the service of a cause that I thought just and it came to nothing. My magic killed thousands and it could easily kill thousands more. I see the children dead in the city yesterday and I remember the children dead in the hostage villages for a hundred years, and I don't know right from wrong. Your cause and your judgment are true, child—" He lifted his hand against her protest. "But people die. And people change. And people—myself included, maybe myself most of all—can be mistaken about what they think is right."

She stood silent for a time, studying him. As she had not really studied him, he thought, when seeking to bend him to her purpose. Then she asked—as if she really wanted to know, "Where will you go?"

"Into the Mire. Maybe to the Lake of Serpents, or to what's left of the City of Butterflies. I don't know. All the people I loved in this world died seventy-five years ago, most of them because they knew me. I don't want to see that happen to anyone else."

He picked up his pack, carried it to her, and set it at her feet. "These are the four oldest books that were in the library of the House of Glass. Tarronis told me which ones to take. I spent part of last night looting the place—put the other really powerful ones in the cellar beneath the infirmary, where your brother was housed. There are spells on the doors and the stair, so that no one will notice them. Your little friend Graywillow should be able to find them easily enough, if she knows they're there. Look after the Sleepers."

He nodded in the direction of the barn where the former mages were. Old men, men who should have been in their prime . . . away from the adamis-soaked environment of the House of Glass they were quiet, huddling together like children, seeking one another's comfort in a world they did not understand. Through the darkness one or two of them could be heard humming, and now and then a voice was raised in the chant of the spells that he recognized, fragments of the power-circle that Khymin must have taught them.

His own power-circle. Spells that he had himself devised.

"I think the magic was burned out of them by the spell they raised," he went on. "As it was burned out of poor Pendri. They had no way to protect themselves against it. They're empty husks. No good to anyone now. Please care for them."

"I will. Rivan also—I'll have him brought back here, to be with his friends."

"Thank you." Once he'd have kept his distance from her—he wouldn't have put it past her, when he stepped forward to touch her bandaged right hand in farewell, to have pulled a blackjack out of her sling and cracked him over the head with it. He'd have woken up in a dungeon with her sitting there and offering some atrocious piece of blackmail for him to serve her again. . . .

But her eyes had changed. When he touched her fingers, they tightened around his own, and he laid a hand briefly on her splinted arm, summoned the strongest spell of healing he knew. He could feel Graywillow's spells there already, and those of the White Ladies.

"Care for yourself as well."

That made her smile, and again she said, "I will."

"My love to Pendri, and Willow, and Hamo."

"Always." She nudged the pack toward him with the toe of her boot. "You'd probably better keep those," she said. "Because you're right. This isn't the kind of power that should be mixed up in fights among the merchant houses. And there *are* going to be fights—about who controls food coming into the city, and what happens to all that adamine, and how do I keep the Kindred from massacring the bastards who made them slaves and stole their land and mutilated their children in the hostage-villages. . . . How do I get everybody to realize that we have to fight these creatures that are appearing, we have to work together, no matter who said or did what?"

A trace of a grin touched her face again and she added, "Hamo says it's like trying to herd wild pigs." And he saw the change in her eyes as she spoke the shepherd's name. Heard the change in her voice, and was surprised to find himself glad for her, as if he'd seen the first green shoots pushing up through earth long barren. "I wish I could change your mind. But we'll manage."

Her fingers tightened on his again, and she turned, and walked out into the stable yard, her boots crunching the gravel. From the doorway, Ithrazel saw Hamo's powerful form detach itself from the dark bulk of the barn and cross toward her, a tiny shape that had to be little Snowball trotting at his heels.

He must have found him in the wreck of the Griffin House. He remembered last night, Hamo had taken a party to search the smoldering ruins for survivors.

Graywillow's slim shape followed a few steps behind. Either she was still limping from her arrow wound, or she deliberately lagged her steps; Hamo's stride lengthened, and he came into the light of Clea's torch, smiling. Asked her something, and she shook her head; Ithrazel heard her say, "Let's go."

Hamo took the brand from her, freeing her hand, which sought his and drew him to her.

A comfort, thought the wizard, on a long and difficult road ahead.

And the gods knew, she'd need all the help she could get.

Children, really, he thought, as he'd thought seeing the three of them together, in the black cold between worlds.

Puppies. Idiots.

With a resigned sigh, he picked up the heavy pack, slung it on his shoulder, and ran to catch up with them in the deepening dark.

About the Author

Barbara Hambly (b. 1951) is a *New York Times*–bestselling author of fantasy and science fiction, as well as historical novels set in the nineteenth century. After receiving a master's degree in medieval history, she published *The Time of the Dark*, the first novel in the Darwath saga, in 1982, establishing herself as an author of serious speculative fiction. Since then, she has created several series, including the Windrose Chronicles, Sun Wolf and Starhawk series, and Sun-Cross series, in addition to writing for the Star Wars and Star Trek universes.

Besides fantasy, Hambly has won acclaim for the James Asher vampire series, which won the Locus Award for best horror novel in 1989, and the Benjamin January mystery series, featuring a brilliant African American surgeon in antebellum New Orleans. She lives in Los Angeles.

BARBARA HAMBLY

FROM OPEN ROAD MEDIA

INTEGRATED MEDIA

Find a full list of our authors and titles at www.openroadmedia.com

FOLLOW US
@OpenRoadMedia

9 781504 079020